NUECES GRIT

ALSO BY MARK GREATHOUSE

The Frontier Chronicles

Perilous Trails

Wyoming Calls

Longhorns North

Warpath

The Tumbleweed Sagas

Nueces Justice

Nueces Reprise

Nueces Deceit

Nueces Blood

NUECES GRIT

TEXANS ANSWER THE CALL

THE TUMBLEWEED SAGAS
BOOK 5

MARK GREATHOUSE

WOLFPACK PUBLISHING
— EST 2013 —

Nueces Grit: Texans Answer the Call
Paperback Edition
Copyright © 2025 (As Revised) by Mark Greathouse

Wolfpack Publishing
1707 E. Diana Street
Tampa, Florida 33610

www.wolfpackpublishing.com

Paperback ISBN 979-8-89567-095-8
Ebook ISBN 979-8-89567-094-1

Dedicated with love to my wife, Carolyn, and to our two sons, Mike and Matt.

THE NUECES STRIP

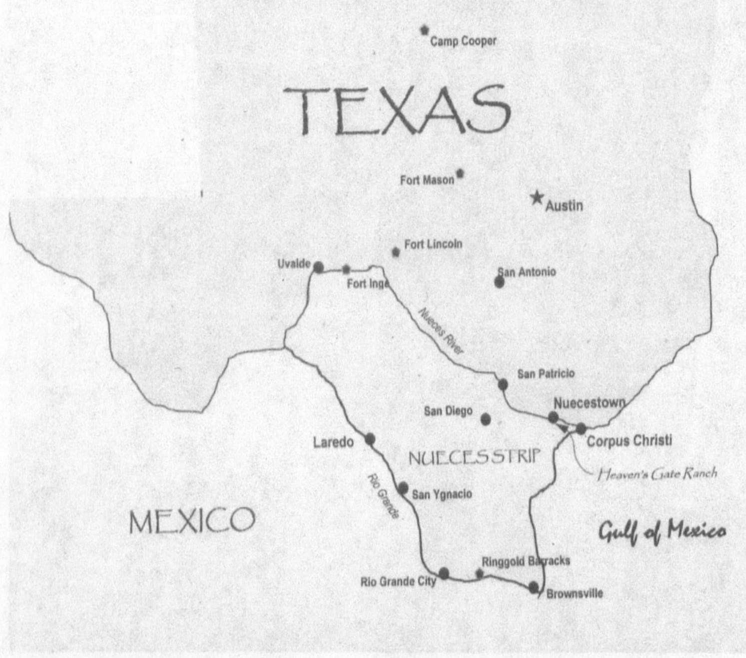

The vast Nueces Strip serves as the primary setting for the
Tumbleweed Sagas. The Strip was also called Wild Horse Desert,
owing to the millions of Mustangs that roamed its prairies. *(Sketch by
Mark Greathouse)*

NUECESTOWN

Nuecestown, Texas, established in 1852 by English and German settlers, was developed by Corpus Christi founder Colonel Henry Kinney along the Nueces River as a ferry crossing. Mostly thanks to the railroad passing it by, it's now a "ghost town" marked only by historical markers. All that remains is a preserved schoolhouse and the old Nuecestown Cemetery. *(Sketch by Mark Greathouse)*

THE CAST

Lucas "Long Luke" Dunn – *Gained notoriety as one of the greatest Texas Ranger Captains ever. He escaped Great Famine in Ireland to seek his fortune on Texas' Nueces Strip. Gained repute as Indian fighter and respected lawman. Conflicted between being lawman and rancher. Comanche called him Ghost-Who-Rides. He finds his true love in Elisa.*

Elisa Corrigan Dunn – *Married Luke Dunn after losing her family to frontier rigors, including fighting off Comanche. She and Luke build the Heaven's Gate ranch and a life on the frontier.*

Scarlett Rose – *Red-headed prostitute from Laredo who seeks to overcome her past, including bad choices of men to run a legitimate business. Searching for redemption in life.*

Walker Carson – *Cowboy and bungling bank robber. Becomes Texas Ranger and then Confederate officer. Gets hitched with Scarlett Rose.*

Doc Andrews – *The formerly alcoholic Nuecestown doctor is the conscience of the town.*

Bernice & Agatha – *Nuecestown town gossips with hearts of gold who run the local boarding house.*

Horace Rucker – *Retired Army Colonel turned preacher. Fights off old ghosts to gain self-respect and support family.*

Rex & Stephen Rucker – *Horace Rucker's sons. Attended Military Academy at West Point. Hold opposing views on slavery issue, and join opposing armies.*

Major Gordon Belknap – *West Point graduate assigned to fight for Union in Texas. Before war, gained battle experience with Luke and the now-deceased Comanche Chief Three Toes.*

William Meaney – *Sheriff of Corpus Christi gives a bit of respect to the lawman role by dressing well. But it belies his toughness.*

Jaime Sanchez – *Works as vaquero at Luke Dunn's Heaven's Gate Ranch. Becomes a valuable asset to Luke. His wife, Julia, helps Elisa with ranch chores.*

Edward Thorpe – *Wealthy Horatio Thorpe's heir to Magnolia Plantation. Frees his slaves. Commits to preserving the Union.*

Jubal Strong – *Cousin to the outlaw "Bad Bart" Strong whom Luke had brought to justice back in 1856 near Laredo. Strong had journeyed from Wyoming and fallen for the opportunities on the Nueces Strip but returns to the War Between the States.*

Chico Sagura – *Mexican rebel loyal to Juan Cortina and determined to accomplish at least some of what Cortina didn't.*

Jake Barber – *Deemed too big and dumb by Confederate recruiters. Earns keep helping Luke keep the peace on the Nueces Strip.*

JD Smith – *A volunteer for Luke's Texas Ranger posse trying to protect the vast reaches of the Nueces Strip from marauding Indians and bandits.*

One Arrow – *Young Penateka Comanche warrior adopted by the now-deceased Comanche Chief Three Toes. One Arrow earned his name killing a buffalo with a single arrow.*

Pablo Ramos – *Leader of Mexican bandit gang. He splits from Juan Cortina and seeks to wreak his own havoc on the Nueces Strip.*

Clay Ashley Bell – *Confederate soldier friend of Walker Carson. Served as a sharpshooter supporting Colonel Yager's Mounted Rifles of the 1st Texas Cavalry.*

Samuel – *Former slave to Horatio Thorpe, father of Edward Thorpe. As a sort of household slave and then an employee, Samuel watched over the family's business interests.*

Snake Collins – *Made reputation as a common thief, claim-jumper, and cold-blooded killer who stalked the gold mines of California. Obsessed with killing lawmen.*

HISTORICAL CHARACTERS

Colonel Henry Lawrence Kinney – *Entrepreneur, rancher, and trader. Founded Corpus Christi. Was leader in settlement of eastern Nueces Strip. Died in Mexico in a gunfight in 1862.*

John Salmon "Rip" Ford – *Soldier, politician, newspaper editor, and Texas Ranger. A renowned Indian fighter, he fought Mexican rebel Juan Cortina. Supported secession, fought in War Between the States, and helped with post-war recovery.*

Sam Houston – *One of Texas' most illustrious leaders. Led fight for independence and served as first president of the Republic of Texas. Served as US Senator and Texas governor.*

Benito Juarez – *Became president of Mexico by the succession mandated by its Constitution when liberal President Comonfort resigned. Served until his death 1872.*

Juan Nepomuceno "Cheno" Cortina – *Mexican rancher, military leader, politician, outlaw, and folk hero. Opposed the Treaty of Guadalupe Hidalgo and fought against Texas Rangers.*

Lieutenant John Kittredge – *Commander, US Navy blockade of Corpus Christi.*

General Benjamin Butler – *Union commander who captured New Orleans early in the War Between the States.*

General Nathaniel Banks – *Successor to General Butler, led three ill-fated campaigns on the Sabine River at the Texas border.*

Colonel William Yager – *Commanded Texas Mounted Rifles and was later commander of the 1st Texas Cavalry.*

Costalites – *Lipan Apache Chief. Caused General mayhem among troops and settlers in Mexico and on the Nueces Strip.*

Colonel William Renshaw – *Union commander who successfully assaulted the strategic port of Galveston in 1862.*

Captain James Ware – *Officer in 1st Texas Mounted Rifle under Colonel Yager.*

THEME

GRIT

Show courage and resolve; strength of character.

INTRODUCTION

Nueces Grit: Texans Answer the Call is the fifth of the Tumbleweed Sagas. The exploits of Texas Ranger Captain Luke Dunn have been at the core of these stories of the taming of the Nueces Strip beginning in 1856. Hopefully, you'll find this contribution to the Sagas an adventure worthy of your time and emotional involvement. This saga takes readers through more troubling and uncertain times for Texans as a devastating conflict had begun to sweep the nation. Texas was very much in its midst.

Visualize the Strip as still mostly a vast prairie of tall grasses and loamy sands that stretched as far as the eye could see and off into some far-off vanishing point. The grasses often grew high enough to reach a horse's withers. The Nueces Strip, called "Wild Horse Desert" by some, reached south from the lazily flowing Nueces River all the way to the meandering Rio Grande along Texas' southern border. Its eastern extremity enjoyed the sea breezes wafting in off the Gulf of Mexico from Corpus Christi all the way to Brownsville. Nestled in hills at its northern extreme was the little town of Uvalde near Fort Inge. The semi-arid rolling terrain of Laredo, with its nearby Fort McIntosh, was generally regarded as the main outpost of the westernmost Nueces Strip. It afforded an easy crossing of the Rio Grande. Corpus Christi founder Colonel Kinney had the foresight to build a road from Corpus to Laredo and another to San Antonio. The roads were rough but serviceable.

The Nueces Strip could be inhospitable six ways to Sunday. The similarities between natural and human dangers were often striking. Imagine the intensity in the yellow eyes and coiled muscles of a lynx stalking an unsuspecting rabbit. Patience. A waft of air stirs the thick fur along his back. The moment of attack must be exactly right. Only an infinitesimal twitch of his bobtail reveals the tension in the beast. He dares not indulge a blink of eyes nor lick of tongue. The rabbit nibbles a shoot of grass and looks about ever so innocently unaware. Now visualize a bushwhacker as he looks long and intensely down the blue-gray barrel of his Winchester. The bead at the muzzle is on the target and cradles in the notch of the rear sight. His finger curls around the trigger. Only a slow bead of sweat rolling down the side of his face reveals his intensity. Patience. The moment must be precise. His breathing; his slow squeeze of the trigger. The bounty hunter tracking him looks about cautiously but unaware. A leap, a snarl, clamped jaws, and the lynx is fed. Breath held, trigger squeezed, and a man lies dead. In its silent vastness, the Nueces Strip sucks it all in.

Inhospitable and uninviting it is in many ways, but the Nueces Strip drew settlers like moths to a light bulb. Mottes or small clusters of live oak or mesquite offered occasional shade relief on the sunbaked prairie. The often-dry creek beds and arroyos eventually filled with rain water and emptied into Nueces Bay and...farther to the east...Corpus Christi Bay. Flash flooding was an ongoing fear. Summers? Well, they tended to be hot and humid. Weather was pretty much whatever you wanted if you waited long enough.

The Nueces Strip up until 1861 had been exploding with growth, as ranches and farms spread ever westward and communities sprung up seemingly overnight. This was despite a creeping drought that had seriously impacted large swaths of south Texas and left it vulnerable economically during the War Between the States. The economic impact on those areas had become serious as livestock perished and settlers were often forced by economics to abandon their spreads. Yet, the telegraph and railroads were expanding their reach, as they'd become an ever-greater contributor to regional commerce. Family, community, faith, and dogged determination were the primary factors contributing to settlement on the Texas frontier, though romantics might be tempted to attribute the winning of the West to a gun or simply a spirit of adventure. Along with settlement came the darker side of human nature —lawbreakers necessitated lawmen to bring justice to the Strip and hostile gangs and Indians demanded larger organizations like the Texas Rangers to keep the peace. However, the Rangers were no longer officially authorized, and lawlessness would get worse.

Slavery figured quite significantly into Texas life, though less so on the vast empty prairies and brush lands of the Nueces Strip. Texas was not immune to the potential social, political, and economic upheaval of slavery. It was estimated that, by 1860, the number of slaves in Texas had reached roughly 180,000, or close to a third of the population. Most of the slave population could be found on the cotton and tobacco plantations of eastern Texas where the soil was especially rich and weather conducive to farming. Cash crops ruled the day, and their financial yields helped fill the coffers in Austin and create powerful politicians. There was a lingering fear of a slave revolt, especially as tempers began to flare nationally concerning slave versus free states. The very institution of slavery had come to near boiling over as an issue and exploded into a full-fledged war in 1861 that tore the nation apart. The Nueces Strip was certainly not immune.

With the break out of the War Between the States in 1861,

life on the Nueces Strip would be changed forever. Such was the dynamic of war. It's notable that Texans preferred not to refer to the conflict as the Civil War. There was nothing civil about it. In any case, the frontier of Texas became ever more vulnerable to predators of the human variety. With precious resources poured into the conflict and manpower in short supply, infrastructure such as roads and railways decayed rapidly. This Texas that Spanish conquistador Cabeza de Vaca had explored way back from 1527 to 1536 was just beginning to manifest the economic giant it was destined to become when the War Between the States hit hard. With war raging and, despite few significant battles in Texas other than Galveston and up on the Sabine River, the Union blockade was effective in causing shortages of many commodities, including coffee, salt, clothing, shoes, medicine, and farm implements. Cotton was a critically important contributor to the Texas economy, and growers were able to skirt the Union blockade by routing it through Matamoros to Bagdad on the coast of Mexico. In fact, the cotton trade with Mexico supplied much-needed iron goods, food, dry goods, liquor, and tobacco to Texans. Coffee is a Texas staple, and Texans in desperation over its scarcity brewed poor substitutes like barley, okra, and peanuts. Transportation was seriously disrupted as railroads deteriorated, stagecoach lines became overcrowded, and the few existing roads suffered from disrepair. The Rio Grande Valley was also home to the Texas version of the Underground Railroad, as many slaves from Mississippi, Alabama, Louisiana, and eastern Texas made their way overland into Mexico. Then, again, it was tough country, and many escaping slaves were either caught by bounty hunters or fell prey to one or more of the natural dangers of the Nueces Strip.

The war slowed commerce in general, as exacerbated by ducking bullets and cannonballs. Beyond places like Corpus Christi, Laredo, and Brownsville, South Texas remained simply an endless prairie of tall grasses and loamy sands or rough brush. There was abundant flora and fauna on the Nueces Strip. If you were on foot, it was advisable to keep an eye and ear peeled for rattlesnakes. They tended to blend in fairly well with their surroundings, so their rattle was often folks' first and only warning of an impending attack. The rattlesnake spawned many a "Texas-ism" like "meaner than a skillet full of rattlesnakes."

The plentiful and accessible longhorn could be called the "low-hanging-fruit" of the regional economy. The longhorns were a hardy breed that could withstand the south Texas heat, fend off disease-carrying pests, and carry just enough meat on their bones to make them reasonably profitable to raise. Originally imported from the Iberian Peninsula by early Spanish priests, the longhorns eventually escaped the mostly failing missionaries, proliferated, and roamed wild and free across the prairies. Millions of the beasts soon covered Texas and especially the excellent grazing lands of the Nueces Strip. They competed with the wild mustangs that had descended from horses also introduced by the Spaniards. Of course, there were the indigenous buffalo, millions of those beasts as well. They were a staple of the Indian way of life. If you liked meat, and any self-respecting folk did, the Texas prairies provided plenty of feed for all.

Despite the roughness of the frontier, the predations of savages and bandits, and a deeply divisive war, the factor that would ultimately win Texas would be the family, the larger the better as children struggled to grow up in the face of all manner of lurking dangers. Families established the ranches and farms popping up not only throughout the eastern portions of the Nueces Strip but across Texas as a whole. The territory east of the 98th meridian that sliced through the very heart of Texas was fast becoming an economic juggernaut, and the Strip was no exception. Its economy was based on growing cotton and raising longhorns and horses. Cotton was bundled and hauled to port for transport to markets in Louisiana and points east. During the War Between the States, sales of cotton helped support the Confederacy. Cattle were still mostly driven to Kansas and Missouri railheads to be shipped to the packing houses of the Midwest, though Corpus Christi would eventually become a hub for the beef industry.

To the west of the aforementioned 98th meridian was the Comancheria. The Indian tribes were pushed ever westward as they were overcome by a deadly cocktail of socio-economic forces and disease. Indigenous tribes of Comanche, Kiowa, Apache, and Ute rode free across this vast region that extended into New Mexico and north into the Texas Panhandle.

No discussion of the Nueces Strip can ever be complete without mention that much of the most significant fighting of the Texas War for Independence was fought on and just north of the Nueces Strip back in 1835 and 1836, and it was scene to the first fighting of the Mexican American War of 1846. The Strip had been officially ceded to the United States by the Treaty of Guadalupe Hidalgo in 1848, though Texas had already laid claim essentially by squatter rights and having kicked Mexican General Santa Anna's sorry posterior. It was likely that this sort of history had prepared Texans for the brutal fighting that would be part and parcel to the War Between the States.

The far reaches of the mostly untamed prairies of the strip beckoned to principled men like our protagonist, Texas Ranger Captain Luke Dunn. While the frontier grew ever westward, there was ongoing worry about the threats posed by Comanche, Kiowa, and Lipan Apache, as well as the rogue marauding bandits from south of the Rio Grande. Those tall grasses and brush of the Nueces Strip were surely high enough to hide a growing population of lawbreakers. This all served to keep early Texans on this wild and often lawless frontier ever vigilant. It was easy to make the case for calling up companies of Texas Rangers to patrol the Nueces Strip, as they took it upon themselves to go where the military found it politically undesirable. On the other hand, the legislators in the state capital in Austin often were unable to pull together the financial means to fund the necessary companies of Rangers. They had to rely on the US Army, which could be chancy at best, as it was subject to the politics of whoever was in power and perceiving real or imagined threats. With the war at hand, they could no longer rely on the US Army, and the Confederate army hadn't the resources to supply meaningful protection.

Nueces Grit takes us to the events and accompanying dynamics in South Texas at the beginning of the War Between the States. In the fourth Tumbleweed Saga, *Nueces Blood*, Texas Ranger Captain Luke Dunn had made significant headway in bringing justice to the Nueces Strip and was just beginning to enjoy the resurgence of the Texas Rangers as a force fighting to bring the rule of law to the region. Luke and Elisa had grown Heaven's Gate ranch both in terms of land holdings and livestock, and the Dunn family had added a son and a daughter to join with their twin boys toward creating their family. But events beyond Luke's control now required a renewed resolve and a major dose of toughness.

Texas Rangers had begun to join the Texas Cavalry units, leaving the law enforcement ranks seriously depleted. With diminished law enforcement, Indians and desperados were quick to take advantage. The Rio Grande Valley became a hotbed of conflict from Brownsville west to El Paso. Occupation seesawed between Yankee and Rebel. Moreover, the civil strife within Mexico often spilled over into Texas.

Luke remained ever-conflicted over his roles of rancher and Texas Ranger, and now war served to complicate his world. Danger lurked whichever Luke chose. Prairie fires, blizzards, floods, stampedes, desperate killers, rustlers, disease, and savages were part and parcel, whether lawman or rancher. Just about anywhere he rode, death could be reaching for his bridle reins. Luke had built considerable notoriety and created enemies by virtue of his successes in bringing lawbreakers to justice, and he had also established reliable allies. Yet the War Between the States pitted friend against friend, brother against brother, and enabled the dredges of society to gain advantage by fair means or foul. When called to continue his role as a Texas Ranger, Luke would be hard-pressed to deliver justice while raising his family. It would take plenty of grit.

While the "Cast of Historical Characters" provides some helpful true-to-life framework to the life and times on the Texas Nueces Strip, woven into the Tumbleweed Sagas are actual settlers of the frontier as drawn from the author's own family ancestry. Peter Dunn immigrated from Ireland in 1850 and established a blacksmith shop in Corpus Christi, John Dunn ranched and grew many acres of cotton, and Nicholas Dunn was a rancher, drover, livestock speculator, and Comanche fighter of some repute. Such real-life characters coupled with actual events have served to reinforce the historical setting for the Tumbleweed Sagas.

My poet/novelist cousin, Mary Maude Dunn Wright (pseud. Lilith Lorraine), in writing the preface to her father John Beamon "Red John" Dunn's biography *Perilous Trails of Texas* back in 1932, posed the question, "Not in the spirit of judging their actions by artificial standards which in their day had no existence, but by asking ourselves if we were in their places, should we have acquitted ourselves as well, and by putting to ourselves the still more potent question: how well have we kept the birthright that have given us, how well have we safeguarded the liberties they purchased through untold privations, how courageously are we meeting the problems that confront us today; in short when we stand before the tribunal of remote posterity, to whom shall the laurel be awarded...?" Whether you live the Old West vicariously through books such as *Nueces Grit* or try your hand at getting outdoors and mimicking frontier life, y'all might think on how you might have handled those challenges of decades ago.

The Old West represents the brave pioneering spirit of

settlers that met the challenges and transcended mere survival to enable America to achieve exceptional growth. The settling of the American West is replete with tales of leveraging freedom for individual achievement. I hope you'll agree that reliving our past—even through history-based fiction—often has the effect of pointing the way to an ever-brighter future. Might we indeed be up to it?

NUECES GRIT

PROLOGUE

"GET BACK HERE, you stupid son of a…!" Luke chased the wayward longhorn as it bolted toward the tall grass and ever-nasty brush. The beast was older than most in his herd and was about as ornery as they came. It was as though the longhorn was taunting Luke, as it would pause, look back at him, and then charge off wildly. Luke's *vaquero* Jaime had taught Luke a popular trick among cowboys aimed at getting escaping beeves under control. The technique was called tailing, and it involved grabbing the tip of the beast's long tail, wrapping it around your saddle horn, and reining in your horse sufficiently to flip the escaping longhorn. The longhorn was plenty sturdy enough to handle it, and tailing was regarded as a highly effective method.

Jaime watched approvingly as Luke grabbed the longhorn's tail. Turned out Luke performed the task with surprising grace for a tall man on a big horse. It helped that Big Horse was swift yet could stop on a dime. Likely had some quarter-horse blood in his line. Jaime had his hands plenty full controlling the half dozen beeves they'd already rounded up that morning, but he managed to let out an approving shout as Luke grabbed the longhorn's tail.

In the split second that Luke began to wrap the end of the longhorn's tail around the saddle horn, the ornery beast came to a sudden halt, hit the ground, bounced up, turned, and narrowly missed goring Big Horse. Much to his disappointment, and to protect the big gray, Luke instinctively released the tail.

The longhorn snorted loudly as though to say, catch me another day. Luke and Jaime would have sworn to about anybody who'd listen that the old longhorn smiled as it ambled off into the tall grass. He'd lay low for now, but he knew they'd get him on another day. The *vaquero* blood in the two men would have liked to have shown the longhorn exactly who was in charge. "Maybe you and Pablo can get his attention on another day, Jaime."

They'd have to satisfy themselves with the cattle they'd already rounded up. Soon enough, they were headed off to the corral Luke and his *vaquero* had built to house the beeves before they were driven to market. Amid the dust and the open landscape, Luke had come to fully love the freedom that was the cowboy life.

They'd built a separate cabin for the new *vaquero* and made sure it was big enough to house a couple of more men as needed.

After tending to Big Horse in the barn, Luke began to walk back to the house. Roughly midway, he paused, turned to his right, and walked up the hill a piece to where Three Toes and other Comanche warriors were buried. It wasn't far from where Elisa's family had been buried under the shade of the live oak motte. Family grave sites were all too common across the frontier, and South Texas was no exception. The stake at the chief's grave was weather beaten but still upright. The bone-bead necklace with its silver cross remained dangling from where Elisa had hung it.

Luke took off his hat and held it in both hands as he reflected on his friendship with Three Toes. He was glad he'd gone off and visited One Arrow at the Comanche encampment. It had been important to show the young warrior the sort of respect that Luke had enjoyed with the chief. He soon enough put his hat back on, stroked his mustache as he thought a moment more on One Arrow, shook his head slightly wondering how the young warrior might be holding up under his weighty responsibilities, and slowly turned back toward the house. He hoped to meet once again with the Comanche, on friendly terms, of course.

ONE
IT BEGINS

A THIN MIST wafted in from the Nueces River as Luke stood on the gallery sipping an early morning cup of coffee. Soon enough, the sun would chase off the mist, absorb the heavy dew, and leave heavy humidity in its wake. He found himself once again ready to set out on what would be a dusty trail from Nuecestown toward Laredo. The telegram from Rip Ford had arrived at Heaven's Gate just a couple of days back.

Elisa was none too happy, but she'd known it'd happen sooner than later. Another idyll was broken. Conflict brought with it the certainty of uncertainty. Despite the war clouds on the horizon and the onset of drought, the ranch had thrived and that translated into ever greater responsibilities. She and Luke had managed to acquire additional small homesteads from folks who'd not been up to meeting the challenge of settling the frontier, much less a potential hostile conflagration among their own people. Heaven's Gate was now home to nearly a thousand longhorns and at least a hundred horses. Coupled with a few pigs, a flock of chickens, and a newly acquired dog, the ranch veritably teemed with life. There was no shortage of trouble for their four-year-old twins Peter and

John to get into, and their two younger siblings taxed Elisa's patience to its limits.

Having recognized the likelihood of the conflict that was now upon them, coupled with their growing holdings, Luke had had the presence to hire a second vaquero to support the ranch. Pablo had become a true asset. Riding the outer reaches of the ranch, gathering strays, roundups, livestock births, and more demanded constant attention. Now, with federal troops lurking on Texas borders, defense had been added to ranch concerns.

"We knew this day would come, Lisa." Lisa was Luke's affectionate name for Elisa. It was special to him, just as she called him Lucas. "So far, the Yankees haven't moved ashore at Corpus." He was referring to the US Navy ship *USS Arthur* and its escorts lurking in the Gulf of Mexico with their ongoing threat of landing federal troops. Apparently, the commander of the *Arthur* was an aggressive lieutenant who was itching to launch an invasion of the city. Every now and then, the ships would lob a few cannonballs. Blessedly, they would give ample warning to the townsfolk. It was as though they were softening Corpus Christi up for a larger effort, perhaps a full-scale landing. Despite a collection of mostly volunteer defenders and the natural barrier of the inland waterway the *USS Arthur*, moored as it was out on the Gulf of Mexico, managed to pretty much keep everyone on edge.

Elisa leaned forward toward Luke, grasped his arm, and stared earnestly into his eyes. "You know they're going to come, Lucas. It's certain they're not going to sit out there forever. Likely as not, they'll do it before you return." She worried that they now had so much more at stake. Their family seemed to be growing fast as blazes. But that was also the way it was on the Texas frontier; large families ensured the ultimate cohesion that marked building civilized communities where disease, dangerous critters, hostile Indians, lawbreakers, and now war tended to create numerous challenges to life.

Importantly, civilization had pretty much been winning until the war got underway in earnest. She knew that civilization as they knew it was now all at extreme risk.

Luke understood her fears. Being a mere 12 miles west of the port city, he fully appreciated that the proximity of the ranch made them vulnerable. When troops landed, the tentacles of their foraging could easily reach out to Heaven's Gate and nearby Nuecestown. He and Elisa were well aware of the perils.

In a way, he regretted having committed to Rip Ford to help keep the peace so far as he could on the Nueces Strip. It was more akin to a choice of keeping the peace near home or join the First Texas Cavalry with his cousins. "I'll try to get this done and be back before the Yankees reach this far." Luke gave her one of those deep kisses that sent her heart to fluttering and a warm shiver of deep passions through her body. If only she could have dragged him up to the bedroom. But the embrace was too brief, and he was already mounting Big Horse, the great gray stallion that served him so well. The horse seemed to sense the adventure that lay ahead.

Luke fondled the telegram, now worn from constant folding. It simply described an attack on a ranch out past San Diego not far off the road to Laredo. According to Rip Ford, now serving as a colonel in the Confederacy and commanding the Rio Grande Military District, Mexicans were suspected. Ford had initiated a trade agreement between Mexico and the Confederacy, but first he'd had to kill a few Mexican invaders loyal to the rebel Juan Cheno Cortina that didn't want Texas to join the Confederacy. In truth, those marked the first deaths in defense of the Confederacy, predating the bombardment at Fort Sumter. Cortina's rebels held hopes of re-annexing the Nueces Strip to Mexico. Ford's telegram to Luke had been delivered about the time Rip left the Rio Grande and rode up to Austin to be in charge of conscription.

Luke figured the attack in San Diego may have been the

last vestiges of the Cortina rebels. Sitting astride Big Horse made Luke seem larger than life. His six-foot-three height had earned him the nickname "Long Luke" from some, but he was partial to the name given him by the Comanche: Ghost-Who-Rides. His ruggedly handsome Irish face framed a well-tended fiery-red mustache. Nine years had now passed since he'd immigrated from County Kildare back in his native Ireland. He still had a hint of Irish brogue on his tongue, but it was now overcome with a bit of the smoothness that was the famous Texas twang. He'd learned a bit of Spanish and had picked up a couple of Comanche words, all delivered with his trademark Irish-Texan accent.

Given Luke's experience, gleaned from having joined rebellious clan factions, he'd learned the use of claymore and firearms and developed a quite self-righteous sense of right and wrong. It was natural for him to gravitate to the lawman profession upon his arrival in Corpus Christi. With a few of his cousins having already immigrated to America, Luke had the advantage of being introduced to Colonel Kinney, the founder of Corpus Christi. Thus, his law enforcement career had gotten underway first as a deputy sheriff and a bit later as a Texas Ranger. He quickly became intimately familiar with the landscape and people of the Nueces Strip, especially given his friendly Irish charm. He'd traded in his weather-beaten, broad-brimmed tan hat for a new chapeau befitting of his Texas Ranger duties. He usually wore a buckskin vest or a coat over a blue shirt with gray trousers stuffed into a comfortable pair of cowboy boots. His gun belt now accommodated his two newly acquired Colt Army Model 1860 revolvers plus plenty of ammunition. Tied to the saddle was his trusty Colt repeating rifle. When on duty as lawman, he pinned the Texas Ranger badge to his shirt, where it stood out so as to be impossible to miss.

His thoughts invariably turned to his personal conflict over being a lawman versus rancher and family man. He'd come to fully appreciate the psychology of dealing with longhorns and discovered it wasn't unlike dealing with desperados. Both were mean and stubborn. As he'd developed his ranching skills, he fully appreciated how the qualities of being a Texas Ranger paralleled those of being a cowboy. Both of those noble professions demanded being observant, alert, loyal, and resourceful. He'd also developed critically important skills such as excellent marksmanship and fine horsemanship. Indeed, the similarities he brought to ranching and delivering justice to the Nueces Strip made his internal conflict between the two roles all the more challenging to choose between—if in fact a choice was necessary.

He rode up the trail from the ranch house and stopped at the entrance to Heaven's Gate. He looked out across Nueces Bay to his right with the Nueces River feeding into it. There was a certain peacefulness that belied the hostilities to come. He could just about make out the house that his cousin John had built. Luke sat a moment and stroked his mustache as he often did during especially thoughtful moments. He wondered how his cousin's cotton business might fare during a protracted war. He shook his head resignedly before he turned the big gray left and began the ride to Nuecestown where he'd find out how many volunteers might have answered his call. He was not exactly optimistic, as most able-bodied men had joined the military to fight with the Confederacy. At best, he hoped the volunteers could ride and shoot with enough accuracy not to put bullets into themselves or other volunteers.

★

Scarlett was a bit tentative as she entered the shop. She'd saved a bit of money, and her new husband, Walker Carson, had urged her to spend a little on herself as a birthday gift.

Perhaps a new dress or new shoes. Little Margaret, her daughter by her ill-fated relationship with now-deceased Sheriff George Whelan, held her mother's hand as they began to examine the beautiful clothing displayed throughout the modestly appointed shop. Scarlett had become more frugal, especially with the prospect of welcoming another child into the world. Her seamstress income, combined with what her husband earned as a sheriff deputy and performing odd jobs, was enough to live fairly comfortably. However, with the coming uncertainties of war…well, she was apprehensive like so many folks around Corpus Christi.

"Look, Mama." Margaret pointed at a young girl that had just entered the shop.

Scarlett's natural reaction was to scold in a near whisper, "Margaret! I've told you never to point at people." With that, she looked to see what had grabbed her daughter's attention.

The young girl was dressed in a fancy black and red dress with a tight corset and bare shoulders. Her lips were painted, and she'd overdone the rouge on her cheeks. She blushed and looked down ashamedly at Margaret's having pointed at her.

Scarlett figured she couldn't be more than fourteen…fifteen at most. Scarlett hadn't been much older when she'd run away from her grandparents' care after having lost her parents in an accident. She'd fallen in love with a couple of ne'er-do-wells before desperation plunged her into the world of prostitution. There was no doubt in her mind that this young lady was already bedding men for money. Men seemed to like the young ones, and the young ones found it easier to pretend to be so very innocent. The shop proprietor was ignoring the girl. Scarlett felt a tug in her heart and decided to reach out to the young whore. "May I help you?" Actually, her question was a deeper one than it appeared. She had risen from that profession and now led a life of married respectability.

The young girl looked up with uncertainty. "I need shoes."

Scarlett looked down at her feet. Despite the fancy dress and makeup, the girl was barefoot. "Where are your shoes, dear?" Scarlett was a mere twenty-three years old herself and was sounding like some grand dame.

The girl looked down sheepishly and mumbled, "A man took them."

Scarlett understood. There were weird customers in the whoring business. "I'm looking for shoes, too. Come join me." She gave a get-over-your-prejudice look to the proprietor and motioned her to come assist them. "What's your name?"

"I'm Martha…but the men have other…" A tear formed.

"Pleased to meet you, Martha. My name is Scarlett Rose Carson and this is my daughter Margaret. My husband is a deputy sheriff here in the city."

At that, the young girl began to perk up and was smiling and talking with Margaret. Scarlett smiled at the girl's apparent ease with children. "Are you interested in…" She paused to think on what she wanted to say, as it would make it clear that she knew what the young girl was. "Are you interested in another line of work?" She could see it register with the young girl's consciousness. She'd have another time to explain how it was that she understood Martha's situation. "I need someone to watch over Margaret on occasion, and I'd like to add another seamstress to my business. Do you know how to sew?" She saw fear creep across Martha's face.

"He'd beat me." Martha said it in a hushed voice that Margaret wouldn't hear.

"Who would beat you, Martha?"

"Him. He'd beat me." Terror edged into her voice.

"What's his name?" Scarlett was nothing if not persistent.

"Rolf something." Beginning to shake with fear, the poor girl could barely get the words out. She didn't even know her pimp's full name.

"Where can he be found?"

"The Longhorn." Martha whispered the name.

"If we get Rolf out of your life, will you work for me?" Scarlett smiled encouragingly.

Martha looked uncertain. "You can do that?"

"We can make certain he doesn't beat you or anyone else. I can take care of that." She was confident that her good Texas Ranger friend could eliminate this problem, but she'd ask Sheriff Meaney first. She asked her question again. "If I take care of Rolf, will you work for me?"

Martha looked deeply into Scarlett's eyes. Finally, her eyes brightened, and she smiled. "I accept."

It brought a warm satisfying feeling to Scarlett as she turned to a nearby table. "Aren't these lovely shoes, Martha?"

★

There was a pinkish glow peeking over the eastern hills where the sun would soon rise. Two men stood outside the rear stairway of the Longhorn Saloon. They'd already hitched their horses and stuffed their spurs into their saddlebags. They slowly and quietly climbed to the second floor. The entry door was open. The barkeep had kept his end of the plan.

The men strode silently down the hallway to Room 12. Each held a Colt revolver in one hand and a branding iron in the other. The larger of the two nodded, stepped back, and opened the door with one heavy kick.

Rolf never had a prayer of defending himself. The shorter man planted the branding iron full onto his nose. The crack could likely have been heard all through the building. Blood gushed from Rolf's face. The larger man brought his iron down on Rolf's knee with sufficient force to break it and bend the iron.

Rolf Gutenhaus was not going to be running anywhere. The larger attacker lifted him bodily and planted him in a nearby chair. His wrists were tied to the arms of the chair. Each attacker went to work on Rolf's hands, smashing them into swollen bloody uselessness. The men's faces were covered by bandannas, so their voices were slightly muffled. "Mr. Gutenhaus, if you are ever seen near Corpus Christi again, you'll be hung or worse."

They untied Rolf's hands, stood for a moment to admire their handiwork, and left the way they'd entered. No one was ever charged with the assault on Rolf. He was never seen in Corpus Christi again.

His whores, if they wanted to continue to ply their trade, would have to find a new master.

★

The nine bandits had ridden confidently up to the cabin. Broad-brimmed sombreros shielded them from the day, and bandoliers crossed over their chests gave them a sinister appearance. They sat astride spirited horses that pranced in seeming anticipation of what was to come. The bandits had already wreaked their carnage on several homesteads. The loot they'd collected was heavy and had become a negative factor as the extra weight slowed them down. There was little reason to continue to raid other than to satisfy a sort of blood lust. The bandits relished the sheer pleasure of what was likely to be their final raid before heading back to Mexico.

The leader raised his arm, pointed at the man on his knees who'd had the misfortune to emerge from the cabin, and snarled loudly. "*¡Mátalo!*" Six rifles responded to the command to kill. The man's body convulsed as he was riddled with bullets. He died before his body hit the ground.

"*¡Qué!*" The leader turned to two of the men whose rifles misfired. "*Limpia tus rifles.*" He would not tolerate carelessness in keeping weapons in working order. "*Mira dentro de la cabina.*" Two men dutifully dismounted and smashed through the cabin door.

The men smiled as they pushed a pretty young blonde-haired woman and two small children before them from the cabin. The frightened woman looked frantically from side to side. There was no avenue to escape. She was trapped. The bandit leader calmly pulled out his revolver and shot each child dead. The woman struggled in the grip of the bandits in her desperation to comfort her boys in their dying gasps, but the men held her tightly.

The bandit leader produced rawhide strips and motioned toward a high corral post. "¡Cuélgala!" The men dutifully bound her wrists and bound her arms to the post high above her head. "¡Desnudala *y violala!*" She was stripped naked. The bandits' smiles and snickers betrayed the evil they were about to do. Trousers were already being loosened in preparation for what was to come next.

The bandy-legged bandit leader was slightly overweight and on the shorter side height-wise. He was a swarthy man in an oversized sombrero. He slouched on a bench in front of the cabin and lit a cigar. A bandolier hung across his chest from the left shoulder and an old Colt 1851 Navy revolver—the one he'd killed the children with—was stuck in his holster. Chico Sagura watched the woman now hanging fully exposed from the post across the yard from him as each of his men had their way with her. Mercifully, each man was quick. Her screams had soon given way to helpless groans. The rawhide cut into her wrists as she pulled and squirmed. Her bonds caused rivulets of blood to flow down her arms and onto her chest. Her ankles had been bound to stakes spread a couple of feet apart so as to make the rapes easier for the men.

"*Ella es muy hermosa, ¿si?*" He egged his men on. The woman was so less beautiful as he'd described. He laughed and shook his head in mock dismay. "*Lástima, supongo que debo mostrarte.*" He would go last and show them how it was done. He pulled himself up from the bench. Sagura strode confidently over to the woman. He clenched the cigar firmly in his teeth and unfastened his pants. He scanned her slender white body from long blonde hair to her now-bloodied feet. He stuck the cigar in her mouth, forcing her to inhale and causing her to cough. He looked straight on into her eyes. He had one gray eye and one brown, but that wouldn't matter to the desperate woman. Didn't matter that some thought it a mark of the devil.

For her part, he was just another one of them. They'd killed her husband and children before her eyes and set fire to the barn. Through the cigar fumes, she could smell the odor of sweat and trail dirt seemingly oozing from every pore of Sagura's body. She didn't know how long she'd been hanging there, but there'd been at least eight men taking turns raping her. They were far from gentle, and her genitals had been rubbed raw. That was the least of her worries.

Sagura pressed himself hard against her and pushed his manhood into her as deep as he could. She winced with pain, as he looked over his shoulder at his men. He jerked the cigar from her mouth, then smiled heartlessly while holding the cigar clenched in his teeth. His head leaned toward her face just enough for her to chomp a piece from his ear. He pulled back. "*¡Eres una luchadora, perra!*" She was a fighter, indeed.

He held his hand to his ear as blood poured down the side of his face. Panting from his sexual effort and now the pain of his wound, he stepped back and looked her over. He turned to his men and laughed out of embarrassment and derision. In a heartbeat, a knife appeared in his hand and found its way deep into her stomach. "*¡Muerte perra!*" Death indeed. It would come as a relief.

The woman screamed in agony. Sagura didn't simply pull the knife out, but rather twisted the blade even deeper into her. He stepped back with a cruel grin to watch her die. The evil smile spread even farther across his face as he realized she was still breathing. He drew on the cigar, blew smoke in the woman's face, and plunged the knife deep into her belly once more. She finally drew her last breath. Sagura turned to his men. "*¡Hombres, vamos!*"

Sagura's men grabbed what they could from the cabin, led the homesteader's horses from the corral, and were soon mounted and on their way.

Sagura turned to the rider next to him to boast of their prowess at having attacked three homesteads in as many days. He figured to steer a bit south of San Diego. Even with manpower reduced in the town, it wouldn't do to tempt fate. Better to head up the road a few miles and make camp.

★

Luke rode easy-like into Nuecestown and pulled up in front of the jail, such as it was. He stopped, sighed, and scanned the little town. Bernice and Agatha, who ran the town boarding house, saw him ride in and alerted the three guests they'd persuaded to enjoy a breakfast while awaiting the Texas Ranger's arrival.

Luke dismounted and hitched Big Horse and the packhorse to the nearest post. He didn't have to wait long for the volunteers to assemble in the street in front of the jail. It had rained just a tad just before sunup, so they did their best to avoid a few muddy patches.

Bernice and Agatha stood on the new gallery they'd added to the front of the boarding house. They'd pretty much figured that Luke would be none too pleased at the ragtag collection his call had brought him. If Texas attracted so-called second-chancers, this array was more like third or fourth chancers.

Five men had finally ambled over to where Luke stood. He'd hardly looked up when he found himself taken aback. "Doc, what are you doing here?"

"I need to contribute, Luke." He'd been sober now for a couple of years, but there wasn't much doctoring going on these days around Nuecestown. He'd lost the rheumy town drunk image and managed to maintain a smart-looking beard. "Thought you might need my medical expertise."

Luke shook his head. "Doc, there's more people that need you here. I appreciate your intentions." He turned to the other four. One man had only one barely serviceable leg. A second volunteer was a big man, while the third and fourth were on the smaller side, one old, one young. Luke could easily figure why the Confederate military had rejected these folks. He considered that they may recruit them if things turned for the worse and they became desperate.

Luke turned to the one-legged man. "I'm sorry, partner, but you know you can't set a horse right. Where we're going is likely to require hard riding. Rather see you stay here and protect the town from Yankees."

The man was saddened, but resigned to his fate. "I'll do the best I can, Captain Dunn."

Luke looked over the other three. "Y'all have horses and weapons?"

"Just what we brung, Captain, sir." The older of the two smaller men spoke up. "We have horses, or at least I have a dang-good mule."

Luke shook his head. "And weapons?"

The youngest of the remaining trio spoke up. He had a rather high-pitched voice, but with just a touch of gravel to it. "Got a Colt and a knife, Captain."

"What's your name?"

"JD...JD Smith, sir."

Luke looked at the young man's short slender frame. "You think you're up to this?"

"Yes. Yes, I am." He was quite definitive.

Luke turned to the big man. "You have a name?"

"Jake Barber, sir. And I've got a rifle and a pistol with plenty of ammo."

Luke nodded and turned to the oldest of the three. "And what of you?"

The man showed a Kentucky long rifle and a flintlock pistol stuck in his waistband. "Name's Rance, sir. These and my Bowie knife are about it, Captain."

Beggars couldn't be choosy, to Luke's way of thinking. At least, they were warm bodies that could likely shoot. He handed each an official-looking form. "Can y'all write? If not, just sign your X." Luke at least wanted to be able to contact next of kin.

With the formalities out of the way, Luke thought on how he was going to deal with this ragtag little group. By now, Dan had brought their horses up from the livery. The mounts were as motley as the volunteers. Of course, one mount was a mule and a tad feisty at that. Luke thought back a couple of years earlier when the Texas Ranger company had paraded with fine horses and full armament. Back then, they looked well-ordered and ready to defeat any Indian or bandit that crossed their path. This crew seemed a different matter. It would take two days to get to San Diego, and then they'd spend a day or so checking out what sort of damage Rip Ford had referred to. Luke actually prayed fervently that they wouldn't run into any hostiles.

"We will be investigating some attacks around San Diego. Most important, don't shoot anything unless I tell you. We might be outgunned, and I'd hate to see y'all get yourselves killed." He looked expectantly from man to man. "We leave from this spot in an hour, so get your gear together and be ready to ride."

★

Sagura's bandits aimed at resting for a couple of days, so their camp had more niceties than usual. Their blood lust had been temporarily satisfied. There was plenty of food, they'd upgraded their horses, and they even pitched a couple of tents. They were disappointed in a perverse sort of way that Sagura hadn't permitted the woman from the homestead to live. She'd have been handy as part of their camp festivities. He seemed to be determined to leave no witnesses to his atrocities. None of the bandits, much less Sagura, considered that, with as clear a trail as he'd cut across the Nueces Strip, witnesses would be the least of their worries.

TWO
MISTAKEN IDENTITY

THE FIRST PART of their journey had gone fairly well along the road toward San Diego, as they made about fifteen miles before the light grew too dim. It gave them some time to begin to get acquainted. With this bunch, Luke thought riding at night might not be the greatest idea.

They hobbled the horses and made camp. Luke and Barber, the big man, unloaded the pack horse with its victuals and cookware. Soon enough, a cooking fire was blazing, and dinner served up. Luke had brought along a bit of bacon and offered it along with spuds and coffee. As he rightly figured, this first night would afford a chance to get even better acquainted.

As they sat around the fire enjoying dinner, Luke opened the conversation. "Jake, how come you decided to volunteer?"

The big man turned serious and paused in his cleaning of the cookware. "Ain't got no gripe with Yankees or Rebels, Captain. Didn't feel led to fight one agin' the other." Implied was that helping Luke afforded him escape from that commitment. "Besides, they didn't have a uniform that'd fit me." He offered up a smile at his own humor. He lowered his voice to a near whisper. "An' I don't cotton much to one man owning another."

Luke nodded. "Ever been in a gunfight or battle?"

"Fought with General Taylor. Didn't shoot nothin' but a couple mangy Mexicans. Don't know if I killed them." He didn't sound as though he wanted to elaborate on the experience.

Luke felt reasonably assured that the man could shoot a gun and might have some hint of battlefield sense. From what he'd heard about the Mexican American War, many battles in Texas and northern Mexico consisted of chasing retreating Mexicans. "Pleased to have you with me, Jake."

Luke turned to JD. The young man seemed at first blush to be the least experienced. He didn't look as though he was old enough to shave yet, and his voice hadn't matured. "How about you, JD, how come you volunteered?"

JD thought a moment, as if never truly having considered a reason. "Don't rightly know, Captain. Jus' seemed like the thing to do."

"Ever been in a gunfight or battle?"

JD forced a smile. "Fought my Pa a few times. He was an ornery old cuss. I used to shoot squirrels and rabbits and such, but never shot a man...or woman." His expression shifted as though there might have been a woman he'd have liked to shoot.

"Just remember not to do any shooting until I say so. Pleased to have you with me, JD."

Luke watched curiously as JD ambled off and bedded down about thirty feet beyond the campsite perimeter. Luke thought that was strange and was concerned as a security issue, though he decided not to raise it as any sort of problem just yet.

Luke repeated his questions with the old man and uncovered nothing especially unusual. He had managed to leave Goliad before the Mexicans massacred the Texans. He had been entrusted to carry a message to Sam Houston, though it didn't matter in the end. As Luke saw it, at least the old man had some sort of fighting spirit and loyalty to Texas.

★

"*Señora* Dunn?" Jaime was calling from the front of the house. The *vaquero* had just returned from Corpus Christi to get supplies that had been unavailable in Nuecestown. Seemed availability of day-to-day goods would be ever more of an issue. He had made a habit of reporting on the status of the Yankee naval vessels sitting offshore.

Elisa appeared on the gallery with baby John held on her hip. "What is it, Jaime?"

"The soldiers are planning to come ashore." He said it matter of factly, though it belied his concern.

Elisa sighed deeply. This was what she feared, especially with Luke away. "Thank you, Jaime. Let's keep the rifles close by. Julia and your son can stay here with me, if you feel that would be safer."

"*Gracias, Señora* Dunn. I will ask her."

Now they'd be left to wait and be as ready as possible if in fact the troops landed and chose to bivouac in Corpus Christi. She wondered where the Confederate military was. What were they doing to defend the city? She knew it was essentially a rhetorical question.

★

Amazingly, Luke's volunteers were mounted and ready to ride at first light. He was pleasantly surprised that the old man's mule had been no problem. The beasts could be ornery, but this one seemed pretty pliable as mules went. It remained to be seen how it might react to gunfire.

They rode at a goodly pace. Luke figured to make San Diego by mid-afternoon.

They stopped once to water themselves and the horses. As Luke dismounted, he quickly took note that JD didn't seem inclined to answer nature's call. "You okay, JD?" He stood, letting the horse drink from the stream.

"Yes, sir. Just have no need, Captain, sir."

Luke shook his head. The dampness spreading at JD's crotch belied the need to relieve himself. "You embarrassed to show yourself among other men?"

"Um…yes."

"Well, JD, you're going to be right uncomfortable riding with wet drawers. Saddle might not appreciate it either."

JD blushed.

Then it hit Luke. JD was not a man. "What does JD stand for?"

JD sighed. The ruse was up. Hadn't taken all that long. "Janet Denise." Barber overheard, and his jaw gaped as his ears perked up.

Luke was stuck with her for now. "Why are you doing this, Janet Denise Smith?"

"My man was beating on me, Captain." A hint of a tear appeared at the corners of each eye. "But…but I can shoot. Really, I can. I can help you."

Luke was of a mind to drop her off in San Diego, but he needed whatever firepower he could muster. If she could shoot, she could stay. For now, they were too close to San Diego to test her marksmanship. It wouldn't do to arouse anyone within earshot. He gazed at her sympathetically. "Well, if you get to feeling the urge again, go on off where we won't be seeing you answer nature's call." He saw Jake start to laugh and quickly dissuaded him with a scowl.

★

Sagura's bandits were groggy from a night of boozing and singing. The bandit leader would be hard put to get them mounted for any purposeful endeavors this day. He decided to sit tight and think on his next attack. There were enough vulnerable homesteads around such that the pickings were right easy. It had become more an issue of how much more loot they could carry.

Sagura and his bandits were among the last of Cheno Cortina's men. Could be said they were the sore losers in the fighting against Texas Ranger leaders Rip Ford and George Stoneman. The Rangers undoubtedly would have kept up the fight had it not been for the arrival of a certain Colonel Robert E. Lee, the US Army's commander of the Department of Texas. Most of the ranches along the Rio Grande from Rio Grande City to Brownsville had been destroyed or abandoned, and Lee was determined to make peace with Mexican officials. The Texas Rangers had brought the Cortina war to a temporary end. Lee had suggested that the Rangers needed to warn Mexicans before they attacked, but the success achieved by Ford was precisely because they gave no forewarning and were thus able to defeat the enemy despite being outnumbered. Sagura had observed Lee and decided he would never win a war, because the man was smart but tended to communicate his intentions to his enemies. Rip Ford surely shared Sagura's perspective. Soon enough, Lee would be headed eastward at the behest of Jefferson Davis.

Despite the inattention by law enforcement and military on the Nueces Strip and most of western Texas, Sagura rightly figured that the Texans would eventually send a force to chase him back to Mexico, if not hang him. He knew he was on borrowed time, but he'd wreak whatever damage he could in the meantime. His raids thus far had been profitable, as hidden caches of coin and jewelry were found on a couple of the places he'd attacked. Thus far, the swath he'd cut from Nuevo Laredo to San Diego had seen eight ranches burned, nearly two dozen settlers killed, several horses captured, and a few hundred dollars' worth of valuables stuffed into the bandits' pockets. Sagura would sit tight for today, but his plan was to turn southward in the next day or so.

★

Luke was tempted to stop in San Diego, but knew it would seriously delay his efforts. His small posse began to skirt the town and head west to see what sort of trouble might have been wrought.

"We're not stopping in San Diego, Captain?" JD was looking for a break from riding all morning, plus had an urge to answer nature's call in a more private setting.

Luke gazed resignedly at her. He knew women could be hardy, as exemplified by his own wife, but also recognized they had special needs now and again. He pulled up. "I don't want to engage the folks in San Diego in any idle chatter. Just take care of your business, and we'll be on our way." With that, he led the trio into the town.

The residents, mostly women and children, lined the street watching out of curiosity as much as anything. Luke tried not to make eye contact. JD made a beeline for the privy behind the general store.

Finally, one of the women was bold enough to step in front of Big Horse. She was middle-aged and well kept. "Who are you?"

"Texas Ranger Captain Luke Dunn, ma'am, at your service."

"Are these…these rabble Rangers, too?"

Luke wasn't exactly pleased at her assessment, though it was fairly accurate. "Ma'am, most Rangers signed up with the cavalry or army. We depend on volunteers." He gave her the steeliest look he could muster. "We heard there were ranches being attacked out this way and have been sent to investigate."

"Little late for investigating, Captain Dunn. Last we heard, the Hackett and Corrigan places were wiped out and everyone massacred. They say it was Mexican rebels."

Luke got to thinking that JD's biological need had yielded a side benefit—he'd learned a bit about his potential foe. "Those places far from here, ma'am? I'd much like to pick up the trail of these bandits and give them a taste of Texas Ranger grit."

"Just keep on heading westward, Captain, and good luck to you."

About this time, JD rejoined the posse with a demure smile that revealed her appreciation for Luke's graciousness in accommodating her needs. "I'm ready, Captain. I'll try not to be a further distraction."

Luke stuck his heels into Big Horse's sides, and they were on their way.

THREE
OUTGUNNED

THE CHILDREN WERE PLAYING BLISSFULLY while Elisa tended to chores inside the house. There was never a shortage of work, and she was trying to tidy up a bit before she'd tackle the deer that Jaime had brought in the night before and left lying alongside the gallery. Of course, the deer had been field-dressed. She and Jaime's wife, Julia, would make short work of it, but it wouldn't do to wait too long. Elisa was of a mind to make some venison sausage, a delicacy that Luke thoroughly enjoyed.

The women were startled by a loud banging at the front door. She peeked out the window to see six heavily armed mounted soldiers in blue coats.

"Open up! Open by order of the United States Army!"

She sighed and wiped her hands on the front of her dress. "Just a minute!" she called out. She motioned to Julia to take the children to a back room. Elisa had rehearsed this eventuality in her mind several times. She leaned the Colt rifle against the doorjamb and slowly opened the door.

The sergeant was momentarily taken aback, likely by the sight of the beautiful woman standing before him. "Er, ma'am, I'm Sergeant Wilson, and we're here to requisition supplies."

"Are you prepared to pay a fair price?"

The question hadn't been expected. "Excuse me, ma'am, but we are at war and this is enemy territory."

"I don't see any enemies here, Sergeant. Do you see enemies?"

The sergeant was totally thrown off his game.

"Sergeant, we raise horses and cattle. If you take any without payment, you'll be stealing. In Texas, we hang rustlers." Elisa knew she had totally confused the young sergeant.

Flustered, Sergeant Wilson bowed slightly, "Sorry to have bothered you, ma'am." He turned, looked at his men, and shrugged. Blessedly, the sergeant was new at foraging in enemy territory.

"Y'all have a nice day, Sergeant." All the while, Elisa had been thinking about the rifle leaning just inside the door and within easy reach. As the sergeant mounted and led his men off, she stepped inside, closed the door, and leaned against it with a huge sigh of relief. She'd won this encounter, but knew it was unlikely to be the first. She turned to Julia. "They'll be back."

★

The odor reached them before the cabin was even in view. The mixed aromas of smoke and carnage caused them to tie bandannas across their faces.

In but a few minutes, they found themselves at the scene. Luke dismounted and grabbed his shovel. As he walked over to the woman still hanging naked and blood-caked, he handed the shovel to Barber. Luke took out his Bowie knife and cut the rawhide straps holding the dead woman to the post. He saw her torn dress nearby and draped it over her.

Luke looked around to find JD, but she was already off in the bushes vomiting.

You'd have thought that with Luke's having seen these kinds of atrocities before, his emotions would have grown numb. But it always touched him deeply. He was ever dismayed over what sorts of monsters torture and maim for pleasure. He could forgive JD her revulsion.

"Let's get on with burying these poor folks. We have some tracking to do." It was clear that he meant to find and likely punish those who had done this. Luke figured it was the Mexican bandits he'd been told about in San Diego, as there was no Indian sign. Had it been Comanche, they'd have mutilated the victims far more.

They dug a single grave, deciding to bury them as a family. Luke fashioned a cross as best he could. From belongings in the cabin, he found their family name and carved it into the cross. They said a little prayer before mounting up. It hadn't taken Luke but a few minutes to find the bandits' track to the south.

"You really aim to bring these sons of bitches to justice, Captain?" Rance was an old codger, but he aimed to live. He wasn't sure what sort of miscreants they'd be facing. "We're likely outnumbered and outgunned."

"I expect we will be, Rance. But I've had just a bit of experience at this sort of thing. We Texas Rangers have a way of evening the odds. Just do as I say, and you'll be fine." Luke knew he was stretching the truth a bit on that last phrase.

Barber had been silent since they'd first discovered the bodies at the little ranch. "Like to kill all them sons of bitches, Captain."

Luke ignored the remark and urged Big Horse into a canter to put a little distance between himself and his modest entourage. He rightly calculated that his prey was burdened with loot from their depredations. It seemed likely they'd catch up with them right quickly.

★

"*¿Jefe, vamos a México?*" One of Sagura's band finally had the courage to ask what they all wanted to know. It'd taken a bit of booze to bolster his psyche, but why not ask?

Sagura smiled. He wondered why they feared him so. "*Si, vamos a México.*"

The man began to turn, then paused. "*¿Ahora?*"

"*Mañana, Carlos. Mañana.*"

"*Atacaremos ranchos. ¿Y las mujeres?*"

Sagura shook his head. He knew it was less about some overarching Mexican cause and more about looting and raping. "*Tal vez.*" It was indeed a maybe. There wasn't much to attack between San Diego and Rio Grande City. He'd decided to head due south rather than cross the Rio Grande further north near Laredo. "*Mañana nos dirigimos a México.*" He smiled at the bandit. "*Ve a celebrar. Bebe ahora, prepárate en la mañana.*" Better to let them celebrate and get drunk. They'd be easier companions riding south with hangovers. Maybe they'd come across another ranch, and the men could have their carnal needs met. Until then…well…they had plenty of whiskey.

As the sun dipped toward the horizon, Sagura picked one of the men who appeared least drunk to stand sentry duty. He hoped he'd be able to catch some sleep before they departed in the morning.

★

Luke actually smelled the Mexican camp before riding to a slight rise on the prairie and seeing it a half mile or so in the distance. He brought his posse to a halt. "Dismount. We're downwind. Tougher to hear or smell us. We walk our horses from here. Watch out for varmints, but don't shoot any. I want us to keep downwind from the camp." He prayed inwardly that they'd not encounter snakes or javelina or the like. The grasses were high enough to mostly hide the posse from sight, and a meandering arroyo made walking a bit easier. He looked up at the vast sky and appreciated that there would barely be any moonlight this night. The sun would fully set in about a half hour.

"We gonna rush them, Captain?" Barber whispered with an intensity that revealed he was anxious to kill all the bandits.

"First, we wait until the sun has fully set. Y'all will stay here while Jake and I dispose of the sentry that's sure to be posted. From the size of the camp and the singing and drunken carrying on I'm hearing, I'd guess there's seven or eight of them. We need to reduce their advantage." Luke looked at Barber. He was nearly as big as Luke, though judged not nearly so intelligent. "Jake, after you and I get back, we'll talk about the best strategy. JD, you and Rance keep the horses quiet."

Darkness finally descended sufficiently that Luke felt confident in approaching the camp. The wind still blew in from the west behind Luke, so he remained downwind from his prey. He stored his spurs in the saddlebag and headed out.

The sentry stood out as a silhouette against the crescent moon, presenting as clear a target as could be hoped for. He was a man of average height with a bit of a paunch. Luke was glad he couldn't smell him. A bit of dew had already settled on the grasses and served to silence their footsteps.

Luke waited patiently until he saw the man unfasten his trousers to relieve himself. Luke had learned long ago that this was the best time to attack. He got to within about three feet when the man heard him. He turned, but too late to avoid Luke's Bowie knife. The bandit stood gasping for a moment as he peed down his pants and crumpled to the ground. Luke slit his throat just to be certain.

"*¿Jorge, dónde estás?*" One of the sentry's companions had decided to answer nature's call and was looking for him.

Luke dropped behind a clump of sagebrush.

The bandit saw the sentry on the ground. "*¿Jorge, te has desmayado?*" He wondered what had happened as he suspected the sentry had passed out. He knelt over the sentry's body and reached out to arouse him. Just as he came to the realization that the stickiness on his hand was blood, Luke's knife found its way into his back.

Luke dealt a finishing cut. He'd been lucky so far. Both bodies were bathed in the odors of sweat, booze, horses, and pee. He guessed they'd been drinking all day. Most were likely more passed out than sleeping. He wished he could feel assured that he had the firepower for a full assault on the camp. Likely as not, he could finish four or five before they even roused from their drunken stupors.

He decided to get a closer look. From 40 or 50 feet away in the moonlight, he counted seven sleeping men in a near-perfect circle around the dying embers of the campfire. Except for occasional snoring, there was silence. The bandits' horses were neatly hobbled and tied on a line like a remuda. It looked as though they were prepared to leave in a hurry at first light. He began to retrace his steps. He wasn't sure about JD and Rance, but perhaps he and the big fellow could finish off the bandits before they even knew what hit them.

"What are we going to do, Captain?" As the eldest, Rance had decided to be spokesman.

"You'd better get that old long rifle primed, Rance." Luke grinned. He turned toward the three of them. "These men are prepared to head out at first light. We need to attack them tonight. If we don't and they discover they've lost two of their gang, they'll do whatever it takes to hunt us down. This will be our only chance. We'll get them while they're in their drunken stupor and asleep around their campfire."

"You killed one of them, Captain?" JD stood with her mouth agape in wonderment.

"Two, actually. There's seven of those mean sons of bitches sleeping in that camp." Luke looked the three over. "We're going in on horseback. A man on a horse always has the advantage in this sort of attack. Jake, you and I are going to ride right on into the embers of the campfire and pick the bandits off one at a time. This will be pistol work. JD and Lance, I want you to be on the right and left to pick off any bandit that runs for it. Am I clear? Y'all stay about thirty feet on either side of Jake and me." Luke thought a moment. "No charity here. Shoot to kill."

The trio was so excited about Luke's call to action that they had no obvious nervousness about them. The adrenaline ran high. Luke checked both of his Colts and Barber checked his old Colt. They mounted up and began to move forward at a trot, then a canter. In what seemed like mere seconds they'd reached the bandit camp. Luke rode the big gray through the campfire, kicking up sparks every which way. The air was quickly filled with the steady sound of explosions rendered by the Colt revolvers. One, two, three...screams and groans filled the air.

Luke alternately fired a Colt in his left hand and then right hand. Each time a bullet hit a body, there was a puff of fabric, flesh, and blood. The carnage took all of a minute. There was no return fire. Barber finished off a couple of the bandits himself, though the image of Luke spitting fire from those two big Colts while astride the huge gray stallion would be indelibly imprinted on Sagura's mind.

The Mexican gang's leader had had the sense to sleep a little farther out than the others. At the first shot, he awakened and bolted for the horses. He could move pretty quick for a man carrying a bit of paunch. Rance aimed his Kentucky long rifle at him and squeezed the trigger. It misfired. The flint had broken off. Sagura managed to leap into the saddle of the nearest horse. He saw the old man trying to insert a new flint, mustered up an evil sort of grin, and calmly squeezed off a well-aimed shot at him.

JD saw Rance fall and sprinted to him. Sagura fired again, the bullet grazing her leg. She half-fell, half-somersaulted onto Rance's body.

By this time, Luke and Barber had completed their death-dealing work around the campfire. Luke saw Sagura's shooting of Rance and JD and turned Big Horse toward the bandit. He could do naught but shout at Sagura. "Halt! You're under arrest!" It was a feeble attempt, but the best Luke could do in the immediate aftermath of the attack. He couldn't yet be certain that all of Sagura's men were dead, and it wouldn't do to be shot by a wounded bandit.

Seeing he was outnumbered and outgunned, Sagura ducked as low as his girth would permit and spurred his mount to a gallop. He'd caught a brief glimpse of Luke's Texas Ranger badge reflected in the starlight, so couldn't be sure that an entire company had descended on him. Sagura quickly disappeared into the thick grasses of the darkened prairie.

Luke turned disappointedly back to the camp. He wouldn't be so foolhardy as to pursue a lone bandit at night in dim moonlight. The Mexican would have too much advantage. He trotted over to where Barber had dismounted to tend to JD. Luke saw that big man had already checked the bandits to be certain they were dead. They were not aiming to take any prisoners. "How's the girl, Jake?"

"She'll make it, Captain. I'm afraid Rance here is done."

"How you feeling, JD?"

"I'll be okay, Captain. Mr. Barber here is patching me up just fine."

Luke saw that the Mexican's bullet had grazed JD's leg. She would indeed be okay. "We're going to bring Rance's body to San Diego. He can be buried properly in their cemetery. We'll load up the bandits' loot and give most of it to the citizens there. The rest pays for our service to Texas."

"We gonna sleep here tonight, Captain?"

Luke looked around the campfire circle. "Can't say as I enjoy sleeping around a bunch of dead bodies, so we'll go off a piece and catch a little shuteye. We'll head out before sunup."

"We gonna bury the dead Mexicans?"

Visions of the ranch where they'd recently buried the murdered family slipped into Luke's consciousness. Such things were unforgettable. It'd be a lot of work burying the six bandits around the campfire plus the two he'd slain out among the grasses. He had to ask himself what made them any different from the dead Comanche he'd laid out respectfully a couple of years back. Maybe it was that the savages didn't know any better and these bandits had made an evil choice. He looked from Barber to JD, who were both standing by expectantly and then at the totally inadequate shovel Barber held.

"Might sound disrespectful to the dead, but the ground's hard and shovel is small. I'd as soon bury a herd of longhorns as these sons of bitches." Luke let a bit of his anger slip out. "Just lay them out in a row and let the buzzards and coyotes have them." He turned his back and began to head to a live oak motte about 100 yards away.

Barber and JD stood with mouths agape. Luke's response had been fully unexpected. They looked at each other and shrugged. JD was a little slip of a thing, so Barber would be carrying the load of moving the bodies. JD turned up her nose. "They're already beginning to stink."

"Hell, they stunk afore they was dead. I don't care what the captain says, we ought to bury them." Barber was riddled through with guilt. He began to dig while JD struggled with her wounded leg but managed to drag three of the bodies over to the shallow graves as Barber dug them.

Luke could hear the chipping and scraping as Barber dug the graves, but he closed his mind to the sounds. This was a tough business, and he didn't always get to do things the way he'd prefer. Every man deserved some sort of burial. After about an hour of listening to the noise from the camp, Luke sighed, strode on over, and took the shovel from Barber. "Haul the last couple of damned bodies over here, Jake. Let the girl get some rest." And he turned to digging the remaining graves.

★

They'd respectfully tied Rance's body over the saddle of the mule he so loved. It didn't take long to ride to San Diego. They stuck around while the town folk graciously found an appropriate box, gave Rance a funeral, and interred him in the San Diego cemetery.

The woman Luke had spoken to the day before was pleased to receive the major share of the bounty Luke had taken from the bandits. She and others were deeply saddened by what had happened to their neighbors.

"Where you headed, Captain?" It was a logical question.

"Back to Nuecestown, ma'am. This is a big territory, and there's lots to tend to."

"You know it's a fool's errand, Captain Dunn. You'll never get them all, and they're as likely gonna get you first. Shoot, they're as plentiful as fleas on a dog."

"Have to try, ma'am." Luke stood beside Big Horse. "I'll try to come through here now and again, but I expect I'll get busier when that confounded war hits our doorstep."

"You didn't join up, Captain?"

"Folks up in Austin needed someone to try to keep law and order on the Strip and the job fell to me. I've been doing this for a bit and know the territory."

"I do confess, Captain, I'd heard about you and must say you fulfilled my expectations." She smiled demurely.

For Luke's part, he'd have none of whatever she was thinking. "It was good to have made your acquaintance." He swung up onto Big Horse and nodded to Barber and JD to follow him eastward.

FOUR
ENEMY

THE JANGLE of military equipment filled the dew-laden morning air. Two dozen blue-coated cavalry rode stood at the entrance arch to Heaven's Gate in the splendor of freshly issued uniforms, yellow bandannas, black broad-brimmed cavalry hats with gold braid hatbands, shining sabers, black boots, and trusty Colt Dragoon revolvers. In the scabbards tied to their saddles were newly issued 44-caliber Henry breech-loading lever-action rifles. If there was anything amiss, it had to be their horses. They rode some of the sorriest nags to be seen. Major Gordon Belknap was intent on correcting that problem and thought he knew exactly where he'd find suitable steeds.

For their parts, the troopers were pleased to be on *terra firma* after weeks at sea. The gentle roll of riding was much preferable to the rocking of a ship. It was a much-celebrated bonus that they could eat and not expect to upchuck food into the Gulf of Mexico.

Belknap was counting on his past alliances with Texas Ranger Captain Luke Dunn. He was put off by having learned that Elisa Dunn had chased off a foraging party a couple of days earlier. He'd had a few words with the sergeant, though was relieved that the man had remained civil and had the good sense not to use force. Belknap and Luke had fought together a couple of times, and he admired the way Luke had even developed a friendship with the savage Comanche Chief Three Toes. Then again, the chief had occasion to have spared the major's life and vice versa. Belknap most admired the way Luke seemed to have figured life out, at times finding peaceful solutions to powder keg moments. Still, when Luke had to use force, the outcome for lawbreakers was never in doubt.

He heard a horse close in behind him and turned to see his lieutenant ride up.

"Pardon, Major."

"Yes, Lieutenant, speak freely."

"Did you see the expressions on the faces of those towns-folk? They'd like to have torn us apart."

"I don't think they view us as friendlies, Lieutenant."

"Sir, do you really think this rancher will sell us horses?"

"He's likely the only one around fair-minded enough. He and I have fought together and hold mutual respect." Belknap's thoughts wandered again to the days fighting Indians, Mexicans, and lawbreakers. He had wondered what Dunn's ranch at Heaven's Gate might be like these days, as it'd been a couple of years since they'd last seen each other. He hadn't even heard about Three Toes's demise.

"Is this the ranch, sir?"

"Yes, Lieutenant...yes, it is." He was thankful that the recently departed Colonel Henry Kinney had built a nice road from Corpus Christi out toward Nuecestown. He'd heard rumors that the colonel had died in a gunfight in Mexico. Still, he admired all that the entrepreneurial founder of Corpus Christi had accomplished.

Looking to his right, he admired the beauty of the Nueces River as it emptied into Nueces Bay. His mind drifted to wondering whether the reef road was still around—that pile of oyster shells that created shallow access across the bay. He'd been told that indigenous tribes used it as a secret escape from attackers as well as a route to shorten travel northward. He considered the circumstances that had brought him back to this place. "Forward!" His harsh tone belied his mixed feelings, as he led his men forward on this distasteful duty.

★

One Arrow appreciated that he'd had the presence of mind to have brought a couple of extra ponies. He knew the journey to find Luke Dunn would entail a long circuitous route to avoid human hazards, and he was pushing hard. Stopping to rest wasn't part of his thinking.

The attack at Heaven's Gate months ago had gone poorly. He'd watched the turncoat War Cloud kill Three Toes, the man who'd adopted him and treated him as his own son. The Kotsoteka Comanche warrior had been insanely jealous of the Penateka Comanche chief. The rivalries between Comanche bands were both lamented and celebrated. When War Cloud had the opportunity in the heat of their attack on Luke's house, the jealous warrior had fired two arrows into the chief. One Arrow witnessed justice delivered mere moments later when the Kotsoteka Comanche warrior went to enter the house. Luke Dunn's wife was every inch the strong frontier woman defending her children as she fired two bullets into the rogue warrior. War Cloud was stopped with the first and felled with second. One Arrow and the others, seeing their chief and strongest warrior fall, beat a hasty retreat.

They'd returned to the camp on the Pedernales River, a slow mournful trek across decidedly rugged terrain. It had been so different when they'd been heading southeastward filled with the adrenaline of impending battles.

As One Arrow and the remainder of his band its wounds at the encampment, he had been first surprised and then impressed with Luke's unexpected visit shortly after the attack on Heaven's Gate.

One Arrow had left Cactus Flower and Bird Woman—these two women would bear the last of Three Toes's children—with the remainder of the band a couple of days earlier. The encampment was secure, it was well off the most traveled routes and even hardened frontiersmen and cattle drovers were hesitant to traverse this part of the Comancheria. The Comanche knew no such boundaries, but it was well-defined in the minds of would-be settlers and brave frontiersmen. The commonly accepted border of the Comancheria was that huge swath of territory west of the 98th meridian that ran north and south through Austin and extended west into New Mexico territory and well north of the Canadian River.

★

Luke and his small band of Rangers had traveled about a third of the way back to Nuecestown when they saw a lone rider roughly a mile off. From his lofty perch on Big Horse, Luke thought he recognized the traveler.

Wasn't but a few minutes before Jubal Strong rode up. "Dang, Captain Dunn. Fancy meeting you out here in the middle of nowhere."

Barber and JD sat their saddles, amazed that Luke would encounter anyone he knew out on the near-desolate emptiness of the Nueces Strip. Other than the approaching rider, there was neither human nor dwelling in sight.

"You tire of the Platte River and Laramie, Jubal? How's the family?"

"Lost 'em, Captain. Fever took 'em. Nothing to stay for, so I headed back here. I hope to make a life on your cousin's ranch." Jubal paused thoughtfully. "Of course, that damned war has messed things up, though I assume the Army just might need beef and horses."

"Sorry to hear about your family, Jubal. You dealing okay with the loss?" Luke wasn't quite sure what to say. Strong seemed to have accepted the loss of his family, but one could never tell, given the reluctance of folks like Strong to reveal their innermost feelings. "Haven't talked with cousin Nick lately. I know he was helping run cotton down to Matamoros for his father. Would have helped them myself but got called to chase down a passel of Juan Cortina's Mexican bandits. Nick will be a great help to his father, as he's already got himself a rep as an Indian fighter and marksman. Hear tell he dispatched a Comanche or two while droving cattle to Missouri a couple of years back." Luke couldn't help a proud satisfied grin crossing his face at the mere thought of it.

"Guess my timing could've been better." Strong gave an ironic sort of grin. "Just couldn't face another icy winter up north, even with that fine squaw, had she been alive to help keep me warm."

"Well, we're headed back to Nuecestown. You're welcome to ride along, given that Nick's likely not home yet."

Strong looked at Barber and JD. The big man and the young girl seemed about as anachronous a combination as could be imagined. "Interesting Ranger company you put together, Captain."

"They have their expertise, Jubal. We lost one of our number to the fight with the Mexicans. I suspect Rance here was killed by the band's leader, given his proximity to where the bandit bedded down near their horses and escaped. Anyway, this here's Jake Barber, a good man with a pistol, and JD Smith, who makes up in feistiness what she lacks in size."

Strong's eyebrows raised at the realization that the little squirt he was looking at was a woman. He now sized her up from a new perspective.

Luke turned to the pair. "This here's Jubal Strong. His cousins Bart and Sam had the misfortune of breaking the law and running into me a few years back. Might say Bart wound up snake-bit in a bad way, and Sam was the main participant at a necktie party." Luke winked at Strong, who'd fully accepted the justness of his brothers' fates.

Strong tipped his hat to Barber, but his eyes lingered a bit on JD. He then turned with his pack mule in tow and fell in with Luke as they headed up the road. They formed a motley crew, though he was pleased that Luke took no umbrage at his having gently characterized the Rangers as interesting.

For Luke's part, he was focused on getting back to Heaven's Gate. He'd be going past his cousin Nick's spread along the way and expected Strong to part ways there to await Nick's return from the Matamoros cotton run.

★

The Mexican bandit had ridden hard all night after having his band wiped out by Luke's attack. At the time of the attack, Sagura had no idea who had hit them and sure wasn't going to hang around to find out. He hadn't seen much but for the man with the long rifle whom he'd shot and the smaller man that had come toward him. With all the gunfire and shouting, he thought an entire Texas Ranger company had attacked him.

He'd experienced the wrath of the Texas Rangers a couple of years earlier as delivered by that damnable Rip Ford. He thought he'd avoided any Ranger interference by skirting wide to the west and attacking from that direction. He'd also heard rumors that the Rangers had been disbanded. At this point, Chico Sagura was no longer inclined to put stock in rumors. He was angry and frustrated. Had he known that his band had been wiped out by such a ragtag crew, he'd have been doubly angry.

Now, he was headed back to Rio Grande City to do some serious recruiting. He still firmly believed that the Nueces Strip was vulnerable. He figured rounding up a new band would take a while. Sagura's mount was well-lathered and now had a loose shoe—the bandit leader would be doing a good bit of walking. He considered letting the horse go free, but he didn't want to give up the tack. Besides, the horse could make the distance at a walk, even with the near-worthless shoe. He felt he owed the horse some degree of loyalty, as the cantle of his saddle sported a couple of bullet holes taken during their escape from the Texas Ranger. He considered the horse a good luck charm of sorts.

It was a five-day ride to Rio Grande City and a far longer walk, but Sagura was determined. However, determination soon gave way to desperation. On the horizon, approaching far faster than he would have liked were, by his count, at least four Indians. He guessed them to be Kiowa or Comanche, likely the latter. What the hell were they doing this far south? The question coursed through his heat-racked brain. All he had was the Colt revolver with a low supply of ammunition and a knife. Out of options, he prepared to meet his fate. He recalled that the very word Comanche was translated to mean enemy. No question, they'd seen him and were headed his way. From the way they held their lances dangling with fresh scalps, they surely intended to deliver a horrific fate.

He stripped the saddle from his horse and tried to get the beast to lie down. He didn't want to kill the horse if he could help it. The Comanche galloped past him. Turned out that killing his mount wasn't his choice, as a half dozen arrows meant for him found their way into the horse at fairly close range. The horse screamed in obvious pain. Sagura dared not poke his head up to put the beast out of its misery with his knife. As the Comanche flew by, he got off a couple of shots and managed to drop one warrior from his pony. His assumption that the Indian was dead turned out to be false, as the savage got up and charged toward him. Another bullet from the Colt finished him. The other three Comanche charged back, firing arrows at Sagura, who'd ducked down by now on the other side of the horse. The warriors grabbed their dead brother, hoisted him behind a pony, and rode off. Sagura was left to assess the aftermath. In the space of thirty seconds, he'd lost a horse, killed a Comanche, and been nicked in his ear by an arrow that glanced off his saddle. He had three bullets remaining. To make matters worse, an arrow had pierced his canteen, and it was leaking water like a sieve. In less than twelve hours, he'd been assaulted by Texas Rangers and Comanche. He dusted himself off, left the tack behind, and renewed his long trek to Rio Grande City.

FIVE
UNDER THE TABLE

LUKE WAS RELIEVED to arrive back at Heaven's Gate. To have accomplished a successful mission with such a ragtag outfit served as testimony to his ability to make the most of resources at hand. Barber and JD had enough reward from the endeavor to enjoy Nuecestown and likely amble on over to Corpus Christi. Luke was still pleasantly surprised by the girl. He decided he'd recruit them both again should the need arise.

As Luke rode up the trail toward the house, he couldn't help but take in the beauty of the landscape. He recalled a time long ago before he and Elisa wed. He'd snuck up behind her, as she was laying flower petals on her parents' graves and quietly began identifying the flowers. It seemed to have impressed her at the time…enough that he'd made it a habit to bring a bouquet for her when he returned from his missions. This return was no different. He considered stopping at the barn, but the few days on the trail made him eager to see Elisa and the children. She just happened to be sitting on the gallery churning butter while the twins played around her. He shifted the bouquet of bluebonnets to his right hand.

It had been a long ride, and he hadn't lingered in Nuecestown. He looked forward to a bit of rest, and Big Horse was certainly tired. Despite the horse's weariness, Luke rode up to the house. The big gray stallion would have to wait just a little longer for a rubdown and the comfort of his stall. Elisa was far and away his top priority. He'd barely dismounted when she flung herself off the gallery and leaped into his arms.

"Lucas, Lucas, you're home safe!"

Luke said nary a word. Didn't have to. He stepped back and thrust the bouquet into her hands.

The twins intertwined themselves around his legs. These days, welcome homes were a family affair.

"Come on inside, Lucas. The butter churning can wait."

"Hang tight, Lisa. That loyal steed out front needs just a few moments of my attention, then…well."

Luke had no sooner headed for the barn than the jangle of sabers and thudding of horse hooves could be heard coming up the trail. Luke hustled over to Big Horse and pulled the Colt rifle from its scabbard.

The troop of blue-coated riders came into view soon enough. It wasn't but a moment later that Luke recognized his old friend, Gordon Belknap.

Belknap stopped the troop about fifty yards from the house. The soldiers would be just out of earshot. The major rode up to the gallery and gave Luke a formal salute, coupled with an uncomfortable smile.

"Dang, Gordon, you've been promoted. Congratulations." Luke tipped his hat and extended his hand.

"Thanks, Luke. I'm on an assignment, so we need to make this look official." He saw Elisa listening from just behind the nearly closed front door. "My apologies to your wife. I understand she had a run in with some foraging troops a couple of days back."

"Care for some coffee?"

"The men back over there likely won't understand, Luke."

"You can tell them that's how we negotiate in Texas, Major."

Belknap smiled and dismounted. "You're still a damned rascal, Luke Dunn."

Luke sat in one of the chairs on the gallery and leaned the rifle against one arm. "Take a seat, Major." Luke cast an eye toward the blue coats. They were a mangy lot, even in their new uniforms and were obviously uncomfortable with whatever Belknap was up to.

Elisa was quick to emerge with three cups of coffee. She rightly figured to stand by while Luke and Belknap talked.

"So, what can I help you with?" Luke pretty much knew, so the question was essentially rhetorical.

"See the horses those men are mounted on?"

Luke scanned the nags, then brought his gaze back to Belknap's mount. "Dang, Gordon, yours isn't much better." He stroked his mustache. "What are you willing to pay?"

"The Army wants us to confiscate your horses, Luke. It's a war thing."

Luke looked grimly at Belknap and then at the dozen soldiers standing a way off. "You know I won't let you take them, Gordon. That simply wouldn't be right, would it? You know what we do to horse thieves here in Texas." He placed his coffee on the table.

"Luke, don't do this to me."

"To you? You come here proposing to steal my horses, and you expect me to just let you do it?" He glanced at the Colt rifle and back at Belknap. "You picked the wrong ranch, Major."

"Luke, I don't want to do this. I've got my orders." Belknap's mind was racing. He'd sort of expected resistance, but Luke appeared adamant. As officer in charge, it was imperative that he look good in front of his troops. "They'll cashier me for certain if they find out about this, Luke…but I've got some money. I'll write you a bank draft and trade you the horses my men are riding. It won't be a good deal for either of us, but it'll save us from bloodshed."

Luke and Elisa looked at each other. She nodded and slipped back inside the house. Even good Texas horseflesh certainly wasn't worth taking human lives. She took the Sharps down from the fireplace mantle just in case.

"What's it going to be, Luke?"

"Jaime and I will cut the horses from our herd. I'll give you solid stock, Gordon, but not my best."

Belknap stood. "Now, we need to make this look like I'm forcing you to give up your horses." He faced out of line of sight from his men and smiled sheepishly.

Luke raised his voice such that the soldiers were sure to hear. "I'll get y'all back one way or another, you damned Yankee trash!" He waved to Jaime who'd been watching from the cabin, mounted Big Horse, and headed out to cut some horses. Luke knew he had to resign himself to this for now. He wasn't about to risk his family.

Belknap ordered his men to dismount, lead their horses into the corral, remove their horses' tack, and then sit and wait. There was a bit of grumbling.

Belknap walked over and took his lieutenant aside. "What's the chatter about, Lieutenant? Speak freely."

"Naturally, the men were curious as to your apparent friendliness with the rancher, sir. They figured you were going to simply seize the horses."

"Lieutenant, I don't expect these men to understand. Eventually, this conflict will end, and we'll all have to tolerate each other again. I knew Mr. Dunn before the war. He was a Texas Ranger captain of considerable repute. He's killed more Indians and lawbreakers than you can imagine, Lieutenant. Mr. Dunn is a reasonable, God-fearing man of honor, but not someone you want to rile. Had we taken his horses without parley, many of these soldiers would surely have died right here on this ground." Belknap glared hard into the lieutenant's eyes to be certain he understood the situation. He wasn't about to share the details of the deal he'd struck, but it was enough. "Now, I suggest you get our troops to stand down."

"Yes sir." The lieutenant strolled purposely over to where the men were milling about and gave the short version of Belknap's explanation. There were still some grumbles, but the atmosphere relaxed a bit.

About this time, Luke and Jamie herded in a couple of dozen horses and guided them into a second corral. Luke looked over to where the soldiers were impatiently waiting and read the expressions on their faces. It was clear to him that the troops were unsettled. "Major Belknap, here are the horses you requested. They're all civilized." By that, he meant they'd been saddle-broken. Luke dismounted and began to lead Big Horse to the barn for a much-deserved currying.

Belknap ordered the men to pick their new mounts as quickly as possible. He was ashamed at having to treat his friend so shabbily, but wasn't in a position to do much of anything about it.

As the men moved toward the corral, a corporal split off and headed toward Luke. He was a big man, though not quite so tall and broad as Luke. He cast a dark sneer back at Belknap and the lieutenant, pushed Luke aside, and grabbed the reins from his hand.

Luke had been caught off guard, and the officers were aghast.

"I choose this here horse. You can all go to hell with those sorry excuses for horseflesh." He slipped his foot into the stirrup.

Before anyone could react, Big Horse reached his head around, clamped his teeth down on the corporal's arm, and yanked him into the dirt. For his part, the man was only slightly bruised but totally embarrassed.

"Damn! What sort of cayuse is this?" The corporal got up and began to take a swing at Luke before Belknap and the lieutenant could sprint over and save the soldier from a certain poor outcome.

Too late. Luke laid out the corporal with a single punch. Everyone heard the sickening crack as the soldier's nose was smashed flat into his face.

Belknap was suddenly thrust into a quandary not of his making. Technically, the punch was a hostile act against a US soldier. On the other hand, the corporal had clearly taken aggressive action. "Lieutenant, have the sergeant arrest this soldier for disorderly conduct." Belknap had made his decision. He wasn't going to have his soldiers provoking Texas citizens.

"Sir?" The lieutenant made the grievous error of questioning the order in front of several other soldiers.

The glaring look Belknap delivered to the officer would have melted steel. "You have this soldier arrested for disorderly conduct, Lieutenant. Now!" He gave an apologetic look at Luke, then turned back toward his troops. "And get the men in order. We're moving out!"

In the few seconds of his men being distracted, Belknap handed Luke a piece of paper. It was a banknote. He shook his head as he mounted up. "Sorry for all of this. God help us all, Luke." Then he rode on out from Heaven's Gate at the head of the column.

★

Nuecestown stood quietly under a leaden sky that hid the full moon's light. Horace Rucker was just preparing to snuff out his pipe and turn in when he heard a horse approaching. As a preacher during wartime, and especially in Texas, he had his revolver handy. He deduced that it couldn't be one of the Yankee soldiers, as they would never travel alone. The horse and rider were clearly headed toward his house. "Who goes there?"

"It's me, Father…it's me…your son." A semi-silhouette-clad in a butternut uniform with golden officer accouterments drew close. It was indeed Stephen Rucker. He pulled up and dismounted.

Rucker, taken aback by the Confederate uniform, hesitated and then raced over and embraced his son. "What…what are you doing here, Stephen?"

"I don't have much time," Stephen said. "How are you and Mother?"

Rucker looked him over top to bottom. The young man before him stood with a tall military bearing. The two years at West Point had at least brought some physical benefit so far as Rucker saw it. "She's fine, son. Let me fetch her."

Stephen wasn't ready to handle another lengthy emotional goodbye. "No, Father. Let her be. I've got orders to report to Colonel Yager with the First Cavalry Mounted Rifles up on the Sabine River. Seems the Yankees aim to invade Texas from up that way." He paused to be sure his father understood. "I heard from Rex, and he's with General Butler in New Orleans."

Rucker had little trouble doing the math. There was a possibility that Stephen and Rex might meet on the battlefield with opposing loyalties. "God help us." He said it more loudly than intended, and it brought Mrs. Rucker to the front door.

"Stephen? Stephen! You're home!" She ran to him.

Stephen was held fast in her desperate motherly embrace. "Mother, I can't stay."

"What? Can't stay? Must you go?" She recalled how she'd been numbed to this sort of thing when her then-officer husband would be called away to duty. But now, it was one of her sons. Stephen was of her. She'd borne him—she'd raised him.

"I've got my orders, Mother." He looked helplessly past her at his father.

Rucker shrugged understandingly. "Sweetheart, let the young man go. He's found his calling, and we mustn't delay his call to duty."

Mrs. Rucker reluctantly released her son. "Be careful, Stephen. Please, you be careful."

Stephen stepped back from his tearful mother, turned, and gave his father a long hug. He stepped back, saluted, and remounted. "I'll stay in touch, Father. Mother, you take care of Father." He hesitated. "If you see Rex, give him my best." He gave a final salute and galloped off in a cloud of dust to the north.

★

Luke enjoyed being back at Heaven's Gate and Elisa's loving arms. It was early morning, and the sun had barely poked above the horizon. The clouds of the previous night had disappeared, giving way to a clear blue Texas sky. He opened the front door. "Lisa!" he called out from the gallery.

Elisa dropped a pan, left her cooking, and rushed to answer Luke's call. "What is it, Lucas?" He didn't often call in such an earnest fashion.

"Look at this!" Hanging from one of the posts on the gallery was a noose with a crude wooden sign that read *Yankee lover*. Luke tore the offensive message down from the post.

Elisa stood back in momentary horror. How could this be? She shared Luke's dismay…and fear. It was the fear of the unknown. "Who would do such a hateful thing, Lucas?"

Luke shook his head and sat down on the edge of the gallery, his boots scuffing aimlessly at the dirt. "War does strange things to folks, Lisa. One thing is for certain—whoever did this is a coward."

"It frightens me, Lucas. What could be next?"

Luke sighed deeply. He thought on all the good he'd done for these people. Was this to be his reward? "I'll let Bill Meaney know about it. I doubt there's much of anything he can do."

Elisa felt terribly vulnerable in a bad sort of way. When she killed a Comanche or a home invader, she'd taken on a very real known threat. An anonymously posted message on what folks around these parts called the *noose of shame* seemed far scarier.

Luke unfastened the noose. It wouldn't do for his children to see the evil thing. He rubbed the sign in the dirt under his boot until the words had disappeared. He looked with a helpless feeling at Elisa. "We should be sure to keep our guns handy, Lisa." He looked off across the ranch. The sun was shining down in all its brightness on Heaven's Gate. "We can't run from this, Lisa. We can't hide. It is what it is. Maybe the coward will show up, but I doubt it."

The War Between the States had added a new dimension to life on the Texas frontier. This death threat had been all too palpable. It certainly wasn't a part of the Texas life that Luke and Elisa had signed up for.

★

Rucker had been fondling the letter all morning while working up the courage to open it. It was from his son Rex. Based on what he'd heard from Stephen, he had a fair idea as to what it would tell him.

He sat back on the bench and finally pulled out his knife, slit the end of the envelope, and coaxed the contents from it. It held no surprise. Rex was assigned to General Benjamin Butler, commander of the Department of the Gulf. He didn't, or more accurately couldn't say, but it seemed clear that Butler was preparing to undertake an invasion of Texas. He'd already gained some notoriety by invading New Orleans and holding it under Union control with the support of a US Navy blockade. Rucker had a sense that Rex wouldn't be in too much danger for the present. But war is a fickle monster, and the preacher yet feared for his sons.

SIX
BANDITS & APACHE

IT'S NEVER good to let dust accumulate, and the changing dynamic facing the Nueces Strip didn't lend itself to piling up any significant dust save what might be kicked up by horses' hooves and caked on sweaty human faces. Like the Mexican rebel Chico Sagura and his band of cutthroats, the Lipan Apache quickly saw the vulnerabilities of the Nueces Strip caused by the distraction of war. While Sagura hid under the uncertain banner of revolution, Lipan Apache Chief Costalites held a more pragmatic view driven by years of broken treaties. The Nueces Strip offered the Apache a veritable cornucopia of opportunity to engorge themselves on rustling, killing, and vengeance.

The Schultz family was no more nor less vigilant than their neighbors. They were defying the odds and the ranching community by farming about fifteen miles north of the tiny village of Rancho in the heart of the Nueces Strip. Hans Schultz kept his old Kentucky long gun near at hand so far as possible, and he ensured that his wife and teenage sons and daughter knew what to do in the event of attack by bandits or Indians. They'd already survived one attack by Comanche a couple of years back, but Schultz's fears were significantly heightened with the vulnerability resulting from most able-bodied men having been called to fight the Yankees.

A stiff wind wafted across the prairie and with it the hint of an odor Schultz didn't recognize. It reminded him vaguely of the smells when the Comanche had attacked. The Indians had a habit of trying to camouflage themselves with buffalo dung. With fewer buffalo on the prairie, that trick was ever less effective. *"Karl, riechst du das?"* He wondered whether his son smelled it, too. It sent a shudder through Schultz's body.

"Reichen, vater?" Karl apparently detected no unusual smells. *"Nein, vater."*

In the next moment, twenty Apache were bearing down on them. *"Lauf, Karl! Lauf."* But it was too late to run. Even had they recognized the telltale odor and realized its meaning, it would have been too late. The cabin was too far. Horses quickly overcame their futile attempt to escape on foot. Schultz didn't even have time to grab his rifle. Both were struck down by the butts of Apache rifles as they ran.

As he and his son groveled in pain among the prairie grasses, Schultz saw the Apache warriors pivot and begin to ride back to finish their work. The cabin could wait.

Schultz felt dizzy, but managed to struggle to his feet. He saw Karl on his hands and knees but unable to stand. As he took a step toward his son, an Apache sped by and struck him again on the back of his head. He fell unconscious.

Karl watched in pained speechlessness, as the Apache warrior scalped his still-living father. The savage finally drove his knife into his victim's heart.

By now, a second Apache had dismounted and started toward Karl to finish him off as he lay in the Nueces Strip dust. The wiry warrior smiled with some perverse pleasure, as he grabbed the semi-conscious young German settler's long blond hair, scalped his helpless prey, and held the hairy flesh high overhead. The Apache warrior dropped the still living boy into the dust and partially cut his throat to let him slowly bleed to death. There was never mercy shown or expected.

The leader smiled and let out a yelp. He motioned the warriors to follow him as he kicked his pony to a gallop and headed for the cabin. This was Costalites himself. The Lipan Apache Chief was every ounce a leader. He'd had his fill of broken Anglo promises. He would show how the Apache dealt with such deception.

Schultz's wife and remaining son and daughter had been working in a vegetable bed beside the house when they first heard the war whoops of the attackers. The daughter made it into the cabin, while the son grabbed the newly acquired lever-action Henry leaning against the nearby chimney.

Lead was flying everywhere as the Apache swooped down on the outnumbered and outgunned family. Mrs. Schultz never had a chance, as she was riddled by Indian gunfire.

The son raised the rifle to fire but, in the excitement, he forgot to work the lever. By the time he remembered, he too had taken multiple death-dealing bullets.

Costalites himself chased the girl into the cabin. He stood menacingly in the doorway as she fumbled with a rusty revolver. She hadn't the strength to pull back the hammer. He grabbed her by the throat, ripped away her dress, and pushed her down onto a table.

She closed her eyes as though being unable to see might make the horror go away. She couldn't have been much older than eleven or twelve. *"Nein! Nein!"* The chief's chokehold made it next to impossible for her to breathe enough to get the words out.

Costalites forced himself into her and was quickly satisfied. Something about rape, the violent shaming of especially a White woman, seemed to heighten his sense of triumph. He released her, grabbed her arm, and tossed her through the front door for the pleasure of his warriors. She tried desperately but in vain to cover her nakedness.

In the end, the girl was stabbed and, like the others, scalped. The Apache had no convenient way to transport prisoners out on the vastness of the prairie. All enemy had to die.

The Schultz's horses were hardly more than underfed broken-down nags that might barely have served as a meal for anyone desperate enough. The Apache shot them both. They gorged themselves on what food was available in the cabin and toyed with whatever trinkets they found attractive among the women's belongings. With their bellies full, enough shiny objects to suit their tastes, and some new scalps, they soon mounted up and rode off. They set the cabin afire to discourage any more White men from using it. It had been a good day…for the Apache.

By pure chance, Chico Sagura traveled in a wide eastern arc on his way to Rio Grande City that would take him near the village of Rancho. He still needed a fresh mount but avoided the village proper for fear of encountering Confederate troops known to be patrolling the region. As he crested a slight rise in the prairie, he saw the still-smoldering ruins of the Schultz homestead. As the bodies came into view, Sagura saw that it was obviously the work of Lipan Apache. He saw the dead nags, but they wouldn't have been any improvement over horse he'd lost.

He held a sort of perverse admiration for the Apache. In his mind, he saw a certain nobility in the savages as they defended their territory from the White man. Sagura felt they had a common enemy in the white invaders, but he chose to overlook the fact that the Spanish had robbed the Indians of their ancestral lands. The Apache answered to Costalites just as he maintained some vague loyalty to the rebel leader Cortina. He had time to think on these things as he walked past the remains of the Schultz cabin and gagged at the sight of the mutilated corpse of the young girl. The buzzards and coyotes had already begun their handiwork on her and the rest of her family. Burying the remains was out of the question, even for Sagura. He wondered what it was that caused these people to defy the odds and try to carve out a life in this desolate place. He found a canteen, filled it, and resumed his trek, now especially on guard for Apache.

Perversely, the savages inspired him and lifted his spirits as he looked forward to recruiting a new band of cutthroats. By his reckoning, he would be extra careful to not fall prey to any Texas Rangers again.

★

"¡Carlos, mira! ¡Es Chico!"

Sagura had gone a scant five miles beyond the Schultz homestead when two riders approached. He'd had the presence of mind to keep his rifle with him. He pointed it in the general direction of the riders. Best to have it handy. *"¿Carlos? ¿Pedro? ¿Qué estás hacienda aquí?* What indeed were these men doing out there on the Nueces Strip? Sagura quickly figured that they were likely up to no good.

The men had been brothers-in-arms on one of Cortina's raids. The men smiled at their old friend's laughable situation. *"Lo que solemos hacer. ¡Asaltar!"* Indeed, they were doing what they usually did, raiding the countryside.

"¿Estás solo?" Sagura knew they were not alone, but had to ask.

Pedro and Carlos smiled at each other. *"¿Necesitas un caballo?"*

Sagura shook his head at their statement of the obvious. He did need a horse. *"Si, amigos. ¿Tienes caballos extra?"*

"¿Viajarás con nosotros?"

It was an invitation to join their band. It was clear to him that to obtain a fresh mount he'd have to join them. *"¿Quien es tu jefe?"* Sagura hoped whoever was leading them was someone he could tolerate. He'd been used to independence and leading his own band.

"Es Pablo Ramos."

Ramos! The name caused an involuntary shudder through Sagura's body. Despite it, he very much needed a horse. He'd tolerate Ramos for a couple of days to achieve that end.

"¿Hay algún problema, Chico?"

"No. No hay problema." It was a necessary lie and said so as to convince Carlos and Pedro that he'd join them. Despite having ridden together, these two would as soon shoot him as look at him. Loyalty was fleeting on the Nueces Strip. *"¡Vamanos!"* He followed the men toward their camp. He was put off that they didn't offer a ride, but then such were the niceties of the bandit life. He made a mental note to not forget them making him walk to the camp.

As they approached the bandit camp, Sagura could see Pablo Ramos inside a circle surrounded by a small cluster of men. He was moving about like a panther stalking its prey. He was fighting someone. Sagura saw the glint of sunlight on a slender knife blade. Moving closer, he could see that Ramos's opponent was getting the worst of it. Blood was all over the man. This was one of Ramos's methods of ensuring loyalty and discipline with his men. It crossed Sagura's mind that escape from this situation might be problematic.

★

"Major Belknap?"

"Sir?" The major exchanged salutes with the young Navy lieutenant.

Kittredge had apparently snuck ashore under cover of

darkness. "Major, I heard a rumor that you were fraternizing with the enemy. Is this true?"

Belknap knew better than to lie. Untruths had a nasty tendency of eventually coming back to haunt the liar. "I traded with an old friend for better horses, sir. Believe me, we got the better of the deal."

Kittredge gazed coldly into Belknap's eyes. "You're supposed to seize them, Major. It's called foraging, not trading."

The lieutenant was beginning to get under Belknap's skin. He didn't need to stand there and be insulted. "Lieutenant, I didn't figure a dozen horses were worth a half dozen or more dead soldiers."

"A half dozen or more?" Kittredge delivered a mock look of amazement. "One man could do that?"

"This man could…and more."

The lieutenant hitched up his pants and cinched his belt a bit tighter. He didn't know quite what to make of the major's claim. "Must be an impressive man, Major. Does this rancher have a name or are you keeping it a mystery?"

"Luke Dunn." Belknap decided not to mention that the rancher was a renowned Texas Ranger captain. It was for Luke's protection as well as his own.

Kittredge made a mental note to check out this Luke Dunn person himself one day soon. "Just don't trade with the locals again, Major Belknap. Orders are orders."

The two saluted, and the lieutenant faded into the night. Belknap's barely audible whisperings wouldn't have been fit for polite company.

★

Costalites and his warriors rode triumphantly into their Texas base camp about thirty miles east of San Ygnacio. It had been hard riding, but their blood lust had been satisfied for the present. A few less homesteaders would be tilling the Nueces Strip soil. Testosterone ran high as the braves sought the welcoming arms of their squaws. The carnality with the women would start the boastful chest-beating and tales of heroism at the evening campfire. Drums, wild dancing, and some peyote would enhance the entire experience.

SEVEN

COMANCHE REDUX

ONE ARROW HAD plenty of time to think about his future. He was still very much a young man. He had begun to think deeply about what the future might hold for him and for his people. Observing Luke's respectful treatment of the Comanche dead had upset many of the preconceived notions the young warrior held.

His companions were older and chided him about his serious demeanor. They respected the young warrior for how he had earned his warrior name, but they had no appreciation for what was on One Arrow's mind. They were still licking the wounds of defeat at Heaven's Gate ranch, mostly at the hands of a White woman. This wasn't something to be boasted about at any council fire.

"What troubles you, One Arrow?" One of the two warriors riding with him moved up to ask the question.

"Comanche."

"You worry about our people?" the man persisted.

One Arrow sighed. How could he get his warriors to understand? Did they not think on such things? "When we reach camp," he announced, "I will go on vision quest."

His companions thought the young man a bit young for a vision quest, but nothing was as it was. "You worry?"

"I have many questions. I must talk with the Great Spirit." One Arrow kicked his pony just enough to move him ahead of the two warriors. The conversation was ended.

One Arrow's mind kept turning over far more questions than answers. As his mind wandered off, he was not being so vigilant.

"One Arrow," one of his companions whispered in alarm. "Look." He pointed to the column of soldiers with gray uniforms riding toward them.

The Confederates had a considerable advantage. Fight or flight raced through the minds of the three warriors. The former meant certain death, while there was a possibility that their ponies were faster than the soldiers' mounts.

"I know a place," hissed One Arrow. He recalled a nearby wooded area not far off in the hill country that Three Toes had shown him.

They'd already been seen by the point rider, who had pivoted and headed back to his unit at a gallop.

One Arrow wasted no time. Reacting quickly, he turned his pony and raced northward with his brother Comanche following close behind.

★

As the point rider rode in, the Texas Confederate army unit was momentarily uncertain about what to do. The delay would cost them any hope of pursuing, much less catching up to the savages.

The officer in charge watched with resignation as the dust of the Comanche ponies faded off into the distance. Frustrated, he went through the motions of pursuit as he rode with a couple of his men to a nearby knoll and looked out with his spyglass just as the three warriors disappeared into a tree line in rocky terrain. It would be futile to try to track them.

Nothing if not practical, the officer lowered the spyglass, shrugged, then headed back to the front of his column. "Not worth the chase," he said, and led his men back on the heading they'd been on when the point man spotted the trio. The officer was slightly irritated, he knew that, with the brief threat behind them, the Comanche would continue their ride back to their encampment safely—for now.

Luke rode out at the crack of dawn to look for strays. Big Horse moved along at an easy walk, likely sensing that his rider was in no hurry.

"What do you think, big fella?" Luke occasionally carried on one-way conversations with the big gray stallion as though attributing some innate intelligence to the beast. "Should we track down that Sagura and end his lunacy? Should we be staying here at Heaven's Gate to protect the homestead?" His self-debate was interrupted as a stray longhorn calf wandered into view.

He figured the calf couldn't have wandered far from its mother. Big Horse knew what to do, and Luke let him urge the little guy along. Sure enough, the mother was in a nearby arroyo looking for her calf. Upon seeing his mother, the calf bawled and sprinted to her. She promptly scolded him for wandering off.

"Good job, Big Horse." Luke patted his horse's neck and chuckled to himself at the nonevent. "I think we know what we've got to do. Let's head home."

For a line officer with battle experience, Major Belknap's

current duty was beyond boredom. What had been friendly territory a mere two years ago had turned decidedly hostile. He was now an invader. His orders amounted to a holding action. He found himself based far north of Corpus Christi at a place called Passe Cavallo at the entrance to Matagorda Bay.

Belknap deeply resented the opportunistic Navy lieutenant onboard the *USS Arthur* who'd dressed him down over the foraging expedition to Nuecestown. The major considered writing a letter to Kittredge's superior officer, Commander Renshaw, but figured it a fool's game as the Navy men would surely support each other.

The major would simply have to endure until opportunity presented itself. He'd begun to feel a bit Texan himself, so had a little inner conflict over fighting against them. Still, they had seceded, and his commander-in-chief had declared that treasonous. Belknap had studied the US Constitution while at West Point and didn't understand President Lincoln's reasoning, as he didn't see secession as prohibited. He sensed this war was about far more than slavery.

★

"Lucas?" They lay together, basking in the afterglow of their passions. Luke's carnality had been extraordinary. He seemed to never tire of consuming her, body and soul. It was with these intense love-makings that he would set her passions fully ablaze. Yet despite his ardor, she felt something was missing. He'd responded to her as always, yet she could feel that something was weighing heavily on his mind.

Luke knew the question and understood. He rolled more closely toward her and gently stroked her shoulders. He began to touch her breasts.

"Lucas?"

He paused. Then he blurted, "I have to finish the work I started with that Mexican bandit Sagura." There—it was out.

She pushed him onto his back and climbed onto him, taking in his quick arousal. She'd married him for better or worse and she wanted as much of the better as she could get. Soon enough, they were lying breathless, bathed in moisture brought on by the sheer wanton lust of their unbridled passions.

As they lay back and could hear the stirrings of children downstairs, she turned to him. There was a glow about her.

Luke recognized that glow. "Really? Again?"

"Those love juices are potent, my love." A fifth Dunn child would be joining their little family in a few months.

He kissed her—a deep forever kiss. He broke away and smiled, then sighed and sat up. "Guess I'd better get started doing what I have to do."

The sex spell had been broken, at least for the moment. "Do you think we'll have trouble from the Yankee soldiers?"

"I don't think so. It sure won't be for horses unless they're looking for broken-down nags." He offered an ironic smile. "I think you'll be safe here at Heaven's Gate. I'll get Bill Meaney to check out here now and again. I have a general idea where this Mexican is, so it may not take very long." He hoped Sagura hadn't recruited more followers.

"What about Comanche?"

"They're unpredictable, but I can't imagine them attacking around here again. I'd be more worried about Apache, but they've been far to the south from what I've heard." In the back of his mind, Luke was more worried about foraging Confederate soldiers but decided not to worry Elisa over much.

Luke figured to ask Barber and JD to join him. He had second thoughts about the girl, but had to admit she was tough and teachable. He judged that the fire in her belly was likely enough to offset her diminutive size.

★

"What is to happen, One Arrow?" Cactus Flower had immersed herself in chores around the encampment as she sought to overcome her grief at losing Three Toes. She would be giving birth to the chief's child any day, and that would ever be a reminder of the Comanche who'd taken her for his woman.

The young Comanche shook his head ruefully. What indeed would be the future of the Penateka Comanche? What was to become of his people? He'd spent days alone reaching out to the Great Spirit as he sought answers to these questions. His meditations invariably brought him to Luke Dunn. One Arrow became convinced that the answers lay with the Texas Ranger friend of Three Toes. Luke Dunn would hold the answer. He snapped from his momentary trance and looked down at Cactus Flower. She was a very pretty woman and young enough to raise lustful thoughts, but she and Bird Woman were several years older than he and both were quite pregnant with the chief's children. "I must find Three Toes's friend."

"What of us?" She felt vulnerable. If One Arrow departed, six women, several children, and two warriors would remain.

Bird Woman overheard them and walked over. "We will be safe here. It is hidden. White men are fighting White men."

One Arrow smiled. "You are wise, Bird Woman." Even as young as he was, the Comanche realized that their enemy was distracted and posed little or no threat. He had no idea as to the huge scale of the White man's conflict but recalled how battles between tribes and even squabbles within the various Comanche tribes disrupted day-to-day life in their encampments.

Three Toes had done an admirable job finding a hidden, well-camouflaged site for the Penateka Comanche encampment. It served to isolate fairly effectively them from what was happening in the world at large. One of the remaining warriors had encountered a couple of Kiowa braves while hunting and learned that the Confederates had signed treaties with Nokoni, Kotsoteka, Tenawa, Yamparika, and Penateka Comanche. It was reassuring to know that there were still other Penatekas around. The treaties apparently included the usual hollow promises of peace and friendship that weren't any better than what the bluecoats had delivered. The Confederates resources were used for fighting a war, not supplying Indians. The warrior also confirmed One Arrow's suspicions that the attention of the whites had been drawn east to fight a war. A bluecoat general named Twiggs had surrendered all federal property in Texas to the Confederates and evacuated nearly 3,000 soldiers from frontier forts. This all served to give the small Comanche band a sense of peace for the present. One Arrow, for one, doubted that the attentions of the whites would be diverted for long. He did feel confident enough in the immediate safety of his people to afford him his vision quest.

One Arrow awoke just as the morning sun broke the horizon. He chose three ponies. He'd already shared his vision quest with his brother warriors. While they didn't understand his obsession with the Texas Ranger, they nevertheless respected a quest blessed by the Great Spirit. Cactus Flower and Bird Woman ensured that One Arrow had adequate supplies.

But for a distracted wave of his hand, the young leader didn't look back as he headed southeast toward Nuecestown to find Three Toes's old friend. The Comanche watched him disappear from view and then turned to resuming their lives there on the Pedernales River. One Arrow was totally focused on finding Luke Dunn.

As he rode, he quickly discovered that the Texas frontier, as established by the whites, had been pushed eastward. He encountered no bluecoats or Texas Rangers for many miles while seeing occasional bands of marauding Comanche and Kiowa. He was mostly successful in avoiding these so as not to distract from his vision quest. One Arrow took some satisfaction from learning that Comanche were exacting revenge against the Tonkawa. The Tonkawa tribe had served as scouts for the bluecoats—the band has earned a special hatred from the Comanche for having killed and eaten the brother of a Comanche chief. One Arrow shuddered at the thought. The Comanche may have been savages, but they were repulsed by the widespread practice of cannibalism. Learning of the justice wrought upon the Tonkawa pleased One Arrow, but he knew intuitively that it wouldn't help his people in the long term. He also knew that the White man's war wouldn't go on forever. The men shedding blood on battlefields to the east would eventually turn west and become a scourge to One Arrow's people.

★

Jubal Strong had found Nick Dunn's little ranch empty save for an elderly Mexican who had been hired to watch over it and a *vaquero* who rode the range checking on cattle and horses. Far as he could tell, Dunn had been spared any incursions by Indians or bandits.

The caretaker told him in halting English that his boss would be back in a couple of days, so Strong made himself at home in a shelter near a makeshift barn. The two Mexicans were happy to share space. The *vaquero* was pleased to have someone to talk with other than the old man. The consequences would be Strong learning some Spanish and the *vaquero* polishing his English skills.

★

Big Horse heard Luke walking down from the house. The big gray stallion seemed to sense another adventure. Men and their horses on the frontier developed special relationships, and Luke and Big Horse were no exception. They'd been together for nearly seven years.

Luke stroked the stallion's neck and fed him an apple that Jaime had acquired in Nuecestown. Big Horse gave Luke a friendly nudge.

"We've got work to do, big fella." Luke could afford understatement with his four-legged friend. Soon enough, he was leading him up to the house where Elisa awaited with some grub for the journey.

Luke picked up the children one by one, telling each that he loved them and would be back soon. It was always an emotionally tough moment. These were times when Luke thought seriously about hanging up his badge. Maybe that day wouldn't be so far off, but he couldn't consider it for the moment. He gave Elisa a deep kiss that sent a surge of passion through her body. "Love you, Lisa." He turned and mounted Big Horse as Elisa regained her composure. The twins giggled at their parents' behavior.

Luke rode up to a rise in the trail leading to the entrance to Heaven's Gate before turning Big Horse to look back at the house. Everyone waved. Goodbyes were hell.

EIGHT
BEHIND THE NOOSE

BERNICE AND AGATHA paused at the entrance to Heaven's Gate. Earlier they'd watched as Luke headed off with Jake Barber and that slip of a girl, JD Smith, to do his duty on the Nueces Strip. The ladies were bubbling over with gossip they dared not share with Luke.

Bernice took a deep breath and glanced sideways at her friend Agatha as they turned the old wagon up the trail.

Jaime's wife Julia was heading up the path to the house to help Elisa when she heard the rickety old wagon. She recognized the ladies and gave them a big smile as they approached.

"Julia, how are you? ¡Buenos *días!*"

Julia appreciated their attempt to toss a bit of Spanish her way, but she spoke impeccable English, the ladies knew it, and so she actually felt just a bit condescended to. She welcomed them nonetheless. "Come on in." She continued her smile and climbed the gallery steps. "I'll let *Señora* Dunn know that you are here."

The seat was a tad high for a couple of elderly widows to be climbing down from, but the ladies managed to disembark without incident. Once they'd gathered their wits and caught their collective breaths from the exertion, they climbed up to the gallery.

Elisa opened the door and stepped out to greet them as Julia prepared to knock. "Bernice...Agatha...welcome to Heaven's Gate." She hugged and kissed each of them. "Do come in and enjoy some coffee." She ushered them inside and motioned them to sit at the newly acquired oaken table.

"My, but you've done wonders with this place, Elisa. You've made it into a true home for your family." It was said from their confidence that, for so long as they'd known Elisa, they'd known she'd make a great wife and mother. It was becoming obvious that she could also handle running a ranch. After the tragic death of most of her family in the Comanche attack on their homestead, Bernice had her early doubts as to the diminutive teen's strength and know-how in running the homestead on her own. Bernice wasn't wrong often so was pleased that Elisa's life was turning out as it was.

Elisa motioned Julia to join them and then poured coffee. "Just one moment, ladies." She picked up baby Michael, sat, loosened her bodice, and began to feed him.

Bernice and Agatha were surprised at her baring her breast to them, but this was just part of life.

"He's going to be a big one like his father, Elisa," Agatha opined.

Though neither of the ladies said anything, they were a shade more disconcerted at a Mexican woman sitting with them as an equal.

"So, what brings you ladies here this fine day?" Elisa smiled and obviously took comfort in Michael being at her breast.

"Well, we heard about that nasty message that was hung on your gallery post. We think we know who put it there." The ladies looked at each other knowingly.

"Really?" Elisa wondered whether they were going to

share their gossip or simply tease her. "And who might that be?"

The ladies leaned forward as if about to deliver some great secret of life, though Agatha abruptly straightened as, with leaning forward, she'd caught a glimpse of a bit too much of Elisa's breast. She found herself embarrassed but envious. Why should smooth firm breasts be wasted on the young?

"It's that new boy down at the Nuecestown stable and his young friends," Bernice whispered. "You know how these kids are today. Have to wonder where they get such behavior."

"Are you certain?" Elisa was surprised. "How do you know for sure?"

"Remember Dan, the young man who married and ran off to Victoria to set up a smithy shop? Well, he was passing through the other day and stopped to say hello." She paused. "Nice boy, that Dan."

Elisa recalled having given him advice on finding a trade so as to increase his chances of attracting a woman and then taught him how to treat her.

"Dan stopped by at the livery to see how it was faring and got to joking and carrying on with the new boy who was tending it." She took a deep breath and glanced furtively at Julia before continuing. "Dan said that the boy laughed about having made a noose and hung it on the gallery post of the house of that Yankee lover Luke Dunn."

"I'm grateful for the information, ladies. Did you mention this to Luke?"

"We thought he might get upset and give the boys a whupping. They're just youngsters, after all. We feared Luke might not know his strength and hurt the boys badly."

Clearly, the ladies didn't know Luke well enough, much less his wife sitting before them. "What makes you think only Luke would be angry?" A bit of redness flushed up into Elisa's face. She disengaged Michael and put him on her shoulder, fully exposing her moistened breast.

The ladies looked at each other. On the one hand, an exposed breast was discomforting to them, but Elisa's obvious anger was a fully unexpected reaction. Where was the young teen girl they'd known?

"What do you mean?" Agatha asked, concern in her voice.

Elisa sat back and sought to relax. "Don't fret yourselves." It was clear that she had something in mind. Now, she needed to change the subject. "I'm so glad y'all came out here to visit." She refastened her bodice and held Michael on her lap. "Isn't this a fine table that Luke brought from Corpus?"

The ladies loosened up a bit. Julia recognized the situation and smiled at their behavior. They meant well. It had been a good time to change the subject.

"Did Luke tell you our latest news?"

"What news?" Bernice put her hand over her mouth. "Oh! Again? A fifth child? My, Elisa Dunn, but you are an amazing woman."

Elisa smiled. "I married an amazing man." No one could dispute that.

Bernice and Agatha were overjoyed to have new gossip to share in Nuecestown. The noose issue and the breast exposure were now quickly relegated to history. Pregnancies rose to the top of the gossip rankings. "My, Elisa, y'all are going to need a bigger house." The house was pretty fair-sized, but they felt there were limits as to how many children could be stuffed in a couple of bedrooms.

"Seems you are the envy of Corpus Christi, Elisa. Your ranch is growing, you've got a much-admired role model of a husband, loving children...yes, I'd say folks are envious...and I mean that in the kindest of ways." Agatha had a habit of accurately perceiving how folks tended to view other folks.

Elisa smiled. She knew Agatha meant well. "If holding high moral values, being self-less, and overcoming tough circumstances makes a role model, then folks can be as envious as they like, dear Agatha. I can only pray that his passion for life and commitment to family and community serve as inspiration."

Agatha's jaw dropped. She'd hardly expected such from a mere 20-year-old girl.

"Yes, Luke Dunn is an amazing man. And he's my man." She lifted her head high with a slight attitude before lowering her chin and smiling friendly-like.

Bernice admired Elisa's feistiness. "Oh, Elisa…you bring back so many fond memories of when I was your age. But you've got something I never had…you have resolve. God bless you, Elisa Dunn."

The ladies spent a couple of more hours chatting before heading back to Nuecestown. Elisa gave them some of her delicious cornbread to take back with them. "Now, ladies, not a word to that livery boy." She smiled at the reminder and what she had in mind as she saw them off.

★

The next morning, Elisa was up bright and early. She arranged for Julia to watch the children and asked Jaime to saddle the roan mare, one of the few decent mounts remaining after the trade with the Yankees. When she emerged wearing pants, Julia gasped. She'd never seen her employer dressed so. Elisa also had Luke's newly acquired Henry lever-action, breech-loading .44-caliber rifle. He'd chosen to take the Sharps on his hunt for Sagura. She hoisted a saddlebag onto the roan, not feeling it necessary to share the contents with Julia. As she was about to mount, she paused to look at the mare. The roan had put on a bit of weight. A ride would be good for her.

"I won't be long, Julia." She saw the concerned expression on her friend's face. "Don't worry. I won't shoot the rascal. He just won't be messing with us anymore." The roan was a fair-sized horse, but Elisa sat her well despite being barely over five feet tall.

"Be careful, *Señora* Dunn. *Via con Dios*."

Elisa turned the mare up the lane and headed toward Nuecestown. She hadn't told Julia of the little secret she'd packed in her saddlebag. Just as well.

It took less than a half hour to ride at an easy trot up to Nuecestown. The river was swollen from a recent rain upriver, so the ferry wasn't operating, that reduced traffic coming through the town. The stable boy was sitting on a bench near the corral gate whittling on what looked to eventually be a whistle.

The uh-oh expression on the boy's face was priceless. Elisa rode up and stopped about six feet from him with the rifle pointed at him. He recognized her.

She was certain he'd peed in his pants. "You know who I am?"

"Er...yes, ma'am. You're Mrs. Dunn." He stood slowly. There was now no question that he'd wet his pants.

Elisa kept the rifle aimed at him as she reached back into her saddlebag. "Put this on." She tossed the noose to him.

"Ma'am?"

"Are you deaf? Put it on!" She worked the lever of the Henry. The click-click sound had a way of getting folks' attention.

The boy dutifully placed the noose around his neck.

"Are you a Yankee lover, boy?"

"No, ma'am."

"Neither am I and neither is my husband. If he knew about you, you'd be bleeding out in the dirt. Whatever you might have heard, you got it wrong...dead wrong." She fired the rifle into the air. She was certain the boy had now crapped in his pants.

The young man was literally shaking with fear.

The blast from the Henry had alerted the townsfolk, who promptly emerged from homes and businesses to see what was going on. "Start walking toward the boarding house."

"Ma'am?" The boy was in tears by this time.

"Must I ask twice?"

He began walking up the street as best he could considering the wetness between his legs and the load of crap in his trousers. She urged the mare along about ten feet behind, still aiming the Henry at him. Folks began chuckling and then outright laughing at the sight. Worse, his friends that had helped him post the noose were among the onlookers and nervously laughing with them.

They'd nearly made it to the boarding house when Bernice and Agatha emerged. Their mouths gaped at the sight of a pregnant Elisa on horseback brandishing a rifle and delivering a well-deserved punishment. "You walk right on up to the jail, boy."

By now, it was all the young man could do to stand. He would have appreciated a hole to crawl into.

"Turn toward me." She paused as he turned. The entire town was watching. "The next time you try some fool stunt, you're going to be lucky to only be locked up in that jail."

"Yes, ma'am. I'm sorry, ma'am."

Elisa smiled at the ladies. "Boy, you can take off the noose now." He did so dutifully and quickly. "Now you git, and don't be making any more trouble around these parts." She looked around at the crowd. "If any of this young man's friends are among y'all, let this be a lesson. Don't you go messin' with Texans."

She tipped her hat to Bernice and Agatha, winked at Doc who'd poked his head out to see the action, and turned the roan mare for home. She had a baby to feed.

★

Luke had decided to take a route due south with his small posse. His gut instinct was that Sagura would have chosen the shortest path to the relative safety of Mexico. A light rain during the night had dampened the landscape, so he was pleased not to be eating dust.

"Do you think he's still traveling alone, Captain?" JD had asked this question at least four times already. She was seeking reassurance that Luke couldn't hope to provide.

He sighed loudly enough for Barber to hear. "Last time, JD. We won't know until we find him." He gave a Big Horse enough of a nudge with his heels to put him well out in front.

Barber smiled at her. "Rest easy, JD. If you can't handle this, we won't think the less of you if you want to go home."

JD wasn't about to be outdone by a man, especially this one. She held a bit of guilt at having been unable to protect the old man back in the Sagura gang gunfight. "I'll be okay." She forced a grim smile, pretending to be confident.

They stopped at an arroyo about midway to Rio Grande City. They'd ridden through the first two nights, so were dead tired. JD still had questions. Finally, she thought of one she hadn't yet asked. She placed a couple of mesquite branches on the small cooking fire. "Captain, excuse me, but what if he made it to Mexico? Will we cross the river?"

This time Luke smiled. "Good question, JD. I expect we just might cross the Rio Grande." He'd done it a few years back under Callahan's Texas Ranger command, but that had caused a lot of hate and discontent among the Mexicans, resulted in engaging the Mexican army, and upset folks back in Austin. "Depends on whether the Mexican army or some of Cortina's men are around to greet us."

They arose bright and early. Barber narrowly avoided a rattlesnake's strike, so he was wide awake.

They'd ridden about fifteen miles when Luke spotted wisps of smoke rising perhaps a mile in the distance. Out here, it was unlikely to be cowboys. There were no ranches nearby to his knowledge. Luke put his finger to his lips and pointed at the smoke. If not cowboys, it would likely be bandits or Indians. Given that the Nueces Strip had become so especially vulnerable thanks to the war, Luke was fairly confident that the smoke meant trouble.

At about a half mile out, the little posse dismounted. Luke took out his spyglass and looked at the position of the sun so no reflection from the lens would give them away. He gazed long and hard at the source of the smoke.

"What do you see, Captain?" It was JD with another question.

"Be quiet," he whispered. "There's about a dozen Mexican bandits. I think Sagura is one of them. I'm thinking they're Pablo Ramos's band."

"Who's he, Captain?"

Luke stroked his mustache as he thought back. He kept his voice low. "As I recall, he ran afoul of that rebel Juan Cortina. Rivals I think. Cortina kicked him out."

Barber whispered. "So, he's a rogue. That's not good for Sagura. He's Cortina man."

"We'll wait here until nightfall."

JD swallowed hard as she realized Luke's intentions. They'd even the odds a bit by picking off any outliers, the ones that went off by themselves to answer nature's call, and then launch a surprise attack on the sleeping bandits.

Luke took another look through the spyglass. "Ramos is no dummy. He's posting a sentry. We'll see whether he relieves them regularly." Luke knew sentries would make eliminating outliers more difficult. Then again, even a sentry could be vulnerable.

The sun was creeping toward the horizon. It hung with its orangey glow for what seemed like forever. To Luke's thinking, nightfall might never come. The sun took its sweet old time.

For JD on the other hand, sunset was arriving all too fast.

At last, darkness arrived. Luke looked thoughtfully at the

mere slip of a girl. "JD, I don't expect you'd have much success taking down a man twice your size even by surprise."

The thought of sneaking up behind bandits and cutting their throats didn't hold much appeal for JD. She vigorously nodded in agreement.

Luke smiled and turned to Barber. "Jake, it's you and me. Let's see what we can do to even our chances." Luke led the way toward Ramos's camp. Ahead lay tall grasses and one dry creek bed that meandered lazily through the landscape. They covered the first couple of hundred yards quickly, staying low and stopping occasionally to listen and pop up cautiously to get their bearings.

Ramos had posted only one sentry, so the challenge for Luke and Barber would be to eliminate bandits without alerting him. To his way of thinking, Luke hoped to eliminate at least four of Ramos's men. Then, he got an idea.

They were about fifty yards from the sentry, when Luke signaled to Barber to stop. The sentry wore the distinctive large sombrero that the Mexicans loved. Luke pointed to himself and made a cutting motion across his throat. He had decided to eliminate the sentry himself.

He moved swiftly through the grasses and was a mere couple of feet from the man, when he was heard. Too late, the razor-sharp edge of Luke's knife swept across the guard's throat. There was no sound save for a noiseless gurgling. Luke retrieved the man's hat, and replaced his own cowboy hat. Barber watched the action with deep admiration. Luke worked like some sort of big cat, delivering the end result swiftly and surely.

As he stood in the sentry's place, it wasn't but a few moments when Luke saw a shadow approach from Ramos's camp. He soon heard a whisper. As the bandit stopped nearby, unbuttoned his pants, and began to relieve himself, the man called over toward him. "*¿Carlos, cómo estás?*"

"*Ven aquí un momento.*" Despite the dim moonlight Luke

could see the man smiling at the invitation as he refastened his trousers and pulled out a cigar while walking over. He was apparently up for a friendly smoke. In the darkness, the man was nearly on top of Luke before he realized the error of his ways. There was a brief flash of silvery steel as Luke was on him before he could utter a sound. Two bandits down and perhaps ten to go. Luke motioned Barber over and handed him the dead man's sombrero. Two men standing in what was apparently friendly conversation might seem less threatening.

Luke and Barber simply had to wait for their prey to come to them. They never expected what came next.

There was a loud rustling in the grasses as a smallish swarthy shadow approached. *"¿Carlos, Domingo, qué está pasando aquí?"*

Luke sensed that it was a command voice demanding to know what was going on. He immediately figured this might be Pablo Ramos himself. *"¿Jefe?"* He offered an urgent-sounding whisper.

It was Ramos! He reached for his gun. As fate would have it, the bandit's foot caught on the body of the dead sentry, causing him to stumble. The split second was all Barber needed to lay the bandit leader out with a single punch.

"Damn, Jake." Luke had no idea Barber could deliver such a blow. He jumped on Ramos, manacled the bandit's hands behind him, and tied a bandanna tightly over his mouth to keep him quiet. "Now, let's see what develops."

Soon enough, another bandit emerged from the darkness apparently to relieve the sentry. *"¿Carlos, dónde estás?"*

"Aquí." This time Luke wasn't so lucky, as the bandit was still several feet away when he realized something was amiss. As he began to draw his pistol, Luke had already cleared leather. His shot was true, but now the camp was alerted.

Barber lifted Ramos onto his feet, and they half-dragged the still-dazed bandit back to JD and the horses. Just about the time that they reached the horses, they heard the bandits riding toward them. By Luke's calculation, they were now outnumbered by eight to three, but held a big chip with which to negotiate. JD and Barber moved swiftly to the horses intending to mount up.

Luke stopped. "No, stay still. They're already mounted and are headed this way." Luke knew they'd likely not get far if they tried to outrun the outlaws. He thrust Ramos in front of them. It'd be a gamble, but these were high stakes. He fired a shot into the air to draw the bandits' attention.

The gang pulled up in front of Luke's little posse. Seeing their leader captured and gagged was a serious attention getter. The Colt pistol held at the bandit's head was like an exclamation point to the matter. With no one stepping up as leader, it was left to Chico Sagura to make a bold move.

"¡*Ranger, eres tú otra vez!*" His words were delivered through teeth clenched in anger. Sagura had quickly recognized Luke.

"*Ah, Sagura. Parece ser así.*" Luke was managing to learn some Spanish lingo. "*Te rindes. Nadie muere.*" Luke made it clear that if Sagura surrendered, no one would die.

Ramos nodded vigorously at his men to give up Sagura.

"*¿Que va a ser?*" Luke challenged the bandits to make a decision. "*Renuncia a Sagura y vas en paz.*" If they gave up Sagura, they could go in peace with no more men getting killed.

For his part, Sagura was astounded that they'd consider trading him for Ramos. After all, the man treated them pretty badly. He started to back his horse as if to make a break. One of the bandits grabbed Sagura's horse's reins and ordered him to stop. "¡*No, détente ahora, hombre!*" Trapped, Sagura lifted his rifle as if to shoot Ramos.

Gunfire echoed across the prairie, half a dozen shots in all. The bandits blasted Sagura from his saddle. One of the stray bullets brought down another bandit. Now, Luke's posse was facing six mounted and fairly well-armed bandits. He still held his ace in the hole: Ramos.

The bandits looked at each other and at the array of guns aimed at them by JD, Barber, and Luke. Clearly, the odds were unattractive. Some of them would surely die.

"¿Ramos? ¿Hablas Inglés?" Luke loosened the gag.

"Un poco, Ranger. A little."

"I think we have a fair trade here. Agree?"

"Si…yes. Fair."

By Luke's figuring, if he were to let Ramos free right then and there, his tiny posse would be brought down in a hail of bullets. "You tell your men to lay down their weapons and give us an hour head start. We'll drop you off up the trail apiece."

Ramos reluctantly gave the orders to his men. He could still feel the end of Luke's Colt pressed into the back of his head.

"Tell them to dismount."

"¡Baje de sus caballos!" Ramos wasn't going to test Luke's patience. Cold steel had a way of encouraging a man to obey orders.

The bandits reluctantly did as they were told. No one was willing to test Luke's trigger finger.

"JD, gather up the leads on the horses and weapons."

She put away her rifle, mounted up, and soon had a veritable remuda of horses trailing her. The guns were stowed on the pack horse.

"Now, we're going to mount up real careful like and ride out of here." Luke roughly hoisted the portly Ramos into Big Horse's saddle and climbed up behind while JD and Barber kept their guns trained on the increasingly itchy bandits. Luke kept his weapon shoved into Ramos's back as his posse mounted up. "Hasta luego, hombres." He headed out at a brisk trot with JD, Barber, and the horses following. At about a hundred yards, Luke glanced over his shoulder. The bandits had not yet moved. Still, something told him to be wary.

After riding a couple of miles, Luke stopped and dismounted. He helped Ramos slide down. It was a long way down for the short, bandy-legged bandit, and he stumbled to his knees upon hitting the ground. "Now, Mr. Ramos, you be careful, you hear?" He looked up to see whether Ramos's men were in sight yet. "Your men should be along soon. If you decide to chase us, know that you're up against Texas Ranger Captain Luke Dunn and I've whupped men far bigger and stronger than you and your sorry gang." He let that sink in. "Next time, I won't be so kind as to set you free. It rubs against my nature, but that was our deal."

Luke unfastened Ramos's manacles and pushed him away. The man turned threateningly. A knife had somehow appeared in Ramos's hand as if from nowhere. Luke stepped back. "You can't be serious," Luke said incredulously.

His comment was followed by a resounding thud. JD had reared back and applied the full force of her rifle butt into the back of Ramos's head. There'd be no knife fighting.

"Whoa, JD. Thanks." He stood a second in amazement at her strength. "Let's get out of here before those bandits get close." Luke hardly expected that sort of strong aggression from so diminutive a human body. He slapped the bandits' horses on their rears and the animals scattered. Luke offered an ironic laugh. "It'll take them a while to gather their horses."

For her part, JD was rightly amazed at what she'd done to Ramos. It sure boosted her confidence.

Now that the business with Sagura had been finished, Luke's Rangers headed for home. Luke had rightly determined that carting prisoners off to jail was too much of a challenge for his small band. They'd let Ramos go off and think on the misplaced wisdom of his gang rustling cattle on the Nueces Strip.

★

The damp darkness was broken by a loud neighing from the barn. Julia lit a lantern and rushed up to the house to awaken Elisa while Jaime went to the barn to confirm his suspicions.

"Señora Dunn, el caballo está de parto." She'd forgotten her English in the excitement, but Elisa understood. The mare had chosen the dead of night to go into labor.

The trio rushed down to the barn to offer what help they could. Elisa had been right a few days back in noticing how the roan mare had put on a bit of weight. The horse likely weighed in at 1300 or 1400 hundred pounds herself and there was no telling how big a foal sired by Big Horse might be. Like the good *vaquero* he was, Jaime had been observing the mare's pregnancy for much of the past several months. He'd been surprised when Elisa had ridden her to Nuecestown a few days ago, but the mare hadn't seemed bothered.

The roan was not in any unusual distress, though this was her first pregnancy. It wasn't but a half hour before the foal's forelegs and head began to emerge from the exhausted mare. Soon enough, the little stallion was curled up in the hay near his mother, and an hour later he made his first efforts to stand. His coat was gray like his sire's. He likely didn't weigh more than 150 pounds or so, but would have big saddles to fill if his lineage was to be any indicator. He finally stood on wobbly legs.

As if on cue, they heard the peal of distant thunder. The mare never flinched at the rumblings, but the foal made an attempt to rear up that nearly caused him to fall.

Elisa looked at Jaime and Julia. They were busy cleaning up the placenta and other birth matter. Seemed the foal had already gotten a name. The two looked up and nodded. No words were necessary. Thunder it would be.

It wasn't long before Thunder was nursing. While new life

was always welcomed at Heaven's Gate, this one was worthy of extra attention. Big Horse's progeny was special. "When Luke gets back, we'll have to celebrate," Elisa said. "You must join us for dinner."

For now, it was nearly sunrise. They were tired, and the roan mare was patiently nursing her offspring.

NINE
SHARPSHOOTER

"WHAT DO YOU THINK, Captain? Have I earned my keep?" JD was parting ways with Luke at Nuecestown. She had babbled about that rifle butt stroke to the back of Pablo Ramos's head on and off for the entire ride back home.

Jake Barber rolled his eyes. He had to admit deep inside that she'd done well. He was just as tired of hearing about it as Luke was.

Luke sighed. "JD, I'll call you for our next job. Trust me. You did good. Now, don't you go wearing the story out." He tried not to sound overly exasperated. In any case, he was anxious to get back to Heaven's Gate and Elisa's loving arms. He bid farewell to his ragtag but capable posse of Rangers and turned Big Horse toward the ranch.

As he began the short ride to Heaven's Gate, his thoughts also turned to what the near future might hold so far as the war. He didn't expect to see Major Belknap for a while, and he was surprised that he hadn't encountered any Confederate troops as of yet. He was certain they were around.

Luke rode through the new archway at Heaven's Gate and nudged Big Horse into a trot. Soon enough the big gray stallion would be relaxing in his stall with oats, hay, and maybe another apple. Luke dismounted and led him into the barn. He did a double-take as he passed the stall of the roan mare and saw that she had company. He led Big Horse over toward the stall. "Dang, will you look at that? You're a daddy, big fella." He watched transfixed as the foal nursed. The newborn was a handsome stallion with the same coloring as his sire. If he lived up to the big stallion's measure, he'd be a prize for sure.

"Come on, Big Horse. Let's get you settled in." He had unsaddled the big gray and was beginning to curry him when he became aware that he had company. Peter, John, and Andrea Anne stood in the doorway, and Elisa followed with Michael on her hip. "Welcome home, Mr. Texas Ranger." She brought an apple for Big Horse and a sweet kiss for Luke.

"Lisa, sweetheart, I love the welcoming party." He picked up each child in turn and gave hugs and secret whispered greetings. He turned back to her, shrugged, and swept her off her feet with baby Michael along for the ride.

"Daddy?" The twins spoke up in unison.

"What is it, boys?"

"We have a new horse."

The twins were now four years old and talking. "Yes, we do indeed have a new horse. Do you think he'll grow up like Big Horse?"

The boys smiled and nodded, then delivered the real news. "Mom has dinner, Daddy."

Elisa laughed and stepped in. "They heard you in the barn and insisted on coming out to greet you. The apple for Big Horse was their idea, too. Come on, Lucas, dinner is waiting." She gathered the children and her Ranger, and herded them back to the house.

Soon enough she'd share the story of the stable boy and the noose. She hoped that, if the folks in Nuecestown had seen Luke ride through, they'd decided it wasn't their place to tell him of his wife's boldness. The story was hers to share with Luke.

"It's time, Scarlett. I've got my orders." Carson held her close to him, his hand on her growing belly.

"Will you be here for him or her?"

"As God is my witness, my love, I'll find a way to be here when your time comes." Over and above the distractions of war, welcoming a new life into the world was Carson's highest priority. He'd survived fighting Apache and Mexican bandits and figured this War Between the States wouldn't last all that long anyway. He'd been assigned to duty around Corpus Christi, and his Texas Ranger experience had earned him a captaincy. It was tough to have to tell Sheriff Meaney that he'd chosen the Army over being a sheriff deputy. It had been even tougher to persuade Scarlett that his duty on the line was of greater importance than making uniforms for soldiers. A leaden cloud of uncertainty hung in the air despite the early confidence of Carson and most of the men who signed up to take on the Yankees.

Scarlett wasn't nearly as confident as her husband. She'd already lost too many men in her young life…father…lovers… clients. It would have been excusable to have become a hard-hearted woman. Luke and Elisa Dunn had given her a path to hope and self-sufficiency, but the loss of another man in her life, especially Walker Carson, might likely dash any vestiges of hope and happiness. "You be sure to be here, Walker Carson. You damn well be certain of it."

"It's Captain Carson, ma'am." He laughed as he often did when she pressed him. He strove to break through this new stress that had arisen between them. He knew where he should be. He and Scarlett were surely not alone in their doubts and worries. Now, if only the uncertainty of war would not stand in his way.

"I love you." Scarlett gave him as crushing an embrace as she could muster. She wanted to be certain he wouldn't soon forget it. She felt his manhood rise to the occasion. She looked up at him and smiled demurely. Oh, yes, he'd remember.

★

Caressing the rifle was a near-constant pastime for Clay Ashley Bell. He'd grown up on a ranch on the Nueces Strip frontier where perfecting marksmanship became a rite of passage for any self-respecting cowboy. But this was an extra special time for the young cowpuncher. His talent with the rifle led to his being called to punch out targets on battlefields as a Confederate sharpshooter.

The rifle? Bell eschewed the .577 caliber Pattern 1853 Enfield rifle popular with most Rebel sharpshooters. In Bell's estimation, the Enfield required too much maintenance. No, his weapon of choice, the one he'd grown up with, was the Sharps breech-loading caplock with a combustible .52 caliber round. His Sharps featured a brand spanking new telescopic sight. If pushed, Bell figured he could nail a target at nearly 1500 yards. Soon enough, he figured to become the bane of Yankee artillerymen and any mounted officers who ventured too close to the front lines.

Bell had signed up at the urging of his good friend Walker Carson. The Texas Ranger had painted an exciting word picture of Confederate glory and how the sharpshooters would be a key to Rebel victory. Carson's picture had been punctuated with verbal pictures of mounted Rebel cavalry with their gold-buttoned and gold-braided gray uniforms, swords, fancy tack, high black riding boots, and rakish hats. No Yankee could possibly withstand an assault by Texas Cavalry.

Clay Bell was itching for an opportunity to show off his very special talent. He'd already impressed army command as he outshot every one of the men they loosely referred to as sharpshooters. He soon got his opportunity. His unit was bivouacked outside of San Antonio. The summer day was warm with clear crisp blue skies. A tall lean jasper broke the idyllic scene, as he rode into the encampment, claiming to have ridden in from the mountains up north somewhere. He carried one of those expensive Enfield rifles, so it was assumed he had money or had acquired the firearm by other means. The man wore mostly black, but seemed up to trading his duds in for the Confederate butternut gray uniforms.

Bell was no shrinking violet. "Howdy, stranger. You fairly good with that fine rifle?"

The stranger offered a crooked sort of smile beneath a full but well-tended growth of beard. "Guess I'm right fair with it, friend. My name's Wills, Colt Wills."

By this time about a dozen members of Bell's unit had gathered 'round. "Pleased to make your acquaintance, Mr. Wills. My name's Clay Bell."

"I gather from your interest in this here Enfield that you're a pretty fair marksman 'round these parts?" Wills began to size up the Rebel sharpshooter. "The sun's high and sighting should be fine. You up for a wager?"

The troops egged Bell on a bit, though it wasn't really necessary. "What do you have in mind?"

"I've got a twenty-dollar gold piece that says I can hit any target you choose at 1,000 yards." Wills smiled again and stroked his beard. "You up to losing 20?" That was a lot of money for any soldier.

About this time, Walker Carson rode up. As a newly minted Rebel captain, he'd taken a few days' leave. After spending time with his now very pregnant wife, Scarlett, he decided to ride up to San Antonio and see his old Texas Ranger friends. He arrived just in time to take in the potential transaction.

Carson locked eyes with Wills. There was a sense of recognition between them, then a light went on for the ex-Ranger. He recalled encountering this man Wills fighting with Apache down near Rio Grande City a couple of years back. Wills was a fair marksman and managed to escape the Texas Ranger assault on Apaches and bandits along the Rio Grande. Carson decided to let this pass for the present. Could be the man had changed his ways.

Bell caught Carson's change in body language. "What's up, Walker?"

Carson took him aside.

"You getting a little coaching, Mr. Bell?" Wills laughed mockingly.

Carson spoke in a whisper. "Clay, I've seen this man before. From what I know, his effective range is just about a thousand yards...or less. I know you're better than that. You might push that Sharps just a tad, but have the target moved out another couple of hundred yards." He looked over at Wills, nodded, and put his finger to his hat as a friendly gesture. "There's a lot of warm moisture in the air, too. Gonna make the bullet fly just a tad faster."

Three of the Confederate soldiers place a two-inch thick wooden plank with a large "x" on it out on a faraway hillside. They'd paced it off at about 1,200 yards.

Wills gave a barely noticeable flinch as he watched the soldiers place the target a bit farther out than he'd have preferred.

"Let's see what you've got with that Enfield of yours, Mr. Wills." Bell suppressed a smile as he invited the challenger to take his position. He was counting on Carson's advice.

Wills thought about kneeling, but dropped to a prone position to better steady the Enfield. He watched a gust of wind hit tall grass a few yards short of the target. This would make things just a bit more challenging. He took his time sighting through the scope, eased out his breath, held it, and squeezed the trigger. An orange flash exploded from the muzzle. It seemed like forever until the bullet knocked a chunk from the side of the plank. The wood still stood. He offered a semi-satis-fied smile.

Bell watched admiringly. "Pretty fair, Mr. Wills. Pretty fair shot for sure." He glanced around at the gathering of what now numbered close to two dozen soldiers. In what seemed like a single choreographed motion, he nonchalantly tossed a handful of grass into the air, watched it, kneeled, raised the Sharps, aimed, and squeezed off a round. His bullet hit the target dead on, exploding it into mere splinters. "Happy to relieve you of that gold piece, Mr. Wills. It's been a pleasure to compete." He nodded his thanks to Carson for his advice. He turned and smiled at Wills. "Pleased to have you join us, Colt." With his reputation intact, Bell extended his hand to welcome the fellow sharpshooter to the ranks.

Carson congratulated him. "Damn fine shot, Clay. I forgot to remind you how the bullet rises when it first comes out of the muzzle, but I expect I didn't need to do that."

Bell nodded. "Appreciate the advice anyway, Walker."

A voice interrupted the welcome. "Sergeant Bell, the major's askin' ya to report. I'm thinkin' he's got an assignment fer ya." The young man looked around at the assembled soldiers. These were mostly sharpshooters—the cream of the Confederate fighting forces. They delivered terror to the Yankee lines, whether picking off a senior officer or elimi-nating a gun crew at a cannon emplacement.

Sure enough, the Rebels had intercepted a courier carrying orders to a Yankee contingent up near Passe Cavallo.

★

Lieutenant Kittredge was relaxing on the deck of the USS *Arthur* sipping a bit of rum. Now and again, he lifted the spyglass and scanned the shoreline. He'd like nothing better than an opportunity to show the Texans the might of the United States Navy. On the other hand, his supply ship was late and visions of his having to lead a party ashore to forage loomed at the forefront of his mind. He'd hoped the rum would help. It wasn't that he lacked confidence—far from it—it was simply such a hassle to deal with the locals. Now and again, he'd lob a shell toward Corpus, knowing it would fall short of the target. Then again, despite his itching for combat, he wasn't up to killing innocent civilians, regardless of which side they were on.

He leaped to his feet. "Boatswain, assemble my officers." His decision was made. His intention was to assemble a shore party and do a bit of foraging. It wouldn't do to have hungry men aboard his ship.

The Army officers gathered around the forecastle. Kittredge looked from man to man. "Where the hell is Major Belknap?"

A pair of lieutenants looked at each other with a hint of exasperation. They weren't especially fond of Lieutenant Kittredge and his treatment of US Army soldiers aboard the *USS Arthur*. "Sir, you set him ashore up near Passe Cavallo on Matagorda Bay."

Kittredge was embarrassed at having forgotten the duty he'd given Belknap as punishment for his having had the audacity to bargain for horses with the Rebels. He looked away distractedly. "Well, I have orders for the major." He handed one of the lieutenants a folded and sealed document. "Take this to Major Belknap. He need not respond...just do as ordered. Stay with the major and confirm that these orders are followed." He looked condescendingly at the group before him. "Dismissed."

★

The Nueces River offered a modicum of cover thanks largely to pecan and Cyprus trees lining its banks. A lone Comanche on horseback with a pair of ponies in tow would have been an unusual sight at any time, but especially with a war underway. Stories of recent Indian raids on the western frontier had folks on guard. Even a lone warrior would be seen by settlers as a serious threat.

One Arrow recognized that the fears of ranchers and farmers worked to his advantage. To that end, he wore much of his war regalia as he traveled. He had already earned three eagle feathers in the headdress he wore over his long black hair with its two braids. His buckskin breechcloth and leggings were complemented by a vest artfully decorated with ornate beadwork. When needed, he had black warpaint to apply over much of his face. Three scalps hung from his war lance and he sported a full quiver of arrows that he'd learned to shoot with considerable accuracy while at a full gallop. His leather shield could easily deflect enemy arrows and lances. As to appearance, One Arrow had become every inch the prototypical Comanche warrior. Like most young warriors in these times, maturity had been thrust upon him at an early age.

He'd now passed into more heavily populated frontier areas, as he skirted around San Patricio. He was ever alert for other Indians, as well as Mexican and Anglo threats.

He was a bit east of San Patricio when he heard voices. He moved to a nearby grove of cypress that offered ample cover. Soon enough, the source of the noise came into view. Half a dozen men in uniforms rode by. One Arrow was especially curious, as these soldiers didn't wear the customary dark blue uniforms he was used to seeing on soldiers. These were a grayish color. The Comanche cocked his head as he tried to determine who these men were. They were White and spoke the White man's tongue. But he remained ever on guard, lest he be discovered.

One Arrow was quite impressed with the weapons carried by the soldiers. To his thinking, these were not ordinary soldiers. They carried the big rifle that the Anglos used to kill buffalo. Some even had some sort of rod mounted on top. He didn't yet know about telescopic sights. In any case, he intuitively knew to give these soldiers a wide berth.

The lone Comanche warrior decided to wait an extra long time for the soldiers to put some distance between them. They were traveling in the same eastward direction, and it wouldn't do for him to overrun them. Wouldn't do at all.

★

"What the hell!" Belknap murmured to himself through gritted teeth as he took the rumpled document the lieutenant had delivered. He ripped it open.

For his part, the lieutenant was too embarrassed to admit to having been waylaid by some non-descript highwayman who'd knocked him from his mount and taken what little money he had. He was unconscious briefly but was relieved upon awakening that he still had Kittredge's orders. The seal had been crushed, but the document was intact.

"Foraging!" the major spat the word aloud so the others could hear. The orders were even specific. He was to head south toward Nuecestown to take food from the locals.

These orders were the icing on the cake so far as the major's displeasure with the current chain of command. "Sergeant, assemble the men. We ride out in an hour." He calculated that it was still early enough that they might reach Victoria by nightfall. He had a rough idea where various Confederate army camps were, so he felt confident they could avoid them. Still, it was a hazardous assignment, and he knew Kittredge was setting him up.

As the men assembled their gear to head off on their foraging assignment, a new officer rode into the camp. The man quickly recognized the command tent and reined in his mount in front of it. Since he wore army blue and everyone was distracted gathering gear, he wasn't challenged and rode directly to the major. Belknap was just finishing saddling his horse. The officer stopped in front of him, dismounted, and saluted. "Lieutenant Rex Rucker reporting, sir."

Belknap's jaw dropped. He offered a cursory return salute. "I'll be damned. Are you Horace Rucker's kin?"

"Yes, sir, yes I am."

"Good man, your father. Had the pleasure of working with the colonel. Preacher now in Nuecestown, isn't he?"

"Yes. I'm sure he'd send his regards, sir."

"So, you were at West Point?"

"Yes, sir."

"Went there myself a few years back. Sort of miss the long gray line." Belknap looked off for a moment as though trying to visualize those days not that long ago. "Welcome, Lieutenant Rucker. The sergeant will introduce you to our command. You can draw supplies and mount up, as we're headed on a bit of a foraging mission." He returned Rex's salute and began to turn away. "You were under General Butler's command?"

Rex nodded.

"Around here, we're taking orders from some wet-behind-the-ears Navy lieutenant sitting on a boat near Corpus Christi." Belknap's tone left no doubt as to what he thought of Kittredge. He waved Rex away. "Draw what you'll need, Lieutenant. Ride with me when we form up."

Once mounted, the troop rode south in a column of twos with two reasonably experienced privates riding point. For most of the soldiers, it served as a great opportunity to escape the boredom of sitting at Passe Cavallo.

Belknap was determined to avoid Nuecestown proper and definitely stay clear of his friends' ranch at Heaven's Gate. There were plenty of outlying homesteads still operating despite having given up their best young men to the war effort. Somewhere in his travels, he'd have to commandeer a wagon.

★

"What do you think, Clay?" The sharpshooters seemed at least by outward appearances to be a happy-go-lucky bunch. Given the macabre nature of their duties, lightheartedness pretty much served as an escape from stress that surely touched their souls.

Bell looked over at the soldier riding next to him. "Think about what?" The man beside him was an important asset to a sharpshooter. He was a spotter, a man whose primary job was to identify potential targets and confirm shooting conditions. Bell hadn't worked with this man before, so wasn't surprised at the questions.

"Well, what do you think about what we'll be doing up the road apiece?"

"Not much, Dan. We've a job to do. That's about the size of it." Bell awaited the expected follow-up question.

"What goes through your mind when you eliminate someone?"

Bell gave him a you-can't-be-serious look. "You mean kill them?"

"Er…yes…kill them."

"I start thinking about the next target." He gave the soldier a grim smile that said not to ask any more questions.

"Sergeant, do you know who we're looking for?"

Bell was becoming a shade put off by the man's questions. "Foragers, Dan. We'll be looking for some Yankees stealing from our Texas brothers." As he said it, he realized he was fighting for Texas, not the Confederacy. Fact of the matter was that Clay Bell didn't give a cow pie for the folks in Richmond. They certainly had no understanding of his world on the Texas Nueces Strip.

They soon heard a rider approaching at a near-gallop from their rear. Bell brought the patrol to a halt and turned to face whoever was riding so hard.

"Clay, wait up!" The rider wore gray, so wasn't seen as a threat. His horse was well lathered.

Bell had last seen the captain a couple of days before at the marksmanship contest. "Well I'll be! You joining up with us, Captain Carson?" He said captain with a bit of attitude. Despite their long friendship, there was just room for envy. Carson's Texas Ranger exploits had earned him the officer commission. It was ironic, given that Carson had always looked up to Bell. They'd even driven cattle together one time before Carson's father kicked him out and his life went awry for a couple of years. Other than their brief reunion at that shooting contest, they had pretty much lost touch.

"Hope you don't mind me tagging along for a while. I'm going to Corpus Christi for a couple of days to see my wife."

"Dang, Walker. You got hitched?"

"Oh, yes. Didn't I tell you? Beautiful red-haired lady. She's carrying our child as we speak."

"Good for you. Sure, you're welcome to ride along at least to a little north of Nuecestown. We'll have to part company there, my friend. By the way, thanks again for that tip that helped me outshoot Wills." Naturally, they dispersed with salutes.

They rode on a bit with Carson alongside the sergeant. Bell turned to him and asked pointedly, "I heard that you tamed a few Apache and outlaws down toward the Rio Grande Valley, Walker."

"Managed to mostly win a few battles, but lost a great Texas Ranger, too. Guy named Bol Richards."

"Yep. Heard of him. Tough, gruff old guy. Must have been an ambush."

"You guessed right. Learned a lot from Bol. He seemed to be able to climb inside an Apache's head and know exactly what he'd do."

The patrol rode on, as Bell and Carson kept up a steady

chatter. Back a mile or so behind, One Arrow kept them ever in his sights. The Comanche wasn't inclined to get involved in the White man's war.

TEN
THORPE'S GAME

WITH PLENTY of money and the power it commands along with its potential for out-sized influence, Edward Thorpe could easily have bought himself a Confederate commission. He'd have been a colonel at the very least. But the Confederate butternut gray uniform and all the trappings that went with it weren't in his constitution.

Thorpe had already pushed his political and social limits by freeing many of his slaves. Had it been revealed that he was secretly paying those who remained, it might have brought the full fury of the Rebel army, not to mention local vigilance committees, down on his head. Thus far, he'd been able to artfully fend off his potential enemies.

He wasn't excited about traveling to Austin, but he still needed to clean up his father's business. It was complicated. He'd hired his father's slave to watch over the offices until he could come to the capital himself. Samuel had been well-treated and had served Horatio Thorpe in what amounted to an administrative assistant role. He had also served as point of contact with Thorpe's nefarious contacts that were engaged to perform work outside the law. It was extra-legal, as it were.

Thorpe's primary mission was to shut down his father's

office. He saw it as an unnecessary business expense. Since Samuel already knew so much of the intricacies of his father's business endeavors, Thorpe figured to possibly bring him back to Magnolia and operate the business from the plantation.

For Samuel's part, he had gotten right comfortable with the current situation. Despite the war mostly to the east, Austin wasn't especially troublesome for him. He'd been under Horatio Thorpe's protection for so long that he'd become a familiar face around Austin. Coupled with his connections in the underworld of lawbreakers, folks shied away from challenging him. Samuel's family enjoyed the fruits of his labors, as Horatio Thorpe had treated him well.

The younger Thorpe certainly recognized the value of Samuel's connections should such a need ever arise. The black man was an invaluable asset. He strode confidently into the Thorpe offices on Congress Street. "Samuel, it's good to see you." He extended his hand.

"Welcome, master."

Thorpe shook his head and smiled. He handed Samuel a piece of paper. "Whoa, Samuel. I'm not your master, but I'd like to be your employer."

Samuel read the paper that gave him his freedom. He knew he needed no paper to be free, but it would matter to some. He cocked his head inquisitively. "What do you mean?"

"You know of my father's business interests, Samuel. I'd like you to oversee the Thorpe international trade interests. I will pay you a fair sum each month."

"Yes. Yes, sir, Mr. Thorpe." The now-former slave smiled broadly.

Thus, it fell to Samuel to maintain the Thorpe international trade interests, such as they were, given the highly effective Union blockades. Samuel also maintained Thorpe's chain of saloons and bawdy houses stretching across Texas. In fact, the former slave was known to dabble on occasion, as some of the young ladies were attracted to black men.

Samuel never did understand his former master's obsession with the whore from Laredo, Scarlett Rose. In any case, it was no longer his concern after the elder Thorpe had been shot and killed by Luke Dunn while attempting to rape the Texas Ranger's wife.

Samuel didn't know Edward Thorpe very well, as the son had been estranged from the father. So far as he could tell, this Thorpe was an honorable man and seemed to truly wish to bring the slave economy to an end. In any case, Samuel knew which side of the bread his future was buttered. He recalled advice his own father had given him back in Georgia to never be so foolish as to argue with your cook. In this case, Edward Thorpe was the cook for Samuel's future.

Thorpe was at peace, as another piece of his efforts to wrestle his legacy from dependence on slave labor was being implemented.

Samuel shook Thorpe's hand to seal their deal, and the black man strode over to the desk outside the executive office. He didn't deign himself worthy of his former master's lavishly ornate workspace.

"Samuel. I will not be here very often. Use my father's desk. You are free to hire someone to sit out here." In Thorpe's mind, it was a fitting justice to have his father's desk taken over by his former slave. Indeed, it seemed the right thing to do.

★

One Arrow spent his days combing the region around Nuecestown. His travels took him near two of the homesteads that War Cloud had attacked. He was extra careful to stay out of sight so as not to scare residents into thinking a Comanche was scouting toward planning some sort of uprising. That he managed to stay out of sight despite having three ponies was a feat Three Toes would surely have been proud of. One Arrow was surprised that he saw no more troops, but assumed they were fighting elsewhere.

It seemed natural that the warrior returned to the scene of the fight at Heaven's Gate. It was partly because it had been among the first of his engagements against the Anglos, but even more, as he'd lost his chief and mentor at the place. For One Arrow, the Dunn ranch held big medicine.

On a particularly dark evening with plenty of cloud cover to hide the moon and stars, he stalked silently onto Heaven's Gate. He felt drawn to the place by some power he had thus far been unable to fully grasp. He wondered what had drawn Three Toes to the Texas Ranger and to the ranch.

One Arrow carefully scouted until he felt confident that he could navigate the area around the ranch buildings in the darkness. He waited until the lights in both the house and the cabin had been extinguished. He'd hobbled his ponies off near the Nueces River and approached the ranch on foot. Despite the nearly pitch blackness, he knew exactly where the chief's grave was.

He knew to stay away from the barn and corral. The last thing he needed was livestock raising a ruckus. He moved silently, gliding swiftly along the hard ground. In but a couple of minutes, the Comanche warrior found himself standing before Three Toes's grave. He found himself unable to breathe. The emotion connected with the place had affected him far more than he'd anticipated. He knelt at the marker that Luke had fashioned for the chief. The bone necklace with its White man's cross was still hanging on the side of the wooden tablet. One Arrow had just begun to understand English as taught by the chief, so recognized Three Toes's name carved into the wood. He lifted the necklace and held it up to gather whatever light he could. He was startled as the clouds parted just enough to cast moonlight onto his upraised hands. The sudden reflection from the white bone beads caused him to drop the necklace onto the chief's grave. He stared at it for a moment as though in awe of some sort of spirit it seemed to hold and then picked it up. Three Toes had told him the necklace was said to possess a very strong power. The young Comanche warrior raised the necklace aloft again and then placed it slowly, almost ceremoniously over his head. He felt it settle gently around his neck. One Arrow felt nothing different.

A coyote stirred in the brush. One Arrow looked around and, as quietly as he'd come, he left the grave.

Now he felt led to take the next step. He truly must see Luke Dunn again. No, more than meet up with the Texas Ranger—his very soul demanded that he find out who the man really was.

★

A man in rather plain clothes accosted Thorpe as he strode up Congress Street toward the capital. He began to walk beside the plantation owner. "Please pay me no never mind, Mr. Thorpe."

It was a tad disconcerting. The man knew whom he was. Was he a threat?

"I'm not here to hurt you, Mr. Thorpe. My name is Barnabas Smith. I'd appreciate a few moments of your time."

Thorpe nodded and was nudged semi-voluntarily toward a nearby bench under a live oak tree.

"Please sit a moment, Mr. Thorpe."

They looked at each other for a moment, each judging the other.

"I'm from the federal government." He showed an identification card to Thorpe. "We are aware of what you have been doing at Magnolia with the slaves, Mr. Thorpe."

Thorpe nodded. He was beginning to suspect what the man was up to. "Is that a problem?"

"To the contrary, the president is quite pleased with such activities. He encourages them." Smith turned deadly serious.

"We would appreciate it, Mr. Thorpe, if we might reach out to you on occasion for a first-hand assessment of goings-on in Texas."

Edward Thorpe was being asked to serve as a spy for the Yankees. If he'd been at risk up to now, being caught as a spy by Confederate forces would mean certain death. "I trust in your total discretion, Mr. Smith."

The agent nodded, for agent he certainly was. "Count on it."

"I'll be whatever help I can, Mr. Smith."

"Thank you." Smith looked around furtively. "We'll be back in touch, Mr. Thorpe. Oh…and I'll be your only contact." The implication was that this was a shady business and contacts necessarily must be limited to protect against double agents or other gnarly activity.

Thorpe's game was on.

ELEVEN
VISION QUEST

THE BREEZE WAFTING across the range was unseasonably warm for the first few days of autumn. Elisa stood on the gallery and let her thoughts drift.

Luke watched her through the window as Peter and John wrestled at his feet. He instinctively knew Elisa needed at least a few moments now and then of peaceful bliss to herself. His eyes fully took in her silhouette and petiteness despite her pregnancy. Much to the envy of the women around Nuecestown, she had managed to keep a slimness about her that belied her having had four children. Luke was aroused at the thought of the soft supple nakedness under her dress. The sometimes harsh sun and winds of the Texas frontier had been ever so kind to Elisa.

The days of summer were dwindling, and cool weather would be upon them soon enough. With the war ever on his mind, Luke did worry about what the future might hold. His gaze drifted from his wife to the prairie beyond, and he couldn't help but think on their safety. The conflict had certainly transcended the relatively carefree days of worrying about stray livestock, rattlesnakes, and weather.

Finally, Elisa broke the spell as she turned and headed to

the door. "Lucas?" There was laundry to be done. "It's a beautiful day, Lucas. I'm going to take the laundry down to the creek." It had rained for better than three days, so the prairie was flourishing and the creeks had come alive. Perfect for swimming and clothes washing. Elisa would apply the age-old techniques of soaping and soaking, wringing, bashing tough dirt out on the rocks, rinsing, and repeating. "Can you watch the children for a bit?" Without the children to tend to, the clothes washing would go much faster.

"Happy to, sweetheart. I've got to clean my guns, so staying up here in the house works out fine. Maybe it's time for the boys to see how to take good care of weapons." He knew it would be a question of holding their interest. They likely wouldn't be fully drawn to the guns until they could shoot. It'd then become a much more meaningful exercise.

Elisa gathered the basket and turned to the door.

"Lisa, don't forget the Colt." She'd almost forgotten. Taking the revolver with her to the creek always brought back memories of the Comanche attack on the homestead when she'd lost her father and a brother. She'd shot a Comanche warrior. The Colt had saved her life. She grabbed it from the fireplace mantle and laid it atop the basket full of clothes.

Luke placed his Colt revolvers and rifle on the table along with the oil and brushes to go about cleaning. John and Peter were curious and came over to watch. Andrea Anne played with a rag doll while pretending to not be interested. Baby Michael simply napped.

Luke watched Elisa leave then turned to disassembling the revolvers. "Now, you boys remember to never ever point a gun at anyone or anything unless you intend to shoot what you're aiming at." The boys blinked as that sunk in.

"It's important to keep your guns clean. All sorts of bad things can happen with a dirty gun." He proceeded to meticulously clean the barrels and cylinders of the Colts. He let the boys hold each piece before he cleaned it so as to give them a sense of what the metal parts felt like.

Finally, Andrea could resist no longer. In the halting and limited speech of a three-year-old, she asked to touch the pieces. "Daddy…gun."

Luke smiled at her curiosity and boldness. She likely got the traits from her mother. Peter and John looked on almost jealously as Luke let her handle each part, just as they had done. She sat and eagerly awaited the next steps in the process.

Finally, the revolvers were assembled. Luke felt as though attention spans were dwindling, so decided to clean the rifle later. He showed each child how to be sure the guns were empty and reminded them not to point at anyone. Each in turn held the empty revolvers, getting a sense of their heft. With a full load of bullets, they'd be just a tad heavier. Andrea Anne nearly dropped the first revolver she held as she was fully unprepared for its weight. She quickly accommodated the Colt, and Luke took note at how comfortably this little three-year-old girl appeared to handle a firearm. Luke decided they were too young to be advised that, in the event of an Indian attack, to always keep a bullet in the cylinder to use on themselves. The Comanche especially earned their description as savages for what they did to captives.

"Tell you what. Michael's still asleep, and your mama's down at the creek." He was about to invite them to watch him shoot, but then realized it just might alarm Elisa and the Sanchez family over in the nearby cabin. It was still early, and there was no point in raising a ruckus unnecessarily. "Let's see what's left of Mama's biscuits from breakfast."

★

One Arrow watched from afar as Elisa wended her way down the steep rocky path to the creek. He knew the Texas Ranger was still in the house, as he'd watched him tend the livestock at sunrise and return, likely to eat a meal. Luke hadn't reemerged.

The Comanche felt intimidated by the thought of approaching the house alone. Three Toes's stories of Luke's strong medicine, coupled with how they'd repelled the attack by War Cloud, left One Arrow more than fearful despite the friendship the chief had with the Texas Ranger. Consequently, he decided to approach what he perceived as the weaker route: Elisa. It occurred to him that it was Elisa's bullets that had killed War Cloud, and he had no idea that she'd killed Comanche before.

He worked his way down to the creek such that he could approach through tall grasses and among a few trees growing on the shore opposite where Elisa had settled in to wash clothes.

For her part, Elisa found herself getting through the washing more quickly than expected. Unencumbered by the children, she was about as blazingly efficient at washing clothes as anyone could hope to be. The day was warming quickly. She looked up at the sun and felt its relaxing penetrating rays course through her body. She recalled the days of bathing in the creek. *Oh, why not?* she thought to herself.

She had not the slightest sense of anyone watching. She could not know that One Arrow was mustering the courage to reveal himself. She slipped from her clothes and immersed herself in the cool running waters of the creek. The water caressing her young womanly and very pregnant body felt invigoratingly luxurious. These sorts of moments were all too rare. She recalled the time when Luke had rescued her from the leering local sheriff who'd been watching her bathe. She especially recalled how Luke's comforting embrace had made her feel. The thought aroused her senses even now, five years later.

One Arrow's jaw gaped as he saw her nakedness. He'd never seen a White woman in this way before, especially a woman filled with child. There was an innocence about it, a certain freedom in her vulnerability. He even envied it.

A deer appeared seemingly from thin air and bounded through the creek. It startled One Arrow enough that he stood up, took a step backward, let out a muffled cry, and nearly fell into the creek.

At the disturbance, a very naked Elisa swiftly waded to the clothes basket and grabbed the old Colt Navy revolver. With her free hand, she snatched up her dress and covered herself as best she could. Standing but a few yards away was a fearsome sight: a young Comanche warrior in nearly full regalia. The memory of the Comanche attacking her family homestead rushed into Elisa's mind.

One Arrow found himself staring down the barrel of a Colt revolver with its hammer pulled back and a very determined-looking young woman at its trigger.

Blessedly for him, Elisa paused.

"Three Toes." The Comanche could barely get out a whisper.

She looked intently at him. Who was this invoking her dead friend's name? "Who are you? Where did you get that?" She held the gun steadily as she nodded toward the necklace.

One Arrow allowed himself a guarded sigh of relief. "Me One Arrow." He pointed to himself. "Three Toes my chief. He say necklace have great power."

She considered this. "Turn around." She pointed up the creek.

Given that she held the gun on him and wore so determined an expression, he complied.

Elisa put her clothes on while keeping an eye on this interloper. "You can turn back toward me. Why are you here?" It occurred to her that this warrior might be telling the truth, as there weren't many places a Comanche might have picked up even a rudimentary understanding of the English tongue. It also occurred to her that he'd apparently been watching her and had ample time to attack her. He could indeed be telling the truth.

One Arrow tried to appear non-threatening. "Want to know Texas Ranger captain. He friend to Three Toes."

Elisa smiled guardedly and motioned toward the path leading up to the house. "Go ahead." She kept the revolver pointed at him. "Here, you carry the basket." Carrying a heavy Colt revolver and a basket of wet laundry would make her a bit too vulnerable for her liking.

He looked questioningly at her. It wasn't in his constitution to take direction from a woman, much less perform woman's work. But this was a friend of his chief, and there was the matter of the revolver she was still pointing at him. From the way she handled the Colt, it was clear she knew how to use it. After a moment of thoughtful hesitation, he placed his bow and arrows on the ground and picked up the heavy basket of wet clothes.

Elisa permitted herself a wry smile at the irony of the situation, picked up the Comanche's bow and quiver of arrows, and followed him up the path to the house.

By now, Luke had finished cleaning his guns and was on the gallery enjoying an all-too-rare moment playing with his children. They'd already savored the last of the breakfast biscuits slathered in butter and jam. The evidence still clung to their lips. He looked up as Elisa came into sight with what appeared to be a captive Comanche warrior walking ahead of her. The humor of her carrying the bow and arrows and him toting her washing wasn't lost on him. "Lisa? What's this?"

One Arrow looked over his shoulder at Elisa, who nodded back at him. He placed the basket on a large flat rock and turned back to Luke. "*Maruawe*, Ghost-Who-Rides."

The Comanche hello, coupled with the name the tribe had given him, took Luke by surprise. He replied with his limited command of the Comanche language by asking the warrior's name. "*Unha hakai nahniska*?" Luke began to come to the realization that he'd met this Comanche before.

"One Arrow." He pointed to himself. "Three Toes my chief. You come my camp."

The formalities were out of the way. Luke recalled his visit to the warrior's encampment on the Pedernales River, when he'd delivered on Three Toes's dying wish. Luke looked over at Elisa, who was still smiling at having captured a Comanche, though it was now tempered with the knowledge that the young brave had come in peace. She stuffed the Colt in her waistband, picked up the clothes basket, and carried it up the steps and into the house. "Ask him if he's hungry, Lucas."

It was clear that there'd be a lot to talk about. It was obvious that One Arrow was intent on learning all he could about the relationship between Three Toes and this Texas Ranger. It was all strong medicine for certain.

Luke winked at her as she climbed the stairs. "We finished the biscuits."

"I'll whip up some fresh ones...maybe some bacon and eggs."

Luke smiled. "Cornbread?"

The children watched with mouths agape as Luke walked over to One Arrow and gave the warrior a handclasp and welcoming hug. It had been quite a while since Luke had visited One Arrow's encampment after the death of Three Toes. In the depths of his heart, he had trusted that the young Comanche warrior's curiosity would eventually bring him to Heaven's Gate.

★

The Apache in South Texas were far from finished. Costalites was unaware of the depredations of the Comanche to the north and the toll that Texas Ranger Rip Ford had taken on them. He had some insight into what some of the

Mexican bandit gangs were up to. He occasionally ran into the likes of Pablo Ramos. He was well aware of Ramos's infighting with Juan Cortina, enough that he could leverage their differences to his advantage by playing one off against the other. He recalled his frustrations against that Texas Ranger Bol Richards a few months back and was relieved to have learned the man had been killed. The Apache chief's motivation, aside from feeding his own Lipan Apache tribe, was to get rid of competitors for the considerable rewards to be had within the Nueces Strip. He sought to open up plenty of space on the Nueces Strip to raid ranches and farms at will.

He and his band of about two dozen warriors were riding at an easy pace across the prairie, when he spotted Ramos limping along with what was left of his bandit gang. They'd seen each other, so there was no avoiding confrontation.

Costalites knew about as much of the Spanish tongue as Ramos did English, which was to say not a whole lot. Since Ramos knew absolutely no Apache, they'd mix Spanish and English. Some folks referred to this as Spanglish.

"*Señor Ramos*...you are injured?" That was the least of the Mexican bandit's concerns, and the chief knew it. He was struck by the physical similarities between Ramos and Cortina. To the chief's thinking, Cortina was what the Mexicans called a *huero* owing to his fair complexion, though he had the same stocky build and evil, sinister facial expressions as Ramos. There the comparison fell apart, as Cortina was reputed to be a superior horseman and had sufficient charisma to maintain a sizable following. However, word had it that Cortina was as dumb as a horseshoe, and Costalites saw the same ignorance in Ramos. The two rebels' egos mostly triumphed over common sense.

Ramos surveyed the scene before him. Two dozen Apache versus his mere handful of men who'd just had their tails kicked by a Texas Ranger and a pair of nobodies. "*Jefe. Buenos dias.* Are you hunting?" He could only pray that Costalites wasn't in a fighting mood.

The chief smiled broadly. He knew he was playing a very strong hand. "¿Dónde *están tus pieles de vaca?*" He knew one of Ramos's chief sources of cash was selling cattle hides. Obviously, the Mexican had lost his hides, had them stolen, or been unsuccessful in obtaining them. "Where are they, *señor?*"

Ramos felt Costalites's symbolic dagger stab deeply and winced as the chief twisted the metaphorical blade with his biting words. "Texas Ranger." It was the best he could offer.

Costalites wasn't finished with his fun. "*¿Una tropa? ¿Cuántos?*" Indeed, how many Rangers were there?

Ramos's face was beginning to flush with a combination of mortification and anger. He was at the Apache's mercy. "*Tres.*" He pretty much whispered it. No point in lying.

"Three?" The chief said it loudly enough that all his warriors could hear.

"Luke Dunn." Ramos said this with more forcefulness as though to justify his having been beaten.

Costalites knew of Luke by reputation. He nodded knowingly for a split second, though his eyes were still laughing. "I think I let you go today, *Señor Ramos.*" He tried to hold back a full-bore laugh as he spat the words out. What was a Mexican bandit to do against two dozen Apache, if he couldn't defeat three ragtag Texas Rangers, even with a force like Luke Dunn? This prey was far too easy for a chief of Costalites's repute.

"*¿Quizás te unas Señor Cortina?*" A jibe to go join his enemy Juan Cortina served as a final insult. Still laughing, the chief turned to his warriors and signaled them to leave. "*Buena suerte, Señor Ramos.*" And Costalites was gone in a swirling cloud of Nueces Strip dust. Indeed, Ramos would need some good luck.

Pablo Ramos looked at his men. They seethed with anger but were helpless. They'd spent most of the previous day retrieving their horses. Ramos had some recruiting to do. If he was to take full advantage of the vulnerable void left by the Texan fighting men that had joined the Confederate army, he needed to move quickly and decisively.

★

With his regalia stored away, One Arrow no longer frightened the children. The warrior relaxed with Luke and Elisa on the gallery across the front of the house. Even Jaime and Julia had come up from the cabin to join in the conversation. One Arrow knew just enough English that he could be understood by Peter and John, who were delighted to talk to this human who looked and acted so differently. They marveled that he walked around half-naked, just as they often did.

They'd had been up late as Luke and Elisa did their best to answer the Comanche's spoken and unspoken questions about Three Toes, the White man, and the future of his own race. Luke sensed One Arrow's deep concern over his own future.

The warrior watched the children play. They were so innocent, so free, so unencumbered with worries. He fondled the necklace as he spoke. "My chief believed your words about power of this gift."

Luke looked at Elisa. She nodded her head ever so slightly. The Texas Ranger looked out over the range stretching before them. "One Arrow, we believe in one all-powerful God. He loves, He forgives…but He can be angry and sometimes seems to permit unfair or unjust things to happen. But we trust in Him and know that He will ultimately protect us. The cross represents Him sending His own Son as a human to us to teach of His love and sacrifice for our evil ways." Luke intently observed the Comanche warrior's reaction. Was his message sinking in? Could a Comanche warrior that worshipped multiple gods grasp a single, all-powerful creator God, greater even than his Great Spirit?

One Arrow thought on Luke's words. The silence became

just a tad uncomfortable. His words had been a lot to take in, and they ran counter to all he'd ever learned. "Comanche have many gods, Ghost-Who-Rides."

Luke had heard Three Toes speak of the Great Spirit and of the evil one. "Our God comes to us as a Father, Son, and Holy Spirit, One Arrow. It is as though He is three in one. He is all-knowing and all-powerful." Luke rightly figured this concept might be challenging for One Arrow to immediately grasp. He awaited the Comanche's response. In the back of his mind, Luke wished all people would love and respect one another and be at peace. He watched intently as the young Comanche warrior processed what he'd just shared. Luke was pragmatic, but held just a touch of optimism. The past few months of drought had been a hard lesson in the real world. True peace was not likely, at least in his lifetime.

One Arrow finally broke the silence. "What of the evil one?"

"Our God triumphs over the evil one. So it is written."

One Arrow's eyes riveted in on Luke's as though he were trying to bore deeply into the Texas Ranger's soul. What he sensed was counterintuitive. This tough frontier lawman's eyes revealed a vulnerability, yet strength that the Comanche had never expected. The young warrior drew Three Toes's necklace from his bag and displayed it to Luke and Elisa. "One Arrow take from chief's grave."

Luke nodded. He was momentarily surprised that One Arrow had already been on their property and at Three Toes's burial place, but then recalled that the Comanche warrior was wearing it when Elisa captured him. He smiled. "Three Toes would want you to have it."

Luke's eyes had a certain aura of honesty and compassion in them. Framed by crow's feet at the corners as tanned from his years in the harsh sun of the Nueces Strip, his blue eyes exuded a true caring for his fellow man. It served to confirm the sense of often violently delivered justice tempered with the seeking of redemption that resided deep within. It was rather anachronistic.

"Me try understand, Ghost-Who-Rides." One Arrow turned to Peter and John. He watched as they played with the small buckskin bags each with an arrowhead inside that he'd given them. This battle-tested warrior wondered whether he might one day have a family and actually live in peace. He was beginning to understand what Three Toes had struggled with. No easy task, as it conflicted with all he'd been taught growing up in Comanche villages. Given his comparative youth, it could be that he might better accommodate his people's future and even help determine it. He looked to Elisa. He sensed the honest caring humanity that filled her being as well. Perhaps, his own vision quest was being fulfilled after all.

Luke and Elisa shared the sense that their message to this wild savage would ultimately prevail.

Lieutenant Rex Rucker rode tall in the saddle alongside Major Belknap. Along with Kittredge's man, they were a bit overmanned with officers. They'd bivouacked late in the day a couple of miles outside of Victoria, as they figured to do their foraging the next morning. Belknap was staying well north of the Nueces River, as he was determined not to ride into territory close to Luke's ranch.

"Major, will we be heading to Nuecestown?" The lieutenant that Kittredge had sent was under orders to encourage the major to do his foraging close to Corpus Christi. Kittredge relished the possibility that Belknap would engage the rancher near Nuecestown again, and he'd be able to file charges with the lieutenant as witness. Belknap suspected as such and would have none of it.

"Are you addressing me, Lieutenant?" He glared at the junior officer.

The lieutenant saluted sheepishly and fell back.

"If I may, sir?" At least Rucker had the courtesy to ask to be recognized.

"What is it, Lieutenant Rucker? Speak freely."

Belknap nudged his heels into his horse to put a little distance between himself and the troop. He motioned young Rucker to do the same. As Rex drew alongside, the major spoke in a low voice. "The naval officer…Lieutenant Kittredge…would like nothing better than to entrap me. It's why we're staying well north of the Nueces River." He let that sink in. "We need to find a homestead that can supply our needs. First order of business, Lieutenant, will be to find a wagon to haul our bounty." They returned to the troop and upon breaking camp resumed their travels.

The troop soon crested a rise where the point riders were waiting. Before them was a fair-sized farm. Given the confidence that just about all capable fighting men had enlisted in the Confederate army, the major wasted no time and led the men toward what appeared to be the main house. It was a ramshackle affair but fairly large as farmhouses went.

As the troop neared the house, Belknap noticed two wagons sitting beside a small barn. Given the time of year, he judged that most crops had been harvested. He was betting that the barn held a treasure trove of food.

"Halt! Who goes there?" An elderly man with a shotgun emerged from the house.

"Major Gordon Belknap, United States Army. We are here to acquire supplies."

"I'm not supplying you damned Yankees with anything!" The old man cocked the hammer on the shotgun.

Belknap recognized the futility of the man's opposition and didn't want to do him harm. "Any womenfolk around, sir?"

With that, a gray-haired woman stepped out and joined the old man. She was unarmed so far as the major could tell. She clung tightly to her husband's arm.

"We don't wish to harm you, ma'am, but we are under orders to take what we need. Please place your gun on the ground."

The old farmer surveyed the firepower before him. It would certainly be suicidal to resist. With defiant tears welling in his eyes, he placed the gun on the ground. "Sons of bitch Yankees." It was all he could manage to say.

★

"Shhhh! Quiet!" Captain Carson's strained whisper had shushed the column. "I heard something up ahead of us." He turned to Sergeant Bell. "We're downwind. Let's dismount." He began to move slowly forward, now vividly alert to his surroundings. "Sounds like soldiers. I swear I heard a saber rattle." The Rebel captain strove to contain his excitement. He felt his hair begin to stand up on the back of his neck. Carson looked out over a slight rise in the landscape where he could see a quarter mile or so off. "Clay, get up here. It's bluecoats… and they look to be foraging. Bring your spotter."

By sheer chance, the little contingent of Confederate sharpshooters had traveled by a route that arched well north of Nuecestown and converged on the Yankee location south of Victoria. For the sergeant, it afforded a chance to practice his specialty on an actual enemy target. Officers and gunners were usually top priority, and this scenario was no exception. They were far enough from the target that they collectively celebrated.

Bell moved forward with his Sharps rifle in hand. He caught up to Carson, raised the gun in the direction the captain was pointing, and looked through the telescopic sight. "Damn, Walker…er, Captain…those Yankees are stealing the farmer's food. I know him; that's old man O'Connor."

"I think we should dissuade them, Sergeant Bell."

Bell smiled and dropped to a prone position. He wasn't showing off for anybody this time. "What do you think, John?"

The spotter took a minute to gauge distance and get a feel for any wind. "Seems like there's a slight breeze, Sergeant, but it's coming at us. I'd guess the Yankee's about eight hundred yards out. Dry day. I'm thinking you can aim straight on... maybe target just a tad above the officer's head." He thought on how the officer had made a bad choice to remain on horseback. "Guess they be writing a letter to his mama."

Carson watched with admiration as Clay Bell inserted a round in the Sharps, peered through the telescopic sight, and carefully took aim at his target. His friend was a cowboy first, but a soldier loyal to the Texas cause. He'd drawn this duty given his reputation as a skilled marksman. While it ran counter to his religious upbringing, this was war and he'd been called to do this distasteful work.

★

"Lieutenant, commandeer the wagon. Hitch up two of our pack horses. Take enough from the barn to fill the wagon, but leave some for these folks." This was more than mercy on Major Belknap's part, as he figured they might have to forage in this region in the future. They'd need the farmers in the area to continue to grow crops. Belknap and Rucker dismounted so as to seem less threatening to the farmer.

"You're leaving food, sir?" Kittredge's damnable man was spouting off out of turn again. He stubbornly refused to dismount.

"You're out of order, Lieutenant. Stand down."

Kittredge's man turned his horse away from Belknap but thought better of it and turned back.

★

Bell was all soldier at this moment. "I'm going to take out the mounted officer." He was silent. He didn't enjoy this. There was no peace to be had in this task. "Got nice shiny shoulder decorations and he's facing us full-on." He breathed slowly, exhaled a little, held his breath, and squeezed the trigger. The sound seemed enough to just about turn a person deaf. The soldiers around the target would hear it far too late. The victim would never hear it.

They all watched as the target was lifted from his saddle. What they couldn't see was the horrific result the sergeant saw through his telescopic sight as the bullet tore half the man's face away.

Bell offered more a grimace than smile at his success. "Nice spot, John."

It had been almost too easy. Killing another human wasn't second nature to any of these men. Killing a thief stealing from pretty much defenseless old folks at least gave the killing act a patina of justice.

Bell looked around. "We'd best get away from here, men. They might figure that the entire Confederate army isn't here after all and give chase. One thing's for certain—they'll think twice about robbing Texans."

★

Soldiers stopped foraging and formed a perimeter without even being asked. As they hunkered down behind anything that seemed protective from water trough to wagon to hay bale, they strained to see anything in the direction from which the shot had apparently come.

Major Belknap didn't especially like the feeling that swept over him, as he'd had a chance to confront the reality of Kittredge's man having been killed. He experienced relief coupled with the horror and sadness accompanying a violent death in wartime.

He surveyed the fields before them. Silence. He realized that the single shot with no follow-up attack likely meant that they'd been the target of a sharpshooter. He'd normally have had a bugler sound assembly, but the company was in hailing distance of his voice and the bugle would tend to stir everyone up. "Sergeant, have the men stand at ease. You and Lieutenant Rucker come with me." He led the two to a nearby dry arroyo a hundred yards away and alongside a struggling live oak.

As the troopers emerged from hiding places, assembled, and stood at ease in front of the farmhouse, Belknap became all too aware of the elderly farmer standing huddled with his wife and still fearing for his life. It didn't take a mental giant to figure out that the sharpshooter had killed the lieutenant to send a message. It had been heard loud and clear.

As he cleared his throat and prepared to address the sergeant and lieutenant, he considered that whatever the farmer had stored in the barn was likely all the couple would have for possibly months to come. The drought was not choosy about its victims. Still, Belknap had a job to do.

"Some of our troops have never been in battle, they've never been shot at before. They're likely a bit scared, though they'd never admit it. Those who've been in battle are probably angry and inclined to pursue whoever shot at us. We know that would be foolhardy." Belknap thoughtfully stroked the beard he'd taken to growing since the start of the war. It was unseasonably hot, and their woolen tunics were not suited to the climate. "That Navy lieutenant sitting comfortably off the coast of Corpus Christi has been a royal pain in our asses, but there's not much we can do about that right now. We've been ordered to forage. Command has not resupplied our forces along the coast, so we must seize food from the locals."

"If I may, sir?" Lieutenant Rucker apparently had a thought.

"Go ahead, Lieutenant."

"General Butler is setting on plenty of supplies in New

Orleans, sir. Perhaps we could…" As he realized how far it was from Victoria to New Orleans, Rucker thought better of his idea. He shook his head. "Sorry, sir. He likely wouldn't supply us anyway."

"Sergeant, we'll commandeer one of this farmer's wagons and fill it with food from the barn. You will seize no greater than two-thirds of his food supply. We're not going to leave folks to starve. Is that clear?"

They followed Belknap back to the troops. He stood a few paces from the farmer. "Sir, we will not take all of your stores, but must borrow your wagon."

There was no nice way of explaining to the farmer. He nodded his understanding resignedly.

"Sergeant, tie the lieutenant over the saddle of his horse. We'll take him back with us."

Within the hour, the major was leading his soldiers toward Corpus Christi to deliver the bounty of his foraging. He seized food from one more farm along the way, but that went without incident.

"You're welcome to stay here, One Arrow, but it may be uncomfortable. Most folks don't understand the Comanche way, and I fear they may seek to harm you." Luke spoke thoughtfully and directly.

"I understand, Ghost-Who-Rides." He watched a tumble-weed blow across the clearing. "I should return to my people. I have much to teach them."

Luke nodded. "We'll get one more breakfast into you, my friend, before the sun rises. I expect you got here with no trouble, so should get to your people safely."

"One Arrow grateful for stories of Three Toes. Understand friendship with my chief." He watched Elisa fetching water with the twins plus Andrea Anne in tow. The Comanche so yearned to live long enough to have and enjoy his own family. His path wouldn't be easy. "One Arrow begin to understand White man." He gave a little laugh. "You strange people."

Luke appreciated that the Comanche felt comfortable enough to find humor in the situation. "When the fighting ends, you should be extra careful, One Arrow. It may take a long time for things to settle down. The loser of a fight holds resentment." Luke hoped the young warrior would understand. "You are always welcome here at Heaven's Gate."

One Arrow stroked the silver cross he now wore hanging from the bone necklace. He didn't yet truly understand it but appreciated the bond it represented between he and these caring White people. It would remain a constant reminder of Three Toes and of the chief's relationship with the Texas Ranger and his family. The warrior had very little to give so far as any gift to show his gratitude and friendship.

Luke recognized One Arrow's discomfort. He vaguely recalled a custom he'd heard of. He grasped the Comanche's hand and pulled him to him. Simultaneously, he pulled out his knife. Before the warrior could react, Luke had made a superficial cut on each of their forearms and pressed the wounds together. The intermingling of blood now made them blood brothers.

One Arrow was brought nearly to tears by the emotion of Luke's act. "We are one people, Ghost-Who-Rides." He was deeply touched. The sense of belonging, of the bonding, had overwhelmed him. He looked from Elisa to Luke and back again. He smiled and raised his brows as a thought came to him. The warrior walked over to the bead-decorated bag he'd left lying on the gallery. He dug deeply into the bag, finally pulling out a buffalo rib bone decorated with two small eagle feathers and painted with various designs. He ceremoniously handed the bone to Luke. "This protect you from all Comanche attack, Ghost-Who-Rides." He demonstrated how to raise it high in the event of such an attack.

Luke was all too aware of the solemnity of the moment. "I am grateful, One Arrow, Chief of the Penateka Comanche."

That Luke referred to him as a chief certainly wasn't lost on One Arrow.

★

Belknap's orders were to deliver the supplies directly to Lieutenant Kittredge. He'd much rather have returned to Passe Cavallo, but orders were orders. He sensed it was another part of Kittredge's plan to hassle him into doing something the Navy lieutenant could nail him for. Discretion being paramount, the major approached from the north out of Aransas Pass. He felt it best to cross to Mustang Island and haul his cargo along the hard-packed sands southward to Corpus Christi. He figured that, with the Gulf of Mexico to his left and Corpus Christi Bay to his right, he significantly reduced any tactical threats. Soon enough, he'd report to the damnable lieutenant sitting out at sea and safely aboard the *USS Arthur*.

The sergeant rode point. They hadn't gone but a few miles down the coast when they caught up to him. He half-turned his mount toward the major. "Sir, can you believe this?" Before them and blocking their path were three longhorn beeves.

"Well, Sergeant, I'm thinking we might deliver some fresh meat to the US Navy." He smiled mischievously at what he was about to say. "We will deliver two cattle to Lieutenant Kittredge." He allowed himself a broad grin. "We will bivouac here tonight, Sergeant. The main entrée will be steak."

Huzzahs went up from the troops upon hearing the major's plan. To Belknap's thinking, there was a certain perverse justice in his decision. It surely endeared him to his men.

They tore some timbers from the wagon box and soon had a roaring cooking fire.

From the deck of the *USS Arthur*, Lieutenant Kittredge

looked north. "Ensign, any idea what that fire is about?" Kittredge aimed his spyglass at the fire, but it was inadequate to enable him to see what was going on. There didn't appear to be any boats, so he assumed it wasn't an enemy planning some sort of attack by sea. "Let's go ashore in the morning and see what it was about."

★

The rough countryside around the Nueces River had long afforded cover for all manner of varmints both wild and domesticated. Longhorns roamed freely and outlaws enjoyed some measure of relief from pursuing lawmen. Luke knew he was going to have to venture back out on the trail to help protect Texas's backside from the depredations of Comanche, Mexican bandits, Anglo lawbreakers, and rogue soldiers. Cattle were another matter altogether, he thought as he wrapped up work on Heaven's Gate in preparation for winter. The drought conditions affected his family as much as folk on spreads for miles around. Crop yields were lighter and livestock was leaner.

With fencing virtually nonexistent, he'd spend a day on the ranch with his vaqueros rounding up as many as thirty longhorns only to discover five or six other brands in the herd other than his **–HG** (Bar HG) brand. Since all brands were registered in the Stock Records of Nueces County, any non **– HG** beeves that Luke sold had to be recorded with credit to their owners. He was entitled to a one-dollar fee for each of those head that he sold. It was a great system so long as folks were honest about selling and registering. Luke had his **–HG** branding irons fired by a cousin in Corpus who ran a smithy shop. Peter Dunn burned the brand from each iron he crafted into the door of his shop, and Luke recalled seeing dozens of brands memorialized there. There were literally hundreds of brands in South Texas, so naturally there were a few ne'er-do-wells that couldn't resist the temptation to modify them and make a few dollars. It was theft, and perpetrators were dealt with harshly, resulting in "necktie" parties. For many, it was worth the risk. Such was the sinful nature of many men.

As Luke rode out from Heaven's Gate toward Nuecestown, he hadn't gone but a couple of miles when a grizzly scene confronted him. Three Mexicans had been lynched. Their bodies swayed in the breeze, as they hung from a couple of oak tree branches. The area was surrounded by the pecan trees for which the river had been named, so the dead men were a stark contrast to the life the pecans represented. Luke could only wonder at what had caused so ignominious an end. Given the way a lot of folks thought of Mexicans, the reason likely might have been as inconsequential as them looking at a White woman. He could only shake his head and move on. Nothing he could do for them now.

TWELVE
WHERE WILL THEY GO?

SAMUEL FELT DECIDEDLY uncomfortable sitting at the ornate mahogany desk that had belonged to his former master. Of a sudden, he was no longer a slave. It had taken a but couple of words spoken by Edward Thorpe and reinforced on a slip of paper, lest anyone doubt his freedom. But could he ever be truly free? His entire life to this point had been as chattel.

As he walked up Congress Street toward the Texas capitol, he knew he was free but he felt the judgmental stares of the White folks he passed. To bystanders, he was still Horatio Thorpe's slave no matter how well he comported himself. Even the few Blacks he saw on the street assumed he was owned. Samuel could see the capitol building off in the near distance. He'd heard rumor that it faced south to memorialize the tragic battles at the Alamo and Goliad during the Texas War for Independence. "Remember the Alamo! Remember Goliad!" had been rallying cries during that war. Some folk now thought it faced south to support the Confederacy. Given that the building had been constructed back in 1853, that sort of thinking didn't hold water for the former slave. But he understood the biases behind such a rumor. Weighing heavily in the back of his mind was the question of where would all the slaves go after the war? He turned into the print shop.

"I'm Sam…"

"I know who you are." The statement was left hanging as though the proprietor had been inclined to add a pejorative term for Blacks. "Here. Give this to your master."

Samuel smiled. This would be neither the first nor the last time he'd encounter this sort of behavior. The free Texans would have to change that thinking, and it wouldn't be easy. Soon enough, Blacks would attain a level on the metaphorical social ladder a rung or so higher than Indians and Mexicans. He politely accepted the envelope. "I'll see that my employer receives this." He said it in a way that the word "employer" might sink in with the print shop proprietor.

★

One Arrow had covered many miles. He now had two mounts rather than three, as he left one pony with Luke as thanks. Thus far, he'd managed to avoid detection. That in itself was quite a feat, given that threats on the Nueces Strip had proliferated.

He emerged into the clearing at the encampment and spotted Cactus Flower and Bird Woman before they saw him. He was so relieved to have finally arrived at the camp that he paid no attention to how easily he'd entered. There were no sentries to challenge him.

The young Comanche quickly dismounted and hugged each of the women in turn. He saw Cactus Flower's baby in a papoose off near where she'd been tanning a deer hide. The women were overjoyed to see him and jabbered excitedly about how wonderful he looked.

One Arrow finally stepped back and then suddenly realized that there was only one teepee. "Where?"

"They leave, One Arrow. Too much danger here. Bad men."

He was initially dismayed and then became angry at the women having been left unprotected.

"They go toward setting sun. We follow when you return."

"When did they leave?" The question was sort of rhetorical, as he saw evidence of them having been encamped there as recently as three or four days ago. He waved off his question.

The women looked at him in anticipation.

One Arrow looked at Bird Woman, as for the first time he became aware that she was not carrying a child. "Where is Three Toes's child, Bird Woman?"

"She is with the spirits, One Arrow."

He didn't ask whether the baby had been miscarried, lost in childbirth, or even killed. The drought had reached the Pedernales River region, and another mouth to feed would have been stressful. As the oldest woman, she might have sacrificed her child so Cactus Flower could begin her family. The warrior tried to show compassion, albeit briefly. "We must go and catch the others."

Cactus Flower noticed that One Arrow wore Three Toes's necklace. "Your vision quest is finished?"

He nodded. "Yes. I have learned much. It is good with us." He didn't yet share his concern as to what would eventually become of the Comanche. It was as though the White man's war had bought his people some precious time. But where indeed would they ultimately go?

"Rest your ponies while we pack. You must eat to keep your strength."

One Arrow felt at home with these women, as they'd become his family. Cactus Flower even smiled winsomely at him. A strange shiver coursed through his loins. He'd never had a woman. He thought back to his amazement at seeing Elisa Dunn swimming back at Heaven's Gate.

★

The soldiers and sailors faced each other on the beach on Mustang Island just north of Corpus Christi.

"Major Belknap? Was that your fire I saw last night?"

Belknap reluctantly saluted. "Yes, sir, yes, it was." He smiled with the awareness that it irritated Kittredge.

"How foolish, Major. Are you trying to give away our position to the enemy?" It had taken a moment, but the Navy lieutenant finally found something negative about what the major had done.

Belknap ignored the arrogant officer's accusation. "We're pleased to have foraged successfully, Lieutenant Kittredge. We've brought you a special gift." He motioned to bring forward the two longhorns. "We hope this will please you, sir."

Kittredge tried to avoid smiling. "Where is...?"

"Our only casualty, sir. A Confederate sharpshooter shot him from his saddle as we foraged a local farm."

"Did you pursue?"

"They were long gone, sir. We had no good information on enemy troops. I felt they might lead us into a trap."

Kittredge knew full well that Belknap's explanation made sense. "Who is this other officer? Are you going to introduce us?"

"I believe Lieutenant Rucker here has a message for you from General Butler."

"Butler?"

"Yes. He commands our forces in New Orleans."

"What's that got to do with Corpus Christi?"

Belknap couldn't suppress a broad smile. "We are under his jurisdiction."

Rucker saluted and handed General Butler's orders to the lieutenant. "Sir." He stepped back alongside Belknap.

"It appears you no longer report to me, Major. Says here I'm to support you in launching an attack on Corpus Christi itself." Kittredge was highly disappointed, as he craved control. He sighed resignedly. "The steamer *Sachem* and naval yacht *Italia* have moved into position, as has the *USS Corypheus*. In fact, word from the *Corypheus* has it that they captured some Confederate schooner. We're to request a truce to let non-combatants escape harm's way before we launch any assault. We'll do the best we can, Major Belknap."

"Thank you, sir." Belknap saluted smartly, relieved that it would likely be the final time he'd have to do that with Kittredge.

As the Navy lieutenant was about to turn away, he gave Belknap a hard look. An air of condescension still hung on Kittredge. The major had won this battle of wills. Kittredge sucked it up. "Thank you for the beeves, Major." And he led his men back to the long boats.

★

The warning to evacuate, coupled with the naval engagements, served as a heavy warning to the citizens of Corpus Christi. In the ensuing two days, the Rebels joined with citizens to occupy some modest earthworks erected seventeen years earlier by General Zachary Taylor.

Major Alfred Hobby was in charge of defending the city. In all, he had roughly 700 soldiers and volunteers backed up with three old smoothbore cannons. As soon as Kittredge's truce expired, Hobby's forces opened fire.

"Mama, what's happening?" Little Margaret had been mostly oblivious to the changes to life in Corpus Christi. The most noticeable factors were fewer merchants plying their trade and the constant parade of ships out beyond Padre Island. Now, there was cannon fire to deal with. Scary indeed.

Scarlett seriously debated evacuating. She was pregnant, of course, and that would make her seem more vulnerable to most folks. But this was the Texas frontier, and she'd already endured plenty of risks in her short life. She made certain the Colt revolver and rifle Carson had left behind were in working order. If there was trouble, she'd go down fighting.

Even Martha seemed to not be especially concerned. Despite any external threats, her life was decidedly rosy since she'd begun working with Scarlett.

"Not to worry, Maggie, Martha. We're safe." It was a lie.

Kittredge was initially angered by the effrontery of the Rebel response to what he considered a gentlemanly offer for Hobby to surrender Corpus Christi. In response, he sent nearly three dozen sailors ashore with orders to destroy the Confederate battery. He rued having failed to embrace Belknap's support. He certainly could have used the manpower. Sailors would have to do. The lieutenant laid down a withering barrage of cannon fire from his ships to cover the sailors.

Walker Carson had seen the sailors land and immediately alerted Captain Ware. "Captain, the Yankees have landed sailors south of our battery." While he held the same rank as Ware, he was nevertheless second in command. The nature of any action would be Ware's decision.

"Just sailors?" Ware knew of Carson's reputation with the Texas Rangers. "Let's go get 'em, Captain."

In moments, the Rebel cavalry was charging headlong at the naval landing party. Hobby's cannon fired over the heads of the charging troop. They managed to do just a bit of damage to the Yankee ships.

The sailors were driven back to their boats and felt fortunate to have escaped what Kittredge characterized as an overwhelming force. He had become the master of exaggeration.

"Mama, the boom-boom stopped."

Scarlett breathed a sigh of relief and held Margaret tightly.

★

The courier arrived at Magnolia Plantation on a well-lathered horse. He'd been ever on guard lest he be waylaid. The message he carried could get him killed were he to be captured. He dressed plainly, but any Confederate captors would likely quickly figure out his mission. "Master Edward?"

Thorpe accepted the envelope. "Go to the barn and take care of your horse. Get some food. I'll have a message for you to deliver by the time you've rested up." He didn't want to know the man's name. This wasn't a personal thing.

The courier observed that the house wasn't so pristine as it had once been. There was now a much smaller but paid household staff. Many of the surrounding fields were fallow. Thorpe had been good to his word about freeing his slaves. On the other hand, he was at great risk. Other plantation owners simply didn't have the resident manpower to come after Thorpe and wreak punishment for his effrontery. Like ranchers and farmers in other parts of Texas, the majority of able-bodied men had joined the Confederate army. Thorpe was all too aware that he was living on borrowed time. He thus felt an immediacy to helping the anti-slavery cause.

★

Sergeant Bell and his company of sharpshooters rendezvoused with Colonel Yager's 1st Mounted Rifles a bit south of Nuecestown. They were ushered directly to the colonel's tent.

The colonel was in uncharacteristically good humor. "Welcome, Sergeant." He returned Bell's salute. "I've heard that you are a fine marksman."

"Some seem to think so, sir."

"I've heard that the Sharps has a range of better than a half mile, Sergeant. Is that so?"

"Why, yes, sir, yes, it does."

"Do you think you could hit a target nearly a half mile away?"

Bell pondered that a moment. The men around him were quiet in anticipation of the sergeant's answer. "I killed a deer once at about a thousand yards, sir."

Yager sat back in his chair and smiled. "Was the deer moving?"

"No, sir." Bell tried to get a read on what the colonel had in mind. "You have a moving target, sir?"

"Setting out in the Gulf off Corpus Christi is a boat that has been quite a bother to us. I'd like nothing better than to send them a message."

"A message, sir?"

The colonel was savoring the moment. He had a strong hunch that the Yankees were thinking of further attacking and capturing Corpus Christi. "About mid-afternoon each day, an officer strolls about the deck of the boat. I don't know whether you can hit him, Sergeant, but you sure enough could scare him."

"I gather, sir, that the boat rocks a bit out there on the open waters and that the officer won't be presenting a stationary target?"

"You up for it, Sergeant?"

"I'll give it a try, sir."

About an hour later, Bell and his spotter had found their way to the top of a sand dune on Padre Island. The boat in question was a gunboat of fair size. It was more than 100 feet long, so was easily rocked by the waves.

"What do you think, John?"

"I'm fixing on the mast, Sergeant. I'd guess it's about 800 yards out."

"Dang, that's a hell of a long shot."

"Breeze is coming toward us."

Bell was pleased that side windage wouldn't have to be

factored in. He looked at the ship through the telescopic sight. "Whew, John…looks far away, even through the scope."

"Worse case, you might get the officer to soil himself, Sergeant." John stifled a laugh. Humor was a necessity in this serious business. The lives of a sharpshooter and target were a personal matter. While a cannon might spew devastating body-maiming canister through an advancing line of soldiers, it was impersonal by comparison. Picking off a single target? Well, it became personal. Sharpshooters had to struggle with putting that intimacy aside.

"Here he comes, John." Bell saw the officer emerge. "Spot?"

"Damn boat is rocking. There are some bad swells out there. It's a blessing he's broadside to us. The boat tends to wallow." John looked through his own spyglass and paused to do his mental calculations. "Sergeant, I think the best time is to catch him is at the bottom of a swell. Aim about a quarter of the way up the main mast just before he passes in front of it."

Bell loaded a round into the Sharps, aimed, breathed out a little, held his breath, and squeezed the trigger.

Lieutenant Kittredge was standing before the main mast amidships when the epaulet on his left soldier was blasted away, a searing heat passed the back of his neck, and a bullet exploded away a chunk from the nearby mast. He immediately dove for the deck along with several sailors in his vicinity. Embarrassed, he slowly got up from the deck and peered out over the railing toward the barrier islands off in the distance.

Bell and his spotter were watching through their scopes. "Damn, Sergeant, I think he did soil himself! That'll teach the son of a bitch not to mess with Texas."

To his further embarrassment, Kittredge realized that the sailors were struggling to avert their eyes from him. A yellow stain had spread from the crotch of his white trousers. He gave them a hard look before beating a retreat to his quarters.

"The colonel should be right pleased, John. From what I

can see, they're raising sail. Gotta bet they'll anchor farther offshore and down the coast a bit." The sergeant permitted himself a smile. Sometimes a near-miss could be as effective as a hit.

★

With Colonel Yager already headed north to the Sabine River with his mounted rifles, the defense of Corpus Christi rested with Major Alfred Hobby and his men. They kept a keen eye on Lieutenant Kittredge's activities, especially since he'd now been given a deep appreciation for his vulnerability should he venture too close to shore. Little did they know that Kittredge was essentially a distraction, as the Yankees intended to launch a major assault farther up the coast at Galveston.

★

The three-masted bark *Endeavor* was docked at its Galveston wharf. Its cargo of cotton reduced its draft such that it would barely clear the sandy bottom of Galveston Bay.

Samuel had journeyed up from Austin to personally supervise the loading of the ship. He knew better than to give direct orders on the wharf. It was not something the workmen on the wharf would tolerate. So far as they were concerned, Samuel was simply a well-dressed slave.

Guffawing bystanders watched as the crew of the Thorpe-owned vessel tossed away the mooring lines, pushed off, and slowly moved toward the channel. Folks on the wharf knew that the Union blockade was out there on the sea waiting to seize the *Endeavor*. Heads were shaking at the foolhardiness. True, a couple of blockade runners had been successful, but the *Endeavor* was a heavy ship.

As the bark sailed by, the crew waved its goodbyes. Once

out of sight of the good citizens of Galveston, the ship's captain had the Stars and Stripes run up the mainmast. Coupled with papers issued by the Union, they'd have no trouble with the Yankee blockade. After a brief stop in Cuba, they'd head to Europe to deliver their cargo.

Samuel watched the bark sail from sight. He didn't know whether to laugh or cry. Perhaps one day these things wouldn't have to be done in secrecy.

THIRTEEN
BROTHER VS. BROTHER

LUKE SAT around the campfire with Barber and JD. Luke felt relieved that JD had stopped her chatter about the time she'd knocked out Pablo Ramos with her rifle butt.

Luke's plan was to travel west to Laredo and then follow the Rio Grande south from there. He figured that Ramos was a creature of habit and would do any recruiting somewhere between San Ygnacio and Rio Grande City. They'd ridden a bit past San Diego on the road that Colonel Kinney had made years earlier. To Luke's thinking, the fact that they were traveling on the road made it seem all the more unusual that they'd not encountered any other travelers. They'd seen virtually no one—not even Confederate patrols.

The sun had set, and the remaining coals of the campfire cast a glow that shed a dim light on their faces. The starlight was shielded by a thin gauze of cloud cover. Of a sudden, Luke's ears perked up. He extended his hand palms down to quiet them. "Listen," he whispered. There was a long silence save for their breathing—then a twig snapped.

"Who goes there? Show yourself plain!" One of Luke's Colts had already found its way into his hand.

A shadowy figure emerged from the darkness. "It's me… Jubal Strong." Strong led two horses and a pack mule.

"Come on in easy-like, Jubal."

"You have coffee for a weary traveler?"

"JD…Jake…this here's Jubal Strong. He'd come to Texas from North Platte River country up north. Jubal, this here's JD Smith and Jake Barber." That took care of formal introductions. Luke had stood up by this time, holstered his Colt, and extended his hand to welcome Strong. "Did you meet up with my cousin?"

"Yes…yes, I did. He wasn't quite ready to hire on another cowboy." Strong paused to take a sip of coffee from the tin. "Damn!" He spit it out. "Hot!"

JD giggled.

"Holy cow, Captain. You have a girl with you?"

Luke smiled. "Yep…and she can shoot."

Strong looked over at Barber and took in the man's size. Even in the dimness of the campfire coals, he could see that he was not someone you'd choose to confront in a barroom brawl. "Can I camp with y'all this evening?"

"Sure, Jubal. Go hobble your horse." Luke suppressed a grin. "Maybe that coffee will cool down by the time you're back."

Strong took care of his horses and mule, then returned to join the campfire conversation. "I hear tell that some Yankee navy officer got hisself in a tither and launched an attack on Corpus Christi."

That got Luke's attention. Heaven's Gate wasn't that far from Corpus. "Any word on what happened?"

"From what I heard, some Confederate major named Hobby sent them packing." Strong took a long sip of the now sufficiently cooled-off coffee. "He commandeered some fortifications left behind by General Taylor during the Mexican American War. He had some small cannon and enough volunteer firepower to soften the Yankees up for a cavalry charge by

Captain Ware that chased the enemy into the sea." Strong was gesticulating excitedly with his hands as he described the victory. "Best part of the story was that some sharpshooter named Bell fired a round that scared the living beejabbers out of that fool Yankee lieutenant."

Everybody had a good laugh at that.

"Jubal, you up for chasing a Mexican bandito? We could use another gun."

Strong sat back. The smile disappeared from his face as he thought on Luke's offer.

In fact, the tenor of the little campfire gathering suddenly changed. Luke had tossed a dose of reality into the mix. "We're chasing a fella named Pablo Ramos. He's vulnerable from an encounter we had with him not so long ago. Want to get him before he rounds up another gang."

Everyone looked at Luke expectantly.

Barber broke the pregnant silence. "Figure he's holdin' a bit of a grudge agin' us, Luke. Never can figure them damned chili-eaters."

Luke nodded. "Likely, he still doesn't get along with Cortina. Most Mexicans are loyal to the Red Robber, but not Ramos. Makes it tougher for him to recruit." Luke acknowledged the understanding nods of agreement. "I expect he's not exactly friends with that Apache Chief Costalites either." Luke looked at Strong. "Sleep on it, Jubal. Meanwhile, I'll take first watch."

"Can't believe that damned Kittredge." Belknap was dismayed at the lieutenant's ill-chosen attack strategy. He'd seen enough of Corpus Christi on his foraging to have realized that it was well-defended against the sort of half-baked attack Kittredge had launched. He'd had the good fortune of being on Mustang Island during the attack on Corpus Christi. One thing for sure, he hoped he'd have a chance to meet the Rebel captain that had chased the lieutenant's forces into the Gulf. He did find himself smiling inwardly at news that Kittredge had been the target of a Confederate sharpshooter. Now, the major had orders to support a Union invasion aimed at Texas's deepest seaport: Galveston.

"Lieutenant Rucker, our orders are to head to Galveston." Belknap didn't elaborate. The fewer who knew of the planned invasion, even Union troops, the better. The major's troops would approach the Rebel defenders from the rear. It'd be a forced march to get north of Matagorda Bay in time, and he'd be dodging Rebel patrols along the way. He relished being free of Kittredge.

★

Walker Carson rode quietly into Corpus Christi. Major Hobby had given him a couple of days leave. He was focused intently on seeing his beloved Scarlett.

"Captain Carson, y'all sure gave those Yankees a handful." Sheriff Meaney stepped out from the sheriff's office and was nearly bowled over by Carson's mount.

Carson pulled up. "Dang. Sorry, Sheriff. Didn't see you."

"Guess you're looking for Scarlett."

"I expect so, Bill. She's at home, isn't she?"

"Sort of." Meaney grinned. "She's taken over that store underneath the apartment. She's taking in a lot of seamstress work. Even hired a young girl to help."

The news got Carson's attention. He raised his eyebrows in surprise. "I hadn't heard."

"Yeah. I hear she saved the young lady from an untoward life." Meaney didn't tell Carson that he and Luke had seen to it that the young girl's whore mongering pimp would be no trouble.

"Thanks, Bill. Maybe you and Clara could come by tomorrow." He laid his fingers aside his hat in a friendly half-salute and turned his horse up the street.

Scarlett had just stepped from the shop. She looked up the street and couldn't believe her eyes. "Walker?" She gave a muffled shout, as she didn't want to wake the neighborhood.

Carson spurred his mount into a canter, stopped just short of her, and fairly leaped from the saddle and into her arms. He lost his senses in the perfume of her long red tresses, as their bodies became as one. "Thank God you're safe," he urgently whispered.

She pushed away slightly and looked down at her belly. "You're going to crush him or her, mister soldier."

The tears of joy in her eyes and wanton smile on her full red lips told Carson all he needed to know. His hands grasped hers. "Shall we go—" He was interrupted mid-sentence, as he caught a glimpse of Martha over Scarlett's shoulder. The young girl had peeked from the doorway, then popped back inside. "I heard you'd hired some help." It broke the romance of the moment, but there'd be time later.

Scarlett glanced back at the door. "Yes, she keeps an eye on Margaret and is learning to sew." She was momentarily disconcerted by the distraction. She strove to recapture those wonderful sensations that had coursed through her body at being held closely in his arms but a moment before. Her ardor was not to be denied. She locked onto his deep blue eyes and leveled her most tempestuous look penetrating into his very soul. "Shall we go upstairs?" she whispered.

He hesitated.

"Now."

Carson threw the horse's reins over the hitching rail and half-stumbled up the stairs in his eagerness.

★

The long gray line wound its way northward through the

subtropical climate of eastern Texas, headed toward Galveston. The cooler autumn weather wasn't a factor, as a warm spell had reinforced the dry effects of the prolonged drought that had gripped Texas for going on two years. The men and horses looked forward to the relief of fording the series of creeks and rivers that crossed their path. Cypress hung with Spanish Moss and remnants of oak forests afforded occasional shady relief from the sun. Colonel Yager was headed up to the Sabine River to support efforts against Major General Banks, who had replaced Butler in New Orleans. They'd be stopping briefly near Galveston, though were as yet unaware that the Yankees were preparing to mount an assault on the port.

Little did Captain Stephen Rucker know that he was following a path parallel to his brother. Barely fifty miles separated the forces as they carved a trail that would converge at Brazoria a bit south of Galveston. Perhaps, ignorance was bliss. The immediate challenge was hauling cannon across the Texas rivers that tended to be broader and shallower as they reached like so many tentacles to the Gulf of Mexico.

The sun crested the horizon and smells of bacon and coffee wafted on what little breeze there was. JD had been given the assignment to cook breakfast, and she wasn't doing a halfway bad job of it. Luke had gone off to check the horses and returned soon enough once the cooking aromas reached him.

With his family gone and it being at least two months before he'd have the prospect of steady ranch employment with Luke's cousin, Jubal Strong had made his decision. He sat up just as Luke strode back into camp. "Captain Dunn, I expect I'll take you up on your offer."

Soon enough, the four were cleaning up after breakfast and preparing to head south to find Pablo Ramos.

As they mounted up, they heard the steady hoofbeats of a rider approaching at a gallop.

"Captain Dunn! Captain Dunn!" It was apparent that the rider knew Luke. The horseman, clothed in telltale Confederate gray, eased up as he drew close. "Captain Dunn, thank God I found you. I've a message from Colonel Ford."

The rider had Luke's full attention. He had to ask himself the odds of his being found out here on the Nueces Strip. "Hold on, soldier. Your horse is pretty well lathered up. Take it easy."

The man handed Luke a sealed envelope.

He began to tear it open. "How the hell did you know where to find me, soldier?"

"They told me back in Nuecestown where you were headed, sir."

Luke read the message. Ford was asking for Luke to join him up in western Texas for a planned Confederate invasion of New Mexico. He reread the message. It was a request, not an order. Luke thought a few moments. He reached into his saddlebag and pulled out a pencil. He wrote a brief note and folded the paper. "Soldier, deliver this to Colonel Ford." He handed him the note and paused. "I'd rest your mount a spell before you head out. You might take him down to yonder creek. There's a little water, and he looks like he could use it. Nothing's so all-fired important to break a horse over."

Luke nodded to the soldier, turned Big Horse toward Laredo, and urged him on at a canter.

JD was naturally the first to break the silence. "If I may ask, Captain? What was that about?"

Luke looked thoughtfully off into the distance before pulling up and turning to his companions. "We were being asked to help invade New Mexico. I judged it to be a dumb idea...a diversion at best and a waste of resources likely conjured up by some politician."

"What did you tell the colonel?" The normally quiet Barber had become curious.

Luke smiled. "Told him no thanks. We have plenty of Yankees, Mexican bandits, outlaws, Apache, and Comanche to worry about."

"Your note didn't seem that long, Captain."

Luke smiled. "Just told him no thanks."

Belknap bivouacked just east of Brazoria near where the Brazos River empties into the Gulf. He awaited orders from Commander William Renshaw, who was to direct the assault. Renshaw expected he'd bring Galveston to its knees by applying his vastly superior firepower. Belknap had force-marched his troops, and now they could do naught but tend to tired bodies and horses while they waited. The major had become used to hurrying up only to have to wait seemingly endless hours for action. Just to be cautious, he set up a defensive perimeter, piling whatever wood the men could gather into an extended breastwork of sorts. With any luck, they might get to Brazoria proper and resupply.

The major was unaware that just a few miles to his east, Rebel Captains Ware and Rucker had been ordered by Colonel Yager to head to the coast and then north toward Galveston. Yager had caught word that there was a lot of activity by US Navy ships in the Gulf of Mexico just beyond gun range of the port. While the colonel continued to lead his 1st Mounted Rifles on toward the Sabine River, the captains knew their jobs would be to support Confederate General Cook in defense of Galveston.

Ware and Rucker followed along the north bank of the Brazos River with Rucker's command in the lead. As the late September sun began to set, Rucker's point men came galloping back to the troop.

"Captain, there are campfires ahead."

Rucker halted the column. "Did you get close enough to find out whether they were Yankees?"

The men weren't trained scouts and hadn't considered taking the initiative to investigate. "No, sir…sorry, sir."

Rucker was just a bit frustrated. He'd have to take charge of reconnoitering.

Soon enough, Captain Ware had ridden up to join him. Together with the point men and a couple of junior officers, they headed out to determine whose campfires were burning.

Belknap had made no effort to make smaller, less obvious fires. He knew there was the possibility of Rebels lurking in the vicinity, but his thinking was to let his men enjoy a night or two of relaxation before being called into battle.

Under cover of a cloudy darkness, the Rebels had moved to within a half mile of the Union troop location. Rucker raised his spyglass, as did Ware. "What do you think, Captain Ware?"

"Damn, they're Yankees all right. Appears we outnumber them. Don't see any cannon either."

Rucker smiled confidently. "I suggest we eliminate these Yankees come morning, Captain."

Colonel Yager had left one cannon behind with Ware and Rucker. It gave the captains a decided advantage, as grapeshot could easily decimate an enemy line. Ware nodded. "From what I can see of the lay of the land, we should be able to bring our cannon close in. Given those bonfires they've lit, they might be stupid enough to charge us."

The Rebels outnumbered their foe by nearly three to one, yet they made a conscious effort not to be overconfident. Rucker's only true experience under fire had been helping his father in an armed pursuit years earlier. Ware, on the other hand, had multiple battle experiences. Rucker gladly handed off command, as two leaders were a guarantee of failure in most any endeavor.

★

The morning sun struggled to peek through a wispy layer of clouds. In the pre-dawn hours, Ware had brought the troops to within a couple of hundred yards of Belknap's camp. The Rebel forces were blessed with a breeze coming toward them, thus making them more difficult to detect. Their butternut gray uniforms were also an advantage, as they blended well with the dry grasses. The captain had found a great placement for the cannon.

Ware whispered over to Rucker. "What say you, Captain? Shall we begin?"

The first cannon shot would be a ball designed to get the Yankees' attention. They'd save the canister for a hoped-for charge. The effectiveness of canister in close combat was horrific, as it was like firing an extremely large gauge shotgun into a line of attackers.

The air was moist and dew lay heavy on the ground, as a dozen Rebel soldiers prepared to charge the Union defense. With the firing of the cannon, they broke into a run toward the Yankees, punctuated by wild Texas Rebel yells. They fired toward the Union troops as they ran.

Belknap's command dropped breakfast plates, tossed aside coffee tins, grabbed rifles, and headed to defend their breast-works. Major Belknap and Lieutenant Rucker unholstered their revolvers in anticipation of close-in combat. Belknap now realized the folly of having made his troops too easy to find. He cursed to himself. "Don't fire until they're close, men."

At that, the Union line let loose with as much gunfire as they were able to muster. A couple of Rebel soldiers fell wounded, but the rest hightailed it back to their line.

"Cease fire! Cease fire!" Belknap looked up and down his line. The men were ready to pursue the enemy. No one had as yet been wounded. "At ease, men." He raised his telescope.

By now the sun had risen and shone full bore into the eyes of the Rebels. Captain Ware hadn't anticipated this eventuality.

Belknap scanned the Confederate battle line. It was well that he'd held his men back. Pursuit would have been suicidal, he saw as he looked into the gaping maw of a trap. Nearly fifty Rebel soldiers and cavalry stood ready to repel any Union assault. The cannon was clearly visible. A single well-aimed canister round would have decimated his small troop.

With his back to the Gulf and the attack on Galveston not yet launched, Belknap's only escape would be to the south back toward Matagorda Bay. Had he been aware that Confederate Colonel Cook in Galveston was pulling his troops and supplies out in the face of the heavily armed Union ships, he might have headed north. Galveston would surrender in a couple of days.

★

Captain Rucker rode over to Ware's position. "What's your plan, Captain?"

"Looks like those damned Yankees are smarter than we thought." Ware wasn't inclined to sit around all day waiting for the Union troops to make a move. "I'm of a mind to lob a few more cannon balls their way. Maybe they'll retreat." Ware rightly figured that by now the Yankees knew they were outnumbered and outgunned.

Stephen Rucker looked through his spyglass. He saw Major Belknap and vaguely remembered the man. "Captain, there's been no attack on Galveston so far as we know. I recognize their commander. He's an experienced Indian fighter. I'm guessing they'll head to more familiar ground to the south. We might use a pincer strategy. I could take my unit to the south to set an ambush while you give chase from the north."

Ware wondered what else they must have taught Rucker at West Point. But it did make sense. "I like your thinking,

Captain. Let's see if we can chase these Yankees out of their nest."

With that, Rucker went off to gather his troop, and Ware unlimbered the cannon.

With cannon balls dropping in every couple of minutes, Belknap's men felt as though they were in some fiery devil's den. The Rebels were too far off to be viable targets for their rifles. Belknap handed his spyglass to Lieutenant Rucker. "Take a gander at what the rebels are up to, Lieutenant. I'm going to reconnoiter an escape route."

Rucker stood to get a better look.

Rebel sharpshooter Sergeant Clay Bell had by now taken a position about 300 yards from the Union line. He saw multiple easy targets. He sighted through the scope of the Sharps rifle and saw an officer stand. "You see that, John?"

"He's all yours, Sergeant."

Bell slipped a round into the Sharps, sighted, took a deep breath, held it, and squeezed the trigger. As fate would have it, the round was defective. The projectile sped out with but a fraction of the firepower typical of the buffalo gun. It was potentially lethal nonetheless.

Rex Rucker reeled as the bullet tore through his shoulder.

Major Belknap had just returned from scouting their escape when he saw Rucker fall. "Damn!" He rushed to the lieutenant's side. "Sergeant, gather the horses. We're getting out of here." He kneeled beside Rucker. "Lieutenant, we're going to get you on a horse. You're going to have to ride." Belknap tied a couple of scarves together to immobilize Rucker's shoulder as best he could. His biggest concern was loss of blood, but there was little he could do save apply pressure to the wound.

Before Ware became aware of the sudden exposure of the Union troops, they were already mounted and headed south along the coast. "Damn! Sergeant, secure the cannon. Get our troops mounted up."

Stephen Rucker had his men mounted earlier and had

begun a mad dash south to head off the Yankees. It had become a question of who'd arrive at Matagorda Bay first. His aim was to dig in at Passe Cavallo to set his trap.

Belknap had Rex Rucker tied into his saddle. The lieutenant was in considerable pain but was determined to survive.

The Union troops had a good jump on the Rebels, and Belknap was intent on maintaining that advantage. The horses had barely had time to recover from the ride north, so he dared not push too hard.

★

From the look of the place, you'd never know there was a war underway. Luke had arrived at the outskirts of Laredo. He hadn't been in Laredo for a couple of years, but it looked as familiar as yesterday. He had actually begun to regret taking on this assignment, as it was promising to take longer than expected. That having been said, he appreciated having Strong join them. There was now the prospect of a fair fight when they caught up with their prey. What weighed on him more than all else was that he wanted to be with Elisa when she gave birth. Still, it wouldn't do to rush his pursuit of Ramos, as it could put his mission in danger. Foolhardiness wouldn't do.

He gathered his band of misfits together. "Anything that happens in Laredo begins at a saloon. Strong drinks tend to loosen tongues." Luke's companions nodded. "Let me do the talking. These things can be sort of sensitive. There's a fair chance someone might recognize me, and that could be to our benefit." Luke counted on his reputation as giving him a decided advantage. No one was likely to pick a fight given his reputation for delivering tough justice.

★

Unbeknownst to Captain Stephen Rucker, he had by far the fresher mounts. Belknap had resigned himself to periodically stopping to rest his travel-weary horses. He continued his escape only when Ware's cavalry came into view behind him. Thus, the Rebel captain was able to arrive at Passe Cavallo several hours ahead of Belknap.

Ware kept up an easy pursuit. It would be foolhardy to risk his men's lives in any attack. He focused on driving the Yankees toward the ambush Rucker would set.

Belknap had quickly realized that the Rebels split their forces. He was savvy enough to figure that there'd be some sort of ambush awaiting him down near Matagorda Bay. He hoped and prayed that there'd still be boats at Passe Cavallo, as his only escape route was likely to be the sea.

Had he not been tied to the saddle, Rex Rucker would probably have slipped into the oblivion of the sands lining East Matagorda Bay. He trailed the main body by at least a quarter mile. He couldn't hear how close Captain Ware's cavalry was nor did he especially care. He was downright miserable. Belknap occasionally looked back to be sure the lieutenant was in sight and not captured by the Rebels chasing them. The major had to consider the lives of the entire unit, not that of one wounded man.

Captain Stephen Rucker had formed up a concave-shaped defensive perimeter designed to force the Yankees into withering rifle fire at its center.

"Sergeant!" Belknap summoned his trusted non-com over to his side. "If I've correctly judged where we are, we should find some boats due east of our position."

"Sounds like a plan, sir. There is one problem."

It's what Belknap had come to like about his sergeant. The man didn't hold back facts or opinions. "What is it, Sergeant?"

"The Rebel defense is in sight, sir. I'm thinking they planned to drive us toward their center. If we're going to reach any boats, we'll have to fight our way around that gray line to our left."

Belknap hadn't realized that they'd already reached the outer part of the Confederate trap. He gazed off to the east, raising his spyglass in an effort to scan the landscape. "No choice, Sergeant. Let's make our break for the coast. Now!"

As a unit, the major's troop turned and bolted toward the end of the Rebel line. Beyond lay the Gulf and escape.

The Rebel soldiers hadn't expected an immediate assault. Caught by surprise, they found Yankee cavalry upon them and through their line before they could bring any rifles to bear.

Belknap never paused. Despite sporadic gunfire, all of his troops made it through and stayed at a full gallop toward the sands of East Matagorda Bay. Had he had the time, he'd have toasted his good luck at finding the boats he'd expected. The men literally flew from their horses and climbed into the boats. In mere minutes they'd shoved well off shore and out of range of Confederate rifles.

Belknap finally stopped to take stock of his men. Only Lieutenant Rucker was missing. He looked back to the shoreline. Rucker had initially ridden into the bay, but the ropes that bound him to the saddle prevented his dismounting. Rebel soldiers soon had him captive. The major could only hope for the best. If the lieutenant survived his wound, he'd surely not survive a Rebel prison camp.

Rex Rucker was untied and roughly pulled from his horse. The Rebel soldiers showed little respect for his golden officer braid. A corporal shoved Rucker to the ground. "Guess we don't have to tie this son of a bitch up, he don't look like he'll see the next sunrise."

Just then, their Captain Rucker rode upon the scene. He'd responded to the sound of gunfire off to his right flank. He looked out toward the Gulf at the escaping Yankees and cussed under his breath.

"We got us a prisoner, Captain." They dragged Rex

forward and shoved him into the sand in front of Stephen's horse.

The captain literally vaulted from his saddle. "Easy with this man, soldier."

"You ain't soft, are ya, Captain?"

"This is my brother." His tough-as-nails glare and firm voice told the soldier to back off.

Rex looked up in his semi-conscious daze. "Stephen?" he asked, then promptly collapsed in the sand.

Captain Rucker moved to his brother's side just as Captain Ware rode up. "What's this, Captain?"

"This is my brother. He's hurt bad."

Ware caught sight of Belknap now far off shore. "Guess we're done here, Captain Rucker."

"I can't let my brother die here, Captain. With your permission, I'd like to take him home to Nuecestown."

Ware gazed compassionately at the Ruckers. War was certainly hell and this likely as not wouldn't be the first-time family tragedies played out. "Do what you have to do, Captain. I'll assume command of your unit until you return."

The two men saluted.

The corporal sheepishly brought the Yankee lieutenant's horse forward. "Sorry, Captain."

Stephen could see the pain ripple in involuntary shudders through Rex's body as he lifted him into the saddle and secured him. He looked into his brother's half-opened eyes. "You damned well better not die on me, Rex Rucker." They wasted no time beginning the journey to Nuecestown.

Belknap had watched through his spyglass at the scene on the beach of East Matagorda Bay. He didn't recognize the Yankee captain who led his lieutenant away, but there appeared to be some compassion. He assumed Rucker would be in decent hands. He was in no position to effect a rescue.

FOURTEEN
RAMOS VENGEANCE?

EMBARRASSED by Texas Rangers and Apaches, Pablo Ramos had been losing sleep. When he did catch some shut eye, he experienced nightmares causing him to writhe, toss, and turn like a nest of angry rattlesnakes. A seething anger welled deep within his core. He barely clung to what remained of his pride.

There'd been trouble on the Nueces Strip ever since the Anglos began to settle Texas, and it had worsened after the Mexican American War and subsequent border upheavals. With most of Texas's fighting men tied up in a war, a tremendous opportunity lay before him. There were plenty of riches to be gathered by mostly foul means. His setback with the Texas Ranger was only temporary, to his thinking. He might yet wreak vengeance on the damnable Luke Dunn and then kill a few Apache to show Costalites who was boss on the Strip.

He found himself holed up in San Ygnacio on the Texas side of the Rio Grande. A half dozen loyal Mexicans shared his hatred for Anglos and Indians, but he'd need three times as many men to accomplish his goals. Rustling and selling hides was slow business. He figured to turn his attention to serious endeavors like banks, stagecoaches, and ranches.

★

JD tended the horses while Luke, Barber, and Strong checked Texas Jack's Saloon. Of course, the place featured the town's best bawdy house, which was enough reason not to have JD tag along. "Jake, you and Jubal fan out to the right as we enter. The bar is to the left, so I'll ease over to it and see what the barkeep can tell me. After we finish at the saloon, we'll go over to the jail and see what Sheriff Stills might know."

They didn't question why Luke wasn't heading to the sheriff first. They didn't know about Luke's grudge with Stills over the escape of Carlos Lopez a couple of years back. The sheriff's lapse had cost lives. The lawman was regarded as more interested in chewing tobacco and filling his spittoon than keeping prisoners in the hoosegow.

Luke eased on into Texas Jack's, pausing just inside the doors to take a read on the customers. He tended to attract attention, as a big man with twin Colts and a Texas Ranger badge would be expected to do. The dealer at a nearby card game paused in mid-shuffle to check out the newcomer. Luke moved toward the bar while Barber and Strong followed and found an empty table just beyond the card game.

Luke sidled up to the bar and motioned to the barkeep.

The card players returned to their game, and a pair of youngish women ventured over to Barber and Strong. "Would you cowboys be interested in a drink?" With their low-cut bodices, long dark hair, and black stockings, they were about as provocative as could be expected for their profession. The prettier of the two brushed against Barber, closely enough to let him get a whiff of her perfume.

Jake rolled his eyes back and breathed deeply taking in the

aroma filling the air beside him. The two men looked at each other before glancing at Luke.

Luke slowly shook his head side to side, as he once again motioned to the busy barkeep.

Back at the table, Luke's deputized Rangers let their jackets fall away revealing their badges. Barber shook his head ruefully. "Afraid tonight's not the night, ladies." The ladies pouted a bit, looked disappointedly over at Luke, and slipped away.

The barkeep finally walked over to Luke's end of the bar. "Can I help you?" He took a long look at Luke. "You're that Texas Ranger fella, ain't you? Luke Dunn, I believe. Yeah, you cleaned a couple varmints from our fine city a while back."

Luke thought calling Laredo a city was a stretch but wasn't going to quibble. "Yes, I'm Captain Dunn. Wondered if you might help me. I'm looking for someone."

"Well, Captain, pretty much anyone around this territory comes through Texas Jack's at one time or another. Who ya got in mind?"

Luke leaned in a bit and lowered his voice. There were Mexicans in the saloon and any one of them could be loyal to Ramos. "Looking for Pablo Ramos."

"Damn, but you missed him by a week, Captain."

Luke slid a coin onto the bar. "Know where he might be found?"

The barkeep pocketed the coin and scratched his rough-trimmed beard. "Seems he was talking about San Ygnacio."

"You've been a great help." He placed another coin on the bar and nodded over at Barber and Strong. "If you'd be so kind…give my men a drink of your fine whiskey."

Luke walked over to the table where his men were sitting. As he walked past the card game, he paused a second. There was something familiar about two of the players, but he couldn't place them. He continued to Barber and Strong. "You stay here and enjoy a couple of drinks. I'll return in a bit."

Exiting the saloon, Luke turned to his right and walked a hundred yards or so up the street to the jail. His ears became attuned to a snoring sound as he drew close. A dim kerosene lantern light cast itself from within. Luke knocked on the door but didn't wait for a response, as he swung the door wide open.

Sheriff Stills slept soundly on one of the jail cell bunks, his steady snoring punctuated by occasional snorts.

"Stills! Rouse your sorry ass!" Luke tossed a rock at the steel bars. The clatter was enough to wake the dead. Stills was hardly an exception.

"What the...who the hell?"

"Luke Dunn here...Texas Ranger Captain Luke Dunn."

Stills sat bolt upright. He blinked his eyes as Luke turned up the lamp.

"Who are those swine down at Texas Jack's? They look familiar."

Stills was shaking the cobwebs out. "Ne'er-do-wells that drifted into town. Um...come south from Uvalde, I think."

Luke was rifling through the helter-skelter wanted posters littering Stills's desk. "Here's one, Sheriff. Zack Carter. Wanted for robbery...murder...rape. How come you're sleeping here and not arresting him?"

"Damn, Captain. I'm sorry. The men who took Perez caught me by surprise."

"You can be thankful he was finally killed." Luke grabbed the wanted poster. "Stay here. I'm going to arrest this man and plant him in your jail. Think you can keep him here?"

Stills nodded.

"Clean up both cells. I think Carter may have company." Luke pivoted and walked out the door and back to the saloon.

He entered Texas Jack's straightaway and walked over to Barber and Strong. "You each take a position in a back corner of the room in line of sight with those men playing cards. I'm going to arrest the dark-haired one, and there may be trouble."

Barber eased up slowly and took a position at the far end of the bar while Strong moved to the opposite side of the room.

Luke walked over to the men playing cards. There were five in the game. Typically, a man on the run from the law surrounded himself with cowards, men perceived as weaker. At the first sign of trouble, their loyalty generally disappeared. Luke looked into the eyes of the dark-haired man in the fancy suit and sporting a goatee. "You Zack Carter?"

"Some call me that." The man started to move his right hand from the table.

"Keep both hands on the table, Mr. Carter." A Colt revolver had appeared seemingly instantaneously in Luke's hand. He placed the wanted poster on the table and looked at the other card players. "I'm Texas Ranger Captain Luke Dunn, and you are under arrest. Any of you men with Mr. Carter here?"

All hands were on the table and shaking their heads in the negative.

"You better drop that gun, Mr. Ranger." A voice appeared from near where Jubal Strong was standing. The men at three tables cleared, as trouble seemed about to be brewing.

"I think not." Luke didn't take his eyes from Carter.

The man who'd spoken felt the hard muzzle of a pistol in his back. Strong had sprung into action. A gun could be heard to thud onto the wooden floor.

Luke held out a set of manacles. "Put these on, Mr. Carter."

At about the moment Carter's hand grazed the top of his gun, a thunderous sound blasted from Luke's Colt. Carter grimaced as he looked over at his right arm now hanging uselessly. "Damn. Goddamn. You done broke my arm!"

"Shall we try the other arm, Mr. Carter?"

Luke had lost patience. He grabbed Carter's left arm, affixed the manacles, and pulled the man up from the chair. He tossed a second set of manacles to Strong. "Bring him along if you'd be so kind, Jubal."

Strong wrenched the second man's arms behind his back and quickly had him in irons.

Luke surveyed the saloon. "Y'all get the word out. There's law in Laredo. Now, let's say we take a little walk up the street." He pushed Carter out the door and headed toward the jail.

Luke figured he'd accomplished three important things. He'd let it be known there was justice on the Nueces Strip, he'd captured a wanted man and his accomplice, and he'd taught Barber and Strong a lesson as to the mission of the Texas Rangers.

★

Stephen Rucker pushed along as fast as he dared. With his brother wounded and still seeping blood, the danger of Yankee patrols, and any possible bandits around, he had to be cautious. To make matters worse, a light rain had begun to fall. He'd wrapped his slicker around his brother, but with the cool damp conditions Rex's breathing had become labored.

The pair were a sight to behold as they came upon the north levee of the Nuecestown ferry: Two forlorn-looking riders, gray shadows in a thickening fog made more miserable by the misty rain. Stephen rang the bell to get the ferryman's attention. There was no response.

After what seemed far too long, the ferryman finally saw them and began poling the craft across the river to fetch them. It seemed like forever as he crossed the rain-swollen Nueces River. "Where you fellas from?"

Stephen was silent and Rex simply was unable to speak.

The ferryman realized they were soldiers with decidedly different uniforms and that the one in the blue tunic was clearly not doing well. He eased them onboard and began the slow crossing.

"You're Saul Duggan, aren't you?"

"Yeah, fella. How'd you know my name?"

"Seen you at church. My father is Horace Rucker."

"Dang, you're the Rucker boys." Stating the obvious seemed in order. "Can I help?"

"Would you fetch my father while I get Rex to Doc's place?"

As soon as the ferry hit the south levee, the ferryman tied up and headed for the Rucker house while Stephen rode on to Doc's.

He unfastened the ropes holding Rex in the saddle and eased his now loudly moaning, semi-conscious brother from the saddle. He almost took solace in hearing sounds of pain. It meant that his brother was alive. Stephen hammered on the door. "Doc! Doc!"

Doc was groggy from his afternoon nap. It had been made all the more relaxing by the patter of rain on the tin roof of his house. "What's the commotion, dammit? Who the…?" He recognized the Ruckers. "Damn, Stephen, what happened?"

"Rex took a Sharps round in the shoulder, Doc. He's in bad shape. Happened a couple of days ago."

"Well, get him in here and get rid of all his wet clothes. Lay him on the table and grab a couple of those dry blankets to keep him warm."

Stephen noticed that there were no whiskey bottles around. Doc had stayed sober pretty much since Pastor Rucker had arrived in Nuecestown. He watched as Doc gently cut away his brother's tunic to reveal an appallingly horrific wound. The bullet had carved away a chunk of shoulder bone and muscle the size of a man's fist.

"Doc?"

"This ain't easy, Stephen. If this was an Army field hospital, your brother's arm would come off first thing." Doc examined closely. "There's just enough bone that maybe…just maybe…I can salvage the arm. If you'd been a day or two later, even I couldn't work that sort of magic."

A knock at the door distracted them. "Come on in," Stephen called.

Horace Rucker stepped into the room. "Oh, my god. What's happened?" A horrified expression swept across his face.

"Good news was that the sharpshooter fired a defective round. Bad news is that he's got a pretty bad wound."

"How'd he fall into your hands, son?" Even as he embraced Stephen and asked the question, he couldn't take his eyes from his eldest son.

"Yankees had to leave him behind to make their escape. Luckily, he was captured by my men."

Doc looked over disconcertedly. "Are you men going to jaw all day? Get out of my way so I can save this young soldier's arm." Doc gave them a stern look and nodded toward the chairs. "Sit a spell. If I need you, I'll holler. He's out like he's been pole-axed, so it's not likely he'll be needing to be held down."

Pastor Rucker took a seat next to Stephen and stared at his younger son, who was gazing numbly off into space while oblivious to his soaking wet gray uniform. The pastor felt helpless. "Anybody winning yet?" He knew the answer before he asked. There was still a bit of retired Army colonel in him.

★

San Ygnacio wasn't much of a town in 1862, despite having been a trading hub on the border for better than three decades. It was located on the site of an old land grant called Hacienda de Dolores made back in 1750. The town was named after the patron saint of Guerrero, Saint Ignatius Loyola. Soon enough, it would be the scene of skirmishes between the Mexican rebel Cheno Cortina and Confederate troops. For now, it afforded breathing room to Pablo Ramos. The Mexican rebel tried to relax as he leaned back in a chair against the sandstone wall.

The place was actually a small fortress named Fort Treviño. The courtyard featured a sundial, boring but offering up a calming effect. Ramos couldn't seem to stop watching the shadow mark the time. He fished a trainman's watch from his pocket and checked it against the sun's ageless accuracy. He'd lost a few pounds and, coupled with newfound physical energy, he was now recruiting a couple of additions to his gang. Eventually, he'd have to brave Apache and Confederate patrols and head toward Rio Grande City to have any hope of serious recruitment. He knew he was in Cheno Cortina territory and that in itself posed a serious risk. He especially had to guard against recruiting Cheno loyalists.

The sun cast a reddish glow on the landscape as the four Texas Rangers rode cautiously into town. JD was back in her disguise, trying once again to give the appearance of being a man. Her diminutive size was such as to make the men seem larger and more imposing. Given their notable size, it was hard to miss Luke and Barber. Strong reflected the serious grittiness that graced the faces of his long-gone, lawbreaking kin. The men looked every bit as tough as they were, and they wore "don't mess with me" expressions as they sought to make a memorable impression on the folks in the little town. Surely, the word of their arrival would get to Ramos.

They didn't have far to go before they saw the man himself still leaning in the chair against the Fort Treviño wall. Ramos peeked from under his broad-brimmed sombrero. What he saw was unsettling, to say the least, and his mind quickly raced to gather his wits as concerned this unexpected development. Not moving a muscle, his eyes darted side to side. None of his band were in view, though he felt confident that at least one sentry was likely watching by now. The sentry that let the Texas Rangers pass through unannounced would be dealt with later.

Luke boldly rode up to within about twenty feet of Ramos. *"Buenos días, Pablo. ¿Estás listo para la cárcel?"*

The sheer boldness of being asked whether he was ready for jail wasn't lost on Ramos. He didn't move a muscle. His options were running through his head. He knew for certain that the Texas Ranger was not to be underestimated. *Where are my sentries? Can I reach my pistol before the Rangers shoot?*

Strong watched in amazement as Luke ordered Ramos to stand and raise his hands. "*¡Levántate y levanta tus manos!*" Like JD and Barber, Luke sat his saddle with his rifle across the saddle horn but ready for action.

Two of Ramos's men appeared off to the Rangers' right in the doorway to the modest fortress. They each held a rifle.

Luke spoke out in a quietly commanding voice to Barber and Strong. "Those two are yours. JD, keep your eyes on Ramos."

Despite the cool late fall air, Ramos felt a couple of beads of sweat run down his temples. He still hadn't budged.

"Perhaps you didn't hear me, you loco son of a bitch. *¡Levanta tus manos!*" Luke was getting impatient. He wasn't looking to mess around. He preferred avoiding gunplay, but it was always an option. Keeping an eye on Ramos's henchmen, he dismounted, grabbed the manacles, and approached the Mexican bandit.

"*¡Es la hora!*" A revolver had found its way into Ramos's hand.

An explosive sound ricocheted off the fortress wall, and a trail of smoke wafted from JD's rifle.

Ramos's eyes grew wide. "*¡Madre de Dios!*" He fired his revolver wildly into the sky as he half-rose, contorted his body in pain, and collapsed in the dirt.

The other two bandits immediately raised their hands as they watched their leader writhing convulsively in the dust.

Luke glanced back at JD and nodded his gratitude.

For her part, she was shaking like a leaf in a strong wind.

"Jake, Jubal, arrest those two. I think San Ygnacio still has a jail."

Ramos looked pleadingly up at Luke. A gut shot was extremely painful. He knew he was going to die. *"Madre de Dios, señor Ranger…por favor mátame."* He begged Luke to put him out of his misery.

Thoughts of compassion mixed with justice swirled through Luke's mind.

Ramos grimaced and groaned as blood spread across his belly and onto the ground. He looked at the sundial. *"Solo… son…las cuatro…en…punto."* With his dying breaths, the bandit was worried about the time of day. *"Cuatro…"*

Luke stood tall, looking down at the bandit. He wondered why four o'clock would mean anything. Seemed the ravings of a madman in pain. Compassion was winning as Luke began to reach for his Colt.

Another rifle blast rang out, the sound echoing from the fortress wall.

Ramos slowly released his grip on the pistol hidden alongside his leg, let out a final breath, and expired.

This time, JD wasn't shaking. She smiled at Luke and touched the muzzle of the rifle to her hat as if to say "You're welcome."

Whatever other recruits Ramos had gathered seemed to have disappeared into the brush and grass of the Nueces Strip as Luke and his Rangers proceeded to march the remaining two bandits down the street to the makeshift jail. Barber had grabbed Ramos by the neck of his shirt and dragged the body along behind. The bandit looked harmless in death.

"Wait, Jake." Luke went over to where Ramos had been seated. The object reflecting the late afternoon sun was an old trainman's watch. He flipped open the lid. JD's bullet had grazed the timepiece such that it was frozen at four o'clock. Luke shook the timepiece. It sounded as though it would never be put back in working order. He tossed it to JD. "Likely isn't worth anything, JD. Seemed to matter to Mr. Ramos here."

JD smiled and pocketed her trophy.

Luke thought about hauling the two bandits up to Laredo, but he'd already had experience with transporting prisoners over any significant distance. The inconvenience of prisoners in transit led to many a delivery of harsh frontier justice, usually in the form of necktie parties. Judges and courtrooms were few and far between. Realistically, Luke's prisoners would likely be set free by the local Mexicans who saw no harm in their association with the likes of Pablo Ramos.

FIFTEEN
APACHE AGAIN

DESPITE THE WIDE expanse that was the Nueces Strip and its sparse population, it was amazing how fast news traveled. The news from San Ygnacio wasn't missed by the Apache. Upon hearing of Ramos's demise, Costalites raised his eyebrows and shrugged. He sat in front of his wickiup staring off into space. He decided he'd like to meet this bigger-than-life Texas Ranger who'd disposed of the Mexican bandit. He'd heard that the Comanche named Luke Ghost-Who-Rides, and the Apache chief wondered what that meant. The fact that the Ranger had befriended a savage Comanche chief was totally lost on the Apache. A raiding expedition to the north seemed to be in order. He just might attract the Texas Ranger's attention.

Costalites looked out over the expanse of his encampment. There were roughly a hundred wickiups. The wickiups were smaller versions of the wigwams, or teepees, used for more established villages. Their small size translated into being more portable, enabling far easier travel for the nomadic Apache. The Apache preferred to travel light, and most of what they needed traveled with them. The dry expanses of prairie over which they ranged, the vagaries of weather, and need for food and water demanded they be as mobile as possible.

In a matter of hours, the Apache were headed northward.

★

Luke gave serious consideration to heading directly toward Nuecestown. The country was rough, but the shorter distance between two points was tempting. To understand his hesitation required an appreciation for the thickness of the brush and grass. Birds, wind, and animals were doing a masterful job of pushing the seeds and resultant growth of non-indigenous brush and trees that made travel ever-more challenging. Travelers generally wound up following dry stream beds or arroyos, so the travel really wasn't as straight as it might seem.

Luke and his little company bedded down beyond the outskirts of San Ygnacio. They were more tired than they'd realized, given the stress of the disposal of Ramos. So long as JD would keep quiet about shooting the bandit, they might even grab some shuteye. Luke was amazed that she could keep up a running chatter about a single topic for so long.

Dawn found the four Rangers headed north on the road to Laredo. Luke had made his route decision. JD had finally shushed up. She'd certainly been hell on Pablo Ramos, having cold-cocked him with a rifle butt weeks earlier and then finally using the business end to kill him. She was certainly earning her stripes and had fully dispelled any reservations Luke might have held at having her along. Special consideration for her womanly needs seemed a small inconvenience, given her well-earned value to the mission.

★

Belknap felt incredibly fortunate to have escaped the Rebels. He was saddened by the loss of Lieutenant Rucker, but experiencing only one casualty in such a situation was quite a feat. He had no idea whether he'd inflicted any losses on the Rebels nor whether Commander Renshaw had begun his assault on Galveston.

They'd rowed well past Matagorda Bay, and Mustang Island soon came into view. The sands appeared deserted. Given that several of the men were suffering from seasickness, he had the boats steered toward the beach. *Terra firma* never felt so good.

A larger problem now loomed for Belknap. His men were cold, wet, thirsty, and hungry. It was a deadly combination by any stretch of the imagination. The good news was that they were alive.

While the boats would afford easy travel down the coast toward Corpus Christi, the men were reluctant to go back to sea. Belknap recognized that they faced a long walk and would be abandoning their most effective means of escape. They were in desperate need of provisions and horses. Given the cool breezes, shelter would be a bonus, though the sand dunes afforded some relief.

"That's about the best I can do, Pastor. God willing, I think he'll keep his arm. Thank God Stephen wasted no time getting here."

Rex still lay unconscious. He clung to life despite a seeming shadow of death hanging over him.

Doc shook his head concernedly as he turned to the pastor. "He's going to be in a lot of pain. Infection is my biggest worry. Let's move him to the bed in the parlor. You can stay if you like. I'll likely need help changing the dressing tomorrow."

Stephen Rucker all of a sudden found himself crying. Great

heaving sobs welled up from deep inside. His head slumped onto his father's shoulder.

The elder Rucker was sympathetic but needed Stephen to buck up. "Come on, Stephen. Let's move your brother and then get home and let your mother know what happened. I expect she'll cook up some special motherly care for Rex."

There'd be plenty of time to talk about the war. That they had so narrowly averted a more serious tragedy was chalked up to the providence of God. Pastor Rucker would be delivering a more personal message on Sunday.

★

The cattle presented a tremendous opportunity. Costalites's Apache looked at their chief almost pleadingly. They could run a few head to Mexico, sell them, and return in a matter of a couple of days.

The Apache chief nodded that the cattle were easy pickings. Then his face took on an aggressive expression. "Seek bigger prize."

His council of warriors reluctantly accepted his decision. They knew he had his mind set on raiding a ranch or two, and that such raids often meant bounty greater than selling a few beeves in Mexico. The risks were greater, but so were the rewards.

Costalites's strategy was to lure the Texas Rangers, especially Luke Dunn, into pursuing him. Bringing down so notorious a lawman would significantly raise his stature among the Apache. With Dunn out of the way and the ease with which the chief avoided Confederate patrols, the Apache could once again become the scourge of the Nueces Strip and even northern Mexico.

They hadn't ridden but a day when they came upon the burned-out ruins of what had been a ranch. The livestock were long gone, and bodies lay about decomposing in the dry southern Texas air. A few warriors snooped around, but the place had been picked clean. Nothing of value remained. The chief quickly recognized this as the work of Mexican bandits. It wasn't the easy bounty Costalites was promising.

Costalites was disappointed but waved his rifle to the Apache warriors to follow, and they resumed their ride. Now, he turned them slightly to the northeast. He was of a mind to reach into the very heart of the Nueces Strip. He'd heard that the White settlers were still building new ranches despite the ongoing war. More importantly, the gray soldiers had turned their attentions to the west.

Three days later, the chief's dogged determination was rewarded. The Apache crested a low rise on the prairie and before them lay what seemed more like a small village than a ranch. Smoke swirled from the makeshift chimney of a large hovel-like cabin.

There was a remuda of at least twenty horses and a half dozen vaqueros visible. A couple of women appeared to be preparing cattle hides for transport. The chief hadn't yet realized that he'd come upon a hider encampment. Costalites's good fortune was that the Mexican cattle thieves were not expecting company. He began to develop a cunning plan.

The chief assumed the cabin was occupied. He needed to lure out whoever was inside. He was tempted to simply launch a straight-on attack, but some of his warriors might be killed. He decided on a more deceptive strategy. He divided his warriors, sending large war parties to his left and right flanks but out of sight of the ranch. Two warriors were sent around to the rear of the cabin for the purpose of blocking the chimney and smoking out anyone inside.

Costalites and three warriors rode slowly toward the main cabin. Two Mexican hiders and one of the women were standing in front of the cabin carrying on some sort of friendly conversation. They were oblivious to the Apache until the chief had ridden to within a mere 50 feet. The chief raised one hand while gripping the rifle lying across his lap with the other. He tried not to seem too threatening. He spoke a little Spanish. "Buenos *días, amigos*."

The woman moved inside the main cabin upon seeing Costalites's approach. Two armed men joined the two facing the chief. Now, four men armed with rifles faced the interlopers. "*¿Qué necesitas?*"

The chief eyed the men. He could see fear in their eyes. "*No es un buen día para morir*." His threat was direct. Not a nice day to die indeed. He could see his warriors beginning to spread a blanket over the smoking chimney top.

The Mexicans sensed they were in deep trouble. As they stood facing down the Apache, several more warriors quietly rode up to the chief's side. Gray clouds of smoke quickly filled the cabin despite the occupants' efforts to extinguish the fire.

Costalites smiled in appreciation of the inevitability of the hiders' situation. "*Caballos y pieles de Ganado*." He would take their hides plus their means to obtain more. Without horses, the Mexicans would be at the treacherous mercy of the Nueces Strip.

The hiders glanced from one to the other. Even if they gave the Apache what they wanted, they might be killed. The Apache could be nearly as savage as the Comanche. By now, eight men and two women were standing in front of the cabin. They knew that a half dozen of their compadres were off somewhere rustling cattle. Little comfort for sure.

The sun glinted from Costalites rifle barrel as he swung it from his lap, fired almost without aiming, and dropped one of the Mexicans where he stood. It was a signal. A withering fire poured into the hiders. It took all of five or six seconds. Ten bodies lay in the morning sun. No Apache had been shot. The chief dismounted. "*Qué lastima*." A pity, indeed.

Their hopes were rewarded as the Apache found some gold coins and plenty of food. The hiders' rifles would also come in handy. Last but hardly least, they captured valuable livestock.

The couple of dozen horses plus the remaining cattle would fetch good prices in Mexico. Any lingering doubts the band had about their chief had been dispelled.

★

On the one hand, Luke was anxious to get back to Heaven's Gate and Elisa's waiting arms. As the four weary travelers passed through San Diego, he paused to watch a few tumbleweeds roll aimlessly on the wind across their trail. He had a sixth sense warning him that trouble lurked to the south. It pretty much went without saying that was a safe assumption any day on the Nueces Strip. He dared not forget that it was home to all sorts of dangers.

Strong was about to ask why Luke had stopped, when a company of Confederate cavalry rode into view. "Lookee there, Captain."

Luke's sixth sense seemed to have been validated. The troop looked right smart in their spanking new gray uniforms with gold buttons and trim. Sabers glistened and jangled in the afternoon sun. Luke stroked his mustache as he wondered where their point riders were. He shook his head at the apparent oversight.

As they approached, Luke raised his hand as a friendly sign and sat more erect so as to let his Texas Ranger badge be seen. "Lieutenant, where you heading?" He gave a salute to show respect.

The lieutenant returned Luke's salute and pulled up. "I'm Lieutenant Atkins."

"Captain Luke Dunn here—Texas Rangers. Pleasure to make your acquaintance, Lieutenant. Where did you say you were headin'?"

"Didn't say." The officer immediately realized that he was being uncivil. "Sorry, Captain Dunn. Meant no disrespect. Heading west to join Colonel Ford."

"Ah, the New Mexico campaign. Rip will have his hands full with that."

"You acquainted with Colonel Ford, sir?"

Luke smiled. "We're old friends, Lieutenant."

"And where are you headed, Captain Dunn?"

"Just took care of a few Mexican bandits down at San Ygnacio. We were heading back to Nuecestown, but I sense serious Apache trouble to the south of here."

"You sense it, sir?"

"Been at this a few years, Lieutenant. I've learned that sometimes you need to listen to your gut feelings. We captured a couple of the Mexican bandit's men, and they babbled about Apache."

"You think they're headed this way?"

Luke smiled. "That's what my gut's telling me."

"Pardon, Captain, were you going to fight Apache with only four men?"

"That's three men and a woman, Lieutenant." He managed to get the words out with a straight face. "And we're used to being outnumbered."

The lieutenant looked over his shoulder at his men. They were anxious to see some action. Moving from bivouac to bivouac had gotten old in a hurry. "We're ahead of our rendezvous schedule, Captain."

"Ever fight Indians, Lieutenant?"

"Can't say as I have, but some of my men have."

Luke smiled knowingly. "Looks as though y'all have kept your scalps thus far. Care to go hunting for Apache?"

"Let me talk with my sergeant." Lieutenant Atkins turned and rode back a few paces to confer.

While the lieutenant rode off to chat with his sergeant, Luke was having second thoughts about chasing the Apache. He was anxious to be getting back to Nuecestown.

As the lieutenant approached his troops, the sergeant

saluted smartly. "Do you know who you're talking with, Lieutenant?"

"Says his name is Dunn. Is that important, Sergeant?"

"Beggin' your pardon, sir, but Texas Ranger Captain Luke Dunn is likely the most feared lawman on the Nueces Strip."

"He's asked us to help him chase down some Apache."

"We can learn a lot from Captain Dunn, sir. And the men are ready for action. At least a half dozen fought with Rip Ford up north whipping the Comanche a few years back." He saluted the lieutenant.

Atkins returned to where Luke was waiting. He had no illusions as to command. "We'd be happy to join you, Captain Dunn."

"I'd like to get some distance from here, Lieutenant. The prairie is pretty flat and you can see a long way. I want to set two four-man patrols riding a mile out at our flanks. They'll be in sight by my spyglass. At first sign of savages, they'll report in. Indians don't tend to adapt well to surprises."

"You have any idea where the Apache might be, Captain?"

"Nope." Luke offered a broad grin. "But I know what they're looking for and I know the Nueces Strip."

Over the next two days, the combined company of Rebel cavalry and Texas Rangers would get acquainted over trail grub and small campfires. They had passed two small ranches still in one piece, but as yet there'd been no sign of Apache.

A hundred or so Apache with women and children raises a bit of dust in the sandy loam soil of the Texas prairie. Their dust cloud could be seen for miles, despite efforts to keep it at a minimum. The extended drought had certainly made its contribution.

They'd not seen a ranch, much less another hider village,

since the attack on the Mexicans a couple of days earlier. Costalites's warriors were once again becoming restless.

Clouds began to form on the horizon portending possible relief from the soul-sucking dryness. Water was a precious commodity, and the Apache were running low. Rain would be deeply appreciated.

As they prepared to make camp for the night, the chief spotted smoke curling into the golden sunset a few miles off. If it was a ranch, there'd surely be water for his people.

The Apache chief assembled a war party of thirty warriors. He figured that should be plenty. If a ranch was out there, it could be easily overcome. He could bring the remaining Apache later.

The moon peeked out from the clouds and lighted the way through the grasses and brush. The cloud front gathering on the horizon was moving toward the chief. He saw a couple of streaks of lightning well off in the distance. The last thing he needed was a fire raging through the dry brittle grasses of the prairie.

The war party traveled perhaps four miles, heading straight toward the rising smoke. Excitement at plunder plus access to water caused a contagion of excitement among the Apache warriors.

Costalites brought the war party to a halt roughly 200 yards from what appeared to be a ranch house. Soft candlelight emanated from the windows. All seemed peaceful. Costalites looked at his warriors and nodded. The usual strategy would be used. Two warriors circled the cabin to cover the chimney and smoke out whoever was inside.

They didn't see a shadowy figure run into the cabin. Of a sudden, the lanterns were snuffed and the fire extinguished. Costalites would have a greater challenge than he'd anticipated. A direct attack would now be in order.

★

Unbeknown to the Apache, a company of Texas Rangers and Confederate cavalry had also spotted the smoke rising from the cabin chimney and were headed toward the ranch.

They were roughly a half mile out when they first heard the distant popping sounds of gunfire.

The lieutenant had tried to persuade Luke to camp for the night, but some inner gut feeling told the Texas Ranger to ride just a little farther. Now, in the fading light, they realized that a battle was underway.

The company of Rangers and cavalry spurred their mounts in the direction of the action. From the amount of gunfire, Luke figured they'd arrive in the thick of the battle.

They reached the top of a slight rise in the prairie floor. Spread before them was an intense battle with Apache having fully surrounded a ranch house and barn. Luke took a count of the number of warriors. He mumbled to himself, "Hmmm… got us three to one." He counted on the element of surprise.

Luke turned to Atkins. "Lieutenant, get ready to spread your men out and make a lot of noise. I want to hear that Rebel yell I've been hearing about. The Apache must think that the entire army is attacking."

"We're going to charge the Apache, Captain?"

"Sure thing. Trust me, Lieutenant. They're going to escape as fast as their ponies can carry them." Luke nodded to Barber, Strong, and JD. "Ready?"

Luke put his spurs to Big Horse, started yelling like a banshee, and charged toward the melee.

This was a horrible turn of events for Costalites and his warriors. They were suddenly in a deadly crossfire between the cabin and a large body of charging horsemen. Cavalry sabers gleamed in the fading light, and the noise of the Rebel yells was deafening to Apache ears. Two, three, six Apache fell. More were wounded and hanging onto their ponies.

Costalites briefly saw a big man on a big horse leading the charge, but it was to be the only glimpse he'd have of Ghost-

Who-Rides. The chief sensed whom he'd finally come up against. Costalites broke off the attack and hightailed it back toward the Apache camp. In a bitter irony, it turned out the clouds he'd seen on the horizon weren't heading his way. He'd suffered from a far different sort of storm.

Luke and the Confederate cavalry pulled up in front of the ranch house. Half a dozen inhabitants emerged. A couple of the men in the cabin were wounded, but they had put up a worthy fight.

"Y'all okay?" Luke dismounted, and Atkins joined him.

"Where'd y'all come from?" The apparent leader of the defenders stepped forward.

Luke kept a straight face best he could. "Just in the neighborhood."

Atkins was still breathing hard, but couldn't suppress a bit of a grin at Luke's humbleness. "Sergeant, see to their wounded."

"My name's Symms." The man stepped forward to shake Luke's hand. "I run this spread for a fella in Corpus Christi named Murdoch. He'll be right pleased."

"Glad we could help, Mr. Symms. I'm Texas Ranger Captain Luke Dunn and this gentleman is Lieutenant Atkins." He looked off toward where the Apache had departed. "I do expect this war party is part of a larger band. If you don't mind, we'll send a couple of scouts out to be sure. We might yet have to persuade them to leave the area."

"Appreciate that, Captain. You're welcome to spend the night here. Happy to cook up some grub for y'all."

★

Costalites would never admit it, but he was relieved to arrive at his encampment. While it wasn't in the chief's nature to be fearful of anyone, he sensed that there was some sort of big medicine surrounding Ghost-Who-Rides. He wasn't especially anxious to do battle again with this larger-than-life legend of the Nueces Strip. The curious part of him still wanted to meet Luke, but fear far transcended that desire. Maybe it was superstition, but this White man's spirit seemed incredibly strong. Costalites made the decision to break camp in the morning and head back toward Mexico. The Apache had plenty of livestock to sell and trade, and there was no point in pushing their luck.

As the Apache began to retire for the night after their ill-fated raid, a party of six warriors rode into camp. Upon questioning a sentry, they headed for Costalites's wickiup.

Costalites had been about to bed down for the night but stopped upon hearing the ruckus. There was an intensity about these newly arrived Apache.

"Chief, we have news from the big river."

The chief gave them an impatient "what are you waiting for" look.

"Pablo Ramos is dead. His bandits are no more."

To Costalites, this meant just a bit less threat on the Texas border. He needed only worry about Cheno Cortina's bandits, the Mexican army, and maybe more Texas Rangers and Confederate soldiers. "How he die?"

A young warrior was bursting with pride at being able to convey the news. "Texas Rangers kill Ramos. Man Comanche call Ghost-Who-Rides."

The chief exhaled audibly. It was hard to maintain composure in the face of such news. What sort of strong spirit did this Texas Ranger possess? He nodded his head in gratitude to the young warrior and entered his wickiup. He felt a desperate need to communicate with the Great Spirit.

SIXTEEN
DAMN YANKEES

MAJOR GORDON BELKNAP found himself frustrated. He'd escaped from a potentially devastating defeat but now found himself in what was effectively a no-man's-land. He had the Gulf of Mexico to his back, but there was no escape now as their poorly moored boats had been carried away by tide and wind. He dared not go far inland, as he would surely encounter Rebel patrols. Belknap desperately needed food and horses. It was frustrating indeed.

By his reckoning, the major's only hope for relief lay with moving south toward Corpus Christi Bay, traversing its northern shore to Nueces Bay, wading across on the shell road, and then skirting Corpus Christi to hail US Navy boats patrolling offshore. If he were able to find food and horses along the way, it would vastly improve his chances. As it was, three of his men were sick.

He figured that he might even sneak into Corpus Christi and learn of the outcome of Renshaw's attack on Galveston.

★

"Thanks for your help, Lieutenant." Luke had arisen early

with the ranch hands and was surprised to see Atkins and his troop preparing to break camp and head west to join Colonel Rip Ford's New Mexico campaign. "Hope we get to work together again sometime. You can surely be proud of your men."

"It was my pleasure, Captain. My troopers will have a great story to tell their children, though I expect it'll get embellished a bit." He finished saddling up and was about to mount. "I will pass your regards along to Colonel Ford. I'll bet he could use your help." The lieutenant swung up into the saddle.

"He asked."

"You turned him down?"

"Lieutenant, I've got the entire Nueces Strip to look after. Nobody's got my backside, and failure isn't an option. Imagine what those Apache would have done to this ranch."

"I hear you, Captain. Ford's going to need all the help he can get. Frankly, between you and me, I'm not sure what folks running this war are thinking. From what I learned at West Point, the invasion of New Mexico makes no sense. We have bigger fights in eastern Texas. Might as well be peeing into a strong wind as we invade New Mexico...but...orders are orders. I'd rather be sharing your duty, Captain Dunn." He offered a salute and led his troop to the northwest.

Luke nodded and returned the lieutenant's salute, then began preparations to head back to Nuecestown. While he'd surely appreciated the help of the Confederate cavalry, the engagement with the Apache served to underscore the increased vulnerability of the Nueces Strip since the start of the war.

"We heading back to Nuecestown, Captain?" Barber had gathered his gear, saddled, and was ready to mount up. "Sure was nice of these folks to feed us."

"Indeed it was," Luke said. "Where's JD and Jubal?"

"Expect she's off doing woman things, Captain." Barber

cogitated on that a moment. "She and Jubal were chattin' up a storm last night."

The same thoughts passed simultaneously with Luke and Barber. "Think there's some sparkin' going on, Jake?"

"He's lost a wife. She's a woman…sorta pretty…could be."

Fraternization hadn't been something Luke had considered when JD joined up. He instinctively reckoned it could become a problem. "See if you can hurry them along, Jake." Luke wasn't going to make a rash decision.

By mid-morning they were finally on the trail.

Whatever might be going on between JD and Strong wasn't evident as the pair rode silently behind Luke with Barber bringing up the rear.

After an hour or so, Strong pulled alongside Luke. The heavy growth of grasses and brush forced them close. "Seems we'll likely be passing close to your cousin's place on the way back, Captain. If it's okay with you, I figure to let him know that I'm still around."

"Up to you, Jubal." Luke struggled to bring himself to open the topic of JD with Strong.

Strong saw that Luke was wrestling with something. "You concerned about JD, Captain?"

"Matter of fact I am, Jubal. Normally wouldn't concern me, but this is Texas Ranger business here." Luke strove to make this non-personal.

"Shucks, Captain. There's no sparkin' going on, if that's what you're worried about." Strong looked over at Luke. "She's a tiny thing, for certain." He looked off thoughtfully. "She's a tough woman and I do find her attractive, but I've got nothing to offer a woman just yet. We were just talking about life and trying to get better acquainted."

"I appreciate you being honest with me, Jubal," Luke said, trying to keep the relief out of his voice. "I do value your contribution to this mission. If you decide not to go back to ranching, I'd be pleased to have you remain with the Texas Rangers."

A live oak motte loomed in the distance. They could just about make out several buzzards circling. The motte was a little out of the way, but Luke felt obliged to investigate.

A single body hung from a rope under the live oak. As they rode closer, it became apparent that it had hung there for a couple of days. Insects flitted about, and half of one leg had been torn off by varmints. A couple of buzzards had been chewing on the upper body, but the vultures had limited access. The branch didn't fit more than a couple of the birds at a time.

"Damn, Captain. From a distance, I thought somebody had hung a Mexican, but this man wears Rebel gray." Barber was approaching with a bandanna over his mouth to filter out the stench of decomposing flesh. He reached out while astride his horse. A swift stroke of his knife cut the body down. Barber dismounted. Still holding the bandanna to his nose, he bent down and rifled the man's pockets. "Nothing here, Captain."

"What's that over there, Jake?" Luke pointed to a rumpled-up piece of paper lying in the grass. It had been trampled by horse hooves and boots, likely from the process of hanging the Rebel.

Barber handed the paper up to Luke. It turned out to be an empty envelope.

"Seems this man was a courier. Doesn't say where he's from, but the name on the envelope is Colonel Ford's." Luke wondered what the message might have said. Was it a warning? Some new strategy? There was no way of knowing. "Damn Yankees," he murmured under his breath.

"We gonna bury him, Captain?"

Luke felt the question needn't have been asked. It irritated him a bit. He gave Strong and Barber an exasperated look, climbed down, and grabbed his shovel.

The soldier was soon buried in a shallow but serviceable grave. Luke hung the man's hat on the makeshift cross.

With the lack of rain, it was easy enough to find the trail of whoever waylaid the Rebel soldier. Luke studied the hoof prints a moment. "Look like shod horses…likely Union. There were only three." The small number of Yankee horses suggested some sort of reconnoitering, perhaps a spy mission to disrupt Confederate initiatives. The horses were headed eastward. "Looks like they're ahead of us." It was obvious that Luke intended to follow, at least so long as the trail headed toward Nuecestown. "Jake, how about riding point? No sense us running into something unexpected."

The fact that the Confederate soldier had been hung gnawed at Luke. He wondered why they didn't simply shoot the man? It occurred to him that he might be dealing with renegade soldiers, if they were soldiers at all.

★

With the Yankees having been repelled in Corpus Christi, Major Hobby had abandoned the city and left it quite vulnerable to another attack. This naturally contributed to feelings of unease among the fine citizens of the port.

The pull-out of Rebel troops concerned Scarlett as much as anyone. Like other residents, she depended directly on the economic engine of Corpus Christi such as it was during wartime. She had plenty of seamstress business, even more when Rebel troops were in town.

Now that Carson was home on leave, she figured he might be able to give her a sense of security. So it was that she awakened to Carson's gentle touch. The sunlight had just broken through the window. The imperfections in the glass cast an artful pattern over their bed. She felt his hand gently trace the outline of her body. She knew his fingers would soon increase their urgency. She turned toward him and opened her eyes.

Her long curly red tresses played out over her delicate shoulders and pregnancy-swollen breasts.

"Good morning." He whispered it as he stroked her face and neck. He pressed his lips forward.

She softened her lips—the better to fully absorb his kiss. For an ever-more hardened man of the frontier, Walker Carson had the capacity to be quite a lover. She fully appreciated how he so naturally responded to her lovemaking needs. Given her whoring background, she'd been subject to the very worst of male depravities. This was so different. Now, despite her thoughts drifting to the defense of her city, she could not deny him—or herself—the pleasure of his sexual ardor. His hands, his lips moved over her naked body. She felt his manhood rise in her hands and soon enough, within her. She felt the baby kick inside her as they worked up an ever-more intense rhythmic motion.

Paroxysms of orgasmic pleasure culminated in a crescendo of passion. She so wanted to cry out but dared not for fear of awakening Margaret and Martha. Soon enough, they lay in warm afterglow.

After a few minutes, she took a deep breath and broke the silence. "Breakfast, my love?"

Carson lay back and smiled. "What's on your mind?"

"Breakfast? Coffee?"

"No, there's something you've been wanting to ask me."

Scarlett sat up. "Well, now that you mention it. Folks around here are concerned that Corpus is not fully defended. What if the damned Yankees come back?"

"Because they won't."

"How do you know that?"

Carson couldn't reveal the nature of tactical sessions he'd sat in on. Major Hobby had his reasons for having pulled out. Forces were needed at other places along the Texas coast, plus there was Colonel Ford's troop needs for the invasion of New Mexico. "You're just gonna have to trust me that I know, Scarlett. Trust that the generals know what they are doing."

His answer didn't exactly give her warm feelings of confidence. "I guess I just have to count on someone knowing what they're doing. This war is already such a mess, Walker. I fear for the future of our children."

He pivoted to the edge of the bed and began to get up.

She pulled him back to her and playfully shoved him onto his back. "Where do you think you're going, Captain Carson?" Soon enough, she was astride him. Breakfast could wait a while longer.

SEVENTEEN
WARPATH

"ONE ARROW, IT TRUE."

"You say gray coats." One Arrow pondered this news. "You sure not blue coats?" He fumbled for words not common to the Comanche tongue.

"Many gray coats…many big guns."

"How far?"

"One day ride."

"What direction?" One Arrow was trying to pin down facts about the potential threat.

"Head toward rising sun, my chief."

One Arrow nodded. "You have done well." With the loss of Three Toes and despite his youth, One Arrow had been chosen as the new leader of the little band of Penateka Comanche. He considered taking Cactus Flower as a wife and adopting her child. He spurned the much older Bird Woman as a wife, but would keep her so long as she contributed. Both had been widowed by the death of Three Toes. Having been wives to a chief, both women still held certain privilege within the band. Bird Woman, for example, was turned to by the younger women for her wise counsel.

The Comanche had set up their village on what the Anglos

called the Llano River in country characterized by rolling hills and forests. It was ideal for hunting game and hiding from the Anglos.

One Arrow had heard that the gray-coat soldiers had been fighting to the west in a place the White men called New Mexico. He understood they had advanced northward not far from Fort Bliss. He had never been there, but he'd heard stories about the rough terrain. Apparently, the gray coats had won an early battle, but failed to capture key military forts. The Yankees defended desperately and successfully, as they depended on New Mexico for much of the gold and silver necessary to finance the war effort.

With a band that now numbered nearly fifty warriors, women, and children, One Arrow felt there might yet be hope for his people to survive. His visit with Ghost-Who-Rides had given him great insight into what Three Toes had been thinking. The Penateka Comanche must remain free. There would be no Fort Cooper or other White man's reservation in their future so long as it was up to him.

He turned to the warrior who brought him the news of the gray coats. "How many?"

"Many, my chief. Many times more than our horses." Since the Comanche had roughly two hundred horses, the warrior was indeed describing a large force. "But they seem sad. Many have wounds. Many sick. Horses tired."

It wasn't difficult for One Arrow to deduce that the gray coats' efforts in New Mexico had been a failure. Did he dare attack the retreating soldiers? Could he hope to avenge Rip Ford's devastating campaigns against his people a few years back on the Brazos and the Canadian Rivers? Despite his attempts to understand Luke, bred into the very marrow of his Comanche bones and an integral part of the Comanche character was the imperative to defeat enemies. The very name Comanche translated to enemy. This left One Arrow in a quandary. His warriors saw an opportunity to display their manhood, their fighting prowess, to count coup and kill enemies. But Three Toes's legacy and Luke Dunn's teachings of understanding and respecting other people left him deeply conflicted.

One Arrow stood before his teepee as his two dozen warriors began preparation for a battle that had yet to materialize. If he was to maintain his leadership role as a chief of the Penateka Comanche, One Arrow had to make a decision. He thought on the likely weakness of the enemy, though feared that they could still inflict great losses among his band. The Comanche could not afford to lose its men. Disease, battles, and the increasing demise of the buffalo had already reduced their number. The Yamparika, Kotsoteka, Nokoni, and Quahadis bands of Comanche had already been decimated by the predations of the Anglos. There were at least eight more smaller bands that had been similarly affected. As he thought on it, there was no upside to attacking the retreating Confederate cavalry other than to salve the blood lust of his warriors.

The older warriors came to One Arrow. They expected him to be mounted with plenty of arrows, his war lance, and the Colt revolver that had belonged to Three Toes. What they found took them by surprise. One Arrow stood before them in full regalia. His face was painted white, not the black traditional with the Penateka. He held his lance pointed into the ground, not up toward the Great Spirit. Three Toes's bone necklace with its silver White man's cross glinted in the midday sun. He stroked the cross, wondering whether it might indeed offer some greater power. He'd need it.

Cactus Flower and Bird Woman stood at the entrance to their teepee several paces behind One Arrow. They too anxiously awaited his words.

"If our people are to grow like the prairie grasses, the mountain trees, the elk and deer, we must live in peace." The last word brought involuntary gasps from the warriors. A couple of the young men instantly began to show signs of anger. One Arrow continued on. "If we are to grow as a nation, we cannot have our best men killed in battles they cannot win. White man comes endlessly like grains of dust. They flow into our lands like many rivers."

His words began to make sense to at least some of the warriors. He could see them relax and nod with understanding.

A small group of warriors were still hot for battle. The prospect of a winter with no escape from the village was fully unappealing. From their very loins, they demanded battle. It was the very essence of whom they were.

One Arrow could see that he wasn't getting through to at least a half dozen warriors. He needed to force their hand. The young chief looked into each of their faces one at a time. The white paint on his own face made him a fearsomely strong spiritual sight. "If you choose to go to fight the gray coats, you are not welcome to return here. I will not lead you to certain death. I will not take away the future of the Comanche." The warriors who had become persuaded to One Arrow's thinking nodded in affirmation.

The Penateka Comanche warriors looked around at each other. The angriest, mostly young and thirsting for first battle, realized they didn't have the numbers to battle hundreds of cavalry, even gray coats in their dispirited defeated condition. Then one smiled. "Stragglers?"

There were a few nods of affirmation. They could attack the rear of the retreating gray coat column. They looked to One Arrow.

The chief sighed and nodded agreement. This was a compromise that might work. "Bring back scalps. Crouching Lion, you lead warriors into battle." One Arrow turned back toward his teepee. Bird Woman smiled her approval. One Arrow was becoming an ever-wiser chief of the Comanche.

★

In the dim twilight, Luke Dunn's Texas Rangers slowly approached the distant campfire. Someone was feeling plenty confident out on the Nueces Strip, as the fire was a roaring enough blaze to be seen for miles. Given the dryness owing to the extended drought, it was likely a considerable danger to spread to the surrounding prairie.

At about 500 yards out, Luke pulled the spyglass from his saddle bag. Five horses were hobbled near a mesquite tree. There were three men huddled near the fire enjoying a meal and from their apparent laughter and wild hand movements also imbibing a bit of spirits. He could make out gold braid on the dark gray hats of at least two of the men. In the bright light of the fire, Luke was startled to find that, despite the gray tunics, they didn't look like typical Anglo Rebel soldiers. Then it struck him like a free-swinging barn door in his face. They were Mexicans. They weren't Confederate soldiers at all.

Luke checked windage. They were downwind. They'd be less likely to be heard. He nevertheless dropped his voice to a whisper. "JD, Jubal, hold here. Jake, come with me."

"We attacking the soldiers?"

"They aren't soldiers. They're Mexicans that stole Rebel uniforms." Luke smiled almost mischievously. "They're drinking a lot, Jake. We'll wait until one of them leaves the campsite to pee." Luke figured to use the old tried-and-true tactic of attacking when nature called.

They split up and headed to within 100 yards of the camp. Sure enough, one of the Mexicans stood. They heard him laugh about answering nature's call and watched him weave and wobble his way to a nearby mesquite tree. Luke watched the man drop his pants, squat with his back against the tree, and begin to grunt. The Mexican was oblivious to his surroundings. Luke moved quickly and silently to no more than two feet from his prey, when the Mexican heard a twig snap. He looked toward the noise, caught sight of a silvery blade in his peripheral vision, and silently fell to the ground with his throat slit.

Luke snuck over toward Barber. He motioned JD and Strong to join them.

A voice arose from the campsite. "*¿Jose, dónde estás?*"

By this time, Luke and his Rangers had approached from the far side of the campfire. They couldn't be seen because of the fire. "*¡Estamos aqui, Mexicanos!*" Luke stepped out from behind the blazing campfire. "*¡Levanta tus manos!*"

Startled but stone cold drunk, one of the Mexicans tried to stand but wobbled and fell as he unholstered his revolver and shot wildly into the air. Always at the ready, JD leveled her rifle and shot him between the eyes.

The remaining Mexican threw his hands high in the air. "*¡Me rindo! ¡Me rindo!*" He left no doubt that he was surrendering.

"You speak English?" By now, Luke had unholstered his newly acquired Colt 1861 Army revolver.

"*Un poco Inglés, señor.*"

"Where you get those horses?"

"*Los compré, señor.*" He looked about furtively. He was a lousy liar.

"Bill of sale?"

The Mexican was beginning to panic. "*Lo perdimos, señor.* Is lost."

Luke turned to his band. "Looks like we have some horse thieves here. Guess we know what to do with their kind."

The Mexican understood Luke's English enough to now be fully panicked. Of a sudden, he dove for his gun.

Luke pulled the Colt's trigger and dropped him before he could reach it. The tall Texas Ranger calmly slipped his revolver back into its home. "Well, that was convenient."

JD and Barber smiled, but Strong didn't quite catch Luke's drift. "Convenient?"

"No tree branches high enough for a good hanging." Enough said on that account.

Strong's mouth gaped. It seemed so unlike Luke to act in such a cold-hearted manner, even against a horse thief.

"What's this?" JD picked up a crumpled piece of paper, looked at it, and handed it to Luke.

Luke scanned the paper. "Looks like the orders that poor courier had been carrying. Guess that's the final piece of this puzzle." He looked around. "Let's break out the shovels. Even thieves deserve a burial."

Strong hesitated. "Convenient, Captain?"

"I know what you're thinking, Jubal." Luke scooped up a shovel full of dirt. "Sorry about my choice of words, but we were saved the task of hauling a prisoner to Corpus Christi. I know that sounds cold-hearted. With JD's discovery of the stolen courier message, it would have been doubly inconvenient. Would we turn him over to civilian authority for horse stealing or military authority for treason?" He paused and tossed another shovel full. "I'm no calloused killer. Had the man not gone for the gun, we'd be taking him to jail."

Strong took up a shovel and dug. "Nasty business bein' a lawman in the middle of a war." He shook his head ruefully.

Barber had been observing the dynamic between Luke and Strong. "If I'd been a hair faster, I'd have shot the Mexican before Luke. My dang gun got hung up in this goldarned holster."

Luke appreciated the big man's support. "Thank God you didn't shoot yourself in the foot, Jake."

The mood was lightened considerably, and they all chuckled a bit.

They camped a short way off for the night, planning to resume their trek back to Nuecestown in the morning.

★

The nine Comanche had ridden hard to the southwest. Their reward was sighting a two-mile long straggling column of Confederate cavalry on spent horses with a few infantrymen mixed in. A couple of caissons had been converted to ambulances to carry the wounded, and these served to slow the procession. Crouching Lion had dismounted near the top of a heavily wooded hill where he had an unobstructed yet concealed panoramic view of the scene below. He watched patiently as the column advanced at a snail's pace along a dry creek bed that effectively formed a gorge and extended several miles. It was vulnerable to ambush and very difficult to defend.

The gray coats were careless in defeat, as they posted no pickets to guard their travels. The Comanche warrior looked at his fellow braves and shook his head. "No guards. White soldiers foolish. They weak." It gave a huge boost to their confidence.

After waiting more than an hour, the rear end of the column came into view. These last straggling gray coats consisted of the more seriously wounded and were escorted by four mounted cavalry nervous at their rear guard duty. Despite their duties to bring up the rear of the column, the cavalry seemed oblivious to their surroundings. There was perhaps a hundred yards between the last members of the column and those in trudging along in front of them. It offered a not-to-be-missed window of opportunity for Crouching Lion and his band. The warrior's mouth began to feel dry with anticipation of what was to come. Coup…scalps…a great story at council fires.

Crouching Lion noted a sharp bend in the dry creek bed where the straggling gray coats would be fully out of sight of the column ahead of them. There was even a convenient trail that led down to an ideal interception point. He signaled to attack from both sides of the gorge. "Kill horse soldiers first," he whispered. "No sound." He dared not attract the column ahead of the stragglers.

They moved slowly and quietly down the trail. They had to be absolutely certain that the main column had passed. Three warriors dismounted and crossed the trail stealthily so as to set the ambush from both sides of the creek bed. They found cover in the heavy brush, nocked their arrows, and waited. The creaking of a wagon alerted the Comanche.

As the group of the four cavalrymen and a half dozen infantry and wounded approached, the air became filled with silent death. To the Confederates, arrows seemed to fly from everywhere. The horses were emptied in but seconds as the Comanche silently swooped down on their prey. In only a couple of minutes, coup were counted, gray coats were killed, scalps were taken, a couple of horses captured, and nine Comanche warriors headed back up the hill from whence they'd come. Their blood lust had been fully sated.

As they crested the hill, Crouching Lion gave passing thought to repeating their strategy. It had worked so well. There'd be more stragglers. On the other hand, it would not likely take long for the gray coats to realize their loss. At least two of the cavalry mounts had taken off riderless up the trail toward the column. That would serve as a vivid warning to the Rebels—enough that they'd not likely be so careless again.

Crouching Lion pointed northward and off they rode at a swift pace until the gray coats were well behind them and they needn't worry about pursuit. They rode swiftly with the wind in their faces and long black hair flowing behind. Their heads were held high.

The Texas Rangers rode at an easy pace into Nuecestown. Strong had taken his leave to check with Luke's cousin, so it was just Luke, JD, and Barber.

Luke pulled up in front of the jail, as he had some paper-work to do before heading on to Heaven's Gate. As he hitched Big Horse in front of the shack that served as town jail, he saw Doc emerge from his house.

Bernice and Agatha had already noted Luke's arrival from their boarding house windows. The ladies felt sure he'd come by for a visit to catch up on the latest Nuecestown news. They rushed out the front door and stood anxiously awaiting his sure visit with them.

Luke waited for Doc to amble over. "Doc, what's new?" Next to Bernice and Agatha, Doc pretty much knew every-thing going on around Nuecestown and even Corpus Christi. The good doctor wasn't getting any younger, as years of rough living and booze had taken their toll on him. Luke recalled how typical it was for Doc to sweep empty whiskey bottles off his operating table before he could treat a seriously injured patient. The mixed aromas of booze, Indian herbal remedies, various elixirs, and vomit used to permeate Doc's little office. Despite it all, he was a veritable magician in his ability to heal wounded bodies and to a lesser extent souls. Since he'd stopped boozing, only patients from long past might still detect the telltale smells embedded in the old plaster walls and woodwork.

"Dang, Luke. Great to see you." He coughed, wiping a little blood onto his crumpled handkerchief. "Got a new patient you might want to visit."

"Who might that be, Doc?"

"Horace Rucker's boy, Rex. Got hisself shot by a Sharps."

Luke felt a slight pang, as he recalled having been on the receiving end of a Sharps bullet. "I'll come by for sure. Just have a couple of things to do here before I head to Heaven's Gate." He turned away, then back. "How'd Rex wind up here? He must have been in a bad way."

"Stephen brought him in. Seems they were in a little battle

up toward Brazoria. Rex was wounded, the Yankees were sent on the run, and they wound up near Passe Cavallo where Rex was captured. By some blessed good fortune, Stephen found him and brought him home. Looks like I managed to save his arm, though it won't be good for much but filling a shirtsleeve. Shoulder was torn up bad."

"Blessed, indeed. I'll stop by shortly, Doc."

★

Crouching Lion and his warriors pranced into camp waving lances adorned with fresh scalps. They'd managed to steal a couple of cavalry horses, pilfer a couple of swords, and acquire three Pattern 1853 Enfield rifled muskets with ammunition pouches. The rifles were relatively ancient, but widely used. Importantly, it meant that ammunition would be plentiful.

One Arrow felt a wave of pride as he stood in front of his teepee observing his victorious Penateka Comanche parade into camp. It was almost like the old days. He still preferred the trusty bow and arrow over the rifles, but was pleased that his braves had the foresight to adapt to new weapons.

Crouching Lion pulled up before One Arrow and dismounted. "My chief, I bring gift." He held out a mahogany box, opened it, and turned a handle on its side.

One Arrow stepped back in delighted surprise as the melodious sounds of musical chimes wafted from the box. "You honor me, Crouching Lion. You have done well." He hesitated at first, but then turned the handle of the music box himself. He couldn't help but smile and begin to laugh. It was infectious, as everyone began to laugh. It seemed to have been a long time since there was any joy among the Comanche. They were as children with simple joys.

One Arrow looked around at his people. "We hold council

fire this night. Crouching Lion will tell us of his battle with the gray coats."

For the first time, the chief felt like he'd truly become the leader of his people. He felt good about having delegated the raid to Crouching Lion. It gave the warrior leadership experience. But in his heart, he knew he must lead an attack himself to cement his leadership role. He needed to offer more than having been in a battle where they suffered defeat and in which their chief and strongest warrior had been killed in what turned out to be a jealous contest for power.

He examined the music box more closely. The wood was a beautiful dark red enhanced by a lacquer coating. The figure of an angel turned on a post above the drum that played the chimes. He saw a cross at the foot of the angel and couldn't help but wonder if it held the same power as the cross he wore around his neck. These Whites worshiped a strange spirit that they thought was all-powerful. The Comanche had many gods that answered to the Great Spirit. Other than what Luke told him and stories shared by Three Toes, One Arrow was clueless.

Crouching Lion and the victorious warriors dispersed throughout the camp, turning out their ponies and returning to their teepees and waiting squaws.

One Arrow felt especially good. He turned to Cactus Flower, walked over, and showed her the box. He looked around. Bird Woman was tanning deer hides and had relieved Cactus Flower of her baby for a while. The chief offered Cactus Flower the music box, nodded his head toward the teepee, and they slipped inside.

Bird Woman watched from afar and smiled as the flap to the teepee entrance closed. She was pleased that One Arrow was maturing so quickly as a leader and more so as a man. Perhaps, the future for the Comanche might not be so dim.

Cactus Flower responded eagerly to the chief's manly arousal. She had wondered what had taken him so long to show sexual interest in her. It had been many moons since

Three Toes had laid with her. So it was that she fully spent her passions on One Arrow. If he were to ask, she would readily be a wife to him. He was a handsome Comanche, taller than most, and had some special power that called him to lead his people. She felt his power course through her as he took her.

EIGHTEEN
ANOTHER DUNN

LUKE MADE the turn through the arch at Heaven's Gate. On the ride from Nuecestown, he'd thought long and hard on his conversations with the Ruckers. The near-loss of Rex had put the war into a very personal perspective. The brother-versus-brother dynamic coursed through his head. Back in Ireland, loyalty to the clan would have prevented such a family tragedy. No Irishman worth his salt would have sided with the British. This War Between the States here in America was a different beast. Tragic indeed.

As he quietly led Big Horse into the barn, he looked up at the house. The hired workmen had begun to set a foundation for the addition. With a growing family, they needed another bedroom or two. Despite the war, life did go on.

Once he'd hung his tack, curried Big Horse, and spent a couple of moments with the foal, he began striding up to the house. He did stop at the water trough to rinse off a bit of trail dust. From the barn, he hadn't seen the dark horse hitched to the rail or the vaguely familiar figure sitting on the gallery.

The front door opened with Elisa holding two cups of coffee and offering one to the visitor. She hadn't yet seen Luke walking up.

As Elisa turned to sit, she saw Luke in her peripheral vision. She nearly dropped her cup. "Lucas!" A huge smile spread across her face. She was ready to run to him, but quickly remembered they had a guest...and a hot cup of coffee. Her shoulders slouched just a bit with disappointment. "Lucas, Rip Ford is here." It was stating the obvious.

Luke was equally disappointed. He'd been looking forward to sweeping Elisa off her feet, carrying her upstairs, and ravishing her with unfathomable passions. "Er...Rip, good to see you."

Ford could sense their discomfiture. "Just stopping by, Luke. I'm heading to Brownsville. Afraid New Mexico didn't go so well for us." He stood to shake Luke's hand. "Sorry to interrupt. Guess you've been away a spell, Luke."

"Been fighting Mexicans and Apache mostly, Rip."

"I'd hoped you'd join me in New Mexico, but seems like you were busy. Just as well." He sat back down and took a sip of coffee. "Did you hear about Colonel Kinney?"

"You mean that he was killed a few months back in some gunfight down in Mexico?"

"Shame. He was quite the impresario."

"I guess I might as well be spitting into the wind as ask you if you'd be interested in joining me in Brownsville." Ford glanced at Elisa's ready-to-bust belly.

Luke smiled for the first time. "No point getting your face all wet, Rip."

Elisa handed Luke the cup of coffee she'd been holding. "I've got some bacon, eggs, and biscuits cooking up, gentlemen." She turned to Ford. "Did you hear about the assault on Corpus Christi, Colonel Ford? Captain Ware chased away a passel of Yankee sailors. But Major Hobby has since pulled out, so we're waiting for the Yankees to attack again." There was a tone of resentment in her voice coupled with a hint of frustration.

"Some Yankee named Renshaw's been too busy assaulting

Galveston to care about Corpus Christi, Mrs. Dunn. I hear our army is getting ready to chase Renshaw back into the Gulf. Meanwhile, we've got Juan Cortina's Mexican rebels and a bunch of renegade Apache to deal with down in Brownsville. I'm charged with keeping our trade route to Mexico open."

Luke stole a glance at Elisa. "Rip, I've had my hands full around these parts. Seems to be no shortage of folks trying to steal, cheat, and kill while most of our best men are off fighting a war. Not sure how long it's going to last."

Ford resisted the temptation to be defensive. He had taken to wearing buckskins and sporting a pair of Colt revolvers, so he looked every bit a frontier-style officer. It pretty much suited his disposition and reinforced his perceived role as successful Indian fighter. He stroked his chin and glanced at Elisa before responding to Luke. "Word has it that the Yankees are squabbling over civil liberties, the conduct of the war, and slave emancipation. Lincoln is frustrated with General McClellan, who allowed General Lee to flank him up into Pennsylvania."

Elisa was tempted to roll her eyes in frustration. "What's that got to do with Texas, Colonel?" Of course, Luke was thinking the same thing.

"Well, Colonel Yager's headed up to Sabine Pass to join with our army and kick General Banks's sorry ass...pardon, Mrs. Dunn...er, rear end back to New Orleans."

Luke nodded. "I'm thinking Texas would have done better to have followed Sam Houston's advice and not joined the Confederacy, Rip. Soon as the Yankee President Lincoln finds a general to whip Lee, it'll all be over and Texas will be a loser despite all our efforts. Shoot, we should have just remained an independent republic." Elisa nodded agreement with Luke.

"I understand, Luke. You make a good point." In his heart, Ford had come to realize that the South would eventually succumb to the North's superior resources. But he'd made his commitment to the Confederate cause and would head to Brownsville and do his duty.

Luke knew that Ford couldn't conscript him into serving. "I wish you well fighting Apache, Mexicans, and Yankees down along the Rio Grande, Rip. I'll look after things around these parts." Unsaid was that he wouldn't be venturing out again until Elisa had given birth.

Rip realized there was no persuading Luke to join him. He nodded to Elisa. "Well, I'm mighty grateful for the coffee. If you change your mind, Luke, you know where I'll be."

"No hard feelings, Rip. Before you go, are you sure we can't stuff some breakfast into you? Lord knows, a good meal can soothe the soul." Luke motioned for Rip to join them, though he knew Ford had already made up his mind to go.

"Well, I'm grateful for your hospitality, but I'd best be letting you folks get on with your lives here. I've got to catch up with my unit and head south." He walked to his horse, mounted up, and with a hand laid to the brim of his hat, took his leave of Heaven's Gate.

To say Major Gordon Belknap was frustrated would be a gross understatement. The Union offensive so far as Texas was concerned consisted mostly of the shipping blockade along the Gulf coast. The unsuccessful assault on Corpus Christi, the tenuous holding of Galveston, and General Banks's failures in northeastern Texas on the Sabine River pretty much summed up the Yankee effort. The Union focus remained back east and the Mississippi Valley. The impact of the War Between the States on Texas for all intents and purposes was to disrupt trade so far as possible. Assaults on major Texas cities weren't part of the strategy. So, despite having scrounged up some serviceable mounts and successfully foraging for enough food to fend off starvation, Belknap found himself basically disconnected from his command. He'd failed to reach Colonel Renshaw, who'd led the assault on Galveston. He'd now been reduced to what could best be termed a rogue unit role on the eastern Nueces Strip.

At night, he could see Corpus Christi through his spyglass, but he dared not venture too close. He had no orders and certainly hadn't a clue as to what the current Union strategy was for Texas. With Lieutenant Rucker lost, he relied heavily on his unit sergeant, though this was a new role for both men. He sure didn't intend to get within sight of the Yankee vessels still lurking offshore. He'd had enough of dealing with the Navy.

"Sergeant, I'm of a mind to head south toward Brownsville. Our way north is blocked, and my sense is that there will be Union troops commanding the Confederacy's southernmost trade hub. You've been in the Army a long time, and I value your experience. Feel free to share your thoughts."

"Yes, sir, Major. To be straight, I think heading to Brownsville makes sense. Can't be any worse than our present situation, sir. And we might make life uncomfortable for Rebel trade caravans along the way." He smiled deviously at the last statement. It was an unconventional strategy, more like what Comanche or Apache might do. "We might even find ourselves better horses, sir."

Belknap nodded with a wry grin. "Might dig up better grub, too, right, Sergeant?"

"Yes, sir. Better grub for sure."

"Order the men to mount up, Sergeant. We're moving out."

★

Luke rolled out of bed just before sunup. "Lots for Jaime and me to get to today, Lisa."

"Y'all might not wander far today, Lucas. I've got a feeling that today's the day." She gently rubbed her belly. She took

Luke's hand and placed it on the distended curve of her tummy. "Feel that? This baby is kicking to get out and greet the world." Luke stroked her stomach gently.

Elisa watched as he stood. "My, oh my, Lucas. Rubbing a pregnant woman's belly..." She couldn't help but observe his aroused condition. "What is this child to think?" She turned toward him and began to sit up.

Luke looked tenderly into her deep blue eyes, leaned down, and planted an intensely impassioned kiss.

Her soft full lips were wont to draw the passion from him. She broke away. "You'd better get to your chores, cowboy. I'll fix you a bit of breakfast."

Luke pulled on his trousers and turned to leave the room.

As he was about to ease out the door, Elisa interrupted with just a tad of urgency. "Lucas, how about fetching Julia?" It was time.

Luke was ever amazed at how Elisa managed to deliver a bit more easily than what he'd heard about most women. She pushed hard and there was certainly pain but, after the delivery, she was amazingly fresh and ready to care for her newborn. He dutifully went off, fetched Julia, and heated up some water. He wasn't certain what the water was for, but recalled Doc asking for it.

Julia coached Elisa through the birth, though it didn't take all that long. "*Señor* Dunn! *¡Sube las escaleras!* Come." Julia called down to the kitchen where Luke was awaiting word while trying to fill four hungry mouths.

Luke nearly dropped the fry pan. "Peter, John, watch after your brother and sister. I'll be back shortly." He climbed up the stairs three at a time.

By now, Elisa was resting with their newborn cradled in her arms. "Lucas, we've got another daughter."

Luke took her from Elisa and looked into the baby's dancing dark eyes. "She's beautiful, just like her mother." Luke saw new life as testament to mankind's triumph over life's threats. The prairie-toughened Texas Ranger looked lovingly down at his wife. "Do you have a name in mind?"

Elisa smiled. "I think Alma would be a sweet name, Lucas."

He looked at the tiny newborn gently cradled in his big arms. "Welcome to our family, Alma." Thus, Alma Dunn entered the world, the fifth of Luke and Elisa Dunn's children. Luke placed the little bundle of new life into Elisa's waiting arms. Alma was ravenously hungry.

"Julia, Jaime and I have to go check livestock. Would you watch our children until we return?" He knew Julia loved to have the Dunn children play with her own child. The Sanchez family had lived in the cabin for a couple of years and had become like part of the family. Of course, Jaime was acknowledged around the region as one of the very best *vaqueros*.

★

Luke headed down to the barn where Jaime was already saddling up. "Got another addition to the family, *amigo*."

Jaime smiled. "Congratulations, *Señor* Dunn. Good that you are adding to the house."

They rode out at a trot. With winter about to descend, the herd was down. Jaime had taken about fifty beeves to market. Another hundred beeves had been sold a month before that. The cattle were on the lean side owing to the drought but brought enough income to live fairly comfortably. They'd delayed hiring another *vaquero* until spring. All told, they had roughly 100 head roaming Heaven's Gate. They had close to 5,000 acres to tend and had the prospect of purchasing more. Land was cheaper due to that infernal drought, but big purchases were nevertheless being delayed because of the uncertainty of the war.

They'd ridden a couple of miles when they were alerted by the unusually loud snorting of a couple of longhorns. Whatever was going on was hidden by grasses and brush. Luke put his spurs into Big Horse and headed in the direction of the ruckus with Jaime close behind.

They came to a halt at a clearing where a longhorn cow was resisting a rope lassoed around her horns. The cow had obstinately dug in. Nearby was a three- or four-month-old calf that had been born after the season. He wasn't especially happy either.

At the other hand of the rope was a desperate-looking man on foot. He'd lassoed more than he'd bargained for. A horse that had seen better days stood nearby.

Luke pulled up a few feet away with Jaime behind and off to his right with his rifle at the ready. Luke pulled back his vest to fully reveal his Texas Ranger badge. "Hey, what do you think you're doing?"

The man desperately wanted to release his grip on the rope but feared losing the longhorn. He thought fast. "I'm helping the ranch owner."

"And who might that be?"

The man had all he could handle with the cow. "I...I don't remember."

Luke realized that he wasn't dealing with a common thief. The man looked to be pretty much skin and bones, likely hadn't had a square meal in quite a while. "This is Mr. Dunn's ranch."

"Yes, that's it." The man got the words out through gritted teeth.

"Well, I'm Texas Ranger Captain Luke Dunn, and you've roped one of my beeves." Luke smiled and winked over at Jaime. "Jaime, please see if you can get this cow under control."

The man was relieved upon realizing he wasn't about to be shot for cattle rustling. "I'm sorry."

"What's your name and where are you from?"

"Callahan...George Callahan. I'm from up the road apiece

near San Diego. I lost all my stock to the dry weather. Most of my crops up and died. My wife's sick. We're terribly hungry, Mr. Dunn."

Luke had a certain compassionate nature about him. "Hunger doesn't give cause to take what isn't yours, Mr. Callahan. If you'd come a couple of miles farther, you might have found my home and asked. I know it's tough to ask for charity, but there's no excuse for thieving." The man Luke looked down at was nearly in tears.

Jaime had the longhorn under control, freeing the man to stand. Callahan stood before Luke with his head hung low and shoulders slumped.

"I don't think this cow is yearning to cooperate with you, Mr. Callahan. Let's let her go back to her calf and head on into the range." Luke was still sizing up the man. He found it hard to imagine what it took to drive a man to such desperation as to steal from others. But then, he'd provided well for his family and Callahan apparently wasn't able to deal with misfortune so well. "You mount up and follow us. We'll give you some food to take back to your wife." He let that sink in. "Now, I'm going to forgive you this time, but rest assured another lawman might punish you according to the law."

Callahan looked up at Luke. "I can't thank you enough, Mr. Dunn. I don't deserve—"

"It's not about deserving, Mr. Callahan. It's about folks helping folks in times of trouble."

The three began the ride back to the house.

Luke leaned over toward Jaime and whispered, "Give one of those Yankee army nags to this fellow. Any of them is better than what he's riding."

★

As twilight descended on Heaven's Gate, a rider trotted on up to the house. "Luke...Luke Dunn! You home?"

Luke peeked from the doorway. "Well, I'll be. Lisa, get some coffee, it's my cousin John."

"Can't stay long, Luke, though I do have time for that cup of coffee."

"Well then, come set a spell, cousin."

John Dunn hitched his horse, climbed the stairs to the gallery, and grabbed a seat next to Luke. "How you been faring with the dryness, Luke?"

One would have thought the first subject of the day might most likely have been about the war, but it was weather that mattered most to ranchers and farmers on the Nueces Strip. "We been holding our own. Beeves were a bit leaner than usual when they went to market."

"How's your cotton been holding up?"

Elisa emerged with coffee and the twins in tow. "Mind if I sit in?"

Luke fetched a chair from the other end of the gallery and offered Elisa a seat. "Here you go, sweetheart. And thanks for the coffee."

"There'll be some cornbread ready in a few minutes."

That grabbed John's attention. "Luke, you keep up this sort of hospitality and I'll be moving my family into that new addition you're building." They all had a chuckle at that.

"So, what brings you to Heaven's Gate?" Luke recalled his having mentioned caravanning cotton to Matamoros a while back, so figured that was what the visit was about.

"We've got a few wagons of cotton bales ready to head to Matamoros, Luke. I've got my crews and some outriders as guards, but I'd feel a lot better if the Texas Rangers were close at hand. I wouldn't expect you to spend weeks on the trail with us. The oxen aren't so fast. I'd be much obliged if you could check on us now and again. As you know, there are nasty varmints between here and there." John didn't have to mention the bandits, Apache, and the like.

"I expect we could do that, cousin. I hear tell Costalites has been raiding, and Rip Ford just headed to Brownsville to keep Juan Cortina under control. Fact is, I've locked horns with Apache and Mexicans in the past few weeks."

"I'll be pleased to pay that bonus we agreed on after we've delivered the cotton, Luke. It'll be worth your while."

Luke smiled. "I'd love to simply do it for family, John, but I'm happy to be rewarded in anything but Confederate paper."

John laughed at that. "Not to worry. Those notes surely won't buy anyone much despite what Richmond would have us believe."

Luke looked at Elisa who nodded back. "I'd be happy to conduct some Texas Ranger patrols along your route, cousin. Maybe we can ease your travels."

Another hour passed before John Dunn saddled up and left Heaven's Gate. Elisa's cornbread had the effect of extending visits. It hadn't been until they heard the plaintive hunger cry of newborn Alma, that they realized how much time had passed.

NINETEEN
TEXAN RECKONING

THREE DOZEN APACHE rode hard along the Texas side of the Rio Grande heading in the general direction of Brownsville. They had plenty of extra ponies, so were pushing along harder than might be normal. Besides, they'd left the women and children behind with the wickiups. Costalites had decided to travel fast and light. He'd learned that the blue coats were in Brownsville and a company of the gray coats were headed south to chase them out. He thought he'd add a dimension of confusion by harassing both armies. But that wouldn't be enough by the Apache chief's way of thinking.

Costalites knew that the Mexican rebel Cheno Cortina had a hacienda near Brownsville and that the Mexican often used it as a base of operations. The Apache chief figured that his warriors could throw further confusion into the South Texas mix by attacking Cortina as well. It would be less risky, since he knew that Cheno had encamped back near Rio Grande City and the hacienda would be more vulnerable. The chief hoped to ultimately pit the Mexicans against the Anglos and come away from his efforts with horses and cattle. He relished the idea of sowing chaos for his own advantage. It seemed well worth eating a diet of Nueces Strip dust toward sating his people's lust for scalps and horses while eliminating the hated invaders from their territory.

*

Things tended to slow a mite around Heaven's Gate during the winter. Given that the Yankees didn't seem inclined to mount any significant offensive just yet around Corpus Christi, Luke thought it was a good time to lead a patrol southward. In part, he'd fulfill his obligation to his cousin with his cotton-laden caravan, but he intuitively knew there was likely to be trouble most anywhere he roamed on the Nueces Strip. He'd persuaded Barber and JD to join him once again, but Jubal Strong had signed on with his cousin Nick. Strong had been immediately assigned duty with the Dunn cotton caravan, thus already committed to guarding it on its entire southward journey to Matamoros.

"What you expecting to dig up this time, Captain?" Barber knew that wherever the trio went trouble would be assured. Any smart betting man would do well never to bet against some sort of danger on the Nueces Strip. They'd departed Nuecestown a couple of days earlier and were traveling easily down the coast. They'd even gotten used to JD's special female needs as concerned answering nature's call.

"No telling, Jake. There's a caravan of wagons loaded with cotton headed to Mexico. The wagons are heavy and the oxen are slow. They're an inviting target, though to be straight I expect they'll be more valuable prey when they head north after selling the cotton. They hired extra men as guards, a couple of cowboys, and a cook. Our friend Jubal hired on with them. Truth be told, I promised John Dunn that I'd check on them."

"They bringing any goods north, Captain?"

"If you mean guns and ammunition, I've been assured that they will only carry trade goods."

JD had been taking in the conversation. "Did you say Jubal Strong had hired on to join the caravan, Captain Dunn?"

Luke smiled inwardly. He'd sensed that JD and Jubal had begun to take a shine to each other. They'd had a couple of private conversations that he'd taken note of. "That's what I was told, JD."

Barber chuckled and boldly asked, "You interested in the cowboy, JD?"

JD blushed a bit. "None of your business, Jake Barber."

With that, Barber slowed his mount and fell back a few paces so he could more fully enjoy his bemusement.

JD stared intently at Luke's back as he rode in front of her. "It's not funny, Captain."

Luke turned back in his saddle to face her. "We're not laughing at you, JD. Hope it works out for you. Jubal seems to be a good man." He turned back to the front, looked ahead, and brought Big Horse to a sudden halt. "Quick! Dismount and stay low!"

They tried to duck down below the tops of the grasses. "Listen," he whispered. Whatever Luke heard must have posed a possible threat.

Luke kept his voice low. "Let's move back into the grasses. Stay quiet."

JD and Barber looked at each other and obediently snuck into the tall grass. They instinctively grabbed their rifles.

Soon enough, a column of bluecoats passed by their position. Luke was amazed that he hadn't been spotted. Far as he could tell, they had no one riding point. They were certainly making too much noise, as he'd heard them before he'd seen them. He watched the tired, travel-weary faces slowly ride on by. By Luke's judgment, these Yankees hadn't seen a real battle yet. On the other hand, this was a six-man patrol which meant that a larger force couldn't be too far away.

Luke waited a few minutes until the column was out of both sight and hearing. "Okay, let's mount up. Keep your eyes peeled. There may be more bluecoats around." Luke decided to head further inland, as he judged the Yankees to be inclined to stay closer to the Gulf shores. Likely as not, the Dunn caravan wouldn't be hugging the coast either.

"Captain, look at this." JD pointed to a broken wheel lying along the bank of a nearby arroyo.

Luke glanced at it but didn't slow down. "Guess those heavy wagons take their toll. It's rough country for sure."

Yankees and a broken wagon wheel were pretty much the extent of the day's excitement.

★

One Arrow looked off from the top of the escarpment. So far as his eyes could see, the vista before him was in a word: majestic. There were no sign of Anglos, Mexicans, gray coats, bluecoats, or other tribes. In his heart, he knew that wouldn't last long, but for now...well, he was grateful for the valuable time his little band of Penateka Comanche had been afforded to regroup. He had time to go off several times to commune with the Great Spirit. It had given him time to think further on Ghost-Who-Rides, his relationship with Three Toes, and what was to become of the once-mighty Comanche.

His band had been blessed with the addition of three more families of Comanche that had escaped Fort Cooper and been wandering around seeking a place to settle. Crouching Lion had become an asset, and the chief and this maturing warrior had hunted deer together several times. Perhaps the best news was that Cactus Flower believed she was carrying One Arrow's child. The Comanche chief's world was good...for the present.

★

The cotton caravan plodded slowly southward. Five

wagons rolled along, each with a driver seated beside an armed guard. A mule-drawn lighter-weight covered wagon was provided for the cook, a dozen heavily armed outriders kept their eyes peeled for danger, and two half-breeds riding point as scouts made for a formidable procession. John Dunn was amazed that they'd traveled more than halfway to the border without incident. They were a huge target for anyone with enough firepower to take them on. After all, there was no hiding such a caravan. So far as Dunn was concerned, the war was right here and now on the Nueces Strip.

His peace of mind wasn't to last much longer.

★

"Empty?" Costalites was incredulous at what his scouts were telling him. His nemesis Juan Cheno Cortina had abandoned his hacienda.

"You certain?" These scouts were among the Apache chief's best warriors. They were his eyes on the prairie. He trusted them. The chief stood perplexed beside his pony. He squinted as he looked eastward as though trying to make an enemy appear.

The scouts weren't finished with their news. "Many blue-coats in city they call Brownsville. Gray coats come and cross big river."

All of this was unsettling news for Costalites. He wouldn't dream of doubting his scouts, but there was much unanswered. Had Cortina truly abandoned his hacienda? Where were the gray coats now? How many bluecoats were in Brownsville? What would the gray coats be doing in Mexico? The Apache had ridden hard to get close to Cortina's hacienda and now appeared to be in a quandary. Costalites really didn't want to hang around, but his warriors lusted for booty and scalps.

Brownsville was well defended by the Yankees. Even Rip

Ford had skirted the city, as he hadn't enough men and weapons to mount an effective assault. The Apache band was even smaller. The best the Apache chief could hope for was to attack any patrols the bluecoats sent out. He paused thoughtfully, every bit the savage turned general working out a new strategy in his mind. He finally turned to his scouts. He pointed northward. He'd decided a full-frontal attack on the bluecoats was out of the question, and he wasn't about to take on armies below the border, whether gray coats or Mexican. "Go north. Now." It was a fishing expedition, but worth a try.

★

"There they are, Captain." Barber had spotted what was surely the caravan kicking up dust about two miles distant.

"I want to go around them, Jake. Let's get ahead of the scout's riding point. I want to see what they're heading into." With that, he turned back toward the east where the ground was more level, rode about a mile on level ground through tall grasses, and then picked up their pace as they headed south.

It didn't take but a couple of hours to easily pass the caravan without alerting it to the Texas Ranger presence. The three soon found themselves several miles ahead. The terrain remained mostly grassy and flat.

"Captain, look to your right." JD had spied riders well off in the distance.

Luke took out his spyglass to get a better look. "Humph! Apache scouts from the look of them. Good eye, JD." This would certainly not be welcome news for the cotton caravan. He dismounted, and JD and Barber followed suit. "Doesn't appear that they saw us." Luke looked northward. "They've surely spotted the caravan."

The Apache scouts rode a bit farther before turning about and scampering south.

"Let's follow them for a bit. If Costalites is around, it'd help to know how many of those damned savages he has with him." They mounted up and began to track the Apache scouts from a distance.

The three Texas Rangers didn't have to ride but an hour, and Costalites's band came into full view.

"What do you think, Captain? Shall we take them on?" Barber was sort of joking, but he'd have charged if Luke was of a mind to.

"Let's head back north and alert the caravan. The Apache haven't seen us. Besides, they have far bigger prey on their minds." He was confident that the Apache chief was too far excited with the news from his scouts to have spotted Luke and his little band.

TWENTY

WAR ON THE PRAIRIE

"HALT! WHO GOES?"

Luke reined in Big Horse a mere 20 yards from John Dunn's half-breed pickets. That he'd managed to get so close without detection had surely unsettled the two men. Luke responded calmly. "Texas Ranger Captain Luke Dunn. We come with news for Mr. Dunn."

The scouts gave them the once-over. Being half-breeds, there was a naturally suspicious side to them owing to the unflattering ways they were often treated. Which side held suspicion was a matter of some debate. They waved Luke through. Had he mentioned that the caravan was headed toward a large band of Apache, the scouts likely would have headed back to the caravan with him.

It didn't take long for the Rangers to reach the caravan as it plodded along. John Dunn was riding a horse out front with his son Nicholas alongside. Luke could see Strong riding beside the third wagon. Luke held his hand up as they approached.

"Captain Dunn, I'd say the look on your face spells trouble ahead."

"You're an observant man, John. There's a passel of Apache hostiles up ahead. They mean to make trouble."

"Well, a few of my men have experience fighting Indians, Captain. Can't imagine the Apache are all that different from Comanche or Kiowa. We kill a handful, and they'll run off for sure. Death is bad medicine."

Luke smiled at John Dunn's confidence. "I'd like to think you're right. The biggest problem is that they have rifles and have learned how to use them."

The upgraded Apache weaponry certainly had to be considered. Luke looked at the terrain surrounding them. "We need a defensive position, John. I'd circle your wagons up on that rise over yonder. It'll make it tougher for them to attack riding uphill. Put all the livestock in the center of the circle. You can't afford to lose any oxen."

By this time, the half-breed scouts had ridden hard to join the caravan. "They are on their way, Captain Dunn. 'Bout thirty or so Apache." Sure enough there was a dust cloud swirling up from the south.

Luke smiled. "They likely know they've been spotted, but not that we'll be ready for them. Let's hurry and get those wagons circled up."

Costalites stopped less than a half mile from the caravan. It was time to think about his next step. His warriors were itching to fight. Having been disappointed by the absence of Cheno Cortina and facing too formidable a foe in Brownsville, the caravan was thought to be easy pickings. However, it was fast becoming obvious that the caravan was aware of their presence.

The Apache chief sent two warriors ahead to scout the caravan. They returned quickly to report that the wagons had been circled in a defensive position. Costalites wondered how they'd been warned. At least he wondered until one of the scouts spoke up. "Big man Comanche call Ghost-Who-Rides is there." The chief shook his head with consternation. The Texas Ranger seemed to be everywhere lately.

Costalites gathered his war chiefs. He might not get another chance to fight Luke. "We set trap here." He pointed to the surrounding ground that formed a natural funnel in the landscape. They all knew the plan. The Apache would lure the Anglos into chasing them and lead them right into their ambush. Once the mounted White men were eliminated, the wagons would be relatively easy. The chief began to feel very confident. "I will lead attack."

The chief led about twenty warriors out at a fast trot. His remaining braves stayed back hidden behind and spread across the two rises that formed the trap. Unlike the Comanche that had mostly bows and arrows, the Apache were all armed with rifles.

★

"They're coming!" Luke raised his spyglass and spotted the Apache approaching. "Do not fire until I give the signal. When they retreat, do not follow!"

The wagons bristled with rifles. The defenders were fairly well protected by the heavy wood wagons and the cotton itself. The oxen, mules, and horses had been corralled inside the defensive circle. There'd be no prizes for the Apache unless they successfully breached the circle.

Costalites's Apache opened fire as they galloped directly toward the wagons, then his force divided and circled the wagon fortress.

Luke returned fire, and the defenders responded with a blistering fusillade.

JD whooped and nearly did a dance as she shot an Apache from his pony. Strong was positioned beside her. He looked admiringly at the fire in her eyes. Her performance confirmed that there could be no other woman in his life. She caught his look, winked at him, and reloaded.

Chief Costalites spotted Ghost-Who-Rides astride the big gray horse inside the circle of wagons. The Texas Ranger had set an excellent defense. This second meeting in battle was going every bit as poorly as the first. If there was an Apache word for "damn," the chief would have uttered it. Nevertheless, Costalites stuck with his plan.

To Costalites's chagrin, four more Apache were shot from their ponies. The chief was undeterred. He reformed his battle line of warriors, turned, and led them off at a gallop toward where they'd set the ambush.

One of the caravan guards was so excited that he took off after the fleeing warriors. He hadn't gone far when he realized he was alone. The man stopped to turn back, but it was too late. He was felled by a hail of Apache gunfire.

Costalites halted his warriors and turned to realize that he'd drawn only one poor soul into his trap. He'd lost four warriors killed in the assault on the caravan and another couple wounded. This was not a good day. He waved his rifle, pointing it to the south. The Apache would escape. Better to do battle another day.

Back at the caravan, Luke was praised with whoops, hollers, and a lot of hat-waving as the defenders had followed his strategy and fended off the Apache attack without losing a single man, except for the one that had unfortunately gotten carried away in the moment. Oxen, mules, and horses were unharmed.

"Mr. Dunn, I believe it's safe to reform your caravan. The Apache won't be back." Luke had learned from experience that the Indians had no stomach for extended battles. Having lost several warriors, he knew the savages would cut their losses and high tail it out of the area. "I'll stay with you for just a little way into Mexico, then you should have safe travels... assuming you can trust the Mexican government."

Dunn nodded. He was all too well aware of the history of broken promises by a succession of Mexican presidents.

★

The noise of battle had attracted Major Belknap. It hadn't lasted long, but it was clear that it hadn't been some hunting expedition. He had been heading toward Brownsville along the coast and investigating the gunfire wouldn't take him out of his way. He was angry and frustrated at being isolated on the Nueces Strip with inadequate food and water and barely serviceable nags for transportation. "Let's go, Sergeant." He wanted to move out at the double, but knew the horses couldn't handle much more than a brisk walk, a canter at best.

The major's troop rode a couple of miles until they crested a hill and could see the cotton caravan off in the distance. From what he could observe through his spyglass, the caravan was slowly wending its way southward with its burst-at-the-seams cargo of cotton. He'd heard that such caravans were being used due to the effectiveness of the Yankee blockade of the Texas coast. He looked long and hard. "Damn!"

"What is it, sir?" The sergeant was right next to him, so Belknap's reaction couldn't be missed.

"I can't believe it. He gets everywhere!"

"Who, sir?"

"It's that Texas Ranger Captain Luke Dunn. He seems to be helping guard the caravan. Can't miss him on that big gray horse." Belknap slipped the spyglass back into its case and looked longingly out across the Nueces Strip toward Luke and the caravan. He was disinclined to confront his old friend in any case.

"Shall we engage, sir?" The sergeant knew that was pretty

much a rhetorical question. The troop was seriously outnumbered and outgunned, as well as in decidedly hostile territory.

"Sergeant, we'll resume riding to Brownsville." He figured his troop might manage to move just a little faster than the ox-drawn wagons and arrive in time to alert the Union force occupying the town. They could choose to send troops out to intercept the caravan. He didn't see warning the garrison as making him any sort of hero, but at least his troop would have served a purpose. More importantly, it would lift the men's spirits.

The caravan continued to wend its way along the rutted trail south. The slow but steady oxen were reliable beasts, to say the least. John Dunn was feeling cautiously optimistic as they approached the Rio Grande. The half-breed scouts had earned their keep by steering them on a route that snaked its way between Brownsville with its Union troops and Santa Rita. Under cover of darkness and fighting the river currents, they'd managed to cross the Rio Grande. They yet had a little way to go to reach Matamoros, but at least the threat of Yankee troops was eliminated.

Luke stuffed his Texas Ranger badge in his pocket and advised JD and Barber to do the same. There was no point in inciting Mexicans who might be harboring grudges against the *Rinches Tejanos*. Luke rode up beside John Dunn and the lead wagon. "Cousin, I expect you won't be needing Texas Rangers from here on. We might be more trouble than help, given the general attitude of these fine Mexican folks toward Texas Rangers. Last time I was down here, I didn't make any friends." Luke thought back to James Callahan's less-than-friendly and near-disastrous depredations nearly a decade back.

"I appreciate your help, Luke. Had it not been for you,

we'd have had a tough go of it against those Apache savages. I'll see that you get your due when we return."

Jubal Strong rode up alongside. "Pardon, Luke…Mr. Dunn. Looks as though you'll be heading back, Captain." He looked over at JD and smiled.

JD blushed at his attention to her. His rapt gaze at her back during the battle had set a fire in her own heart.

"Seems the right thing to do, Jubal. No point in overstaying our welcome, and we need to tend to business back in Corpus." Luke had long ago figured the reason behind Strong's ongoing interest in what the Texas Rangers were up to. He'd obviously been developing a man-sized hankering for JD.

"I expect I'll be back up to Nuecestown in a few weeks. Nick Dunn is going to hire me as ranch foreman. It'll be solid steady work."

It was easy for Luke to figure where this conversation was headed. "That's great, Jubal. Hope you'll stop by Heaven's Gate from time to time."

Strong leaned forward and lowered his voice to a near whisper. "To be straight, Captain…well…Janet…I mean JD says she's missed her monthly bleeding. We're planning to hitch up when I get back." Strong glanced at JD and then back at Luke.

Luke shook his head friendly-like. He'd thought that hint of a bump at JD's belly wasn't from overeating. "Kinda figured you two had a little something going, Jubal. You seemed to get things out of order. You're supposed to hitch up first, but I'm happy for you both. I expect you'll make a good life for her. If JD needs any advice, feel free to have her visit Elisa."

Strong was relieved. His journey had taken him from the North Platte River country up north to Texas to investigate how his outlaw brother had died to falling in love with Texas. Having lost his wife and children to freezing cold and starvation back near Fort Laramie, he returned to fight beside his new friend Luke Dunn before finding himself blessed with a new love to begin life anew. In a sense, he'd experienced a sort of redemption from the difficult challenges that the dangers of the hostile western frontier had thrown his way. He motioned for JD to join them.

JD nudged her pony forward with just a touch of trepidation. She looked from Strong to Luke. "Y'all talkin' 'bout me?"

Luke gave up a gentle smile. "You are an amazing woman JD. I thought you were out to shoot bandits and Apache, but what you were really doing was showing off for Jubal here." He gave an infectious laugh.

John Dunn couldn't help but overhear and joined in the laughter. "Y'all are welcome to come marry at my spread."

"Jubal, Jake and I will take good care of her on our ride home. See you soon." Luke turned Big Horse away, and the trio headed back toward Texas. JD gave a few over-the-shoulder looks back at Strong as they rode off. She'd wanted to plant a goodbye kiss on him, but there were simply too many men around, and she saw no point in embarrassing her man.

The caravan restarted its journey to Matamoros.

There were about two dozen of the Mexican dragoons resting in the shade of a small cluster of cypress trees a few miles south of the Rio Grande. A bit of Spanish Moss hung lazily from the tree branches. They were resting their horses to the extent that they'd removed the saddles, and they'd pitched a couple of tents. Tunics had been tossed nonchalantly over the saddles lying about near clusters of saltgrass and a few prickly pear cacti.

"*Si, teniente, vi una caravana a medio día al sur.*" The scout had just returned from reconnoitering the region and had seen the Dunn cotton caravan. Mexico had a treaty with the Confederacy, but sought to be sure that any goods passing through were accounted for such that any tariffs…also known as bribes…could be collected.

"*¿Cuanto?*" The lieutenant was having to work at pulling the information from the scout. He lamented the poor training the scouts must receive that they were unable to provide full reports at the outset. He thought information like knowing how many wagons there were would make perfect sense.

"*Cuatro vagones, teniente.*" The scout thought another moment. "*Cargado de algodon.*" He at least anticipated the lieutenant's question about a cargo of cotton.

The lieutenant scratched his head and sighed. Four wagons filled with cotton. "*¿A dónde van ellos?*" Of course, the officer needed to know where they were headed, though he intuitively knew. All such caravans were destined for Matamoros. From there, goods were sent down river to the coast for loading onto ships docked in Bagdad. It was a port big enough to handle major trade, and the Union Navy dared not blockade the Mexican coast.

"*Van a Matamoros, teniente.*"

The lieutenant sighed again. It was a warm muggy day. They'd been riding for several hours, and he was not inclined to chase down even a slow-moving trade caravan. "*Gracias.*" He waved the scout away and sat down to lean against his saddle.

"*¡Teniente!*"

Just as he was about to relax, a dragoon shouted out. The man was pointing off into the distance to the east of where they were resting.

El Teniente Valdez jumped to his feet and peered out toward where the dragoon was pointing.

"*¡Caramba!*" Valdez motioned to his dragoons to saddle up.

★

"Doesn't that just figure, Luke? Just a couple of miles from the Rio Grande and safety of Texas and here come the damned dragoons." Barber was first to see the low-lying dust cloud off to their west.

"Think we can outrun them?" JD was up for a run. "My horse feels pretty good, Captain."

Luke spurred Big Horse to a gallop. "What y'all waiting for?" Luke especially didn't want to deal with any Mexican military. He'd had plenty of that back in his days riding with Texas Ranger Captain Callahan.

The three leaned forward low in the saddle and urged their horses northward. They soon found themselves gazing into the brown waters of the Rio Grande.

Luke looked over his shoulder. The dragoons were closing, but the trio would be getting across with plenty of time to spare. Luke turned to look at the Texas side of the Rio Grande. He urged Big Horse into the water. Barber and JD followed suit.

"Damn!" As Big Horse began to climb from the river, Luke saw a Yankee patrol off to his right. With tired mounts, Mexican dragoons behind them, and now a half dozen mounted Union soldiers too close for comfort, Luke was in a major quandary. He hoped Big Horse had more hard riding in his heart. His bigger worry was JD's and Barber's horses. He looked across the river. To Luke, the redcoats on the dragoons were like waving a red cape in front of an angry bull. He fought the temptation to throw caution to the winds and charge the Mexicans. He glanced over his shoulder. The Yankee patrol had seen him and had begun to give chase.

The dragoons whooped and hollered and fired from across the river, but the Texas Rangers and even the Union troops were beyond their accurate range. *El teniente* was fuming in his frustration, but there wasn't really much he could do. Nevertheless, bullets ricocheted in the shoreline dirt between them and the river.

There was plenty of tall grass to ride into. Luke restrained his urge to turn and fight the red-coated dragoons, waved his hat at *El Teniente*, and spurred Big Horse deeper into Texas. He hoped to find a mesquite or live oak motte where they could defend against the Yankees.

Of a sudden, Luke pulled up short, turned and headed back to the riverbank. JD and Barber shot past him before stopping a few feet beyond. They perplexedly looked back. Luke was obviously angry at the dragoons firing into Texas. They couldn't know that he was struggling to put from his mind his momentary flashback to the barbarically cruel British redcoats in Ireland. Instead, he became the picture of cool calculation.

JD and Barber watched in amazement, as Luke calmly drew his Sharps rifle from its scabbard, dismounted, and sat on the bank between two large clumps of grass. He slipped a cartridge into the breech, took careful aim across the river, exhaled slightly, held his breath, and squeezed the trigger.

El Teniente Valdez's horse dropped from under him. Luke smiled, leaped onto Big Horse, and galloped past the jaw-gaping JD and Barber. They could hear the jangling of swords, as the Yankees drew closer behind them.

A motte loomed ahead, and Luke led them straight to it. From there, the three of them could hold off most any attack the size of the Yankee patrol. They dismounted and quickly crouched beneath the mesquite branches, rifles at the ready.

"Luke, why the hell did you shoot the dragoon's horse?"

Luke kept his eyes on the spot where he expected the Yankees to emerge. "Just sending a message, JD. In my heart, I wanted to kill the dragoon."

JD looked puzzled. "Why didn't you?"

"He hadn't done anything to warrant it. It'd have been revenge, JD, not justice. I'll explain it to you sometime."

Just then the Union patrol pulled up perhaps fifty yards from the Texas Ranger hiding place. A sergeant led the contingent. He held up and peered intently at the mesquite motte. He knew at least a couple of folks were in it, but couldn't quite make out who or what he was up against. "Yo, there! Identify yourselves!"

Luke reckoned to cast some doubt in the sergeant's mind. Without moving a muscle and keeping his finger alongside the rifle trigger, he retorted, "Who wants to know?" His thinking was that the sergeant wouldn't expect to be challenged.

"Sergeant Johnson, United States Army. Lay down your weapons and come out with your hands high." The sergeant still sat astride his horse as did his troopers.

Luke was amazed that the bluecoats remained mounted. They were easy targets. "Dang, Sergeant Johnson, you've just happened to come upon the damnedest luck anyone in these parts could ever hope to have run into. I'm Texas Ranger Captain Luke Dunn, and I've got two Rangers with me. It's your misfortune, Sergeant, to be a mounted target with three rifles aimed at you and your troopers. We are excellent marksmen, and you would lose at least three of your men in a mere heartbeat. I suggest you lay down your weapons and dismount."

The sergeant's jaw dropped as he realized the Rangers had the drop on him. He slipped his rifle back into its scabbard and motioned his men to do the same before dismounting. "Truce, Captain Dunn. Please...don't shoot."

Luke, JD, and Barber came out from under the mesquite with rifles still at the ready.

The sergeant saw Luke, and his eyes widened as he looked up at the big well-armed Ranger. "Damn, I've heard one of our officers talk of you, Captain." The sergeant's men looked at him in bewilderment. "Er...what you planning to do with us now that we're looking down the barrels of those fine Sharps rifles?"

"You know Major Belknap, sergeant?"

"Yes, yes, I do, sir."

"Give him my regards. I've had the pleasure of fighting alongside him." Luke thoughtfully stroked his mustache for a moment. "Tell you what, Sergeant, given that y'all are our prisoners and, with all due respect to Major Belknap, let's all take a stroll back down to the river."

JD and Barber led the horses while Luke kept his rifle at the ready. Once at the banks of the Rio Grande, Luke had them stop. He scanned across the river, but the dragoons had gone. The only evidence was *El Teniente's* dead horse. "Sergeant, you and your men remove your boots and wade a piece out into the river." Luke turned to JD and Barber. "Unsaddle their horses and put the boots with the saddles. Hobble the horses, so at least they won't have to chase them far."

The sergeant knew he was getting off light. "I hope we meet again under better circumstances, Captain Dunn." He'd been shown mercy at a time of war and deeply appreciated his situation.

"I do hope that happens, Sergeant. I expect y'all don't like this war any better than we do. I pray you make it through safely." Luke mounted Big Horse and turned back to Sergeant Johnson. "And watch out for those confounded Apaches, Sergeant. By my estimation, y'all look better keeping your hair on top of your heads." He gave a wry smile and led JD and Barber away.

★

Edward Thorpe read and reread the message Samuel had handed to him. "Where'd you get this, Samuel?"

"She didn't say her name, Mr. Thorpe."

Thorpe thought on that. A woman spy? He smiled. "Was she pretty, Samuel?" He didn't know why he asked, but he was curious.

Samuel wasn't quite sure what to say. "I guess for a White woman, Mr. Thorpe. I'm not a good judge." He looked down, then looked back up at Thorpe. "She was young, sort of smallish, well-dressed, and had dark hair."

Thorpe tried to visualize that. A young, good-looking, classy woman likely could pass through enemy lines more easily than a man. She'd get attention but not the same as might be reserved for a man. "The note says I'm to take a room in San Antonio at the Menger Hotel. Let's get me packed up, Samuel."

Thorpe had no idea what lay in store for him. As he was learning, there were quite a few folks that didn't support the Confederacy or the war. He'd found this especially true among those of German descent who'd settled largely in central Texas. Given that most of the action was occurring along the coast and up the Sabine River, places like Austin and San Antonio were relatively insulated from the actual fighting.

His plantation managers were handling affairs at Magnolia, so he didn't have that burden weighing on his mind. He remained driven to be what his father was not...except for being wealthy. He simply had different intentions for his wealth. Thorpe figured it would be more worthy to be remembered for good works than feared as some evil threat. In any case, he had no idea how long he might be waiting in San Antonio or for what. He couldn't help but wonder at the woman who'd delivered the message to Samuel.

Luke and his Rangers moved northward toward Corpus Christi as quickly as their horses would allow.

Early on, the ever-curious JD peppered Luke with questions like why he'd shown mercy to the Yankees and what was he thinking when he ordered the sergeant to surrender. But the big question on her mind finally had to gush from her lips, as she simply couldn't hold it back. She feared it might be too personal to Luke. "Captain, if you don't mind...why didn't you kill the dragoon lieutenant?"

"Guess I said I'd tell you, didn't I, JD?"

Barber was all ears as he rode alongside. He earnestly wanted to profit from what his Texas Ranger boss and mentor had to teach.

Luke sat his saddle straight and tipped his hat back just a tad. He took an easy breath. "Well, it began back in Ireland about ten years ago. Americans had right nasty battles with the British here in America not so long ago and so did my clan back in County Kildare. The British oppressed us at every turn, taking our crops at a whim and torturing my countrymen for sins as little as stealing a bit of bread to feed a starving family. The potato famine came, went, and came again. I joined a band of rebels. I was a sight, JD, with my kilt, claymore, and musket."

"A kilt?"

Luke smiled. "It's a knee-length skirt that fighting men wore. It had a lot of advantages."

She tried to picture Luke in a kilt. "What's a claymore?"

"Ah, it's a type of sword. Very effective in close quarters battle. 'Twas bigger than a Bowie knife but shorter than a cavalry saber." Luke made a motion in the air as if swinging a claymore. "Well, the British didn't like our standing up for our rights as supposedly free men. They were even trying to get us to give up our Celtic language, our heritage."

Luke rode on silently for another minute. "One day, a rider came and warned us that British warships had landed at Dublin and soldiers were marching toward Kildare. We were full of ourselves and confident we could whip them in their spit-and-polish brass with their fancy scarlet coats. 'Course they were equipped with rifles featuring long bayonets."

"So, a bunch of your countrymen were going to fight the British?" JD shook her head. She'd heard about the American Revolution and had found how amazing it was that the ragtag Americans had won.

"We plunged headlong at them, JD. But they stood in long rows and began to march forward toward us with bayonets fixed. 'Twas a fearsome sight, but no matter that to us. We were like wild men desperate to protect our homes and families. I likely slayed a couple of soldiers. My claymore was covered slick with blood. It was spattered all over me. But the redcoats kept coming and killing...and killing. They even killed the helpless wounded and the dying. We began to retreat. We ran, and they began to hunt us down. I saw my fellow clansmen captured, tortured for British sport, and killed." Luke paused as though he was re-experiencing the struggle. A bit of the red that comes with anger colored his neck, and he set his jaw firmly. He took a deep breath. "By the grace of God, I survived. I made it to the coast, found a small boat, and rowed across the Irish Sea." He pinched his nose between his eyes, as though trying to make a headache go away. "At a port called Liverpool, I snuck onto a sailing ship with a cargo headed to America. Only when I'd gotten onboard did I discover that it was headed to a faraway place some cousins had told me about. It was called Texas. We arrived at Galveston, and the rest is history as I made my way to Corpus Christi and found my cousins. That's pretty much the story. Those redcoats get my dander up. Seems it brought me to the attention of the Texas Ranger leaders in Austin for my effectiveness in fighting with James Callahan." Luke gave JD and Barber a now-you-know look, gently kicked his heels into Big Horse's flanks, and moved ahead. "Thinking on it, it was a shame that Callahan was killed— some say murdered—a couple of years later in some sort of affair of honor." He shook his head ruefully. "A shame indeed."

JD and Barber had listened with rapt attention. Luke generally wasn't one to string more than a couple of sentences together. It was clear to them from the intensity of how he spoke that what he'd experienced with the troubles in Ireland had fully shaped the successful lawman he had become in Texas. He was about justice...and redemption.

★

Brownsville was a bustling town, to say the least. There was an understandable tension between the mostly Hispanic citizens and the occupying Union soldiers. For the Mexicans, it was both a trade mecca as well as a beachhead of sorts should the Treaty of Guadalupe Hidalgo ever be relegated to the trash heap of memories most would like to forget.

Major Gordon Belknap sat on a bench and smoked a cigar as he enjoyed a bit of relaxation after having endured his travails up the coast near Matagorda Bay. He took long tugs on the cigar and would occasionally hold it out at arm's length before him and wonder how it seemed to foster an easier spirit within him. He'd sent word of his whereabouts to Colonel Renshaw, the commander occupying Galveston, and hoped his explanation of the encounter with Rebel forces was sufficient.

"Major Belknap?" An orderly interrupted the major's quietude.

Belknap gave a barely audible sigh of resignation to his fate. He casually returned the salute. "What do you have, soldier?"

"This just arrived for you, sir." He handed Belknap an envelope, gave a snappy salute, and left the major to do as he would with the message.

Belknap broke the seal, took a deep breath, and opened the envelope. "Damn," he whispered under his breath. He snubbed out the cigar on the porch railing, grabbed his hat, and headed out to find his commanding officer.

★

An unseasonably warm wind wafted in from the southwest. The prevailing winds through central Texas generally came from the south, unless a winter norther charged through with cold winds gestated up in the Colorado Rockies. One

Arrow stood at the perimeter of his encampment deep in thought. He heard Cactus Flower approach. She stirred the surrounding leaves to avoid surprising him.

She reached out and touched his arm. "One Arrow. I have news."

His train of thought broken, he looked distractedly at her. It was unusual for her to disturb him when he was obviously contemplating serious matters. "What is it, Cactus Flower?" He forced his expression to soften. "What news do you bring?" He looked down at her growing belly.

She noticed where his eyes were looking. "I'm sure child is boy. He kick strong."

One Arrow's immediate thought was, why had she disturbed him with this not so significant news? He looked inquiringly at her. Her eyes said there was something more. He glanced back at the small collection of teepees that comprised the village. His people were busy with the multitude of chores that represented the life of their culture. One Arrow turned back to Cactus Flower and placed his arm around her shoulder, pulling her closer. She didn't resist. "What is your news?" He repeated the earlier question.

She turned serious. "There is talk among Crouching Bear and the warriors to hunt horses."

The chief thought a moment on this news. He knew that a horse hunt either meant stealing from a ranch or scouring the prairie for wild mustangs. Both would place his warriors at risk. "Thank you, Cactus Flower. This is council matter."

She was pleased that he found her news important and that she was appreciated. Smiling softly, she pulled away, leaving only her hand in his. Cactus Flower had the chief's undivided attention. She felt a surge course through her body. She wanted him. Her eyes fell to the rising response at his loins.

One Arrow allowed her to lead him to a sheltered clear area behind the cypress. Her buckskin dress fell easily from her shoulders as his hands sought and gently stroked her pregnancy-swollen breasts.

Spasms surged through her body like a cascading river of passion. She pulled him tightly, taking him deeply to her inner core. She locked her legs around his hips as their rhythmic motions built to a crescendo. She felt she might burst as his love exploded within her.

As their bodies parted, One Arrow lay on his back and stared up into the bright blue sky. A warm breeze played across the clearing. He stared admiringly at Cactus Flower. She was a beautiful woman made even more so by the child all too obviously evidenced by her growing belly. "You are good woman, Cactus Flower." Love was implied but somehow never spoken. There really wasn't a Comanche word for it.

"I must help Bird Woman," she whispered. She rose and pulled herself together before heading back to the village.

TWENTY-ONE
WINNERS & LOSERS

THORPE STRODE down into the lobby of the Menger Hotel. The hotel was well-appointed, conjuring a more civilized image of frontier Texas. And San Antonio in the winter wasn't half bad. It occurred to him that the weather was generally milder than what he'd experienced back east yet not so warm and humid as his Magnolia plantation in east Texas.

He helped himself to a cup of coffee and took a seat on a settee in the lobby. Whoever he was to meet was to appear that morning.

Two gray-clad officers walked past and out the entrance. They were clearly of no immediate concern. The men were engaged in intense conversation and didn't even look his way.

An hour passed, and Thorpe refilled his coffee. Maybe his contact was not going to show. Travel could be uncertain and this was enemy territory for this person he was to meet. His mind strayed to wondering about the woman who'd delivered the message to Samuel. Perhaps, when all of this was ended, he'd venture to meet her.

Edward Thorpe's musings were interrupted soon enough by a visitor who sat in the chair at right angles to the settee he occupied. The man was dressed in a gray three-piece suit as was the fashion of the time. Yet, there was a military bearing about him.

The visitor looked Thorpe's way. "Pardon, do you know when the next train arrives?"

That was the code Thorpe was looking for. This man was his contact. Now he had to remember the response. "Expecting it soon, sir."

Both men relaxed and breathed a bit more easily, despite the air being thick with anxiety.

The visitor, who was none other than Major Belknap, spoke in low tones. There was no one nearby that could hear. "The Germans are mustering a resistance. They plan to recruit freed slaves." The major fully disliked this assignment. He hadn't signed up to military service to be a spy. The furtive trip up from Brownsville had contributed to his annoyance. He was supposed to be fighting enemy soldiers and Apache, not coddling a growing resistance to the Confederate rebels.

"Where?" Thorpe asked.

"Up on the Guadalupe River west of San Antonio," Belknap replied. "They need perhaps two hundred."

Thorpe cogitated on that. "That's an exposed place…likely crawling with Rebels." He sat back. "I can't move a lot of Blacks all at once. It's a long way from Magnolia."

At first, neither man saw the two Confederate officers re-enter the hotel.

Thorpe spotted them first. He had a view out into the street and saw several gray-clad soldiers forming in the street outside the hotel. He strove not to reveal any notion of panic. Apparently, the officers' earlier walk-through was to confirm Thorpe's presence. He lowered his head and at just louder than a whisper advised Belknap, "Sir, I fear we've been discovered. We must leave, and quickly."

One of the Rebel officers had moved to a position blocking the rear entrance. It was clear from their demeanor that they wanted to capture Thorpe and Belknap without endangering hotel patrons.

Major Belknap was at greatest risk, as he was a soldier out of uniform. As a spy, he'd be hanged right promptly. "I am armed, sir. Shall we overpower the Rebel guarding the rear entrance?" Belknap slowly drew his revolver, keeping it hidden beneath the folds of his coat. He recognized that Thorpe was not a military man, and would likely need protecting. It would tend to hamper their escape…if escape was possible. He saw that the officer standing closer to the front door was getting up the courage to move in on them. "When I get up, follow me. Stay close. I've got a horse outside." He hoped the Rebels hadn't posted soldiers behind the hotel.

Belknap stood, sent two bullets into the officer standing at the front door, turned, shot down the officer guarding the rear entrance, and yanked Thorpe behind him. Patrons scattered in the lobby. Belknap crashed through the rear door of the hotel. As they emerged from the hotel, they found that Dame Fortune had smiled upon them. There were no Rebels in sight.

Belknap leaped into his saddle and pulled Thorpe up behind them. They made a dash up the alley. Fortune smiled once again as the major spotted a saddled but riderless horse ahead. Horse stealing wasn't an issue at this moment. As he pulled alongside the horse, the apparent owner standing nearby started to protest. Belknap leveled his gun at the man, and he stopped long enough for Thorpe to mount the horse. Belknap waved his revolver threateningly. "Sir, you'd best forget you ever saw us." The man had begun to pull his own gun but thought better of it. Belknap spurred his horse to a gallop, and Thorpe followed close behind.

★

"One Arrow, my chief, there be no bluecoats or gray coats." Crouching Lion was trying to make his case for stealing horses from a couple of nearby ranches that his warriors had scouted. "Weak men, many women." The implication was that the ranches were extremely vulnerable.

One Arrow had a bit more respect for women, having learned from Three Toes of the capabilities of the wife of Ghost-Who-Rides. He was nevertheless resigned to the band having a horse hunt. It was a question of the best strategy to minimize risk. He couldn't afford to lose any warriors. Crouching Lion had invested his thinking in raiding a ranch. One Arrow was more inclined toward hunting among the thousands of wild horses in the region. The bounty of the Great Spirit was there for the taking. "We are a small band, Crouching Lion. Hunting among the wild horses is better." He found himself fondling the cross dangling from the necklace he'd taken from Three Toes's grave.

Crouching Lion's gaze focused on the White man's symbol hanging from the chief's neck. He had begun to think it was weakening One Arrow's warrior spirit.

The chief saw where the warrior's eyes were looking. It was a challenge for which he had no response. The only understanding he had of the White man's faith was what little he'd gleaned from Three Toes and Ghost-Who-Rides. He knew only that it represented some powerful force. "We hunt wild horse." It was a definitive statement. He paused. "Penateka Comanche must think of future." He was trying to get Crouching Lion to understand that he was concerned with the long-term welfare of the Comanche. They could not afford to lose any more warriors. They'd not raid any ranches.

Crouching Lion grudgingly accepted his chief's decision. He smiled at One Arrow and nodded his acquiescence so the other warriors could see. "We hunt horses tomorrow."

They watched the smoke curl its way up and out the teepee vent as they talked of old times and dreams of what was to come.

★

John and Peter sat playing on the gallery. Elisa had cautioned them not to venture beyond its confines, and the boys had learned to obey their mother. She was loving, but they knew better than to test her patience, especially when she was feeding their newborn sister Alma.

They heard the noise of battle long before it arrived almost literally on their doorstep. Shouting and gunfire were fast approaching Heaven's Gate. The boys sat transfixed. On the one hand, they had the urge to run inside while on the other they had the curiosity that tended to grip young boys on the frontier. Perhaps it was why children of settlers of the west seemed to grow up more quickly than those back east.

A half dozen or so gray-clad soldiers were soon running past the house. Panic was written across their faces. They whooped and hollered bravely as though trying to muster some sort of courage. A wounded man was being helped along by his comrades. Two of them stopped, turned, and returned fire. They'd barely made it past the clearing and out into the tall grass of the prairie when at least a dozen pursuing blue-coats ran by the house. They too were hollering and stopping now and then to load and fire.

It was as though the Dunn house and cabin didn't exist for them, as the soldiers were so focused on each other. Bullets flew, but none toward the house.

By the time Elisa had heard the shooting and shouting and run onto the gallery to deliver her protective motherly instincts, the fighting had already moved well away from the ranch buildings. "Boys, why didn't you come inside?" She looked sternly at them.

"But, Mama, we stay on gallery." They were doing as they'd been told.

Exasperated, Elisa sighed. "Well, come inside now. It's dangerous. They may come back." She hustled them inside.

Once inside, she stuffed her Colt revolver in her apron waistband. It was unwieldy, but made her feel safer.

Whatever happened with the skirmish or became of the soldiers would remain a mystery, as they never passed back through Heaven's Gate. At least, they didn't pass by the ranch buildings again. For Peter and John, the fighting passed as entertainment of sorts, though it would likely be a while before they'd be old enough to grasp what it was about. Elisa could only shake her head and wonder when it might all end. She was grateful that so far as she could tell none of the soldiers on either side had fallen during their passage through the ranch.

It wasn't but an hour later that the twins, along with their sister Andrea Anne, peeked from the doorway and found their way back onto the gallery. There was no sign of soldiers of either side. It was a warm day and the sun and light breezes begged them to come out and enjoy it. Besides, it was an opportunity to tease Andrea without Elisa around to protect her.

"Look, John." Peter pointed to a couple of caps the soldiers had lost as they ran across the clearing. There they lay, not fifty feet from the gallery. One was gray, the other blue.

John gazed longingly at the caps and then to Andrea Anne and Peter. They knew their mother would not be pleased were they to venture from the gallery. But John's eyes were lit up. He was feeling adventurous. He put his finger to his lips, listened to be sure his mother was busy inside, and made a determined dash to grab the caps. He returned triumphantly, handing the blue one to Peter.

If a child's look could kill, Andrea Anne would have delivered a death blow to her brother. "Where's my hat?" She almost spoke loudly enough that the boys feared their mother might hear.

"Shush, Dre." John laid his finger aside his tensed lips. Dre was their nickname for her, as it came easily off a five-year-old's tongue. John was desperate to find something to quiet his sister, to buy off her silence. He scanned the clearing. There were no more spoils of war to be seen.

Peter was ahead of his brother. He was just pulling from his pocket the rabbit's foot that Three Toes had given him when Elisa emerged onto the gallery. There was no chance to hide the caps. John already had the gray one on his head. It was justice time, mother-style.

"Where did you get those caps?" Elisa's voice boomed out loudly enough that the horses in the corral neighed in fear.

Andrea Anne couldn't erase the smug grin that swept her face from ear to ear. She stood looking vengefully at her brothers, raised her arm, and pointed straight at John. "John did it, Mama."

The pleasing look John initially gave Andrea Anne turned to an "I'm going to get you for this" glare. "Dang it, Dre."

Elisa looked sternly down at them. Peter became guilty by association. She grabbed both boys firmly by their ears and led them back into the house. "Do you boys see those pots? Now, you get to clean them. Make them shine."

Andrea Anne stood in the doorway, smirking.

Elisa turned to her daughter. "And you let this happen."

Andrea Anne's smile disappeared.

"Here." She handed her a pot, then strode across the kitchen and out the front door. The tough pioneer woman leaned against a gallery post, sighed, and let her motherly protective juices flow. She cried softly with the relief that her children weren't hurt. Deep inside, she cursed the war and the troubles it brought.

Luke looked to the west as the sun began to sink below the horizon and knocked on the boarding house door. JD and

Barber sat astride their mounts at the hitching rail alongside Big Horse.

The door cracked open, and Bernice's smiling face appeared. "Why, Luke Dunn. What brings you here at this hour?"

"Just back from handling some squabbles down south, Bernice." He shifted his stance from one foot to the other in an uncharacteristically uncomfortable way. "I need a favor, Bernice."

"Come in, Luke." She stepped back and motioned him inside.

Luke looked back at his erstwhile Rangers and stepped through the doorway. "Bernice, you see the smaller of my companions?"

"Small lad for a Texas Ranger, Luke. What about him?"

"He is a she, and she's pregnant."

Bernice's mouth gaped just about the time Agatha joined her at the foyer in time to hear the news. "She needs a temporary place to stay, ladies. Her lover is intending to make an honest woman of her when he gets back from helping John Dunn deliver cotton to Matamoros. He'll be working on Nick's ranch."

The ladies knew that the Dunn family wouldn't truck with any of their hired hands dallying with women and then not marrying them. They felt there was a fair chance that Luke was right. Bernice and Agatha looked at each other and nodded in unison. "Well, don't be letting the little thing set all night out there, Luke. Bring her on in."

Luke smiled. "Ladies, I'm grateful. But be forewarned."

The ladies looked inquisitively.

"She can likely shoot the tail off a squirrel at a hundred yards. She's tougher than she looks, but she's had some rough times and does have a gentler side. Maybe mothering will bring that out." He waved at JD to join them.

JD promptly jumped from her horse and walked gingerly up to Luke and the ladies. "Yes, sir, Captain?"

"Ladies, meet Janice Denise Smith…JD for short. She's betrothed to a fella named Jubal Strong." He turned to JD. "JD, meet Bernice and Agatha. These fine ladies run this establishment and would be pleased to have you as their guest."

Luke dug into his pocket and fished out a couple of coins. "This should about cover things until Jubal returns. The coins are compliments of some Mexican ne'er-do-wells."

JD looked with amazement at Luke and caught him fully off guard as she wrapped her arms around him and planted a kiss on his cheek. Not a word needed to be spoken.

"See y'all," Luke said after he'd gotten over the surprise of the hug and kiss from JD. "I've got to get to Heaven's Gate before it gets too dark."

★

"Damn!" Sheriff Stills muttered under his breath. A bit of drool from his tobacco chaw had puddled on the spanking new wanted poster. He straightened up and spat into the ever-present spittoon near the jail cell. He pulled out his stash and freshened his chaw. Stills was actually more annoyed that a certain Snake Collins had been seen in west Texas. It made sense that the man would eventually find his way to Laredo. "Billy Bob Collins." The sheriff muttered again. Wasn't anyone around to hear him. But there were no illusions as to what might be expected should Collins find his way to Stills's jurisdiction.

He read Collins's description. The outlaw sounded to be about as evil as they came. Stills slipped the poster in a desk drawer with other posters, grabbed his gun, took a final spit, and headed to Texas Jack's Saloon. He'd grab an out-of-the-way table and try to put the new threat from his mind. A drink or two seemed in order.

★

The rider slipped from the saddle and hitched his horse. He wasn't sure just how long he might spend in Laredo, so there was no point in finding the local stable. Night had already fallen, and a silvery moon floated lazily just above the distant horizon. He heard the sharp moaning cry of a coyote as he climbed the steps of the saloon. The light inside looked to offer a welcome as contrasted to the brisk evening air. He could smell the saloon's acrid aromas before he'd even stepped through the door. A beer or two would soon compensate for that.

The bartender shifted uncomfortably as he took notice of the stranger who strode into Texas Jack's. The saloon in Laredo seemed to naturally attract folks that didn't seem…at least upon initial appearances…to be upstanding citizens.

The man swaggered up to the bar, turned with his back to it, and leaned with his elbows on it. He surveyed the room. He wore a black brocaded vest over a dark shirt. His black boots and dark gray, pin-striped trousers were topped by holsters with Colt 1861 Army revolvers. Seeing no one he recognized, or perhaps vice versa, he looked over at the barkeep. "You got beer?"

Sheriff Stills sat in the shadows off in one corner taking in the arrival of the stranger. His break from reading wanted posters and spittoon target practice looked to be ended. He took a swig of whiskey as he kept the newcomer in his sight. The whiskey served to cleanse the tobacco juice from his teeth as well as his mind. The stranger sure fit the description he'd just seen of Snake Collins. He had hardly expected the man to show up so soon. He felt an uncharacteristic nervous chill. Stills made a mental note to review wanted posters more frequently.

The barkeep placed the beer on the bar alongside the stranger. "You got a name, friend?"

The stranger turned and faced the bartender. "That matter?"

"Just askin'. We try to be friendly 'round here."

"Well, then, call me friend." The man glared with his dark eyes as though to fully dig into the barkeep's very soul. He gave an evil sort of half-smile. "You have a sheriff in this flea-bit town? A slip of a man named Stills?"

"You mean the sheriff that has his gun aimed at you as we speak?"

"In the corner?"

"Sure 'nuf, friend."

The aromas in the room seemed even more pungent than usual. Sweat, liquor, body odor, and piss can tend to stink a place up such that even the booze and the smell of the whores' perfumes couldn't neutralize it. The stranger looked into the mirror behind the bartender and saw that he was telling the truth. Sheriff Stills did have a big Colt revolver aimed at him. He sighed. Every town. Seemed like it was pretty much always the same. There was invariably a lawman who had heard about him and looked to take him down. He took a long drink of beer. In the split second following setting the beer glass down on the bar, the air was shattered with the sound of one of Collins's Colts. No one had seen him clear leather...no one had seen the third Colt hidden in his waistband.

The barkeep gaped.

Sheriff Stills's eyes grew wide for a moment as he gurgled up blood from the wound in his throat. The bullet had torn half his neck away. He slumped in his chair as his gun clattered to the floor. His eyes stared lifelessly into space.

"Damn, I hated to do that." The stranger returned the Colt to its holster, turned back to the bar, and quaffed the rest of his beer. He threw a coin on the bar. "This should cover your trouble, barkeep." The stranger pushed away and headed for the door but stopped before stepping outside. He turned toward the barkeeper. "Anyone asks, tell them Snake Collins visited Laredo and settled an old score."

As the barkeep watched, Collins walked out and disappeared from sight. Two other Texas Jack's patrons got up and tended to Stills. "Damn, he sure does stink of tobacco juice. Crapped in his pants, too." They dragged his body out to the livery with its stash of coffins.

"Looks like we'll be needing a new sheriff, boys." The barkeep went over with a wet towel to clean up the bloody mess where Stills had been sitting.

★

Luke sat across from Elisa at breakfast. He'd gotten in late, but she was still awake when he'd arrived. They were both tired and simply enjoyed falling asleep in each other's arms. The peace was only broken by Elisa having to get up to feed baby Alma.

"I'm thinking it's time, Lisa."

"Time? Time for what, Lucas Dunn?" She'd already told him about the pass-by skirmish of a couple of days earlier.

Luke looked over at Peter and John. Each sported a military cap. "My, but those pots sure look nice and shiny, Lisa." He winked at the boys.

For Elisa's part, she wasn't liking Luke's possibly undermining her punishment of the children. "What do you have in mind, husband?"

Luke scraped the last bit of breakfast from his plate. "Let's go out to the barn."

"Let me clean up, Lucas."

"No, that can wait." He was firm. "Let's all go out to the barn."

The barn wasn't all that big, so it was next to impossible to hide anything. The foal that Big Horse had sired had been put out in the corral along with its mother. Luke led them inside and walked them past Big Horse's stall.

"What are you up to, Lucas Dunn?"

Luke stepped to the next stall and swung open its door. "Well, lookee here. How did these critters get here?" Two geldings stood nervously at the rear of the stall. They weren't nearly so large as Big Horse, but full grown for sure.

By now, Elisa had figured out what Luke was up to and pushed Peter and John forward.

"You boys are growing like there's no tomorrow. I figure it's high time you had your own horses to care for." Luke fished a couple of apples from inside his shirt and took each son forward to meet his horse for the first time. "Go ahead, men. Say hello to your horses."

For Peter and John, it was all they could do to contain their sheer joy. "Papa, thank you!"

"You are responsible, boys. You've watched and helped your mother and me care for the livestock, so you know what to do." Luke let them get acquainted with their new gifts for a few moments while he and Elisa stood arm in arm and watched. Alma was at her breast, while Andrea Anne and toddler Michael peeked out from the folds of her skirt.

"Both these broncs are saddle-ready, boys," Luke told his sons. "They've got their own personalities, so you'll need to get acquainted. Oh, and you might think on giving them names." Luke well knew that a man and his horse were essential to life on the frontier, and so far as his sons, it was the sooner the better.

"What about a horse for me, Papa?" Andrea Anne as ever was looking to match whatever her older brothers were doing.

Elisa gave Luke a questioning glance.

"If you keep being real good and help me and your mother with chores, we'll look into one for you, Andrea Anne…next year." She was pint-sized and likely wouldn't grow any taller than Elisa, but she was already showing signs of being as feisty as her mother. He saw her disappointment. "We'll keep an eye out for a good horse, sweetie. It's got to be just right, doesn't it?"

Andrea Anne forced a smile. "Yes, Papa. I suppose it does."

Luke stroked her hair. "After we've cleaned up from breakfast, we'll take a ride, boys." He looked at Andrea Anne. "And you can ride with me, darlin'."

They all strolled back to the house.

Elisa spoke softly to Luke. "Is there another message here, Lucas?"

"Don't know. Could be." Rancher or lawman? Was he close to making a decision?

They persuaded Peter and John to leave the horses and strolled on back to the house. The horses tried to follow, but Luke closed the stable door. It seemed like the horses didn't want the boys leaving them, they'd bonded that quickly.

"Looks like the new rooms will be done in a couple of weeks, Lisa. Nice to let Andrea Anne and the boys have their own space."

TWENTY-TWO
NO SECRETS

IT HAD BEEN A LONG DAY. Samuel had devoted most of it to reconciling the business accounts for Thorpe's still far-flung empire. Even though revenues were down from Magnolia plantation and shipping interests, the former slave's experience with maintaining the finances kept the operations profitable. He filed away the books and walked over to the massive credenza along the far wall of the office. He opened one of the ornately decorated mahogany drawers and drew out a Colt revolver. It had been owned by Edward Thorpe's father, Horatio. He recalled the man who'd owned him, to his days as a house slave. He slipped the gun into his waistband. Next to where the revolver had been lying was a stiletto. It was a nasty-looking weapon. He shrugged and slipped it into his waistband beside the gun. He put on his coat. There was still a bit of winter chill, so the coat served a dual purpose of keeping Samuel warm and concealing the weapons from curious eyes. It wouldn't do for a man still perceived as a slave to be seen sporting a gun. He locked the heavy office door.

Samuel made the short walk to his house. It was a humble dwelling befitting his perceived stature in the Austin community. Until recently, Samuel had been just one of roughly 180,000 slaves residing in Texas.

As he went to grab the latch, the door opened and his wife Martha greeted him. She put her finger across her lips and whispered, "We've got company."

Inside, Samuel was taken aback to find Edward Thorpe and Major Gordon Belknap seated at their kitchen table. "What?"

Thorpe was first to speak. "It was a trap, Samuel. There were a bunch of rebel soldiers at the Menger Hotel ready to capture us. They wanted to make us examples of what happens to Yankee lovers."

Samuel shook his head. "I don't understand, Mr. Thorpe. The woman that gave me the message for you seemed to be honest. She had papers."

"Likely forged papers, Samuel, but you couldn't know that. She was apparently a very persuasive young lady, good at her craft." Thorpe smiled at his recollection of how charming she'd been, according to Samuel's description. "She certainly had my interest."

"The damage seems done, Mr. Thorpe. We likely need to get you and the major here out of Texas. I hear that some of the neighbor landowners near Magnolia have damaged the big house and outbuildings. You may do well to head to New Orleans. General Banks is in command there."

Belknap nodded. "Seems to make sense. I'm a dead man if I'm captured. The Rebs don't take kindly to spies."

"What about that woman?"

"I'll take care of that, Mr. Thorpe. First, we must get you fresh horses and supplies for your journey."

★

"Walker?" She'd cautiously opened the door. "What are you doing here?"

"It's Major Carson, ma'am." He doffed his gray hat with its gold braid. "I talked the general into giving me a couple days of leave before we head up to go run the Yankees out of Galveston."

"Why, I think I like Colonel Hobby, Major. Come on in. Congratulations on the promotion." She smiled mischievously.

Carson stood back to better take her in. "You're sure a sight for sore eyes, Scarlett."

"I'm a very pregnant sight for your eyes, Walker. Could be giving you a son or daughter any day now. I'm betting it's a boy."

"You know?"

"Call it intuition. Do you really have to head to Galveston?"

Carson nodded. "Looks like there's a lot of war still ahead for us, my love. The Yankees have come to realize that the South intends to fight to our last breath." A look of concern swept his face.

"I don't sense you are confident that the Confederacy will win, darling."

"The Yankees have more resources. Emotion and patriotism to a cause only gets you so far in war, Scarlett. Unless there's a quick victory, it becomes a war of attrition. I fear they will outlast us. It's the cold hard reality of it all."

"Well, reality for me is having a few precious hours of you being here with me and Margaret." Never had Scarlett imagined when she'd first met the dashing Texas Ranger that she'd have to see her man off to war. Thus far, he'd managed to avoid being wounded or, God forbid, killed. She drew him to her, and they embraced silently for a long time.

★

"Luke, what brings you into Corpus?" Sheriff Bill Meaney

was pleasantly surprised. "Come on in." He held open the front door to the Corpus Christi jail.

Luke stepped inside and plunked himself in a chair opposite the sheriff's desk. "Figured to see how you're doing, Bill, what with those Yankee ships watching from the Gulf."

Meaney smiled. "You better keep your head low. Now and again, they lob a shell our way." His smile broke into a chuckle. "They do warn us first."

"How's Clara?"

"We hitched up while you were gallivanting around the Nueces Strip." The sheriff turned serious. "You heard about Collins?"

"Texas Rangers hear about pretty much everything, Bill. Understand Snake Collins killed Sheriff Stills in Laredo. Not sure whether he'll head this way."

"I'm watching for him, Luke. Got to think of Clara's welfare, too. As a new bride, she sure doesn't deserve widowhood yet."

"I expect if Rip Ford wasn't tied up down south, he'd likely be asking me to hunt Collins down."

Meaney thought on Luke's comment, looking past him and out the window. Clara hung in the back of his mind. As capable a lawman as he was, the thought of possibly facing Collins was not the least bit attractive. "Would you take that assignment, Luke?"

Luke smiled and tugged a bit at his mustache. "Ever known me to avoid the chance to bring justice, Bill?"

★

It was a little before mid-morning when Sergeant Clay Bell set up at the top of a low ridge overlooking Fort Brown. There were two cannon emplacements within range. Each day, the cannon would be unlimbered as part of a practice routine.

Unfortunately, the exercise was performed at precisely the same time each day.

As Bell understood it, his role as a sharpshooter was to help soften up the Yankees toward enabling the recapture of Brownsville. "What do you think, John?" Bell peered through the telescopic sight. His instincts as a marksman kicked in. He noted the cloudless sky and bright sun to his left.

"No wind, Sergeant."

Bell thought on that. No wind. It would be an easy shot, sort of like plunking squirrels back in the old days growing up. His mind wrestled with what he'd been called to do. He kept reminding himself that this was war. The targets happened to be human. He couldn't afford to think of their human qualities, of mothers, fathers, wives, children, faith, livelihoods.

"You going to do it, Sergeant?" The spotter sensed what was going through Bell's mind—sensed why he was hesitating. Part of his job was to remind the sharpshooter of his duty. It was about eliminating Yankee cannoneers to make attack safer for their fellow Rebel soldiers and make the enemy think twice about manning cannon and practicing at the fort parapets.

"Yeah, I've got them." He stabilized his grip on the Sharps rifle, inserted a round, and slipped his finger onto the trigger. He relaxed, took a breath, exhaled just a bit, and squeezed off the round.

The spotter watched through his own spyglass. "My god, Sergeant!"

Bell knew the outcome without looking. The cannoneer loading and tamping the round had been aligned through the sergeant's sight with the soldier behind him ready to light off the cannon. Two Yankees had fallen with a single shot.

"Damn, you're good, Sergeant…very very good." John shook his head in admiration. Then again, he'd seen it before.

Bell started slipping the Sharps back into its scabbard.

"Can't wait 'til it's all over, John." His mind was deeply conflicted. Two men had fallen with no chance to defend themselves. They'd likely eaten a regular breakfast that morning and enjoyed the camaraderie of fellow soldiers. They could never have known what was to happen. Bell sighed, as he watched the flurry of activity around the distant cannon emplacement. "We'd best get out of here. They'll be sending out a patrol for sure."

★

A heavy early morning mist hung around Samuel's cabin. There was barely a hint of sunrise as he watched Belknap and Thorpe mount up and gallop away. Samuel's wife had seen to it that the men were sufficiently supplied for their journey. With any luck, they'd make Galveston in a couple of days and connect safely with Colonel Renshaw.

Samuel turned to his wife. "I'm going away for a couple of days. If anyone inquires, just tell them I'm away on business."

"Where are you going, Sam?"

"I can't tell you. It's safer that way."

She tried to understand. "What are you going to do?"

He gave her a "don't ask" expression. "If you don't know..."

She placed her fingers over his lips. "...I can't tell."

"I shouldn't be more than a couple of days. If it takes longer, there's a note on Mr. Thorpe's desk. You know where the key is hidden."

She'd gotten used to Samuel acting differently ever since Thorpe began freeing his slaves. "Be safe."

And he disappeared into the mist.

★

Luke and the sheriff had tipped a whiskey or two at the

Longhorn before calling it a night. Luke spent the night sacked out in one of the jail cells. With the little wood stove, it was rather toasty on a chill winter evening. Still, it was a tad uncomfortable as the tiny bed didn't accommodate his long frame.

Luke awoke and fixed himself a cup of coffee. He wasn't especially impressed with Meaney's well-seasoned coffee pot, but he wasn't in a position to be choosy. He strolled up the street to Scarlett's place, as he'd promised to check in on her from time to time. He'd found Scarlett comfortably ensconced with Walker Carson, as they were enjoying the major's leave and making plans to reopen the haberdashery at war's end. After briefly visiting, he fetched Big Horse and returned to the jail to meet with Meaney before heading back to Heaven's Gate.

"Take it easy, Bill. I figure this Collins fellow will find his way through Nuecestown if he's aiming to head this way."

"I'd ask how the son of a bitch got the way he is, Luke, but that's what they call one of those rhetorical-type questions. Bad home…messed-up brains…revenge-minded?"

"I recall Bol Richards telling me how many of the Texans that fought for independence back in 1836 were called second-chancers. They came to Texas from rough situations elsewhere to seek fresh beginnings. I don't think Collins is looking for any second chance, Bill. He's plain and simple a cold-blooded killer."

"Maybe he'll head to Uvalde or San Antone first." Meaney knew it was wishful thinking.

"I'll keep my eyes peeled, my friend. Meanwhile, keep your head down and don't let any Yankee cannonballs get you." Luke bade farewell and headed home.

★

There she was. Samuel was close enough to almost reach

out and touch her. He kept his hat low to hide his face. The gloves on his hands caused no particular notice given the chill winter air. In any case, a black man in this place was likely to not get out alive. He inched closer. She was laughing and flirting with the five men pressed closely around her as she leaned against the bar. They'd heard of some big battle way off in Virginia that the Rebels had won and were in a wild celebratory mood. They were convinced that the Yankees would soon surrender. They were laughing and toasting and paying no never mind to anyone around them.

Samuel was close enough to smell her perfume. For his part, you couldn't cover the stink of a double agent with sweet fragrances. He sidled next to her. The gun would have made far too much noise. He didn't want to draw attention to himself. His stiletto plunged deep through corset, flesh, and ribs. She gasped.

Samuel slipped away as inconspicuously as possible. He could see her trying to breathe. She couldn't fall right away due to the press of those around her. He took a final look as he exited. She breathed her last before crumpling vertically to the surprise of those around her. There was the expected mayhem, but no one had seen her killer.

Samuel rode eastward. He'd be safe at Magnolia until the incident blew over.

★

It hadn't taken but a couple of days ride. There before them on the vast prairie were hundreds of wild horses. One Arrow and Crouching Bear looked at each other. This was exactly what they'd hoped for.

It was easy to spot the lead stallion. Big and spirited, it was clear he had his way with all the mares and no other stallion would dare challenge him.

From the crest of a hill, the two Comanche laid out a

strategy while the other warriors excitedly awaited the round-up. Just as One Arrow was pointing to a natural depression to which the horses could be driven and trapped, he caught movement in the distance off to the west. "Look, Crouching Bear." The chief pointed to what appeared to be a band of Indians.

"I see nothing, my chief."

One Arrow was insistent. "Look again! Kiowa!"

The Kiowa could be friend or foe, depending on circumstances. One Arrow suspected that the competition for horses this day likely made them foes.

Crouching Lion's first reaction was to prepare to fight.

One Arrow ignored him and kept his eyes on the Kiowa. He could ill afford to lose any warriors, as his band was small in numbers. The chief tried to focus on the long-term good of his people, much as Three Toes might have done. He looked at Crouching Lion and extended his hand palm downward toward the warrior as a sign to be at ease.

The warrior stared at the cross hanging from the chief's necklace, then shifted his gaze upward to fixate on One Arrow's own hardening gaze. Crouching Lion began to sneer disrespectfully. "White man gift make you weak."

The chief's expression shifted to anger, as the warrior sought to embarrass him before the other Comanche in earshot. He stared down the warrior. "Great Spirit has spoken to me. For Penateka Comanche to grow, we must not be foolish." He ignored the inference about the necklace.

Crouching Lion wasn't finished, or so he thought. "What of the…" He stared again at the cross at the chief's neck.

"This belonged to Three Toes. He was great chief." He rose as high as possible astride his pony. "Too many Kiowa. We go find other horses." He was intent on not engaging Kiowa in battle, especially as he was outnumbered by at least two to one.

Crouching Lion looked from the chief to the warriors. He

reluctantly nodded agreement with One Arrow. They would live to fight another day. They'd look for more wild horses.

★

Luke turned from the road and passed under the arch to Heaven's Gate. The ranch was doing well despite the ongoing conflict. He'd hedged his bets so to speak by accepting payment for his cattle in gold and silver rather than Confederate paper. Something deep within, a sort of intuition, told him that the Rebel cause was doomed.

A sunny mild late winter day on the Nueces Strip was cause for joy. He tied his winter coat behind his saddle as he eased Big Horse up the trail to the barn. "What do you think, big fella? We'll be out rounding up strays before you know it." Luke found Big Horse to be a great listener. As if on cue, the big gray stallion launched into a canter that didn't end until he stood before the barn door.

Luke had dismounted and was about to swing the door open when Big Horse pulled back and neighed loudly. His eyes grew wide and wild. Danger was at hand. Luke knew his horse well, and this was a warning sound, much as years before the big gray had alerted him to Bad Bart Strong's ambush intentions. He reflexively pulled one of his Colts and cocked the hammer. "What is it, big fella? What's spooking you?"

Luke carefully pulled the door open. No obvious threat he could see as yet. No rattlesnakes, at least so far as he could see or hear. He took a tentative step inside.

A voice came from the shadows. "Move another muscle and you're a dead man." There was the telltale click of a cocked and ready pistol.

Luke dove back outside as a bullet tore through the door where he'd been standing. The bullet grazed Big Horse's neck, sending him into a panic. Luke calmed him, grabbed his rifle, and then slapped the big gray's behind to send him out of danger. He heard Elisa appear on the gallery to the house a couple of hundred feet away.

"Stay there, Lisa. Go inside." He waved her back.

He hadn't heard another sound from inside the barn. "Who's there?"

There was no response. Luke looked up the front of the barn, figuring he might climb up to the loft and see exactly what was lurking inside. Before he could move, there was a crash as a man mounted on Elisa's mare rode through the door, bowled Luke over, and lit on up the trail out of Heaven's Gate.

Luke picked himself up. He was initially stunned.

"Luke, he's got my horse!" Elisa had reemerged onto the gallery.

The last thing Luke wanted to do was give chase. He didn't know who the attacker was, much less how well armed. The pleading expression on Elisa's face didn't leave him much choice. He corralled Big Horse and vaulted into the saddle. The gray stallion's long legs would make short work of closing ground on the much smaller mare.

Luke felt the blood oozing from Big Horse's neck. It was a superficial wound, but it angered Luke nonetheless. For all the dangerous encounters they'd faced over the years, his steed had never taken a bullet. Thorns, yes. Cattle horns, yes. But never a gunshot.

The escaping rider soon drew into sight. The mare simply didn't have it in her to go too far at a gallop, so Luke was closing right quickly.

Luke eased up as he rode to within fifty yards of the rider. He stopped and whistled. The mare came to such a sudden stop that the rider was tossed over its head. Well-lathered and breathing heavily, the mare likely welcomed stopping.

The rider wasn't so fortunate. He landed nearly head first in a cluster of cacti. The wind was knocked from him and the pain from the cactus spines was palpable. He'd lost his gun in the process of being summarily dismounted, so he lay moaning and gasping.

Luke rode Big Horse up to him. Towering over the man, he took a breath or two after the tough ride. He dismounted, keeping his Colt trained on the man. "What the hell did you think you were doing, mister?" About this time, Luke noticed that the man had gray trousers and a gray kepi that had fallen from his head. It didn't take a mental giant to figure that the man was likely a deserter.

"Please don't shoot." He was still trying to catch his breath.

"You've had the misfortune of running into Texas Ranger Captain Luke Dunn, soldier. You are under arrest." Luke didn't have it in him to pity the man. If he was a deserter, that was bad, but horse thievery was a hanging offense. "You holed up in the wrong barn, and you definitely stole the wrong horse."

The soldier looked up pleadingly at Luke. "I'm tryin' to get back to my family. My momma's sick an' dyin'."

"You aren't going anywhere with my wife's horse, and you need attention to those cactus spines. We're going to visit Doc back in Nuecestown, so get off your butt and mount up." Luke retrieved the soldier's pistol and slipped it into the saddlebag on Big Horse. "What's your name?"

"John Smith."

"Oh, come on, soldier. What is your name?"

"I'm tellin' the truth, sir."

"Okay, John. Head on out." Luke pointed the way. They didn't have all that far to ride and had soon pulled up in front of Doc's place.

Luke dismounted, held both horses' reins, and knocked on Doc's door. Smith winced as he got off the mare.

"Luke! What's up, my friend?" Doc threw open the door.

Luke ushered Smith in. He hadn't manacled the deserter or

mentioned that he'd stolen Elisa's horse or shot at Luke. Yet. "This man needs some tending to, Doc."

Doc saw the Rebel trousers and began to put two and two together. Taking the man's shirt off was a painful process, as some of the cactus spines came loose. Doc spoke up as he began to yank out and treat the remaining spines. "What you running from, soldier?"

Luke rolled his eyes.

"My momma's dyin', Doc. I'm goin' to my momma."

"Where's she at?"

"Galveston."

"You know the place is crawling with Yankees?"

Luke interrupted and looked over at Doc. They exchanged understanding looks. "Doc, I'm inclined to believe this man. I could turn him over for desertion or could arrest him for horse thievery and assault. I expect that would be justice…of sorts." He stroked his red mustache thoughtfully.

Smith looked pleadingly at Luke. Doc was finishing up dressing his wounds, and they'd be departing soon.

"You got an extra shirt and pants around, Doc?" Luke was working on seeing the redemptive side of the situation. He wouldn't have been questioned had he taken the deserter horse thief behind the jail and hung the man.

Tears began to well up in Smith's eyes.

"I think there's a decent nag up at the livery. Dan should be able to fix us up with some tack." Luke stared hard at Smith. "You going back into the fighting after you see your momma?"

"I promise, Captain. I do promise."

"If we loan you a horse, can we trust you to bring it back?"

"Yes, Captain. I promise I will."

Doc nodded approvingly at Luke.

Soon enough, Luke parted ways with the Rebel soldier and was on his way back to Heaven's Gate with Elisa's mare in tow. He was anxious to put a poultice on Big Horse's wound. It was one of those handy medicinal things he'd learned from

Three Toes. He looked forward to Elisa's pleasure at his recovering her mare and likely her understanding at what he'd done for the thief. He'd thought how he might have behaved had his own mother been sick and dying. 'Course that led to a bit of homesickness coursing through him, as he realized he'd never even know whether he'd even see his own mother again back in County Kildare. That sure didn't seem likely.

TWENTY-THREE
FRONTIER TAKES GRIT

SNAKE COLLINS SAT astride his black horse in the middle of the main street running through San Diego. It had been a long ride from Laredo. He looked out curiously over a town that was pretty much empty, as the few cowboys not fighting Yankees were out on the ranches around the region preparing for spring roundups. The local sheriff was a part-timer who occasionally worked as a wrangler on a nearby ranch, when he wasn't tipping beers at the only saloon. He hailed a woman who was scurrying across the street toward a wagon. She carried an armload of brightly colored fabric bolts that contrasted with Collin's rather somber appearance. "Excuse me, ma'am?"

She stopped and looked with a touch of trepidation at the man before her. He was rather intimidating to look at. It wasn't that he was so big as he was dark and foreboding. The black leather coat and matching felt hat coupled with long dark hair and a beard contributed to enhance what might be regarded as a considerably less-than-angelic image. "Yes? Can I help you?" She tried to be cordial, though her nerves resulted in just a touch of quiver in her voice.

Collins forced a smile. It might have been a friendly smile

had it not been punctuated by a gold tooth. "Would you be so kind as to direct me to Corpus Christi?"

Slightly relieved, she placed her goods in the wagon and pointed eastward. "Just follow the road, mister. It's about a long day's ride from here, maybe two. You'll find Nuecestown between here and Corpus."

"Does this Nuecestown have a sheriff?"

The woman thought it a strange question. Why was this man concerned about sheriffs? "They have a jail. Sheriff Meaney in Corpus Christi stops by now and again."

"Sheriff Meaney. He's a fine lawman." Collins didn't have a clue who Meaney was but figured to sound like his question had been innocent with no intended threat. There was no point in causing any alarm. "Thanks for the directions, ma'am. Have a nice day." He turned his horse toward Nuecestown and gave a bit of a nudge to the steed's flanks.

The woman watched him ride on by. An involuntary chill coursed through her body.

★

Luke was enjoying a rare relaxing moment sitting on the gallery with Elisa and the children. He'd begun to think about the spring and rounding up most of the beeves foraging around the ranch. Heaven's Gate needed ever more of his attention. Of a sudden, movement off to his left caught his eye, and he looked off up the trail. "Lisa, look there. It's Pastor Rucker coming to visit."

"I'll fetch some coffee, Luke." She got up and headed into the house.

Horace Rucker still maintained his military bearing as he rode up to the house. He sat straight in the saddle. Old habits don't break easily, as his thirty years in the Army attested. He pulled up at the gallery, dismounted, and casually hitched his horse. "Beautiful day, Luke. How are you and the family?"

"Looking forward to neighborly visits, pastor. What news do you bring?"

Elisa appeared with cups of coffee and some cornbread.

"The Lord sure has blessed us with your cornbread, Elisa Dunn." He savored a bite while Elisa blushed. "I got a letter from Stephen. He's doing well. He's up on the Sabine getting ready to fight the Union Army led by General Banks. I knew Banks, and he's a good man. But the Confederates are familiar with the ground and will likely put a whipping on him." Rucker chuckled at that.

"I guess Stephen's doing what he was aiming to do, pastor." Luke knew Rucker was distressed over the divided loyalties of his sons.

As a retired Army colonel himself, the pastor tended to be loyal to the Union. "I'm concerned about Rex. His wounds have pretty much healed, but he'll be doing no more fighting. In fact, his military days are doubtful." Rucker clasped his hands as though in prayer. "He's of a mind to head to Washington and apply his skills toward helping President Lincoln at the War Department."

"Sounds worthy, pastor. You should be proud of him." Luke strove to muster up some compassion. "I understand your concern over your sons, pastor, but they're grown men and it seems you've taught them well. I'm sure you'd agree that they're old enough to make their own decisions. If I was in your shoes, I'd be hard pressed not to bless Rex's ambitions."

Luke's words seemed to bring some comfort to Rucker.

Elisa placed her coffee aside and leaned toward Rucker. "I think it's toughest on the mothers, Pastor. You should comfort your wife." Wizened by years on the frontier and despite her youth, Elisa brought her unique motherly perspective to the conversation.

Rucker looked around him at Heaven's Gate and at the children playing at his feet. A peacefulness settled over him.

"You've done well, Luke…Elisa. I pray that all will be good with you and your family when this infernal war is ended." He got up to take his leave.

"You fixing to leave already, Pastor?"

"Actually, I'm on my way to Corpus. Figured I'd poke my head in with y'all along the way."

"Good to see you."

"I do appreciate your advice…and the coffee and corn-bread. Oh, and don't be so scarce on Sunday morning." He knew that Luke hadn't let loose of the Catholic faith he'd brought with him from Ireland.

"Thanks for the invite, Pastor."

★

The buckboard filled with Elisa and the children pulled up in front of Scarlett and Walker Carson's little place. The captain had returned to duty with the 1st Texas Cavalry, so Scarlett was left home to deal with their livelihood. The Dunn family had decided to see first-hand what were the latest goings-on in Corpus Christi. From Luke's point of view, he was curious as to how dangerous it might be. The Yankees had reportedly taken a break from lobbing occasional shells into the city, so the street along the coast had become a tourist attraction of sorts. Visitors and residents would stroll along and keep watch for Union picket ships that plied up and down the coast.

Elisa hustled the children into Scarlett's home. There was no point in exposing them unnecessarily. Luke was bemused by her heightened caution but didn't object.

"Let's go down to the wharf." Scarlett was almost insistent. "It drives me crazy to be cooped up in here day after day while those Yankees laugh at us from their ships."

"Is it safe?"

"Everybody's been doing it. It's been pretty warm the past few days."

"So, there's nothing to fear?" Elisa was more worried about the children. Luke had gone off to see Sheriff Meaney, so she was on her own. She wasn't concerned about Scarlett's pregnancy, as she was as tough as she was beautiful. Elisa very well knew that women on the frontier were simply never slowed down by pregnancies.

"Maybe a few early-season mosquitos." Scarlett laughed. "Some say they're oversized in Texas."

After an hour or so strolling the wharf and keeping rambunctious kids corralled, Elisa and Scarlett returned to the house. They made small talk about the little haberdashery business the Carsons had started despite the ongoing war.

"I think it's great that y'all found a business you could enjoy together, Scarlett. I wish Luke could be around more, but Heaven's Gate has surely been a blessing for us."

Scarlett glanced out the window. "I see Luke coming up the street. Y'all care to join us for a bit of dinner?"

Elisa scanned the offering of cookies and cakes Scarlett had spread on the table. "You've already fed us plenty, Scarlett. Likely, Luke will want to be home before dark." She scratched at a couple of mosquito bites. Scarlett was rubbing her bites as well. "You might put a bit of liniment on those to relieve the itch. Dang pests are ahead of their season."

As Luke was about to knock, the door swung open. "Why, thanks, Scarlett." He stepped inside. "Lisa, darling, you about ready to head back to Heaven's Gate?"

Soon enough, they were all seated in the buckboard and headed home. Elisa tried to ignore her mosquito bites. "You get your business with Sheriff Meaney finished up?"

"Pretty much. We're keeping our eyes peeled for some outlaw named Collins who has a strong dislike for sheriffs. If he comes to Corpus Christi, he's likely to pass through Nuecestown."

"Should we worry?"

Luke smiled and let his eyes scan her diminutive body.

"Nope. I don't see you wearing a sheriff's badge." It was good to see Elisa laugh at his humor. The trip into Corpus had been a good opportunity to get away from the ranch for a day.

★

Snake Collins could barely make out the silhouette of Nuecestown, camouflaged as it was among the low rolling hills and the sinking of the sun below the western horizon. In all his journey from California across several mountain ranges, he hadn't been quite prepared for the broad, mostly flat expanses of the Nueces Strip.

Far as he could tell, it'd be another couple of hours ride to Corpus Christi. It would be getting right dark soon, and he was unfamiliar with this part of the country. Collins decided to seek lodging overnight in Nuecestown.

As he approached the edge of town, he removed his guns and holsters and stuffed them into his saddlebag. There was no point in stirring up unnecessary attention.

In the ever-dimming light, he nearly didn't notice the man that rode past him heading west. The two tipped hats as they went their separate ways. Jubal Strong had made it back from Matamoros and had just visited with JD. She would be staying at the boarding house a few days more as Strong arranged for their marriage. They sought to minimize the possibly ugly talk about her being pregnant out of wedlock. Collins rode on, oblivious to such local private concerns.

He pulled up at the boarding house and was pleased that some lights were lit. He glanced around. There to his left and up the street a bit was the jail that the woman in San Diego had mentioned. It was unlit, but appeared to be reasonably well-maintained so far as he could tell. He dismounted and hitched his horse.

Bernice answered Collins's knock. She was momentarily

taken aback by his dark presence framed in the doorway with a night sky behind him. "Yes, sir. How may I help you?"

"Looking for a room for the night, ma'am." He gauged Bernice as likely being the town busybody, the person who knew everything about everybody. She might also know who he was. He wouldn't take that chance.

"Come on in, traveler. Where are you headed?" She thrust a register in front of him and followed his hand as he signed in. "Mr. Jones from Santa Fe. Welcome. We'll have our man come take your mount down to the livery."

Agatha appeared. "I'll let Dan know." She gave Collins the once-over. He looked a bit suspicious to her, but then being wary of strangers was pretty much her nature.

"Much obliged at you looking after my horse. I've got my saddlebags here, so he's ready to be stabled. Is there someplace I can grab some grub?"

"I think I can rustle up something, Mr. Jones." She wanted to add "or whoever you are." She felt the same suspicious feelings as Agatha. "I'll see you to your room. You can come down for dinner in about an hour."

As Bernice and Collins went upstairs, JD stepped from hiding behind a drapery and confronted Agatha with a whisper. "I was nosing around the jail yesterday, Agatha. That man? He's a wanted man. I recognize him from the drawing on the poster. Name's Snake something." She heard Bernice returning and repeated her concerns in a low murmur lest Collins overhear. "You should get Dan to ride out and warn Luke."

JD's news confirmed the suspicions Bernice already had. She spoke furtively. "Those saddlebags looked mighty heavy. Guns? Gold? Could be both."

Agatha went to fetch Dan, leaving JD behind at the boarding house. She was just a tad frustrated. In her very pregnant condition, she wouldn't or shouldn't be pursuing desperados.

Always observant, Bernice figured what she was thinking. "No, JD. Not here. Not now. This is strictly men's business this time." She looked at JD's belly. "You're gonna be a momma afore long, woman."

JD went to her room and pulled her rifle from behind the chest of drawers. She leaned it against a chair by the window where it just might prove handy.

★

Luke and Elisa had just bedded down when they heard the banging at the front door. Jaime had gone with Julia to visit cousins, or the person knocking would have answered to the *vaquero*. Groggily, Luke came to the door. He resented the interruption of his whisperings of sweet love notes in Elisa's ear.

He peeked out and then opened the door to Dan. "What is it at this hour, Dan?" He knew from experience that it could only mean trouble.

"The ladies tell me Snake Collins has come to town. He's a wanted man staying at the boarding house, and I've got his horse and tack down at the stable."

"You sure it's Collins?"

"He said he was on his way to Corpus. Something about business with the sheriff. I saw the poster on him, Captain Dunn. It says Collins isn't especially beholden to sheriffs."

Dan had Luke's full attention. Soon enough, Elisa came downstairs and joined Luke at the front door. "What's going on, Lucas?"

"Seems we have a bit of a problem, Lisa." He turned to Dan. "Thanks. I'll head out early and figure how best to handle this. Can you be so kind as to ride into Corpus and warn Sheriff Meaney? This Snake Collins fellow apparently has an obsession with killing sheriffs."

As Dan tipped his hat to Elisa and departed to warn

Meaney, Luke turned to her. "Not sure what sort of varmint this Collins fellow is, Lisa." He saw the deep concern written on her face. How many more times would he go out and return safely? Telling her not to worry rang hollow. He tried to muster a comforting look.

★

"Thanks to you, ladies, for your fine hospitality." Collins had an intuitive feeling that the law in Corpus had been fore-warned. It was time for a change in plans. "When does the ferry master begin his day?" He had begun to think that Victoria just might make better sense. Surely, they had a sheriff up there.

"When his first customer shows up, Mr. Jones." Bernice was relieved but concerned that the opportunity to apprehend Snake Collins was slipping from their grasp. "We'll get Dan to bring your mount over from the livery." She saw this as an opportunity to delay with the hope that Luke or Meaney would show up. They didn't yet know that Meaney was holed up in the jail sleeping off the residual but not debilitating effects of some whiskey, or that Luke wasn't far off. They'd met up aforehand and snuck into Nuecestown unbeknownst to Bernice and Agatha. It was likely just as well that the ladies didn't know.

"That'd be just fine, ladies." He stepped out from the boarding house and saw up the street to where his mount was being led up from the stable. However, it was the twist of smoke rising from the chimney at the jail that now caught his undivided attention. It set all manner of alarms off in his head. Was this going to be a chance to add another sheriff to his list of lawman victims? He noted the roan tied to the hitching post in front of the jail but was concerned as to who might be riding the large gray stallion beside it.

Collins waited patiently until Dan handed him the reins to

his horse. He threw his saddlebags behind the saddle and tied them down.

Bernice and Agatha watched from a front window of the boarding house.

Meanwhile, JD had taken a position seated by the windowsill from her room overlooking what served as the town square. The window was open despite the chill early spring air. Drapery flapped slightly in the breeze, though not so as to be noticed from the street. It served to screen her from view. The rifle had found its way into her hands.

Collins thanked Dan, placed a coin in his hand, and made sure the farrier had walked away a distance that met his liking. He turned his horse to put it between himself and both the boarding house and the jail.

The ladies could barely see Collins reach into a saddlebag and pull out his holsters with their twin Colt revolvers. Collins, like the snake he was, stayed behind his steed while he ensured that his guns were loaded and ready. He strapped the belt around his waist while keeping an eye on the jail. He took a quick but careless glance around him. Still behind his horse, he moved over toward the jail. "Hey, Sheriff! You in there?"

"He might be."

The deep voice behind Snake Collins was enough to freeze the most hardened killer.

"Bill Collins, raise your hands high and turn around real easy-like."

Collins's hands went up about shoulder high as he turned to face the source of the voice. He found himself looking down the cavernous barrels of Luke's own Colt revolvers.

"I'm Texas Ranger Captain Luke Dunn, and you are under arrest for murder."

Collins's mind was racing despite his outwardly calm appearance. Could he get to his guns before the Texas Ranger could react?

Luke shook his head ever so slightly. "I know what you're thinking. Don't be stupid."

Collins had vaguely heard about some damned Texas Ranger on the Nueces Strip but never had imagined he'd meet the man. The outlaw was now so focused on Luke and trying to decide his next action that he hadn't heard Sheriff Meaney come up behind him and lift the Colts from his holsters. Now Collins was in a serious fix. But it also gave him an opportunity. He stepped back hard, threw a shoulder into Meaney, rolled both of them to the ground, and came up with one of his Colts.

With the sheriff so close, Luke had no clear shot at the man.

Collins slipped under his horse and aimed his gun at Luke. "You damned son of a bitch Ranger!" He shouldn't have taken the time to say anything.

The sound of a single rifle shot reverberated off the surrounding buildings. A bullet from a high vantage point penetrated Collins's shoulder and drove down into his gut. The killer fell where he was kneeling, and Luke and Meaney looked up to see a wisp of gun smoke wafting from a second-floor window of the boarding house.

JD hollered down at the ladies. "Bernice…Agatha…come help. The baby's coming!"

Bernice and Agatha dashed to the stairway and were beside her in what seemed a heartbeat to them and an eternity to JD.

Luke and Meaney stared at each other and then down at Collins lying in the dust of the Nuecestown street. Luke reacted first. "Damn, Bill. Don't that beat all? That little fireball has saved me again."

Meaney offered the obvious. "Guess Snake Collins won't be killing any more sheriffs, Luke." He looked down at Collins's pitiful-looking body curled into a fetal position. "Those evil ones sure don't look like much when they're all bled out dead-like." He looked over as Dan approached. "Hey, Dan, how about taking this horse back to the stable? Oh, and we'll be needing one of those fine boxes you're keeping out back."

"Bill, I'll let Doc know he's got a birthing to tend to. I expect I'll hang around to see whether it's a boy or girl." Luke began to head off to Doc's place while Meaney dragged Collins's very dead body around to the back of the jailhouse.

As though on cue, Jubal Strong rode into town. He'd started out to visit Luke's cousin's new ranch and stopped by Pastor Rucker's place to arrange for him to officiate at his marriage to JD. Just by happenstance, he'd decided to double back to Nuecestown.

Luke sported a sort of wry grin. "Jubal, grab a seat on the steps. Your bride-to-be is working on delivering your family. She's early, so we'd all better pray there are no problems."

Strong leaped off his horse and headed to the boarding house, but was stopped at the front door by Agatha. "You go help Luke fetch Doc. Nothing else you can do here, young man."

Agatha tried not to show her worry. She knew that the baby was coming far too early and, with JD being just a little slip of a thing, it would likely be a tough labor in the best of circumstances.

Luke let Strong have the honors of getting Doc. He finally found himself with a moment to relax. As he surveyed the scene, he was struck by his witnessing to death and life on the Texas frontier. It all seemed so very fragile.

Not an hour later, Nuecestown was treated not to the plaintive cries of a newborn life but the agonizing wails of a woman who had lost her baby. Strong and JD would have had a son, but it was not to be. Life and death were harsh realities and frontier Texas was no exception to delivering on good and bad.

Luke did his best to comfort Strong, putting his hand on the grief-stricken man's shoulder while assuring him that there'd be a next time and encouraging him to be strong and help JD in her grief. "It's God's timing, Jubal. You'll yet have family." Somehow the words resonated hollow.

"Mr. Strong...come quick." Bernice was frantically beckoning Strong to come. "You must console JD."

Soothe? Console? Comfort? These feelings weren't natural to Jubal Strong. On the other hand, he loved JD and was determined to make their relationship work. He was in shock and hurting deeply, but knew he had to show strength. He dashed into the boarding house, rushed to the top of the stairs, paused, and entered the room hat in hand.

She was holding their dead child, wrapped in a blanket as though it still breathed with life. The baby was barely bigger than the palm of Strong's hand.

Strong fought back his own tears. "JD...Janet...it's not the end, darling. We've got to be strong. We'll bring new life into this world. We'll do it together." Strong really didn't know what to say, much less how to say it. He felt as though he was rambling in hope that something would connect with JD. He wrapped his arms around her.

JD's tears still flowed. She sighed deeply, kissed the tiny baby, and handed him up to Strong. "We gotta bury him, Jubal."

"Do we give him a name?"

The thought of identity began to take JD from her crying. "Let's call him Texas. Texas Strong."

Strong managed the beginnings of a smile. "I like that, JD. Texas Strong it is." He leaned down and kissed her on the forehead.

JD gave him a funny look and pointed to her lips.

Strong didn't miss a beat as he gave her the sweetest kiss he could muster. "When you're well...we'll make another baby, darling." He intuitively knew she wasn't fully up to hearing that, but he had to let her know where his heart lay. He watched her grow heavy-lidded and stroked her hair as she drifted off to sleep. He departed to find Dan and have him fashion a small coffin for baby Texas.

Luke and Meaney respectfully watched as Strong walked slowly up the street toward the stable with the tiny bundle in his arm. Jake Barber had just arrived from a visit to San Patricio and stood with the two men, though he was a bit bewildered as to all that had occurred.

Luke knew that Elisa would want to know all the goings-on. He'd thank JD later...much later...for shooting Snake Collins. He patted Big Horse on his neck before mounting up, stroked his mustache as he took a final look around the scene, and headed toward Heaven's Gate. He took comfort in knowing that Jubal Strong and JD would put tragedy behind them and be starting a happy new future, Meaney and his wife Clara could sleep soundly, and a peacefulness of sorts had settled over Nuecestown. He could also take bemused comfort in knowing that Bernice would have the news of the morning's happenings all over town by midday. As he left Nuecestown behind, a couple of tumbleweeds rolled across the road on a strong breeze. Were they aimless? Were there choices to be made? For now, Luke had longhorns to tend to. Elisa and the children awaited him. No telling what lawbreaker might yet come into his life again. He thought on how much longer that goldarned war would continue. That war remained by far the greatest uncertainty in their lives.

★

The days had gone by swiftly. The weather was warming. The war seemed far off, at least for the present. They hadn't heard cannon fire from Corpus Christi in weeks. Flowers were just beginning to bud. Now and then, an early-season mosquito would make an appearance. The livestock seemed oblivious to the pests.

Luke was up at the crack of dawn. "Gotta get going, Lisa. I'm burning sunlight."

She looked up at him through reddened eyes. "Lucas, I'm feeling off this morning. Could you look after the children? And please close the curtain—it's too bright in here." It wasn't like Elisa to stay in bed or to complain. She would usually be a bundle of energy, even when she didn't feel especially well.

Luke leaned over and placed a hand on her forehead, then drew it back quickly. Coulda fried eggs on her forehead. She was burning up with fever. "How long you had the burn, Lisa?" He could see right away that his plans for the day were about to change.

She leaned over the side of the bed and threw up into the pan on the floor. She looked up wanly. The headache had come on that night, and she was aching all over.

"Lisa, sweetheart, I'm going to feed the children and then go fetch Doc."

"Don't fix anything for me, Lucas." She rolled on her side and tried to go back to sleep.

Luke stopped at the cabin on his way to the barn. "Jaime, please have Julia look in on the children. Lisa's not feeling well, so I'm going for Doc."

"No problem, *Señor* Dunn." Jaime's expression turned to one of deep concern. "I don't mean to make you worry, but I have heard of the *la fiebre amarilla*, the yellow fever, in Corpus Christi. Some have gotten sick. Doc will know."

"*Gracias*, Jaime. I appreciate your concern." Luke headed to the barn, threw a saddle on Big Horse, and headed to Nuecestown. The stallion could sense Luke's worry and picked up his pace with nary a nudge to his sides.

★

One Arrow stood triumphantly at the outer boundary of the

encampment. There were nearly a hundred wild horses milling about in the roped-off clearing but a few yards away. It filled the Comanche chief's heart with a mix of pride and joy. To his inner self, there was something about horses that equated to freedom. Indeed, they were beautiful animals, tossing heads and swishing tails, stallions hunting for ready mares. They'd have them ready to ride soon enough. He wasn't certain what they'd be ready for, but that mattered not. It was all about the hunt, the capture, and the breaking. Comanche without horses were not true warriors.

Crouching Lion had been a true asset on the hunt and had long since forgiven the chief for not being willing to fight the band of Kiowa that challenged them for the first horses they'd found. The warrior clearly had ever more respect for One Arrow.

Cactus Flower walked up behind the young chief. "It is nearly time. I feel it." She placed his hand on her belly.

The chief drew his hand back with a look of wonderment. "Must be warrior. Kick strong!" One Arrow smiled. He'd not had enough reasons to smile in several moons. Perhaps the necklace with its White man's cross had great power after all.

Cactus Flower's smile turned to a look of surprise. Her water had broken. "It is time." She ran to the teepee and Bird Woman.

★

Doc took Luke aside on the gallery. It had taken him but seconds to deduce Elisa's illness. He placed his hand on Luke's arm, as Doc wasn't especially tall, and Luke's shoulder was a reach. There was no lily-coating the diagnosis. "It's the yellow fever, Luke." He shook his head. "Not much you can do but keep her comfortable as possible. Use wet cloths on her forehead to keep the fever low."

Luke looked out on the gentle rolling hills of Heaven's

Gate. Everything had seemed so peaceful. Alas, it was to be but an interlude. "Will she recover, Doc?"

"We caught it early, Luke." He hesitated. "Some folks in Corpus have passed. If her skin turns yellow or she starts bleeding, that'll be bad…very bad. Call me if she turns for the worse." He headed to his buckboard. "She's a strong woman, Luke. I think she'll be okay." He tried not to look overly grim. He wasn't a religious man, but Doc crossed himself and pointed skyward.

Luke waved as Doc drove off. Fighting Comanche and other dangers he'd faced over the years on the Nueces Strip didn't seem to match up to the invisible threat he and Elisa were now facing. He looked up to the sky in follow-up to Doc's silent appeal to God, then sighed deeply and went back inside the house. Peter and John played quietly in a corner of the parlor. They seemed to sense that it wasn't a good time to be teasing Andrea Anne. Michael and Alma slept peacefully.

He felt blessed to have Jaime and Julia Sanchez living in the cabin nearby. She was well along with child again, so would be readily able to feed Michael and Alma. Julia's *vaquero* husband would carry an extra workload with the spring round-up as Luke took the time to care for Elisa.

Luke slowly climbed the stairs and was soon standing silently over Elisa. She looked so fragile. As he replaced the damp cloth on her forehead, he felt the raging heat from the fever radiate from her. The rims of her eyelids remained the telltale red that told him the yellow fever was still within her. Her breathing was shallow. Sleep belied the illness that racked Elisa's body, as a nerve-racking fragility had imposed itself over her tough frontier woman essence. Helplessness strove to sweep its paralyzing spell over Luke, to cast doubt in his mind. He could only wonder what fate the future might hold. This choice wasn't his to make. It was in God's hands. He fought back a tear, as he whispered, "Lisa…Lisa…I love you."

Luke slipped on his hat, took another resignedly hopeful look at Elisa, and quietly closed the bedroom door behind him. What indeed did the future hold?

ACKNOWLEDGMENTS

Authoring books simply doesn't happen in a vacuum. The author provides the creative talent and crafts the stories, but there's so much more that demands acknowledgment. So it is with the fifth Tumbleweed Saga: *Nueces Grit: Texans Answer the Call*. I've been blessed with many friends and family who have supported my writings. My wife Carolyn's reviews and encouragement were a huge help, along with very important tech support from our sons Mike and Matt.

Other supporters have included Cara Miller, Jim May, Ernie Angell, Chris Haug, and my dear cousins Johnny Dunn, Jim & Cindy Holmgreen, and Eddie Thornton. Many more friends have contributed support at some level to the creation and publication of *Nueces Grit*, be it encouragement or advice.

Naturally, I am major grateful to the great folks at Wolfpack Publishing. The team they bring to publishing is first rate from promotion to editing, cover design, narration, and the myriad tasks that lead to successful book sales.

Most of my authoring has occurred in my office as decorated to channel my inner Texan, but my creative juices have often been inspired and imagination stoked in cafés and coffee houses across America. My favorites were Hester's Café & Coffee Bar in Corpus Christi, TX; Nueces Café in Robstown, TX; Java Ranch Espresso Bar & Café in Fredericksburg, TX; PAX Coffee & Goods in Kerrville, TX; Ragged Edge Coffee House and Bantam Coffee Roasters in Gettysburg, PA; 1889 Coffee House in Helena, MT; Dunn Brothers Coffee in Rapid

City, SD; Postmasters Coffee & Bakery and Brio Coffeehouse in Waynesboro, PA; Birdie's Café and American Ice Co Café in Westminster, MD; Deja Brew Coffee House, New Oxford and Deja Brew at Miney Branch, Carroll Valley, PA; and Baltimore Coffee & Tea Co., Frederick Coffee Company & Café, and Dublin Roasters in Frederick, MD. I must admit to also frequenting a few Dunkin Donuts and Starbucks around our fine nation. The décors and easy listening music in these fine establishments combined with savory cups of coffee tended to set me in the right creative frame of mind.

Last but not least, I'm especially thankful for the many folks who have read and enjoyed my books.

I do believe it's important to acknowledge how the old west represents the brave pioneering spirit of settlers that met the challenges and transcended mere survival to enable America to achieve exceptional growth. The settling of the American frontier west is replete with tales of leveraging freedom for individual achievement. I hope you'll agree that reliving our past—even through history-based fiction—often has the effect of pointing the way to an ever-brighter future. Might we be up to it? I hope that the inspiration I've drawn from my having walked the very earth my characters have trodden coupled with my extensive historical research will enable readers to fully experience the grit, adventure, and passion of my characters while sensing aromas of gunsmoke, trail dust, leather, and bluebonnets.

A LOOK AT BOOK SIX
NUECES TRUTH

The Nueces Strip bares its unforgiving soul.

In the turbulent final years of the Civil War, the Texas frontier is a powder keg of lawlessness and survival. Texas Ranger Captain Luke Dunn, known to the Comanche as "Ghost-Who-Rides," is caught in a relentless battle against bandits, rogue soldiers, and the unforgiving wilds of the Nueces Strip. With most of Texas' best men fighting a losing cause, Dunn stands as a lone beacon of justice, his every ride shadowed by death.

As cannonballs rain on Corpus Christi and turmoil engulfs the region, Luke must navigate a treacherous path where love, loyalty, and law collide. With the spirited Elisa by his side, the truths uncovered in the chaos of war threaten to alter everything they hold dear.

Can one man's dedication to justice withstand the relentless tides of war?

AVAILABLE MARCH 2025

ABOUT THE AUTHOR

Award-winning author Mark Greathouse's love for the Western genre draws upon his deep family roots and love of the outdoors, honed from teen years spent hiking the Appalachian Trail and family travels across America's frontier. He hopes his work reveals his passion for America's western history.

A member of Western Writers of America and the Wild West History Association, Mark also contributes articles on the history of America's west to Western-themed magazines. He was recognized as a 2024 Finalist in the Western genre by the American Literary Book Awards for his sixth Tumbleweed Saga, *Nueces Truth: Texans Face War's Realities*.

Mark began writing full time after a successful career as a business executive and later as an entrepreneurial investor and advisor. His service as president of several business and community nonprofits led to their extraordinary growth. He holds a BA in English and MBA in marketing.

Mark also donates time and books annually to support wounded military warriors. He was a Boy Scout leader (Eagle Scout) and served on a local school board earlier in life.